Fire Ice

CLIVE CUSSLER
with PAUL KEMPRECOS

A NOVEL FROM
THE NUMA® FILES

PENGUIN BOOKS

PENGUIN BOOKS

Published by the Penguin Group

Penguin Books Ltd, 80 Strand, London WC2R ORL, England

Penguin Group (USA) Inc., 375 Hudson Street, New York, New York 10014, USA

Penguin Group (Canada), 90 Eglinton Avenue East, Suite 700, Toronto, Ontario,
Canada M4P 2Y3 (a division of Pearson Penguin Canada Inc.)

Penguin Ireland, 25 St Stephen's Green, Dublin 2, Ireland (a division of Penguin Books Ltd)

Penguin Group (Australia), 250 Camberwell Road, Camberwell, Victoria 3124, Australia
(a division of Pearson Australia Group Pty Ltd)

Penguin Books India Pvt Ltd, 11 Community Centre, Panchsheel Park,
New Delhi – 110 017, India

Penguin Group (NZ), 67 Apollo Drive, Rosedale, Auckland 0632, New Zealand
(a division of Pearson New Zealand Ltd)

Penguin Books (South Africa) (Pty) Ltd, 24 Sturdee Avenue, Rosebank, Johannesburg 2196,
South Africa

Penguin Books Ltd, Registered Offices: 80 Strand, London WC2R ORL, England

www.penguin.com

First published in the USA by G. P. Putnam's Sons 2002
First published in Great Britain by Michael Joseph 2002
Published in Penguin Books 2003
Reissued in this edition 2011

005

Copyright © Sandecker, RLLLP, 2002
All rights reserved

The moral right of the authors has been asserted

Printed in England by Clays Ltd, St Ives plc

ISBN: 978-0-241-95585-7

www.greenpenguin.co.uk

Acknowledgments

With thanks to Arnold Carr for his helpful suggestions on that remarkable research vessel, the *NR-1*; to John Fish of American Underwater Search and Survey for sharing his considerable technical expertise; and to William Ott and the staff at the Weston Observatory, who answered fanciful questions about undersea earthquakes with patience and alacrity.

Prologue

Odessa, Russia, 1918

The dense fog rolled into the harbor late in the afternoon, nudged by a sudden change in wind direction. The damp gray billows washed over the stone quays, swirled up the Odessa Steps and brought an early nightfall to the busy Black Sea port. Passenger ferries and freighters canceled their runs, idling dozens of sailors. As Captain Anatoly Tovrov groped his way through the bone-chilling mists that enveloped the waterfront, he could hear bursts of drunken laughter from the crowded dives and brothels. He walked past the main concentration of bars, turned down an alley and opened an unmarked door. Warm air, heavy with the smell of cigarette smoke and vodka, invaded his nostrils. A portly man sitting at a corner table beckoned the captain over.

Alexei Federoff was in charge of Odessa Customs. When the captain was in port, he and Federoff made it a habit to meet at the secluded watering hole, frequented mostly by retired mariners, where the vodka was cheap and not usually lethal. The bureaucrat satisfied the captain's need for human companionship without friendship. Tovrov had steered a lonely course since his wife and young daughter had been killed years before in one of Russia's senseless outbursts of violence.

Federoff seemed strangely subdued. Normally a boisterous man who could be counted on to accuse the waiter jokingly of overcharging, he ordered a round by silently raising two fingers. Even more surprising, the frugal customs man paid for the drinks. He kept his voice low, nervously tugging at his pointed little black beard, and glanced nervously at other tables where weather-beaten seamen hunched over their glasses. Satisfied that their conversation was private, Federoff raised his drink and they clinked glasses.

'My dear Captain,' Federoff said. 'I regret that I have little time and must get directly to the point. I would like you to take a group of passengers and a small amount of cargo to Constantinople, no questions asked.'

'I knew something was odd when you paid for my drink,' the captain said, with his usual bluntness.

Federoff chuckled. He had always been intrigued by the captain's honesty, even if he couldn't comprehend it. 'Well, Captain, we poor government servants must exist on the pittance they pay us.'

The captain's lips tightened in a thin smile as he eyed the corpulent belly that strained the buttons of Federoff's expensive French-made waistcoat. The customs man often complained about his job. Tovrov would listen politely. He knew the official had powerful connections in Saint Petersburg and that he spent his days soliciting bribes from shipowners to 'smooth the seas' of bureaucracy, as he put it.

'You know my ship,' Tovrov said, with a shrug. 'It is not what you would call a luxury liner.'

'No matter. It will suit our purposes admirably.'

The captain paused in thought, wondering why anyone would want to sail on an old coal carrier when more appealing alternatives were available. Federoff mistook the captain's hesitation for the opening round of a bargaining session. Reaching into his breast pocket, he withdrew a thick envelope and placed it on the table. He opened the envelope slightly so the captain could see that it held thousands of rubles.

'You would be well compensated.'

Tovrov swallowed hard. With shaking fingers, he dug a cigarette from its pack and lit up. 'I don't understand,' he said.

Federoff noted the captain's bewilderment. 'What do you know about the political state of our country?'

The captain relied on scuttlebutt and out-of-date papers for his news. 'I am a simple sailor,' he replied. 'I rarely set foot on Russian soil.'

'Even so, you are a man of vast practical experience. Please be frank, my friend. I have always valued your opinion.'

Tovrov pondered what he knew about Russia's tribulations and put it in a nautical context. 'If a ship were in the same condition as our country, I would wonder why it is not at the bottom of the sea.'

'I have always admired your candor,' Federoff replied, with a hearty laugh. 'It seems you have a gift for metaphor as well.' He grew serious again. 'Your reply is entirely to the point. Russia is indeed in a *perilous* state. Our young men are dying in the Great War, the tsar has abdicated, the Bolsheviks are ruthlessly assuming power, the Germans occupy our southern flank and we have called upon other nations to snatch our chestnuts from the fire.'

'I had no idea things were that bad.'

'They are getting worse, if you can believe it. Which brings me back to you and your ship.' Federoff locked his eyes on the captain's. 'We loyal patriots here in Odessa have our backs to the sea. The White Army holds territory, but the Reds are pressing from the north and will soon overwhelm them. The German army's ten-mile military zone will dissolve like sugar in water. By taking on these passengers, you would be doing a great service for Russia.'

The captain considered himself a citizen of the world, but deep down he was no different from the rest of his countrymen, with their deep attachment to the motherland. He knew that the Bolsheviks were arresting and executing the old guard and that many refugees had escaped to the south. He had talked with other captains who whispered tales of taking on important passengers in the dead of night.

Passenger space was no problem. The ship was practically empty. The *Odessa Star* was the last choice of sailors looking for a berth. She smelled of leaky fuel, rusting metal and low-end cargo. Sailors called it the stench of death and avoided the ship as if it carried the plague. The crew was mostly wharf rats no other ship would hire. Tovrov could move the first mate into his quarters, freeing up the officers' cabins for passengers. He glanced at the thick envelope. The money would make the difference between dying in an old sailors' home or retiring to a comfortable cottage by the sea.

'We sail in three days with the evening tide,' the captain said.

'You are a true patriot,' Federoff said, his eyes glistening with tears. He thrust the envelope across the table. 'This is half. I will pay you the balance when the passengers arrive.'

The captain slid the money into his coat, where it seemed to throw off heat. 'How many passengers will there be?'

Federoff glanced at two sailors who entered the café and sat at a table. Lowering his voice, he said, 'About a dozen. There is extra money in the envelope to buy food. Purchase the supplies at different markets to avoid suspicion. I must go now.' He rose from his seat, and, in a voice loud enough for all to hear, said sternly, 'Well, my good Captain, I hope you have a better understanding of our customs rules and regulations! Good day.'

On the afternoon of departure, Federoff came to the ship to tell the captain the plans were unchanged. The passengers would arrive late in the evening. Only the captain was to be on deck. Shortly before midnight, as Tovrov paced the fog-shrouded deck alone, a vehicle squealed to a halt at the bottom of the gangplank. From the guttural sound of the motor, he guessed it was a truck. The headlights and engine were turned off. Doors opened and closed, and there was the murmur of voices and the scuffle of boots on wet cobblestones.

A tall figure wearing a hooded cloak climbed the gangway, stepped onto the deck and came over to the captain. Tovrov felt unseen eyes boring into his. Then a deep male voice spoke from the dark hole under the cowling.

'Where are the passengers' quarters?'

'I'll show you,' Tovrov said.

'No, *tell* me.'

'Very well. The cabins are on the bridge one deck up. The ladder is over there.'

'Where are your crew?'

'They are all in their bunks.'

'See that they *stay* there. Wait here.'

The man silently made his way to the ladder and climbed to the officers' cabins on the deck below the wheelhouse. Minutes later, he returned from his inspection. 'Better than a stable, but not much,' he said. 'We're coming aboard. Stay out of the way. Over there.' He pointed toward the bow, then descended to the quay.

Tovrov was ruffled at being ordered about on his own ship, but the thought of the money locked in his cabin safe smoothed his feathers. He was also wise enough not to argue with a man who towered above him. He took up a post on the bow as instructed.

The group huddled on the quay filed onto the ship. Tovrov heard the sleepy voice of a young girl or boy being shushed by an adult as the passengers made their way to their quarters. Others followed, lugging boxes or steamer trunks. From the grunts and curses, he guessed that the baggage was heavy. The last person onto the ship was Federoff, who huffed with unaccustomed exertion from the short climb.

'Well, my good fellow,' he said cheerily, clapping his gloves together for warmth. 'That's the last of it. Is everything ready?'

'We sail when you give the order.'

'Consider it given. Here is the rest of your money.' He handed Tovrov an envelope that crackled with new bills. Then, unexpectedly, he embraced the captain in a bear hug and kissed him on both cheeks. 'Mother Russia can never pay you enough,' he whispered. 'Tonight you make history.' He released the astounded captain and descended the gangway. After a moment, the truck drove off and disappeared into the gloom.

The captain brought the envelope to his nose, inhaling the smell of rubles as if they were roses, then he tucked the money in a coat pocket and climbed to the wheelhouse. He went into the chart room behind the wheelhouse, then through a door into his cabin to roust Sergei, his first mate. The captain told the young Georgian to wake the crew and cast off. Muttering incomprehensibly to himself, the mate went below to follow orders.

A handful of human flotsam staggered out onto the deck in various states of sobriety. Tovrov watched from the wheelhouse as the mooring lines were cast off and the gangway pulled up. There were a dozen crewmen in all, including two men hired at the last minute as stokers down in the 'junkyard,' as the engine room was called. The chief engineer was a competent seaman who had stayed with the captain out of loyalty. He wielded his oilcan like a magic wand and breathed life into the piles of scrap metal that powered the *Star*. The boilers had been warming up and were building up steam as well as could be expected.

Tovrov took the helm, the telegraph jangled and the ship moved away from the dock. As the *Odessa Star* inched her way out of the fog-bound harbor, those who saw her crossed themselves and invoked ancient prayers to ward off demons. She seemed to float above the water like a phantom ship doomed to wander the world in search of drowned sailors for her crew. Her running lights were veiled in a gauzy glow, as if Saint Elmo's fire danced in the rigging.

The captain steered the ship through the winding channel and around fog-shrouded boats as easily as a porpoise using its natural radar. Years of steaming between Odessa and Constantinople had engraved the route in his brain, and he knew without resorting to charts or channel markers how many turns of the wheel to make.

The *Star*'s French owners had purposely neglected her maintenance for years, hoping one good storm would send the ship to the bottom and pay out its insurance. Rust dripped from the scuppers like bleeding sores and streaked the blistered hull. The masts and cranes were splotched by corrosion. The ship listed drunkenly to port, where water from a leaky bilge had settled. The *Star*'s engines, worn and long in need of an overhaul, wheezed as if they suffered from emphysema. The choking black cloud that poured from its single smokestack stank as if it were sulfur emanating from Hades. Like a terminal patient who somehow existed in a wasted body, the *Star* continued to plow through the seas long after she should have been declared clinically dead.

Tovrov knew that the *Star* was the last ship he would ever command. Yet he strove to maintain a spit-and-polish look. He buffed his thin-soled black shoes every morning. His white shirt was yellowed but clean, and he attempted to keep a crease in his threadbare black trousers. Only the cosmetic skills of an embalmer would have improved the captain's physical appearance. Late hours, poor diet and lack of sleep had taken their toll. His sunken cheeks gave even greater prominence to the long, red-veined nose and his skin was as gray as parchment.

The first mate went back to sleep, and the crew

settled in their bunks while the first shift of stokers fed the coal into the boilers. The captain lit up a potent Turkish cigarette that triggered a coughing fit that doubled him over. As he got his fit under control, he became aware that cold sea air was coming in an open door. He looked up and saw he was no longer alone. A huge man stood in the doorway, dramatically framed by wisps of fog. He stepped inside and shut the door behind him.

'Lights,' he said in a baritone voice that identified him as the figure who had been the first to come aboard.

Tovrov pulled the cord for the bare bulb that hung from the overhead. The man had thrown back his hood. He was tall and lean and wore a white fur hat known as a *papakha* at a rakish angle. A pale dueling scar slashed his right cheek above the beard line, his skin was red and blistered with snowburn and sparkling drops of moisture matted his black hair and beard. His left iris was clouded from an injury or disease, and his staring good eye made him look like a lopsided Cyclops.

The fur-lined cloak had fallen open to reveal a pistol holster at his belt and in his hand he carried a rifle. A cartridge bandoleer crossed his chest and a saber hung from his belt. He was dressed in a muddy gray tunic and his feet were shod with high, black-leather boots. The uniform and his air of barely repressed violence identified him as a Cossack, one of the fierce warrior caste who inhabited the rim of the Black Sea. Tovrov stifled his revulsion. Cossacks had been involved in the death of his family, and he always tried to avoid the belligerent horsemen who seemed happiest when instilling fear.

The man glanced around the deserted wheelhouse. 'Alone?'

'The first mate is sleeping back there,' Tovrov said, with a jerk of his head. 'He is drunk and doesn't hear anything.' He fumbled with a cigarette and offered the man one.

'My name is Major Peter Yakelev,' the man said, waving the cigarette away. 'You will do as you are told, Captain Tovrov.'

'You may trust me to be at your service, Major.'

'I trust *no* one.' He stepped closer and spat out the words. 'Not the White Russians or the Reds. Not the Germans or the British. They are *all* against us. Even Cossacks have gone over to the Bolsheviks.' He glared at the captain, searching for a nuance of defiance. Seeing no threat in the captain's bland expression, he reached out with thick fingers.

'Cigarette,' he growled.

Tovrov gave him the whole pack. The major lit one up and drank in the smoke as if it were an elixir. Tovrov was intrigued by the major's accent. The captain's father had worked as a coachman for a wealthy landowner, and Tovrov was familiar with the cultured speech of the Russian elite. This man looked as if he had sprung from the steppes, but he spoke with an educated inflection. Tovrov knew that upper-class officers trained at the military academy were often picked to lead Cossack troops.

Tovrov noticed the weariness in the Cossack's ruined face and the slight sag to the powerful shoulders.

'A long trip?' he said.

The major grinned without humor. 'Yes, a long, hard trip.' He blew twin plumes of smoke out of his nostrils and produced a flask of vodka from his coat. He took a pull and looked around. 'This ship stinks,' he declared.

'The *Star* is an old, old lady with a great heart.'

'Your old lady still stinks,' the Cossack said.

'When you're my age, you learn to hold your nose and take what you can get.'

The major roared with laughter and slapped Tovrov on the back so hard that sharp daggers of pain stabbed his ravaged lungs and set him coughing. The Cossack offered Tovrov his flask. The captain managed a swallow. It was high-quality vodka, not the rotgut he was used to. The fiery liquid dampened the cough, and he handed the flask back and took the helm.

Yakelev tucked the flask away. 'What did Federoff tell you?' he said.

'Only that we're carrying cargo and passengers of great importance to Russia.'

'You're not curious?'

Tovrov shrugged. 'I have heard what is going on in the west. I assume these are bureaucrats running

12

away from the Bolsheviks with their families and what few belongings they can bring.'

Yakelev smiled. 'Yes, that is a good story.'

Emboldened, Tovrov said, 'If I may ask, why did you choose the *Odessa Star*? Surely there were newer ships fitted out for passenger service.'

'Use your brain, Captain,' Yakelev said with contempt. 'Nobody would expect this old scow to carry passengers of importance.' He glanced out the window into the night. 'How long to Constantinople?'

'Two days and two nights, if all goes well.'

'Make sure it *does* go well.'

'I'll do my best. Anything else?'

'Yes. Tell your crew to stay away from the passengers. A cook will come into the kitchen and prepare meals. No one will talk to her. There are six guards, including myself, and we will be on duty at all times. Anyone who comes to the cabins without permission will be shot.' He put his hand on the butt of his pistol in emphasis.

'I will make sure the crew is informed,' the captain said. 'The only ones normally on the bridge are the first mate and myself. His name is Sergei.'

'The *drunk*?'

Tovrov nodded. The Cossack shook his head in disbelief, his good eye sweeping the wheelhouse, then he left as suddenly as he had appeared.

Tovrov stared at the open door and scratched his chin. Passengers who bring their armed guards are not petty bureaucrats, he thought. He must be carrying someone high up in the hierarchy, maybe even members of the court. But it was none of his business, he decided, and went back to his duties. He checked the compass heading, set the helm, then stepped out onto the port wing to clear his head.

The damp air carried a perfume laden with scents from the ancient lands that surrounded the sea. He cocked his ear, straining to hear over the erratic *thrum-thrum* of the *Star*'s engines. Decades at sea had honed his senses to a sharp edge. Another boat was moving through the fog. Who else would be so foolish as to sail on such a terrible night? Maybe it was the vodka at work.

A new sound drowned out the boat noise. Music was coming from the passengers' quarters. Someone was playing a concertina and male voices sang in chorus. It was the Russian national anthem, *'Baje Tsaria Krani.'* 'God Save the Tsar.' The melancholy voices made him sad, and he went back into the wheelhouse and closed the door so he could no longer hear the haunting strains.

The fog vanished with the dawn, and the bleary-eyed mate stumbled in to relieve the captain. Tovrov gave him the course orders, then stepped outside and yawned in the early-morning sunlight. He swept his eyes over the blue satin sea and saw that his instincts had been right. A fishing boat was running parallel to the *Star*'s long wake. He watched the boat for a few minutes, then shrugged and made the rounds, warning every crewman that the officers' quarters were off-limits.

Satisfied that all was well, the captain crawled into his bunk and slept in his clothes. His first mate was under strict orders to awaken him at the first sign of anything unusual. Nevertheless, Tovrov, who had mastered the art of the catnap, rose several times and returned to a deep slumber in between. Around midday, he awoke and went into the mess, where he ate bread and cheese, plus sausage purchased with his newfound wealth. A stout woman was there, bending over the stove, and standing by was a tough-looking Cossack who helped her carry the steaming pots back to the passenger section. After his meal, Tovrov relieved the mate for a lunch break. As the day wore on, the fishing boat fell back until it could have been any one of the dots visible on the horizon.

The *Star* seemed to shed years as she glided over the mirrored surface of the sunlit sea. Eager to reach Constantinople, Tovrov ordered the ship kept at nearly top speed, but finally, the ship paid for its coltish behavior. Around dinnertime, an engine broke down, and though the first mate and the engineer tinkered with the engine for hours, their only accomplishment was to coat themselves with grease. The captain saw that further effort was futile and ordered them to push forward on one engine.

The major was waiting in the wheelhouse and roared like a wounded bull when the captain laid out the problem. Tovrov said they would get to Constantinople, only not as soon. An extra day, perhaps.

Yakelev raised his fists in the air and affixed the captain with his baleful eye. Tovrov expected to be smashed to goulash, but the major suddenly whirled and swept from the cabin. The captain exhaled the breath he had been holding and returned to his charts. The ship was moving at half speed, but at least it was moving. The captain prayed to the icon of Saint Basil on the wall that the good engine would hold out.

Yakelev was calmer when he returned. The captain asked how the passengers were doing. They were fine, the major said, but they would do better if the stinking rust bucket they were on got to where it was going. Fog moved in later, and Tovrov had to reduce speed by a couple of knots. He hoped Yakelev was asleep and wouldn't notice.

Tovrov had the nervous mental tic that comes to men who have spent their lives on the water, his eyes constantly darting here and there, checking the compass and barometer dozens of times in an hour. In between, he walked from wing to wing to observe weather and sea conditions. About one o'clock in the morning, he went out onto the port wing . . . and his neck began to tingle. A vessel was overtaking them. He listened intently. It was closing fast.

Tovrov was a simple man, but he was not stupid. He cranked the phone that connected the bridge to the officers' cabin.

Yakelev answered. 'What do you want?' he snapped.

'We must talk,' Tovrov said.

'I will come by later.'

'No, it is very important. We must talk *now*.'

'All right. Come down to the passengers' quarters. Don't worry,' Yakelev said with an evil chuckle, 'I'll try not to shoot you.'

The captain hung up and woke Sergei, who reeked of alcohol. He poured the mate a mug of the strong black coffee.

'Keep a heading due south. I will be back in a few minutes. Any mistakes and I will take away your vodka until we reach Constantinople.'

Tovrov hurried below and cautiously pushed open the door, half expecting to be met by a hail of bullets. Yakelev was waiting. He stood with his legs wide apart and his hands on his hips. Four other Cossacks were asleep on the floor. Another sat cross-legged with his back to the cabin door and a rifle balanced on his knees.

Yakelev glared accusingly. 'You woke me up.'

'Come with me, please,' the captain said, leading the way outside. They descended to the fog-shrouded main deck and made their way to the stern. The captain leaned over the fantail and peered into the wooly darkness that swallowed their broad wake. He listened a few seconds, blocking out the burble and hiss of the water.

'A boat is following us,' he said.

Yakelev looked at him with suspicion and cupped his hand to his ear. 'You're *crazy*. I hear nothing but the noise from this stupid ship.'

'You're a Cossack,' Tovrov said. 'You know about horses?'

'Of *course*,' the major replied, with a contemptuous snort. 'What *man* doesn't?'

'*I* don't, but I *do* know ships, and we're being followed. A piston on that boat is missing a stroke. I think it is the fishing boat I saw earlier.'

'So what of it? This is the sea. Fish swim in the sea.'

'There are no fish this far from shore.' He listened again. 'No doubt. It's the same boat and it is moving in on us.'

The major uttered a string of curses and pounded the rail. 'You must lose them.'

'Impossible! Not with one engine down.'

Yakelev's hand grabbed the front of Tovrov's coat and he lifted the captain onto his toes.

'Do not tell me what is impossible,' he snarled. 'It took us weeks to come from Kiev. The temperature was thirty degrees below zero. The wind lashed our faces like whips. There was a *burin*, a blizzard like none I have ever seen. I had a full *sontia* of one hundred Cossacks when I started. These pitiful fellows are all I have left. My other men stayed behind to watch our backs when we came through German lines. If not for the Tartars' help, we would all be dead. We managed to find a way. You will, too.'

Tovrov stifled the urge to cough. 'Then I suggest we change our course and cut the lights.'

'*Do* it then,' Yakelev ordered, releasing his iron grip.

The captain caught his breath and dashed back to the bridge, with the major close behind. As they approached the ladder that led up to the wheelhouse, a bright square of light appeared on the deck above. Several people stepped out onto the open platform. The light was from behind, so their faces were in shadow.

'Inside!' Yakelev shouted.

'We came outside for air,' a woman said, speaking in a German accent. 'It is stifling in the cabin.'

'Please, Madame,' the major said in a softer, pleading voice.

'As you wish,' the woman said, after a moment. She was clearly reluctant, but she herded the others back inside. As she turned, Tovrov saw her profile. She had a strong chin, and her nose was slightly curved at the tip.

A guard emerged from the ship and called down. 'I couldn't stop them, Major.'

'Go back inside and shut the door before all the world hears your stupid excuses.'

The guard vanished and slammed the door behind him. As Tovrov stared up at the empty platform, the major's fingers dug into his arm.

Yakelev's voice was harsh and low. 'You saw nothing, Captain.'

'Those people –'

'*Nothing!* For God's sake, man. I do not want to kill you.'

Tovrov started to reply, but the words never left his mouth. He had felt a change in the ship's movement, and he jerked his arm away from Yakelev's grip. 'I must go to the bridge.'

'What is wrong?'

'There's no one at the wheel. Can't you feel it? My stupid first mate is probably drunk.'

Tovrov left the major behind and climbed to the wheelhouse. In the light from the binnacle, he saw the wheel slowly spinning back and forth as if moved by invisible hands. The captain stepped inside and stumbled over something soft and yielding. He swore, thinking that the mate had passed out. Then he turned on the light and saw how wrong he was.

The mate lay facedown on the metal deck, a puddle of blood around his head. Tovrov's anger turned to alarm. He knelt beside the young officer and turned him over. A wound grinned at him like a second mouth where the poor wretch's throat had been cut.

Eyes wide with horror, the captain stood and edged away from the corpse, only to back into a wall of solid flesh. He whirled and saw Yakelev.

'What has happened?' the major said.

'It's incredible! Someone has killed the first mate.'

Yakelev nudged the bloody corpse with his boot. 'Who could have done this?'

'*No* one.'

'No one slaughtered your mate like a pig? Come to your senses, Captain.'

Tovrov shook his head, unable to take his eyes off the mate's body. 'I meant that I know all the crew well.' He paused. 'All except the two new men.'

'*What* new men?' Yakelev's good eye blazed at Tovrov like a spotlight.

'I hired them two days ago as stokers. They were in the bar when I was talking to Federoff, and they came by later looking for berths. They looked like ruffians, but I was short of crew –'

Uttering a curse, Yakelev pulled his pistol from its holster, shoved Tovrov aside and vaulted through the door, shouting commands to his men. Tovrov glanced at the first mate and vowed not to let the same thing happen to him without a fight. He tied the wheel, then he went into his stateroom and with trembling hands turned the combination dial on the ship's safe. Pulling out a 7.63-millimeter Mauser automatic, he unwrapped the soft velvet cloth protecting the gun, which he had acquired years before in a barter in the event of a mutiny, loaded the magazine, stuck the pistol in his belt and peered out the cabin door.

Descending to the lower deck, he peeked through the small circular window in the door that led to the passengers' quarters. The passageway was empty. He went down to the main deck and crept forward. In the glow of the deck lights, he saw the Cossacks crouched near the rail.

Suddenly, a small, dark object looped over the gunwale, bounced once and skittered along the wet deck, leaving a trail of sparks.

'*Grenade!*' someone yelled.

Moving like quicksilver, Yakelev dove for the sputtering grenade, rolled onto his back and snapped the metal pineapple over the side. An explosion sounded, and the screams of pain that followed were drowned out as the Cossacks poured rifle fire into the mist. One guard leaned over with a sharp knife and slashed the lines tied to several grappling hooks, then a boat engine roared, as if it had been given full throttle. The Cossacks continued to fire until the boat was out of range.

The major turned and his rifle snapped up to firing position. Then a grin crossed his face as he recognized the captain.

'You'd better put that toy away before you shoot yourself, Captain.'

Tovrov tucked the gun into his belt and walked over to Yakelev. 'What happened?'

'You were right about being followed. A fishing boat came alongside and some impolite fellows tried to invite themselves on board. We had to teach them manners. One of your new crewmen was signaling them with a light until we put a knife in his heart.' He indicated a body lying on the deck.

'We gave our visitors a warm welcome,' another Cossack said, and his companions joined in the laughter. The guards picked the body up and threw it over the side. The captain was about to ask where the other stoker was. *Too late.*

The missing stoker announced his arrival with deadly force. Rifle fire cut short the Cossacks' mirth, and four men were mowed down as if by an invisible scythe. A round caught Yakelev in the chest, and the force slammed him against the bulkhead. He refused to go down and mustered the strength to push the captain out of the line of fire. The remaining Cossack dropped to his belly and crawled along the deck, firing as he went, but he was killed before he gained the protection of an air vent.

While the attacker was diverted, Tovrov and the major made their escape, but after a few steps, the major's knees buckled and his great body dropped to the deck, his tunic soaked in blood. He gestured toward the captain, who brought his ear close to the Cossack's mouth.

'See to the family,' he said in a wet, guttural voice. 'They must live.' His hand groped for Tovrov's jacket. 'Remember. Without a tsar, Russia cannot exist.' He blinked in astonishment that he should be in such a position, and a soggy chuckle escaped his frothy lips. 'Damn this ship . . . give me a horse any day . . .' The life went out of his fierce eye, his chin slumped forward and his fingers went limp.

Just then, the ship was rocked by a tremendous blast. Crouching low, Tovrov ran to the rail and saw the fishing boat a hundred yards away. A bright flash from the muzzle of a deck gun, and a second shell slammed into the freighter. The ship rocked violently.

A muffled thud came from below, as the fuel tanks caught fire, and burning fuel gushed from the tanks and spread in flaming sheets across the surface of the water. The second stoker decided to abandon ship. He ran across the deck, threw the rifle over the side, then he climbed onto the rail, leaped into a clear section of water and stroked for the fishing boat. He underestimated the speed of the spreading fuel, however. Within seconds, it caught up with him, and his screams were drowned out by the loud crackle of flames.

The cannonade had dislodged the rest of the crew from their hiding places. Men ran in desperation toward the lifeboat on the side away from the fire. Tovrov went to follow them, then he remembered Yakelev's dying words. Gasping as he tried to pull air into his ravaged lungs, Tovrov climbed to the passenger quarters and threw the door open.

A pitiful sight greeted his eyes. Four girls in their teens cowered against the wall, along with the cook. Standing protectively in front of them was a middle-aged woman with sad blue-gray eyes. She had a long thin nose, slightly aquiline, with a firm but delicate chin. Her lips were closely pressed together in determination. They could have been any group of refugees huddling in terror, but Tovrov knew they weren't. He fumbled as he tried to decide on the right form of address.

'Madame,' he said finally. 'You and the children must come to the lifeboat.'

'Who are you?' the woman said, with the same German accent the captain had heard earlier.

'Captain Tovrov. I am master of this vessel.'

'Tell me what has happened. What is all that noise?'

'Your guards are all dead. The ship is under attack. We must abandon it.'

She glanced at the girls and seemed to gain renewed courage. 'Captain Tovrov, if you guide me and my family to safety, great rewards await you.'

'I will do my best, Madame.'

She nodded. 'Go, and we will follow.'

Tovrov checked to see if the way was clear, then held the door open for the family and led the way across the deck away from the fire. The *Star* tilted at a pronounced angle and they had to climb up a slanting slippery metal surface. They fell, helped one another up and pushed on.

The crew was piling into the lifeboat, struggling to work the davits. Taking control, the captain ordered the men to help the family. When everyone was in the boat, he told the crewmen to look smart and lower the boat. He was worried that the ship was at such an angle that the davits would not work, but the boat began to descend, although it bumped against the slanting hull.

The lifeboat was a few yards above the water when one of the men shouted. The fishing boat had come around from the other side and the deck gun was leveled directly at the lifeboat. The gun fired and the shell smashed through one end of the boat, and then the air was filled with flying splinters of wood, hot steel and body parts.

Tovrov had stretched his arm around the girl nearest to him. He still had his arm around her when he came to in the freezing water, calling out the name of his long-lost daughter. Spotting a wooden hatch cover floating nearby, and moving slowly so as not to alert the attackers, he swam toward the debris, hauling the semiconscious girl behind him. He helped her climb aboard the precarious raft, gave it a shove, and the cover and its cargo drifted away from the light of the dying ship and merged with the darkness. Then, frozen and exhausted, with nothing to keep him afloat, Tovrov slipped beneath the embracing waters, taking with him his dream of a cottage by the sea.

I

Off the Maine Coast, the Present

Leroy Jenkins was hauling in a barnacle-encrusted lobster trap aboard his boat, *The Kestrel*, when he looked up and saw the giant ship on the horizon. He gingerly extracted a fat pair of angry crustaceans from the trap, pegged the claws and tossed the lobsters into a holding tank, then he rebaited the trap with a fish head, pushed the wire cage over the side and went into the pilothouse for his binoculars. He peered through the lenses and silently mouthed the word 'Wow!'

The ship was huge. Jenkins examined the vessel from stem to stern with an expert eye. Before retiring to take up lobster-fishing, he had taught oceanography for years at the University of Maine, and he had spent many summer breaks on survey ships – but this vessel was like nothing he had ever seen. He estimated its length at about six hundred feet. Derricks and cranes sprouted from its deck. Jenkins guessed it was some sort of ocean mining or exploration vessel. He watched until the ship vanished from sight, then went back to pull the rest of the string of pots.

Jenkins was a tall, rangy man in his sixties, whose rugged features mirrored the rockbound coast of his native Maine. A smile crossed his deeply tanned face as he hauled in the last trap. It had been an exceptionally good day. He had found the honey hole by accident a couple of months earlier. The spot produced an endless supply of lobsters, and he kept coming back even though he had to go farther from land than normal. Fortunately, his thirty-six-foot wooden boat was seaworthy even with a full load. Setting a course for land, he put the boat on autopilot and went below to reward himself with what they used to call a Dagwood sandwich when he was a kid. He had just layered in another slice of baloney on top of the pile of ham, cheese and salami when he heard a muffled '*Boom!*' It sounded like a thunderclap, but it seemed to come from below.

The boat shuddered so violently the jars of mustard and mayonnaise rolled off the counter. Jenkins tossed his knife in the sink and sprang up to the deck. He wondered if the propeller had broken off or if he had hit a floating log, but nothing seemed amiss. The sea was calm and almost flat. Earlier, the blue surface had reminded him of a Rothko canvas.

The boat had stopped vibrating, and he took a wondering look around, then, shrugging, went below. He finished making his sandwich, cleaned up and went out on the deck to eat. Noticing a couple of lobster traps that had shifted, he secured them with a line, then as he stepped back into the wheelhouse, he experienced a sudden unpleasant stomach-sinking sensation, as if someone had pushed the Up button in a fast elevator. He grabbed onto the mechanical hauler to keep his footing. The boat plunged, then levitated again, higher this time, plummeted once more and repeated the cycle a third time before sinking back into the sea, where it rocked violently from side to side.

After a few minutes, the motion stopped and the boat stabilized, and Jenkins saw a flickering movement in the distance. Retrieving his binoculars from the wheelhouse, he swept the sea, and as he adjusted the focus ring, he saw three dark furrows extending from north to south. The ranks of waves were moving in the direction of the coast. A long-dormant alarm bell clanged in his head. It *can't* be. His mind raced back to that July day in 1998 off the coast of Papua New Guinea. He had been on a ship, making a survey, when there had been a mysterious explosion and the seismic instruments had gone crazy, indicating a disturbance on the seafloor. Recognizing the symptoms of a *tsunami*, the scientists aboard the ship had tried to warn the coast, but many of the villages had no communication. The huge waves had flattened the villages like a giant steamroller. The destruction was horrifying. Jenkins never forgot the sight of bodies impaled on mangrove branches, of crocodiles preying on the dead.

The radio crackled with a chorus of hard-edged Maine accents as fishermen set the airways abuzz.

'Whoa!' said a voice Jenkins recognized as that of his neighbor, Elwood Smalley. 'Hear that big boomer?'

'Sounded like a jet fighter, only underwater,' another fisherman said.

'Anyone else feel those big seas?' said a third man.

'Yup,' replied a laconic veteran lobsterman named Homer Gudgeon. 'Thought for a time there I was on a roller coaster!'

Jenkins barely heard the other voices chiming in. He dug a pocket calculator out of a drawer, estimated the time between the waves and their height, did some quick calculations and glanced with disbelief at the numbers. Then he picked up the cell phone he used when he didn't want personal messages to go over the marine channel and punched out a number.

The gravelly voice of Charlie Howes, Rocky Cove's police chief, came on the phone.

'Charlie, thank God I got you!'

'In my cruiser on my way to the station, Roy. You calling to crow about whippin' me at chess last night?'

'Another time,' Jenkins said. 'I'm east of Rocky Point. Look, Charlie, we don't have much time. There's a big wave heading right toward town.'

He heard a dry chuckle at the other end. 'Hell, Roy,' the chief said, 'town like ours on the water is bound to get *lots* of waves.'

'Not like this one. You've got to evacuate the people from near the harbor, especially the new motel.'

Jenkins thought the phone had gone dead. Then

came Charlie Howes's famous guffaw. 'I didn't know today was April Fool's.'

'Charlie, this is *no joke*,' Jenkins said in exasperation. 'That wave is going to slam into the harbor. I don't know how strong it will be, because there are lots of unknowns, but that motel is right in its path.'

The chief laughed again. 'Hell, some people would be real happy to see the Harbor View washed into the sea.'

The two-story edifice that extended into the harbor on stilts had been a source of controversy for months. It had gone up only after a bitter fight, an expensive lawsuit filed by the developers and what many suspected were bribes to officials.

'They're going to get their wish, but you've got to get the guests out first.'

'Hell, Roy, there must be a hundred people staying there. I can't roust them out for no reason. I'll lose my job. Even worse, I'll be a laughingstock.'

Jenkins checked his watch and cursed under his breath. He hadn't wanted to panic the chief, but he had reached the end of his self-control.

'Goddamnit, you old fool! How will you feel if a hundred people *die* because *you're* afraid of being laughed at?'

'You're not kidding, are you, Roy?'

'You know what I did before I took up lobstering.'

'Yeah, you were a professor at the university up at Orono.'

'That's right. I headed up the Oceanography

31

Department. We studied wave action. You've heard of the Perfect Storm? You've got the perfect tidal wave heading your way. I calculate it will hit in twenty-five minutes. I don't care *what* you tell those motel people. Tell them there's a gas leak, a bomb threat, *anything*. Just get them out and to higher ground. And do it *now*.'

'Okay, Roy. *Okay*.'

'Is there anything open on Main Street?'

'Coffee shop. Jacoby kid is on the night shift. I'll have him swing by, then check out the fish pier.'

'Make sure everybody is out of the area in fifteen minutes. That goes for you and Ed Jacoby.'

'Will do. Thanks, Roy. I think. 'Bye.'

Jenkins was almost dizzy with tension. He pictured Rocky Point in his mind. The town of twelve hundred was built like the seats in an amphitheater, its houses clustered on the side of a small hill overlooking the roughly circular harbor. The harbor was relatively sheltered, but the town's inhabitants had learned after a couple of hurricane-driven storm surges to build back from the water. The old brick maritime buildings on the main street bordering the harbor had been given over to shops and restaurants that served tourists. The fish pier and the motel dominated the harbor. Jenkins cranked up the throttle and prayed that his warning had arrived in time.

Chief Howes immediately regretted agreeing to Roy's urgent pleas, and was overcome by a numbing sense of uncertainty. Damned if he did, damned if he didn't. He'd known Jenkins since they were kids and Roy was the smartest one in class. He had never known him to fail as a friend. *Still.* Oh hell, he was near retirement anyhow.

Howes switched on his flasher, nailed the accelerator and, with a smoky screech of tires, roared toward the waterfront. While he drove the short distance, he got the deputy on the radio and told him to clear out the coffee shop then to go along Main Street with his PA system blasting, warning people to get to high ground. The chief knew the diurnal rhythms of his town: who would be up, who would be walking a dog. Luckily, most businesses didn't open before ten.

The motel was another story. Howes pulled over two empty buses on their way to pick up school-children and told the drivers to follow him. The cruiser squealed to a stop beneath the motel's canopy, and the chief huffed his way to the front door. Howes had been on the fence about the motel. It would spoil the integrity of the harbor, but it might bring in jobs for locals; not everyone in town wanted to be a fisherman. On the other hand, he didn't like the way the project was rammed through to approval. He couldn't prove it, but he was sure there had been bribes at town hall.

The developer was a local named Jack Shrager, an unprincipled land raper who was building condos along the river that ran off the harbor, further despoiling the town's quiet beauty. Shrager never did hire locals, preferring foreigners who worked long and cheap.

The desk clerk, a young Jamaican, looked up with a startled expression on his thin, dark face as the chief burst into the lobby and shouted: 'Get everyone out of the motel! This is an emergency!'

'What's the problem, mon?'

'I've been told there's a bomb here.'

The desk clerk gulped. Then he got on the switchboard and began to call rooms.

'You've got ten minutes,' Howes emphasized. 'There are buses waiting in front. Get everyone out, including yourself. Tell anyone who refuses that the police will arrest them.'

The chief strode down the nearest hallway and pounded on doors. 'Police! You must evacuate this building immediately. You have ten minutes,' he yelled at the sleepy faces that peered out. 'There has been a bomb threat. Don't stop to gather your belongings.'

He repeated the message until he was hoarse. The hallways filled with people in bathrobes and pajamas or with blankets wrapped around them. A swarthy man with an unpleasant scowl on his face stepped from one room. 'What the hell is going on?' Jack Shrager demanded.

Howes swallowed hard. 'There's been a bomb threat, Jack. You've got to get out.'

A young blond woman poked her head out of the room. 'What's wrong, babe?'

'There's a bomb in the motel,' the chief said, becoming more specific.

The woman's face went pale and she stepped into the hallway. She was still in her silk bathrobe. Shrager tried to hold her, but she pulled away.

'I'm not staying here,' she said.

'And I'm not moving,' Shrager said. He slammed the door.

Howes shook his head in frustration, then guided the woman by the arm, joining the throng heading for the front door. He saw the buses were almost filled and yelled at the drivers.

'Get out of here in five minutes. Drive to the highest hill in town.'

He slid behind the wheel of his cruiser and drove to the fish pier. The deputy was arguing with three fishermen. Howes saw what was happening and yelled out the window, 'Get your asses into those trucks and go to the top of Hill Street or you'll be arrested.'

'What the hell is going on, Charlie?'

Howes lowered his voice. 'Look, Buck, you know me. Just do as I say and I'll explain later.'

The fisherman nodded, then he and the others got into their pickups. Howes told his deputy to follow them and made one last sweep along the fish pier, where he picked up an elderly man who sorted through the rubbish bins for cans and bottles. Then he scoured Main Street, saw that it was quiet and headed for the top of Hill Street.

Some of the people who stood shivering in the cool air of morning shouted at him. Howes ignored their insults, got out of his cruiser and walked partway down the steep hill that led down toward the harbor. Now that the adrenaline rush was over, he felt weak-kneed. *Nothing.* He checked his watch. Five minutes came and went. And so did his dreams of a peaceful retirement on a police pension. I'm dead, he thought, sweating despite the coolness.

Then he saw the sea rise above the horizon and heard what sounded like distant thunder. The towns-people stopped shouting. A darkness loomed out near the channel entrance and the harbor emptied out – he could actually see bottom – but the phenomenon lasted only a few seconds. The water roared back in with a noise like a 747 taking off, and the sea lifted the moored fishing boats as if they were toys. It was reinforced by two more waves, seconds apart, each taller than the one before. They surged over the shore. When they receded, the motel and the fish pier had vanished.

The Rocky Point that Jenkins returned to was far different from the one he had left that morning. The boats moored in the harbor were jumbled together along the shore in a tangled heap of wood and fiber-glass. Smaller craft had been thrown up onto Main Street. Shop windows were smashed as if by a gang of vandals. The water was littered with debris and seaweed, and a sulfuric smell of sea bottom mixed with the odor of dead fish. The motel had vanished. Only pilings remained of the fish pier, although the sturdy concrete bulkhead showed no sign of damage. Jenkins pointed his boat toward a figure waving his arms on the bulkhead. Chief Howes grabbed the mooring lines and tied them off, then he stepped aboard.

'Anybody hurt?' Jenkins said, his eyes sweeping the harbor and town.

'Jack Shrager was killed. He's the only one as far as we know. We got everyone else out of the motel.'

'Thanks for believing me. Sorry I called you an old fool.'

The chief puffed his cheeks out. 'That's what I would have been if I'd sat on my ass and done nothing.'

'Tell me what you saw,' Jenkins said, the scientist reasserting itself over the Samaritan.

Howes laid out the details. 'We were standing at the top of Hill Street. Sounded and looked like a thunderstorm, then the harbor emptied out like a kid pulling the plug in a bathtub. I could actually see bottom. That only lasted a few seconds before the water roared in like a jet plane.'

'That's an apt comparison. On the open ocean, a *tsunami* can go six hundred miles an hour.'

'That's *fast*!' the chief said.

'Luckily, it slows down as it approaches land and hits shallower water. But the wave energy doesn't diminish with the speed.'

'It wasn't like I pictured. You know, a wall of water fifty feet high. This was more like a wave surge. I counted three of them, each bigger than the last. Thirty feet, maybe. They whacked the motel and pier and flooded Main Street.' He shrugged. 'I know you're a professor, Roy, but how exactly did you know this was going to happen?'

'I've seen it before off New Guinea. We were doing some research when an undersea slide generated a *tsunami* thirty to sixty feet tall, and a series of waves lifted our boat off the water just like what I felt today. The people were warned and many made it to high ground when the waves hit, but even so, more than two thousand people were lost.'

The chief gulped. 'That's more than live in this town.' He pondered the professor's words. 'You think that an earthquake caused *this* mess? I thought that was something that happened in the Pacific.'

'Normally, you'd be right.' Jenkins furrowed his brow and stared out to sea. 'This is absolutely incomprehensible.'

'I'll tell you something else that's going to be hard to figure. How am I going to explain that I evacuated the motel for a bomb scare?'

'Do you think anyone will care at this point?'

Chief Howes surveyed the town and the crowds of people cautiously making their way down the hill to the harbor and shook his head. 'No,' he said. 'I don't guess they will.'

2

The Aegean Sea

The miniature research submarine *NR-1* rocked gently in the waves off the coast of Turkey, almost invisible except for the bright tangerine color of the conning tower. Captain Joe Logan stood with his legs wide apart on the sea-washed deck, holding on to one of the horizontal wings that protruded from the sides of the conning tower. As was his custom before a dive, the captain was making a last minute visual check.

Logan let his eye range along the 145-foot length of the slender black hull whose deck was only inches above the surface of the water. Satisfied all was shipshape, he removed his navy baseball cap and waved at the cream-and-orange *Carolyn Chouest* a quarter of a mile away. The superstructure of the muscular support ship rose several levels, like the floors in an apartment house. A massive crane capable of lifting several tons jutted out at an angle from the port side.

The captain climbed to the top of the tower and squeezed through the thirty-one-inch-diameter opening. His flotation vest made for a tight fit and he had to wriggle to get through. He ran his fingers along the seal to make sure it was clean, then secured the hatch cover and descended into the confined control area. The space was made even more cramped by the dials, gauges and instruments that covered every square inch of the walls and overhead.

The captain was a man of unassuming appearance who could have passed for an Ivy League college professor. A nuclear engineer by training, Logan had commanded surface ships before being assigned as the officer in charge of the *NR-1*. He was of medium height and build, with thinning blond hair and a slight fleshiness around the jaw. The navy had long ago dispensed with the rawboned John Wayne type who ran a ship by the seat of his pants. With computerized firing controls, laser guidance and smart missiles, navy vessels were too complicated and expensive to entrust to cowboys. Logan had a sharp mind and the ability to make a lightning-quick analysis of the most complex technical problem.

His previous commands had been much bigger, yet none came close to the *NR-1* in the sophistication of her electronics. Although the boat had been built in 1969, she was constantly upgraded. Despite her cutting edge technology, the sub still used some older but time-tested techniques. A thick twelve-hundred-foot towline ran from the support vessel's deck to a large metal ball clutched by metal jaws on the submarine's bow.

Logan gave the order to release the towrope, then he turned to a thickset bearded man in his fifties and said, 'Welcome aboard the smallest nuclear submarine in the world, Dr Pulaski. Sorry we don't have more elbowroom. The shielding for the nuclear reactor takes up most of the sub. My guess is that you'd prefer claustrophobia to radiation. I assume you've had a tour.'

Pulaski smiled. 'Yes, I've been checked out on the proper procedure for using the head.' He spoke with a slight accent.

'You might have to stand in line, so I'd go easy on the coffee. We've got a ten-man crew, and our facilities can get busy.'

'I understand you can stay submerged for up to thirty days,' Pulaski said. 'I can't imagine what it must be like sitting on the bottom a half-mile down for that length of time.'

'I'd be the first to admit that even the simplest task, such as taking a shower or cooking a meal, can be a challenge,' Logan said. 'Luckily for you, we'll only be down a few hours.' He glanced at his watch. 'We'll descend one hundred feet to make sure all systems are working. If everything checks out, we'll dive.'

Logan stepped through a short passageway slightly wider than his shoulders and indicated a small padded platform behind the two chairs in the control station. 'That's normally where I sit during operations. It's all yours today. I'll take the copilot's seat. You've met Dr Pulaski,' he said to the pilot. 'He's a marine archaeologist from the University of North Carolina.'

The pilot nodded and Logan slid into the right-hand chair beside him. In front of him was a formidable array of instruments and video display screens. 'Those are our "eyes,"' he said, pointing to a row of television monitors. 'That's the bow view from the sail cam on the front of the sail.'

The captain studied the glowing control panel and after conferring with the pilot, he radioed the support ship and said the sub was ready to dive. He gave the order to submerge and level off at one hundred feet. The pump motors hummed as water was introduced into the ballast tanks. The rocking motion of the sub ceased as she sank below the waves. The sharp bow pictured on the monitors disappeared in a geyser of spray, then reappeared, looming dark against the blue water. The crew checked out the sub's systems while the captain tested the UQC, an underwater wireless telephone that connected the sub with the support ship. The voice from the ship had a drawling, metallic quality but the words were clear and distinct.

When the captain was assured all systems were go, he said, 'Dive, *dive*!'

There was little sensation of movement. The monitor pictures went from blue to black water as the sunlight faded, and the captain ordered the exterior lights on. The descent was practically silent, the pilot using a joystick to operate the diving planes, the captain keeping a close eye on the deep-depth gauge. When the sub was fifty feet above the bottom, Logan ordered the pilot to hover.

The pilot turned to Pulaski. 'We're in shouting distance of the site we picked up with remote sensing. We'll run a search using our side-scan sonar. We can program a search pattern into the computer. The sub will automatically run the course on its own while we sit back and relax. Saves wear and tear on the crew.'

'Incredible,' Pulaski said. 'I'm surprised this remarkable boat won't analyze our findings, write a report and defend our conclusions against the criticism of jealous colleagues.'

'We're working on that,' Logan said, with a poker face.

Pulaski shook his head in mock dismay. 'I'd better find another line of work. At this rate, marine archaeologists will be doomed to extinction or to simply staring at television monitors.'

'Something else you can blame on the Cold War.'

Pulaski looked around in wonderment. 'I never would have guessed that I'd be doing archaeological research in a sub designed to spy on the Soviet Union.'

'There's no way you *could* have known. This vessel was as hush-hush as it gets. The amazing part is that the ninety-million-dollar price tag was kept a secret. It was money well-spent in my opinion. Now that the navy has allowed her to be used for civilian purposes, we have an incredible tool for pure research.'

'I understand the sub was used in the *Challenger* space shuttle disaster,' Pulaski said.

Logan said, 'She retrieved critical parts so NASA

could determine what went wrong and make the shuttle safe to fly. She also salvaged a sunken F-14 and a missing Phoenix air-to-air missile we didn't want anyone getting their hands on. Some of the stuff involving the Russians is still classified.'

'What can you tell me about the mechanical arm?'

'The manipulator works like a human arm, with rotation at all the joints. The sub has two rubber wheels in the keel. It's not exactly a Harley-Davidson motorcycle, but it allows us to move along on the seabed. While the sub rests on the ocean floor, the arm can work a nine-foot radius.'

'Fascinating,' Pulaski said. 'And its capacity?'

'It can lift objects up to two hundred pounds.'

'What about cutting tools?'

'Its jaws can cut rope or cable, but they can also hold a torch if the job is tough. As I said, very versatile.'

'Yes, evidently,' Pulaski said. He seemed pleased.

The sub had been moving in a classic search pattern, back and forth in a series of parallel lines, like mowing a lawn. The monitors showed the seafloor moving beneath the submarine. Vegetation was non-existent.

Logan said, 'We should be closing in on the location we spotted from above.' He gestured at a screen. '*Hul*-lo. Looks like the side scan picked up a hit.' He turned to the pilot. 'Resume manual control and bring her down around twenty degrees to port.'

With gentle bursts of the thrusters, the *NR-1* glided

on a shallow angle. The battery of two dozen exterior lights illuminated the sea bottom with a sun-bright intensity. The pilot adjusted ballast tanks until the sub achieved neutral buoyancy.

'Hold steady,' Logan said. 'We're coming into visual contact with our target.' He leaned forward and peered intently at the screen, his features bathed in the blue-green light. As the sub moved forward, bulbous shapes appeared on the screen, singly at first, then in groups.

'Those are concentrations of *amphorae*,' Pulaski said. The clay jars for wine or other liquid cargo were often found on ancient sunken ships.

'We've got the still and video cameras making a three-dimensional record for you to analyze later,' the captain said. 'Is there anything you'd like to retrieve?'

'Yes, that would be wonderful. Can we bring up an amphora? Maybe from that pile.'

Logan ordered the pilot to put the sub on the bottom near a pile of clay jars. The four-hundred-ton vessel touched down like a feather and rolled forward. The captain called for the retrieval crew.

Two crewmen came forward and lifted a hatch in the floor behind the control area. Beneath the hatch was a shallow well. A trio of four-inch-thick acrylic viewing ports in the floor offered a view of the bottom. One man squeezed into the space and kept watch so the sub wouldn't run into the pile of jars. When the targets were within reach, the sub stopped. The manipulator arm was housed in the forward end of the keel box. Using a portable control panel, the man in the well extended the arm and worked the jaws. The arm rotated at the shoulder.

The mechanical hand gently grabbed a jar around the neck, lifted and placed it in a storage basket below the bow. The arm was retracted and Logan ordered the crew to raise the sub off the bottom. While the sub made another photo run, Logan called the support ship, described their find and said they were about to surface, then ordered the sonar turned on to locate the support ship on the surface. A measured *ping-ping* echoed throughout the sub.

'Prepare to surface,' Logan told the pilot.

Dr Pulaski was standing directly behind the captain's chair. 'I don't think so,' he said.

Preoccupied with the task at hand, Logan was only half listening. 'Pardon me, Doctor. What did you say?'

'I said we're not going to the surface.'

Logan spun his chair around, an amused expression on his face. 'I hope you didn't take my bragging about the ability to stay down for a month at face value. We only brought enough food for a few days.'

Pulaski slipped a hand under his windbreaker and pulled out a Tokarev TT-33 pistol. Speaking calmly, he said, 'You will do as I say or I will shoot your pilot.' He brought the weapon around and placed the muzzle against the pilot's head.

Logan's eyes focused on the gun, then darted to

Pulaski's face. There was no hint of mercy in the rock-hard features.

'Who *are* you?' Logan said.

'It makes no difference who I am. I will repeat this only one more time. You will follow my orders.'

'All right,' Logan said, his voice hoarse with tension. 'What do you want me to do?'

'First, switch off all communications with your support ship.' Pulaski watched carefully as Logan clicked all the radio switches off. 'Thank you,' he said, checking his watch. 'Next, inform the rest of the crew that the sub has been hijacked. Warn them that anyone who comes forward without permission will be shot.'

The captain glared at Pulaski as he got on the internal communications system. 'This is the captain. There is a man with a gun in the control area. The sub is now under his command. We will do what he says. Stay out of the control area. This is not a joke. Repeat: This is not a joke. Remain at your posts. Anyone coming forward will be shot.'

Startled voices could be heard coming from the aft section, and the captain issued the warning a second time to make sure his men knew he was serious.

'Very good,' Pulaski said. 'Now you will bring the sub up to the five-hundred-foot level.'

'You heard him,' Logan said to the pilot, as if reluctant to give the direct order.

The pilot had been frozen in his chair. At Logan's

command, he reached for the controls and pumped water from the variable ballast tanks. Working the planes, he elevated the sub's nose and moved the *NR-1* upward with short bursts of the main propulsion. At five hundred feet, he leveled the sub off.

'Okay,' Logan said. '*Now* what?' His eyes blazed with anger.

Pulaski glanced at his watch like a man worrying over a late train. 'Now we wait.' He shifted the gun away from the pilot, but kept it leveled and at ready.

Ten minutes passed. Then fifteen. Logan's patience was wearing thin. 'If you don't mind, could you tell me what we're waiting for?'

Pulaski put his finger to his lips. 'You'll see,' he said with a mysterious smile.

Several more minutes passed. The tension was suffocating. Logan stared at the sail cam monitor, wondering who this man was and what he wanted – and the answer was soon in coming. A huge shadow moved beyond the sharply pointed bow.

Logan leaned forward and peered at the screen. 'What the hell is *that*?'

The shadow glided under the sub like a monstrous shark coming up for a belly bite. A horrendous metal clang reverberated from one end of the sub to the other as if the *NR-1* had been slammed by a giant sledgehammer. The vessel shivered from the shock and rose several feet.

'We've been *hit*!' the pilot yelled, instinctively reaching for the controls.

'Stay where you are!' Pulaski barked, bringing his gun to bear.

The pilot's hand froze in midair and his eyes stared at the overhead. Those in the sub could hear scraping and dragging as if big metal bugs were crawling on the hull.

Pulaski beamed with pleasure. 'Our welcoming party has arrived to greet us.'

The noise continued for several minutes before it stopped, to be replaced by the vibration of powerful engines. The speed dial on the control panel began to move even though no power had been given to the thrusters.

'We're *moving*,' the pilot said, his eyes glued to the speed indicator. 'What should I do?'

He turned to the captain. They were up to ten, then twenty knots and still accelerating.

'Nothing,' Pulaski answered. Turning to Logan, he said, 'Captain, if you would give a message to your crew.'

'What do you want me to say?'

Pulaski smiled. 'I think that is fairly obvious,' he said. 'Tell them to sit back and enjoy the ride.'

3

The Black Sea

The sixteen-foot Zodiac inflatable boat sped toward the distant shore, its flat bottom thumping against the waves like a hand beating a tom-tom. Hunkered down in the bow, hands clutching the lifeline to keep from being bounced out, Kaela Dorn looked like a finely carved figurehead. The spray that splashed over the blunt prow stung her face and her dusky features dripped with water, but she turned away only once, and that was to yell at the man who knelt in the boat with his hand on the tiller.

'Mehmet, crank this thing up, crank it up!' She made circular motions with her hand as if she were twirling a lariat.

The wizened Turk answered with a toothless grin that was wider than his face. He goosed the throttle and the Zodiac porpoised over the next wave and slammed down with even greater gut-wrenching force. Kaela reinforced her grip on the lifeline and laughed with delight.

The two men jouncing around in the boat like dice in a shaker were less enthusiastic. They held tight to keep from being thrown into the sea, their teeth clacking with every jolt. Neither passenger was surprised to hear Kaela tell Mehmet to kick up the speed. After three months of working with the young reporter on the *Unbelievable Mysteries* television series, they were accustomed to her recklessness.

Mickey Lombardo, the crew's senior member, was a short, thickset native New Yorker with arms made powerful from hefting sound and light equipment in and out of every conceivable means of transport around the globe. A wave had extinguished the cigar clenched between his teeth seconds after their wild ride began. His assistant, Hank Simpson, was a blond and muscled Australian beach boy Lombardo had nicknamed 'Dundee.'

When they'd first learned that they would be working closely with the beautiful reporter, neither man could believe his good luck. That was before Kaela had led them through a dung-filled bat cave in Arizona, down the rapids in the Green Hell of the Amazon and crashed a voodoo ceremony in Haiti. Lombardo said Kaela was living proof of the old axiom: Be careful what you wish for, because you might get it. She'd turned out to be a cross between Amelia Earhart and Wonder Woman, and their libidos had diminished in direct proportion to their growing respect for her audacity. Instead of regarding Kaela as a potential conquest, they now guarded her like a precocious kid sister who had to be protected from her own impetuousness.

Lombardo and Dundee could hardly be classified

as shrinking violets themselves. The crews that worked for *Unbelievable Mysteries* had to be physically fit, aggressive in pursuing a story and preferably brain-dead. The cable TV series had a high turnover and injury rate. With its emphasis on high-risk adventures, the series was tough on production crews – in fact, the misadventures of the crews, rather than their main assignments, often became the topic of each episode. It was the logical continuation of the 'true-life' adventure inspired by the success of the *Survivor* series and its clones. If a reporter or technician were swept into the sea or pursued by cannibals, it made for a better story. As long as a crew didn't lose expensive equipment, management didn't care how hazardous working conditions were.

They had arrived in Istanbul a few days earlier to launch a search for Noah's ark. The ark was an overworked cliché that even the supermarket tabloids had consigned to the back section with Elvis sightings and the Loch Ness monster, so Kaela had kept a sharp eye out for other leads in case the ark story didn't pan out. Their first day, while Kaela was looking for a fishing boat to take them into the Black Sea, she'd struck up a conversation with a colorful old Russian seaman she met on the docks. He had served on a Soviet missile sub and told her about an abandoned submarine base, even drew her a map showing the base's location in a remote corner of the Black Sea, after hinting that a gift of money might refresh his failing memory.

When Kaela approached her colleagues and excitedly poured out the story of the abandoned Soviet submarine base, they lost no time planning a side trip. The sub base might make a good backup if the search for Noah's ark fell apart, as it probably would. The fishing boat had been hired to take them to a rendezvous with a research vessel from the National Underwater and Marine Agency.

Captain Kemal, the boat's owner, was paid by the day, and said he knew of the sub base and would be happy to go there before they hooked up with the NUMA vessel. However, the fishing boat had engine trouble as they neared the base and the captain wanted to turn back to port – he'd had a similar problem before and it would take only a few hours to fix it once he had the part – but Kaela had persuaded him to drop her and her crew off and come back for them the next day. Mehmet, who was the captain's cousin, had volunteered to run them ashore in his Zodiac.

Now, the Zodiac was approaching a wide beach that rose gradually to a ridge of sand dunes. The waves grew higher and closer together, and Mehmet reduced their speed to half. The old Russian sailor had said that the base was underground, near an abandoned scientific station, and they would have to search for telltale air vents. Kaela wiped the water from her sunglasses and squinted toward the grassy hills, but saw no sign of human presence. The countryside was bleak and desolate, and she began to wonder if they had bitten off more than they could chew. The bean counters at *U.M.* frowned at unproductive expenditures.

'See anything?' Lombardo shouted over the buzz of the outboard.

'No billboards, if that's what you mean.'

'Maybe this isn't the right place.'

'Captain Kemal says this is it, and I have the map from the Russian.'

'How much did you pay that scam artist for the map?'

'One hundred dollars.'

Lombardo looked as if he had sucked on a lemon. 'Wonder how many times he's sold the same map.'

Kaela pointed toward land. 'That high spot over there looks promising.'

Thut!

Kaela jerked her head back at the weird sound. Then she saw the ragged hole that had opened in the rubberized fabric a foot to the right of her head. She thought one of the many patches on the inflatable's skin had popped off from the beating the Zodiac was taking, and she turned to tell Mehmet – but the Turk had risen from his kneeling position, an odd expression on his face, his hand clutched to his chest. Then he crumpled as if the air had gone out of him and pitched overboard. With no hand to steady the tiller, the boat went broadside and was caught by an incoming wave. The breaker lifted the boat at a sharp angle, when it was caught by another wave and flipped over, spilling the passengers into the sea.

The sky whirled over Kaela's head, then cold water shocked her body. She went under a few feet, and when she came up, sputtering, to the surface, the lights had gone out. She was under the overturned raft. She ducked her head and came up in the open. Lombardo's bald head bobbed up, then Dundee surfaced.

'Are you okay?' she yelled, swimming closer.

Lombardo spit out the remnants of his cigar. 'What the hell happened?'

'I think Mehmet was shot.'

'*Shot?* Are you sure?'

'He grabbed his chest and went over the side.' With Lombardo following, she swam over to the front of the boat. 'This is where the first bullet hit a second before the second one got Mehmet.'

'Jeez!' Lombardo said, sticking his finger in the hole. 'Poor bastard.'

Dundee breaststroked over to join the other two and they all drifted together, holding on to the raft. They agreed to stay with the raft where Kemal would find them, rather than risk going ashore. The Zodiac was low in the water, but some compartments still held air. Several times they tried to flip the boat over, but the weight of the outboard and the slipperiness of the rounded sides made it impossible. They were tiring fast and the waves were pushing them ever closer to the beach.

'That's it,' Lombardo said, after an unsuccessful

effort that left them all breathless. 'Looks like we're going in after all.'

'What if the guys who shot at us are still there?' Dundee said.

'You got a better suggestion?'

'The gunshots look as if they came from directly ahead,' Kaela said. 'Let's hide under the raft and move it off at an angle.'

'We don't have a hell of a lot of choice,' Lombardo said. He ducked underneath.

When the other two joined him, he was smiling. 'Look at this,' he said, grabbing onto the waterproof bags that were suspended from the seats, where they had been tied. 'The cameras are okay.'

Kaela let out a whooping laugh that had a damp echo in the enclosed space. 'What are we supposed to do if somebody points a gun at us, Mickey, take their picture?'

'You'll have to admit it would make a good story. What'ya think, Dundee?'

'I think you two Yanks are bloody crazy! But so am I, or I wouldn't be here with you. Tell me, luv,' he said to Kaela, 'didn't your Russkie friend say this place was abandoned?'

'He said the Russians had left a long time ago.'

'Maybe it's like one of those islands in the Pacific where the Japanese soldiers hid in the jungle, not knowing the war was over,' Lombardo suggested. 'Maybe the guys here haven't heard the Cold War ended.' He was clearly excited at the prospect.

'Sounds pretty far-fetched,' Kaela said.

'Yeah, I agree, but do you have a better idea of who took the potshots at us?'

'No, I don't,' Kaela said. 'But if we don't start kicking, we're going to find out real soon. I'll check things out.' She disappeared for a few moments. When she returned, she said, 'The beach looks deserted. I suggest we start moving this thing off to the right. Otherwise we'll drift straight in.'

They grabbed onto the boat, and began to kick. The Zodiac moved, but the rollers pushed them toward shore. The muffled roar of waves breaking on the beach grew louder. No more gunshots came their way and they began to hope that the shooters were gone. That optimism would have eroded quickly if they had been able to see beyond the grass crowning the dunes. A line of razor-sharp sabers was raised high in the sun like the blades of a giant threshing machine, ready to cut them to ribbons as soon as they crawled ashore.

4

High above the overturned Zodiac, a turquoise aircraft that resembled a winged canoe wheeled in a lazy circle. The broad-shouldered man at the controls rolled the ultralight airplane into a tight banking turn and peered down through tinted goggles, squinting against the reflected glare with eyes the color of coral underwater. His wind-burnished face was creased in a look of puzzlement. Moments before, he had seen swimmers in the water next to the overturned inflatable. He glanced away to get his bearings, and when he looked again the swimmers were gone.

Kurt Austin had been chasing the Zodiac like an aerial motorcycle cop hot on the tail of a speeder, and had seen the boat flip over. He couldn't figure out why it had gone out of control. The seas were moderate, and no rocks or other submerged objects were visible. Austin wondered if the inflatable, or the fishing boat he had seen steaming away from the coast, had anything to do with the television crew he was looking for. Probably not. The crew should be on its way to meet the NUMA survey ship *Argo*, not heading for this desolate stretch.

Austin was aboard the *Argo* as a deep-ocean consultant on loan from his duties as leader of NUMA's

Special Assignments Team. The other members of the team, Joe Zavala and Paul and Gamay Trout, had been given different and undemanding assignments in scattered projects around the globe. NUMA director James Sandecker had insisted that they take working vacations after the team had crossed swords with the hired killers of a megacorporation that wanted to take over the freshwater resources of the world. He had been particularly worried about Austin's attachment to the beautiful, brilliant Brazilian scientist who had sacrificed herself to bring down the conspiracy.

The *Argo* was in the Black Sea, collecting information on wave and wind action for an international data bank. With his master's degree in systems management from the University of Washington and his vast practical knowledge as a diver and undersea investigator, Austin had been invaluable in helping to set up the sophisticated remote-sensing survey instruments.

As the cruise had gone on and systems were set in place, however, his expertise became less necessary. He read some philosophy books he'd brought from his extensive library, but he started to grow bored and restless. The ship seemed like a prison surrounded by a very wide moat. Austin was aware that his psyche had been bruised and that Sandecker had his best interests at heart, but he needed strenuous physical and mental activity, not a cruise ship atmosphere.

The serious scientists aboard the ship had been grumbling about the impending visit from the TV crew. They saw them as intruders who would interrupt their work with dumb questions. The fact that they were from a tabloid show on a mission to find Noah's ark didn't add to their appeal. Austin's outlook was the exact opposite. He looked forward to their arrival as a diversion from his shipboard boredom.

The television people had been due that morning, but they'd never arrived and attempts to reach them by radio were unsuccessful. After lunch, Austin had climbed to the wheelhouse to run an idea past the skipper. The *Argo*'s commander, Captain Joe Atwood, was clearly annoyed at the TV crew's failure to show up or contact his ship. He'd paced from one side of the bridge to the other, scanning the sea with binoculars. The *Argo* was supposed to be moving to another station, and the captain was unhappy about the delay.

'Any word on our guests?' Austin said, although he knew from Atwood's dour expression what the answer would be.

Atwood scowled at his watch. 'I think they're lost,' he declared sharply. 'The next time those idiots in public affairs want me to entertain some crazy TV people, I'm going to tell them to stick their request where the sun don't shine.'

The captain was in no mood to be told that the job done by NUMA's public affairs department in proclaiming the agency's accomplishments helped loosen the congressional purse strings and attracted grants for projects like the Black Sea survey.

'I've got a suggestion,' Austin volunteered. 'I'm not busy. What say I take a spin around the neighborhood and see if I can spot them?'

The captain's frown dissolved into a knowing grin. 'You're not fooling me, Austin. You've wanted to get the Gooney into the air since the day you stepped aboard.'

'It would serve a dual purpose. I could test-fly the bird and look for our wayward guests at the same time.' And it would be a perfect antidote for his developing case of cabin fever.

Atwood ran his fingers through his pale red hair. 'Okay, pal. *Go* for it. But keep us appraised of your position every few minutes. I've got enough trouble with those missing TV types. I don't want to chase you all over the Black Sea as well.'

Austin thanked the captain, and, with a noticeable spring in his step, went down to get the Gooney ready. The ultralight seaplane had been developed as a way to extend a boat's visual reach. The radar that most NUMA ships carried could pick up a gnat at ten miles, but at times there was no substitute for the human eye. Joe Zavala, whose mechanical mind bordered on brilliant, had designed the aircraft. Zavala had asked Austin to take the plane aboard the *Argo* to test it under real-life conditions, but the ship had been on the go for most of its mission and Austin had been reluctant to ask the captain for time to make a test flight.

The single-seat plane was named after the gooney bird, the nickname sailors gave the albatross, a seabird known for its exquisite beauty in flight, and clumsiness taking off and landing. Austin inspected the aircraft in its deck hangar. The stubby, ungainly appearance didn't bother him. Austin had flown ultralights before, and what was important was stability and ease of operation.

The letters NUMA were painted in black on the side. The flat-bottomed fiberglass hull had an upturned canoe nose, and fiberglass floats supported by aluminum struts hung from both sides of the hull. Attached to the floats and flanking the hull was the manually operated retractable landing gear that allowed the Gooney to set down on waterways or runways.

The plane was hauled out onto the deck and its narrow, thirty-foot Dacron-covered wings were unfolded and locked in place. Austin eased into the snug cockpit, and some of the *Argo*'s crew pushed the Gooney down the ship's broad, slanting stern ramp into the sea. Austin started the power plant, threw off the safety line and taxied to open water to get the feel of the controls. The aircraft handled well on water, and he decided to see what it would do in the air. He pointed the Gooney down an imaginary airstrip and gave it the throttle.

Powered by the compact forty-horsepower engine,

the Gooney got on plane quickly with no skidding. The aircraft skimmed the wave tops for about a hundred feet, then lifted into the air and climbed until it was above the survey ship. Austin circled the *Argo* once, tipped his wings in salute, then headed in a line toward the Bosporus Strait that connected the Black Sea with the Mediterranean. He reasoned that the TV people, based in Istanbul, would be coming from that direction.

The Rotax two-stroke, twin-cylinder engine driving the rear-mounted propeller could push the blunt-nosed plane at a top speed of sixty-five miles per hour. Not exactly supersonic, but the plane handled like a dream, turning, climbing and diving without a hint of a stall. Austin felt as free as the seabirds he'd seen wheeling high above the *Argo* in search of scraps from the galley. He flew at about a thousand feet, an altitude that allowed him to see miles in every direction, cruising at fifty-five miles per hour. The five-gallon tank gave the plane a range of about one hundred and fifty miles.

The air was as clear as fine crystal, and the bright sun cast a silvery sheen on the rippled surface of the water. He set up a rough search pattern, running a series of parallel lines that would cover the greatest amount of territory in the shortest time. The TV people had sent a short radio message before they'd left Istanbul, requesting the *Argo*'s position and giving their estimated time of arrival. They said they would be traveling on a fishing boat. Austin saw a number of trawlers, but none appeared to be on a direct course for the *Argo*.

The back-and-forth flight pattern quickly used up his fuel. He was down to a third of a tank, enough to get back to the ship with a narrow margin of error. He checked his compass and was about to turn back to the ship, when he spotted the wake of a boat approaching the Russian coast at a high rate of speed. Curiosity got the best of him, and he decided to make a swing close to land. He brought the Gooney down so that he was flying less than five hundred feet over the water, and had almost caught up with the boat when suddenly it was caught by a wave and flipped over.

As Austin circled, pondering his next step, he noticed that the capsized inflatable was behaving oddly. Although it was caught in the pull of waves, it was moving toward shore at an angle.

Austin picked up his microphone and clicked the On button.

'Gooney to NUMA ship *Argo*. Come in, please.'

'*Argo* here.' Austin recognized the voice of the ship's captain. 'How's the little seabird handle?' Atwood said.

'Like a trained pterodactyl. She practically flies herself. I'm just along for the ride.'

'Glad to hear that. Any sign of those unbelievable TV idiots from *Unbelievable Mysteries*?'

Keeping his eye on the boat below, Austin said, 'The only mystery out here is an overturned Zodiac.

I saw some people hanging on to it, but they're gone.'

'What's your position?'

'I'm right off the coast.' Austin scanned a craggy point of land that jutted into the sea. 'I'm looking at some medium-high sea cliffs, with a beach and dunes in between them. There's a rock profile on a headland that reminds me of Admiral Sandecker's profile. Beard and all.'

'I'll ask the navigator. He's sailed these waters hundreds of times.' After a pause, the voice came back. 'That's Imam's Point. Supposedly the face of an old holy man.'

'The boat's drifted into the surf line. Too rough for me to set down at sea.'

'What do you want us to do?'

'I'm going down for a peek. I'm going to need help if I find anyone. The Gooney wasn't made to carry passengers.'

'We're on our way. ETA in about an hour.'

'Roger. Will land and see if I can find a bar that serves a decent Stoli martini.'

Austin clicked off the mike and checked the boat again. He smiled tightly. He hadn't been imagining things. Three swimmers had broken away from the Zodiac and were stroking toward the beach.

The ultralight landed best into the wind, which was coming off the water. Austin dropped down to a hundred feet and headed toward shore, setting his sights on a long rolling dune overlooking the beach.

He intended to make a U-turn over the dune and bring the aircraft down lightly onto the sand.

The Gooney flew over the figures struggling through the surf. The swimmers were making good progress, riding the crests to save their strength. Austin had a brief glimpse of some low-lying buildings inland, but a brilliant flash of light from the ground caught his eye. The Gooney could turn on a dime. Taking advantage of its quick handling, Austin pushed the rudder control. The plane seemed to spin in midair, and he had a clear view of the shallow valley behind the dune.

Hidden behind the dune were a dozen mounted men spread out in a single line with swords held high in the air. The silvery-red brightness Austin had seen was the sun reflecting off the sword blades. The Gooney's sudden and noisy appearance startled the horses, however, and they milled around in fright while the riders fought to bring them under control. Austin only caught a glimpse of the scene as he passed directly overhead, then he was above the beach again. The swimmers were only moments from shore.

Suddenly, pieces of Dacron began flying past his face. The horsemen were carrying more than swords. The wing over Austin's head looked as if a tiger was sharpening its claws in the fabric – someone on the beach was shooting at him. The thin fiberglass cockpit was no protection against bullets. Even worse, Austin was practically sitting on the Gooney's gas tank. The shots were high, but one lucky round in the propeller would drop him like a wounded duck. He pushed forward on the stick, and the plane dove. Even wearing earphones, he heard the sharp *thwack* of a bullet striking one of the hollow aluminum struts that connected the cockpit to the wings. He felt a sharp sting on his right temple. A splinter of flying metal had hit him, and blood was trickling down his face. He was wearing a neckerchief, and he pulled it up around his forehead to catch the blood.

The same volley that had also hit the strut had shattered a fiberglass wing float. Austin jammed the stick as far forward as it would go, and the ultralight dropped like a runaway elevator and tilted dangerously, the plane thrown off-balance by the loss of the float. Austin had to compensate by leaning his weight to one side. He flew out to sea until he was out of range, then put the plane into a turn that took him parallel to the shore.

The swimmers had hit the sand on their bellies when the gunfire broke out. Now they were up again and running along the water's edge. He picked out a slim, dark-skinned woman and two men, one short and the other tall. As they ran, they glanced over their shoulders, trying to keep an eye on the Gooney, only to see the mounted men crest the dune with swords raised. Spurred on by the new threat, the trio dug their feet in, but it was impossible to run faster in the soft sand. The mounted men would make short work of the defenseless runners caught between them and the deep blue sea. The open expanse of beach offered no shelter. It was a perfect killing field.

The horsemen spurred their mounts and galloped along the dune to outflank their prey. Austin reached into an emergency chest behind his seat and pulled out the Orion 25-millimeter signal kit for offshore boats. He fit one of the 10,000-candlepower Red Meteors into the pistol launcher. Then he cranked up the throttle to full speed. Wobbling dangerously because of the damage, the Gooney hurtled toward the beach at sixty-five miles per hour.

The runners dove onto their bellies again as the ultralight buzzed overhead like a large, angry hornet. Austin was operating on pure reflex, more machine than man. Holding the control stick between his knees, he leaned around the curved Plexiglas sheet that served as a windshield and sighted on the center of the mounted line. He squeezed the trigger and the flare streaked toward the horsemen like a miniature comet.

The awkward angle of the aircraft threw Austin's aim off. The missile struck the dune a few feet below the grassy crest and exploded in a bright scarlet shower. The horses nearest to the fiery burst reared in panic. Those animals that managed to maintain their calm lost it as the plane grazed their heads like a giant buzzing insect.

Austin made a quick turn for a second run. The chaotic scene atop the dune reminded him of the famous Picasso mural, *Guernica*. It was hard to know where the horses ended and their riders began. He smiled grimly and slid another flare into the launch gun. Again he came in, attacking from the rear this time.

A ragged hole surrounded by a lacework of cracks appeared in the windshield. One of the riders had gotten off a lucky shot. Austin felt the bullet whistle by his ear. He made a superhuman effort to keep a grip on his concentration as he aimed the pistol and squeezed the trigger.

The second flare streaked toward the confusing mass of horse and human bodies and slammed into a rider with a burst of red phosphorus. He fell from his horse and was dragged off with one foot still caught in the stirrup.

The beach flashed by in a blur, and again Austin was out to sea. He came around at an angle until he was behind the dune once more. The grass was on fire and black smoke billowed into the sky. Riders who had been thrown by their mounts were trying to roll out of the way to avoid being trampled. Others had dismounted and held tightly to the reins as they tried to calm the terrified animals. The horses bumped into one another, and the contact only served to increase their terror.

A lone horseman broke away from the others and spurred his mount into a gallop. Kaela and her friends heard the thunder of hooves and turned to see the rider bearing down on them with sword held high. Austin swung around until he was facing the horseman. He brought up the flare gun, but had a problem keeping it steady for proper aim. Instead, he put the Gooney into a low dive that took him a few feet above the heads of the runners and aimed directly at the horseman, a big man with a flowing red beard. At the last second, Austin pulled up. The float missed the man's head by inches. The horse whinnied in terror and broke into a wild run. The rider struggled to hang on as the horse took matters into its own hooves, climbed the dune and chased after the other riders, who had lost their stomach for the attack and were galloping for the woods.

Meanwhile, Austin was fighting a losing battle to keep the damaged plane level. He sat half out of the cockpit, like someone hiking out on an angled sailboat, gritted his teeth – and braced himself for the hard landing that he knew was coming.

5

Kaela Dorn held her breath as the strange little aircraft plunged from the sky in a spiraling tailspin. At the last second, the plane swung up in a wild G-force swoop. It soared and dipped like a kite on a string, then leveled off, although the wings quivered and the aircraft pitched and yawed as if it were on an invisible roller coaster.

The pilot finally brought the plane under a semblance of control and put it in a landing glide. He held it steady, but before he could touch down, the left wing dipped sharply and dug into the soft sand. The wing snapped off where it joined the fuselage and the plane slammed into the beach at an angle, skidding several yards before it came to a jarring halt, tail section high in the air. The engine shut down, and the beach was suddenly quiet except for the lap of waves and the crackle of burning grass.

The reporter and her colleagues stared like zombies at the plane wreck. They were too exhausted to move, drained by their swim to shore, still panting from the run for their lives. Kaela was in the best shape of the three, and her legs felt like putty. When the stubby plane had first appeared, they hadn't known whether it was friend or foe, but there had been no question as to the intentions of the horsemen with their wild yells and drawn swords: They had been out for blood.

The plane looked like a bird that had flown into a fan, and it seemed impossible that its pilot could have escaped without harm, but someone moved in the cockpit. The pilot got one leg, then another over the cockpit combing and climbed out. He seemed to be all right as he walked around the aircraft, hands on hips, inspecting the damage. He kicked a buckled wheel as if he were checking out a used car and shook his head. Then he turned to the television crew, gave them a friendly wave, and started in their direction, walking with a slight limp.

Lombardo and Dundee moved in and stood protectively at Kaela's sides. She was more interested in appraising the stranger. He was tall, slightly over six feet, and the broad powerful shoulders of a nightclub bouncer filled out the navy sweatshirt. He wore tan shorts, and his muscular legs looked as if they could propel the husky body through a brick wall. As he came closer, he removed his baseball cap to reveal his steel gray, almost platinum hair. His bronzed face was unlined, except for laugh crinkles around the eyes and mouth. She guessed his age at around forty.

Dried blood dripped down one cheek and soaked the bandanna around his forehead. The aircraft landing must have been hair-raising, yet he seemed as if he were coming off a game of tennis.

'Good afternoon,' he said, with a wide grin. 'Are you folks okay?'

'Yes, we're fine, thank you,' Kaela replied warily. 'What about you? You're bleeding.'

He touched the wound absentmindedly. 'It's only a little cut. I'm still in one piece, more or less.' He jerked his thumb at the battered ultralight. 'Wish I could say the same for my transportation. They just don't make them like they used to. You don't happen to have a roll of duct tape?'

Kaela ventured a smile. 'Your plane has gone beyond the duct tape stage,' she said. 'I believe the term insurance people use is *totaled*.'

The stranger grimaced. 'I'm afraid you're right, Ms –'

'Dorn. Kaela Dorn. This is my producer, Mickey Lombardo, and his assistant, Hank Simpson. We're with the *Unbelievable Mysteries* television series.'

'I thought so. My name is Kurt Austin. I'm with NUMA.'

'*NUMA*.' Lombardo stepped forward and pumped Austin's hand. 'Boy, are we glad to see *you*. Lucky you came by.'

'It was more than luck,' Austin said. 'I've been looking for you folks. You were supposed to rendezvous with the *Argo* this morning.'

'Sorry about that,' Lombardo said. 'We took a detour to check out an old Russian submarine base that's supposed to be around here.'

'The captain of the *Argo* isn't too happy. You've

73

delayed his departure schedule. It might have saved us some grief if you had let us know that your plans had changed.' Austin was smiling, but the gentle scolding tone of his voice was unmistakable.

'It's *my* fault,' Kaela said. 'We thought we'd only be a few hours. We intended to call you at sea, but the fishing boat we hired didn't have a workable radio. The captain had to return to port for engine repairs, and he planned to get the radio fixed and give you a call.'

'That must be the fishing boat I saw steaming away from here.'

She nodded. 'He was going to pick us up in the morning. Thank you for saving our lives. I apologize for putting you through so much trouble.'

'No trouble,' he said, reluctant to chastise the bedraggled group any further. He gazed at the wrecked aircraft. 'Maybe a *little* trouble. What made your boat capsize?'

'Someone on shore shot at us and killed the Turkish man who was bringing us in,' Kaela said. 'A wave caught us broadside and the boat went over. We hid under the Zodiac and tried to move it away from the beach, but the surf was too strong and we came almost straight in.' She glanced toward the dune where she had first seen the attackers. 'Do you know who those men on horseback were?'

Austin didn't reply. Although he seemed to be studying her face, Kaela became aware that her wet T-shirt and shorts clung to her lithe figure. She self-consciously plucked at the sand-caked front of the shirt, but the fabric insisted on plastering itself to her skin. Austin sensed her discomfiture and stared off at the smoke rising from the dune.

'My guess is that they weren't the local equestrian group out for a jaunt,' he said. 'Let's take a look.'

He climbed up the sloping beach, with the others trailing tentatively behind. The fire had almost burned itself out. They walked through the charred stalks of grass at the top of the dune. Austin saw sunlight glinting off something on the ground and went over to investigate. It was a saber. He picked the weapon up and tested the heft and balance. The sword's long, curved blade was perfectly weighted to give the arm greater striking power. Austin's jaw muscles clenched as he contemplated the terrible damage the scalpel-sharp edge could inflict on human flesh. He was examining the Cyrillic writing etched into the blade when the Australian called out. Dundee was standing in a knee-high patch of unburned grass staring at something at his feet.

'What is it?' Austin said.

'Dead guy.'

Austin stuck the saber point into the sand and waded through the thatch. Dundee pointed to the body of a man who lay on his back, glassy eyes locked in a death stare. A black beard and mustache matted with sand hid most of his features. He could have been in his forties. His head was twisted at a wrong angle. Blood soaked one side of his face, which had a caved-in look to it.

Austin said, 'I'd guess he fell off his horse during the fight and was kicked in the head.' He was not a callous man, but he felt no pity for the dead horseman.

Lombardo had retrieved his camera from the beached Zodiac and was filming the battle site. He and Kaela came over to see what the others were looking at. Lombardo let out a low whistle. 'What kind of a getup is that?'

Austin knelt by the body. 'Looks like something out of *The Wizard of Oz*.'

The dead man wore a long muddy-gray coat that buttoned up the front and baggy pants tucked into black boots. His black fur pillbox hat lay a few feet away. Red epaulets decorated each shoulder. A pistol holster and scabbard hung from the wide leather belt that encircled his waist. Slung across his chest was a cartridge belt. A sheathed dagger hung from a cord around his neck.

'G'day!' Dundee said with wonderment. 'The man's a walking arsenal.'

Austin searched the grass around the dead man. A few yards away, he found a rifle and he put the stock against his shoulder and worked the well-oiled bolt. Like the saber blade, the barrel was etched with Cyrillic writing. Austin was a collector of dueling pistols, and he had accumulated a general knowledge of antique guns. The rifle was a Moisin-Nagant, more than a hundred years old, and in mint condition. He uttered a silent prayer of thanks that the horsemen weren't carrying modern automatic weapons. A single

Kalashnikov would have ripped him and the Gooney to shreds.

Austin handed the rifle off to Dundee and went through the dead man's pockets. Nothing. He unpinned the metal starburst emblem from the front of the hat and pocketed it. Lombardo had finished filming the battle scene, and Kaela suggested shooting some footage around the one-story cinder-block buildings farther inland.

'Not a good idea,' Austin said, pointing to the trail of hoofprints leading toward the structures. He'd been worried that the horsemen would make a return appearance, but hadn't said anything because there wasn't much they could do about it. 'In fact, I'd suggest that we get out of here as soon as we can.' He rested the rifle on his shoulder, retrieved the saber and started walking back toward the beach. Kaela caught up with him on the crest of the dune.

'Do you have any idea what this is all about?' she said breathlessly. 'Why these men would want to kill us?'

'You know as much as I do. I thought they were filming a movie until somebody took a few shots at me.'

'It's a good thing for us that their aim was bad.' She paused. Austin was studying her face the way he had earlier. 'Is there anything wrong?'

'I'm almost embarrassed to say.'

'I find it hard to believe that you'd be embarrassed. You hardly seem the shy type.'

Austin shrugged. 'Well, in a manner of speaking, you might say we've met before.'

'Sorry, I'm sure I would have remembered.'

'Not literally. Believe me when I say this. You bear a striking resemblance to the face of a princess I once saw painted on the wall of an Egyptian temple.'

Kaela was tall, with a good part of her height invested in long shapely legs. She had a smooth mocha complexion and ebony black hair that she kept long with a natural tight curl. Her mouth was full and almost perfect, and her eyes were a dark amber. As an attractive woman working in a man's profession, she thought she had heard every male line invented – but this was a new one. She gave Austin a sidelong glance. 'That's funny, I was thinking that you looked as if you'd fallen off Captain Kidd's pirate ship.'

Austin laughed and ran his fingers through his disheveled hair. 'I suppose I do look like a pirate, but I'm not joking. You're a ringer for the young woman in the temple. You're quite a bit younger than she is, though. I believe her portrait dates back to about four thousand BC.'

'I've been called a lot of things,' she said, 'but never an Egyptian *mummy*. Thanks for the compliment, if that's what it was. And for saving our necks. There's no way we can ever repay you, Mr Austin.'

'You can start by calling me Kurt. And may I call you Kaela?'

She smiled. 'Of course.'

'Now that we're old friends, how about being my guest at dinner?'

She glanced up and down the deserted coast. 'What did you have in mind, something out of the Boy Scout handbook? Roots and berries?'

'I only made it as far as Cub Scout, and foraging was never my forte. I was thinking more of something like *duck à l'orange*. I can almost guarantee a table with a water view.'

'Here?' she said, going along with the game.

'No, *there*.' He pointed out to sea, where a turquoise-hulled ship could be seen steaming in their direction. 'Casa *Argo*. They say the chef used to work at the Four Seasons before NUMA stole him.'

'My mother didn't raise any stupid kids,' Kaela said. 'I'd be a fool to refuse an invitation like that.' Conscious of her unkempt state, she said, 'I don't think I'm dressed for a fancy dinner.'

'I'm sure we can find something appropriate aboard the ship. I'll ask when I call for reservations. My radio is the only thing that wasn't smashed when I landed. Maybe you can round up your friends while I hail the boat – but you might want to hurry them along. We're on Russian territory, and I don't have my passport. We shouldn't overstay our welcome.'

Kaela followed Austin with her eyes as he made his way back to the damaged ultralight. She sensed a story. Who *was* this guy? This was no nerd. She called out to Mike and Dundee and told them to wrap up their filming. Then she hurried to catch up with Austin.

6

Moscow, Russia

Wielding iron self-control, Viktor Petrov replaced his telephone in its cradle, tented his fingers and stared into space. After a moment lost in thought, he rose from his desk and went to the window. As he gazed out at the city, letting his eyes linger on the turnip-shaped spires of St Basil's in the distance, his hand came up and brushed his right cheek. He hardly felt the touch of his fingers through the parchment-like scar tissue that covered the dead nerve endings in his skin. How long had it been? *Fifteen years.* Strange. After all that time, a single phone call brought back memories of the searing pain.

Petrov watched the crowds of pedestrians swarming in the summer heat and yearned for winter. Like many of his countrymen, he had a poignant attachment to snow. The Russian winter was harsh and unforgiving, but it had protected the country from the armies of Napoleon and Hitler. Petrov's love of snow was more prosaic, as well. Winter covered the city's flaws, hushed its noise and hid its corruption under a white blanket of purity.

He returned to his battered metal desk, the largest

object in the small, drab room. At one elbow was an old-fashioned black dial telephone. At the other, a fax machine. An empty filing cabinet stood in a corner, there mainly for show. The cramped office was one of dozens of cubicles that made up the tenth-floor warren of the agricultural building, a soaring gray monument to the banality of socialist architecture. Printed in small letters on the door were the words SIBERIAN PEST CONTROL. Petrov rarely had visitors. Occasionally, a lost soul blundered into the office, only to be told that Siberian Pest Control had moved.

In spite of his spartan surroundings, Petrov exerted wide power in the Russian government. The key to his influence was the anonymity that kept him from view. He remembered the old days when *Pravda* had dutifully printed photos of the Soviet hierarchy reviewing the May Day parade from Lenin's tomb. Any hint that someone in the lineup was a possible successor to the reigning tyrant of the day marked the unfortunate individual for liquidation. Petrov had mastered the art of fading into the woodwork. He was the bureaucratic equivalent of a shape-shifter, a legendary being that can change form at will. He had survived three premiers and countless Politburo members with his ability to avoid definition. He hadn't allowed himself to be photographed in years. The photos clipped to his personnel files were of dead men. He resisted attempts to give him a title. In the various evolutions of his long career, he was known simply as an *aide*.

In keeping with his façade, Petrov enclosed his athletic physique in one of the baggy monotone suits that had long been the uniform of the Kremlin's faceless gray men. His pepper-and-salt hair was worn over the collar of his cheap shirt as if he could not afford a regular haircut. The glass in his wire-rimmed spectacles was plain and intended to give him a professorial look. Disguise had its limitations, though. He could cover his scar, but no sartorial sleight of hand could hide the lively intelligence that glinted in the slate-blue eyes, and his chiseled profile projected a ruthless determination.

The caller was an earnest young man named Aleksei, whom Petrov had personally recruited as an agent. 'There is a new development in the south,' he said, making no effort to hide his excitement.

The four cardinal directions had become a rough verbal shorthand in alerting Petrov to the general location of trouble in the vortex of assassinations, murders, rebellions and unrest that swirled around in the far corners of the old Soviet empire. Petrov thought he was about to hear more bad news from the Republic of Georgia.

'Go ahead,' Petrov said automatically.

'An American ship violated Russian territory in the Black Sea earlier today.'

'What sort of ship?' Petrov said, with barely disguised irritation. Far more weighty matters occupied his mind.

'It was a survey vessel from the National Underwater and Marine Agency.'

'*NUMA*?' Petrov tightened his grip on the phone. 'Go on,' he said, trying to keep his voice level.

'Our observers identified the vessel as the *Argo*. I checked on the ship's permit. The vessel is only allowed to conduct operations in the open sea. Several communications were picked up between the ship and an aircraft. The pilot of the plane indicated his intention to enter Russian territory.'

'Did the plane actually cross our borders?'

'We don't know, sir. There were no radar sightings.'

'Well, this is not exactly an invasion, Aleksei. Is it not a matter that should be taken up with the US State Department?'

'Not in this case, sir. The plane gave its positions, so we were able to chart its course. It was flying near Department Three Thirty-one when the pilot made plans to rendezvous with the ship.'

Petrov's lips parted in a silent curse. 'You're *certain* of their position?'

'Absolutely.'

'Where is the NUMA ship now?'

'The coastguard's dispatched a helicopter to the scene. The ship has left Russian territorial waters and appears to be on its way to Istanbul. We're continuing to monitor radio messages.'

'What about the aircraft?'

'No sign of it.'

'There was a thorough visual inspection of their landing site, I assume.'

'Yes, sir. The landing party reported seeing about an acre of burned grass. There were many footprints and evidence of horses.'

Horses. Petrov had the feeling someone had walked on his grave.

'I want you to follow the progress of the ship. If it makes port, place it under twenty-four-hour surveillance. Alert me to any development that has to do with this vessel.'

'Yes, sir. Is that all?'

'Send me the printed conversations between the pilot and ship.'

'I'll do that immediately.'

Petrov praised the agent for his thoroughness and hung up. The fax machine hummed a few minutes later and spat out several sheets of paper. Petrov studied the double-spaced transcript of the conversation between the *Argo*'s captain and the man in the aircraft. His fingers stiffened as he read the first sentence.

'Austin to *Argo*.'

Austin. It couldn't be.

Petrov took a deep breath to steady his nerves. Austin was a common name in the United States, and NUMA was a large organization. He tried to persuade himself that it was sheer coincidence, but as he read the transcript, his lips curled into a

84

grim smile. There was no mistaking the pilot's wise-cracking tone. The irreverent reference to the director of NUMA clinched it. He was reading pure Kurt Austin.

Petrov reached into a dusty file cabinet and extracted a thick folder marked *NUMA, Kurt Austin.* The dossier's well-worn pages told him what he already knew by heart. Austin had been born in Seattle, his father the wealthy owner of a marine salvage company. The sea had shaped his adventurous personality. He could sail as soon as he could walk, and as he grew older, he acquired a taste for racing speedboats, although in recent years he had taken up sculling on the Potomac. He lived in a converted boathouse below the Palisades in Washington, D.C., less than a mile from the Central Intelligence Agency at Langley. He enjoyed philosophy, collected dueling pistols, listened to progressive jazz . . .

Petrov read further, though his eyes barely registered the words. After studying for his master's in systems management at the University of Washington, Austin had attended a highly rated Seattle dive school and trained as a professional. He'd brought these skills to bear working on North Sea oil rigs, then returned to his father's salvage company before being lured into government service by a little-known branch of the CIA that specialized in under-water intelligence-gathering. At the end of the Cold War, the CIA had closed down the branch and

NUMA director Admiral James Sandecker had hired Austin to head up a special assignments team being assembled for oceanographic research.

Their backgrounds couldn't have been more different, Austin and Petrov. Like the American, Petrov had salt water in his veins, but his beginnings were more humble. He'd been born the only son of a poor fisherman. As a Young Pioneer, his intelligence and athletic ability were noticed by a visiting political commissar, and he was taken to Moscow and made a ward of the state. He never saw his parents or siblings again. Even worse, he didn't care to see them; the Soviet state had become his new family. He attended the finest Soviet schools, excelling in engineering, served a stint in the KGB as a submarine officer, and later moved to naval intelligence. Like Austin, Petrov had also served in a little-known ocean intelligence branch. Unlike Austin's group, which concentrated on oceanographic research, Petrov's people were authorized to carry out their duties by *any* means, including force.

Their paths had first crossed after an Israeli submarine clandestinely sank an Iranian container ship carrying nuclear weapons. Petrov was ordered to retrieve the weapons at all costs: The container ship could be an embarrassment, because the weapons had been stolen from the Soviet arsenal. Meanwhile, the US was performing a balancing act between its Arab allies and Israel, and Washington had worried that if Iran knew how the ship had been sunk, they would declare a holy war that would spread around the region. Austin had been made the director of an attempt to salvage the container ship and destroy the evidence.

Ships from the USSR and the US had arrived over the sunken container ship at about the same time. Neither ship would give way to the other. The stand-off dragged on for days. Warships from both countries hovered on the horizon. It was a tense time. Petrov was awaiting orders from Moscow when he was called to the bridge to hear a message from the American ship.

'This is the US vessel *Talon* calling unknown Soviet salvage ship. Come in, please.' The caller spoke in heavily accented Russian.

'Soviet salvage ship to *Talon*,' Petrov replied in the American-accented English he had learned at the state schools.

'Do you mind if we speak in English?' the American said. 'My Russian is a little rusty.'

'No problem. I assume you called to let us know you will be moving off-site.'

'No, actually I called to check on your caviar supply.'

Petrov smiled. 'It is more than adequate, thank you. Now let me ask a question. When will your ship be departing?'

'Your command of English isn't as good as I thought. We have no intention of leaving inter-national waters.'

'Then the responsibility for any repercussions will be on your head.'

'Sorry, we're not accepting repercussions.'

'Then we have no alternative but to force the situation.'

'Let's see if we can settle this thing amicably, *tovarich*,' the American replied casually. 'We both know what's on that wreck and what a pain it could cause our respective countries. So here's my suggestion: We pull back while you go down and retrieve your, uh, stolen property. We'll even give you a hand if you'd like. When you're finished with your salvage work, you leave and we'll dispose of the evidence. What do you say?'

'Interesting proposition.'

'I think so.'

'How do I know I can trust you?'

'Action speaks louder than words. I've given the order to move back a half mile.'

Petrov watched the American ship lift anchor and reposition itself farther from the salvage site. Petrov judged that despite the American's lighthearted manner, he was determined to carry out his mission. The alternative to a deal was an escalation of force. Petrov was no gambler. If the American reneged, Petrov could use the armed men on his ship and the Soviet navy was on call. No matter what the outcome, however, he would not look good for letting the confrontation get out of control.

'Very well,' he said. 'Once we are finished with our salvage, we will leave and you may move in.'

'Fair enough. What's your name, by the way? I like to know whom I'm dealing with.'

The question caught Petrov off-guard. In a sense, he had no name, having been given one by the Soviet government. He chuckled and said, 'You may call me Ivan.'

His answer was greeted by a deep laugh. 'I'll bet half the guys on your ship are named Ivan. Okay, you can call me John Doe.' He wished Petrov good luck in Russian and hung up.

Petrov lost no time sending divers down to the container ship. The torpedo blast hole allowed for relatively easy access to the hull, and two nuclear devices were extracted. There were a few dicey moments when currents snagged the lifting line, but they worked on rotating shifts and got the job done in less than twenty-four hours. Petrov ordered the ship to move out and signaled the Americans. The vessels passed within a few hundred yards of each other, going in opposite directions. Petrov stood on the deck and looked through binoculars at the American vessel. Through the lenses, he saw a husky man with gray hair looking back at him. At one point, the American lowered his binoculars and waved. Petrov ignored him.

Their next encounter was not as friendly. A commercial airliner from a third-world nation had been mysteriously shot down in the Persian Gulf. Paranoia was the reigning national psychosis of the Cold War, and for reasons as vague as they were far-fetched, both countries suspected the other of complicity. Again, Petrov and Austin located the plane at the same time. Petrov's ship came close to ramming the American vessel, shearing off at the last second so Austin could see the heavily armed men on deck. Austin called Petrov and warned the Russian to improve his driving or he'd get a traffic ticket. Austin stubbornly refused to move out. An international incident was avoided only when ships from the plane's home nation showed up at the site to claim the jetliner.

As the rival vessels steamed off in opposite directions, Austin radioed a good-bye message.

'So long, Ivan. 'Til we meet again.'

Petrov had a short fuse in his younger days, and this arrogant American was annoying him. 'You better hope that won't happen,' he said with chilling directness. 'Neither one of us will be happy with the outcome.'

Eight months later, Petrov's prediction came true.

During the Cold War, the United States pursued a daring intelligence operation. When the secret was finally unveiled years later, one writer called it *Blind Man's Bluff*, a dangerous game played by a few intrepid sub commanders and their crews whereby they would bring their subs within a few miles of the Soviet coast to gather intelligence. One scheme involved planting an electronic pod to listen in on underwater communications cables.

In his drab Moscow office, Petrov lit up one of the thin Havana cigars he had made on special order and puffed out a mouthful of smoke. His mind drifted back through the years, and in the purple cloud that swirled in front of him, he saw the morning mists rising off the dark, cold surface of the Barents Sea as his ship cut through the water at full speed.

He had been in Moscow trying to extract funds for new equipment from a strategically placed *apparatchik* who was complaining about tight purse strings. One of Petrov's assistants had called and said that a strange message had been picked up from an unknown ship close to Russian shores. The coded message was short, as if the operator were in a hurry. The Soviet cryptographers were trying to decipher the message. The only reason someone would risk sending a message would be if he were in trouble, Petrov thought, as the bureaucrat blathered on. Petrov was well aware that American subs had come into the Barents Sea. Could one of these boats be in trouble?

He broke off his meeting and caught a plane to Murmansk, where his survey ship was waiting. The vessel had supplemented its scientific gear with depth charges, guns and a trained complement of armed Marines. By the time his ship was under way, the code had been broken. The message consisted of one word: *Stranded.* He ordered all ships and aircraft to be on the lookout for strange vessels on or under the surface.

Despite the Soviets' vigilance, however, the *Talon* carried out a picture-perfect rescue operation. The American ship came in during the night with a Russian-language expert on board who gave a phony identification when the ship was picked up on radar. The ID wasn't perfect, but it bought time. Another American submarine, whose propeller had been made to operate noisily, drew the Russians' attention away. The stranded submarine was in about three hundred feet of water, sitting flat on the bottom, its power out after an electrical explosion. The hundred-man crew was rescued in a matter of hours, using a special diving bell.

Petrov had finally figured out the decoy ruse and was speeding in his ship to the rescue site. The ship followed the communications cable until magneto-meter readings showed a huge mass of ferrous material. It could only be the US sub. A ship was rapidly moving out of the area, and Petrov recognized the *Talon*. Speaking in English, Petrov hailed the ship by its name and ordered it to stop.

A familiar voice responded over the radio. 'Ivan, is that *you*?' said the man who called himself John Doe. 'Nice to hear your voice again.'

'Prepare to be boarded or your ship will be sunk.'

A roar of laughter burst from the radio. 'Hell, Ivan, I thought you Russians were better chess players than that.'

'Frankly, I prefer stud poker.'

'Which is obviously where you learned how to bluff. Nice try, comrade.'

'This is your last warning. Aircraft will be overhead in five minutes, and your ship will be destroyed if you don't stop.'

'Too little and too late. We'll be in international waters in *three* minutes. Our State and Defense Departments are aware of the situation. Looks like you're out of luck.'

'I don't think so. We still have your submarine and its contents, Mr Doe. Our scientists will have a field day dissecting your top-secret equipment.'

'That's not going to happen, old pal.'

'I think it will. The *Glomar Explorer* isn't the only boat that can raise a submarine.' Petrov was referring to an earlier US salvage of a Soviet submarine.

'I wouldn't get *near* that boat if I were you. It's heavily mined.'

'*Now* who's bluffing, Mr Doe?'

'I'm dead serious, Ivan. The sub carried two hundred pounds of HBX explosives in case something like this happened.'

'Why would you care if I were killed?'

'Look, Ivan, the Cold War's not going to last forever. Someday we'll bump into each other in a bar and you'll buy me a Stolichnaya martini.' His voice lost its levity. 'No joke. This thing will self-destruct in about twenty minutes. I set the timer myself.'

'You're lying.'

'People like us don't lie to each other, old pal.'

It was Ivan's turn to laugh. 'You've seen too many episodes of *Mission Impossible*, old *pal*.'

He clicked off the radio. There was no way the crew could have been evacuated and set charges. He didn't know about Austin's expertise. He could have waited twenty minutes to see if Austin was telling the truth, but he seethed with anger. His rage overcame his good judgment. Petrov's ship carried a one-person minisub that could be launched quickly for reconnaissance, and Petrov ordered the sub readied for a dive.

Sitting in his office years after that day, he examined the grayish-red glow of cigar ashes. How impetuous and foolish he had been as a younger man. He had jammed the bomb-shaped sub almost straight down. Within minutes, his lights had outlined the black hulk on the bottom, and he saw the pod near the cable and landed near it. The minisub's retractable metal arm had the pod in its grip – when there was a blinding flash of light and a muffled roar. Petrov felt himself flying into space. Then he blacked out.

He awoke to the antiseptic smell of a Soviet hospital. His broken and mangled leg was in traction, and the right side of his face was heavily bandaged where jagged shards of plastic or metal had torn his skin as the minisub had been blown to the surface, where it had been retrieved with him inside it. He had had to wear a hearing aid until his damaged eardrums healed. He spent four weeks in the hospital before being released to the care of a nurse at his *dacha*, the country home he maintained outside of Moscow.

Petrov had been sitting in the sunroom reading Tolstoy when the nurse brought him a bouquet of red, white and blue carnations. Tucked in with the flowers was a small card.

Thinking back to that day, Petrov pulled an envelope from the dossier. The card he extracted had yellowed with age, but the large block letters in English were clearly visible.

'Sorry you got nailed, Ivan. Can't say I didn't warn you. Get well soon so we can have that drink. First round's on me. John Doe.'

Austin had almost ended his life and career. Now the same man was poking around where he could derail Petrov's carefully laid plans. Austin could not know how dangerous his meddling was. How precarious the situation was in Russia. Throughout his country's history, it had been afflicted with uncaring, inept, even psychopathic leaders. Petrov was one of thousands of faceless clones who did the bidding of their masters without question and kept them in power. Now his fragile nation seemed poised for another orgy of self-destruction. The furies welling up in the soul of Mother Russia would soon sweep across the country from Siberia to Saint Petersburg.

Petrov read the card again, then lifted the phone.

'Yes, sir,' answered a trusted assistant who occupied an office in another part of the agricultural building.

'I want a plane ready to leave for Istanbul in one hour.' Petrov gave orders to call his mistress and cancel their dinner date.

'Is there any particular message you would like me to give Miss Kostikov?' the assistant asked.

Petrov pondered the question. 'Yes,' he said after a moment. 'Tell her I must go to repay a favor to an old friend.'

7

Novorossiysk, The Black Sea

The bearded man sat on the carpeted floor of the darkened cabin, legs folded in a lotus position, his rough peasant's hands clasped loosely in his lap. He had been locked in the same pose for more than two hours, the only sign of life the slight rise and fall of his narrow chest. His pulse was barely discernible, and his lethargic heartbeat would have alarmed a cardiologist. The heavy-lidded eyes over the prominent nose were closed, but he was neither asleep nor awake. The thick lips were curled in a beatific smile. Unseen, behind the thorny brambles that guarded the dense thicket of his mind, lurked the unfathomable musings of a madman.

A soft knock came at the door. The bearded man showed no sign that he had heard it. The knock repeated, louder and more insistent this time.

'Yes,' the man said in Russian. His deep voice sounded as if it issued from the depths of a catacomb.

The door opened a crack and a young man dressed in the uniform of a ship's steward peered into the room. Light from the passageway fell on the face of the sitting man. The steward murmured a silent prayer his grandmother had taught him to ward off demons. Mustering the courage to speak, he said, 'Forgive the interruption, sir.'

'What is it?'

'Mr Razov asks to see you in the main cabin.'

Deep-set eyes of pale yellow opened and stared out of the bony skull. They were the hypnotic eyes of a predator, large and lustrous.

A pause. Then, 'Tell him I will be there.'

'Yes, sir.' Under the spell of the unrelenting gaze, the terrified steward felt the strength start to leave his legs. He slammed the door shut and bolted along the passageway.

The man unfolded his body and stood to his full height of six feet four. He was dressed in a belted tunic of black cotton. The military collar of his shirt was tight against the neck, and his pants were tucked into low boots of shiny black leather. His dark brown hair was worn long over the ears, blending into a full beard that spilled down to his chest.

He worked the stiffness from his muscles joint by joint and took great gulps of air into his starved lungs. When all his vital systems were operating normally, he opened the cabin door, ducked his head, and stepped out into the corridor. Moving silently, he followed the passageway and climbed onto the deck of the four-hundred-foot yacht. Crewmen who saw him coming stepped aside.

The yacht had been designed with a wide uncluttered deck and low, streamlined superstructure that minimized wind resistance. Based on a design for a FastShip freighter, the vessel was built with a deep V-shaped hull that cut through the waves and a concave stern that reduced drag. Powered by gas turbines and using an innovative water jet propulsion system, the vessel could go at speeds that were twice those reached by vessels of comparable length.

The bearded man came to a door, opened it without knocking and stepped into a spacious stateroom as big as a small house. He walked through the living area with its sofas, chairs and a dining table of medieval size. The floors were carpeted with antique Persian rugs, any one of which was worth a small fortune. On the walls were priceless masterpieces, most stolen from museums and private collections.

At the far end of the room was a massive desk made of the finest mahogany inlaid with gold and pearl. On the wall behind the desk was a stylized logo that depicted a military fur hat crossed by an unsheathed saber. Printed in Cyrillic letters under the symbol were the words: ATAMAN INDUSTRIES. Seated at the desk, talking into a telephone, was Mikhail Razov, president of Ataman.

Although Razov hardly spoke above a whisper, his seemingly gentle tone couldn't mask the cold menace in his voice. His pale white face could have been carved from Carrara marble, but no one would mistake the hard-edged profile as the work of a Renaissance sculptor. It was a face that countless victims had seen with their dying breath.

Two lean, white Russian wolfhounds lounged at his feet. When the tall man approached, they began to whimper. Razov hung the phone up and shushed the dogs, who crawled under his desk. Razov underwent an astounding metamorphosis. Unexpected warmth came into the slate gray eyes, the cruel lips widened in a smile and the rough-hewn features softened. Razov could have been anyone's favorite uncle. Career criminals like Razov become accomplished actors if they live long enough. Razov had cultivated his natural chameleon's talent under the tutelage of professional actors. In an instant, he could transform himself from a murderous thug into a hard-driving businessman, a charming host or a charismatic orator.

Razov's powerful shoulders and muscular thighs offered a hint of humbler beginnings. Born on the steppes of the Black Sea, the son of a Cossack horse breeder, Razov had ridden from the time he was big enough to climb into a saddle. He'd had a keen mind and quickly saw the disadvantages of the brutal farm toil that had killed his mother and was ruining his father's health.

He ran away to the city and put his muscle to work as an enforcer for a gang of extortionists. Razov's skill as a bone crusher and killer earned him top wages. He had forgotten how many times he had put a bullet into the kneecap of a recalcitrant merchant or the head of a tardy loan customer. He'd lost count of the wayward prostitutes he had strangled. In fact, he'd used his newfound wealth to buy a house of prostitution for himself.

Soon, by eliminating his former employers, he gained control of a network of brothels. He protected his investment with a private army of ruthless thugs and branched out into gambling, drugs and loan-sharking. With generous bribes and strategic killings, Razov put himself beyond the reach of Soviet authority and became a multimillionaire. He'd become the quintessential Soviet mobster, and it seemed as if he would go on until a more aggressive rival surfaced.

The bearded man came over and stood in front of Razov's desk, hands clasped in front of him. 'You called for me, Mikhail?'

'Boris, my dear friend and advisor. I'm sorry if I disturbed your meditation, but there's important news.'

'The test was a success then?'

Razov nodded. 'The early damage reports are most impressive, considering the small scale of the experiment.' He hit a button on the desk and an orderly appeared, as if by magic, with a tray, two glasses and a bottle of vodka. Razov poured the glasses full and handed one to Boris. Dismissing the orderly, he indicated a chair, took a seat opposite and raised his glass in toast.

Boris's large Adam's apple bobbled as he noisily slugged his drink down. He drained the glass as if the contents were no stronger than herbal tea and wiped his mouth with the back of his hairy hand. 'How many dead?' he said, hardly able to control his eagerness.

'One or two,' Razov said, with a shrug. 'Apparently, there was a warning.'

The monk's strange eyes blazed with a killing anger. 'An *informer*?'

'No, it was completely unanticipated. A fisherman warned the townspeople, and the harbor was evacuated.'

'A pity,' Boris said, with genuine sadness in his voice. 'We must be sure next time that there is no warning.'

Razov nodded in agreement and pointed to a large computer-generated monitor on one wall. The screen displayed a map of the world. It sparkled with lights that showed the positions of the far-flung Ataman fleet. Using a remote control, he zoomed in on the map to bring up a line of lights assembling off the East Coast of the United States.

'Our assets are moving into position.' His eyes grew colder. 'I can assure you that when we have accomplished our work, there will be many dead to count, and much more.'

Boris smiled. 'Then the North American project is on schedule?'.

Razov refilled their glasses. He seemed troubled. 'Yes and no. There are some matters of vital importance that I want to discuss with you. They have a bearing on our plans. We must deal with an unexpected problem. There have been intruders at our Black Sea operation.'

'Moscow has heard of our activities?'

'The fools in Moscow are still unaware of our plan,' Razov replied with unveiled contempt. 'No, it was not the central government. An American television crew landed near the old submarine pen.'

'*Americans?*' He lifted his arms toward the sky. 'A gift from heaven,' he said, eyes glittering. 'I hope their necks felt the sharp edges of the Guardians' blades.'

'To the contrary. There was a fight and the Guardians were driven off. Some of your men died in the struggle.'

'How could that be, Mikhail? The Guardians are trained to kill without mercy.'

'True, they are superb horsemen, Cossack warriors in the finest sense. Their weapons are traditional but effective.'

'Then how could an unarmed television crew resist?'

'They were not alone,' Razov said, scowling. 'Apparently, they had help from an aircraft.'

'Military?'

Razov shook his head. 'My sources tell me the aircraft was launched from a ship called the *Argo*. The vessel is supposedly in the Black Sea to conduct a scientific survey for *NUMA*.'

'What is this NUMA?'

'I've forgotten that you were isolated from the outside world for many years. The National Underwater and Marine Agency is the largest oceanic science organization in the world. They have thousands of scientists and engineers spread across the globe. The pilot of the aircraft, the man who killed the Guardians, was one of those scientists.'

Boris stood and paced the cabin. 'This report concerns me. How could scientists or engineers defeat armed warriors?'

'A good question. I don't know. I'm certain of one thing, however. This is not the end of it. I have ordered preparations made to move our operations. Meanwhile, extra guards will be posted. I have taken the liberty of arming them with more contemporary weapons. I'm sorry. I know how you feel about preserving the purity of our traditions.'

'I understand the need to be ready to face impure forces. What of your source in Washington?'

'His power is limited, but I have asked him to do what he can without jeopardizing his role.'

'We must know who and what we are dealing with,' Boris said. 'This NUMA may not be what it says it is.'

'Agreed. It would be folly to underestimate them, as the Guardians did.'

'Tell me about these television people.'

'I have confirmed that they were from an American network. Two men and a woman.'

Boris stroked his beard in thought. 'This is no accident. The television people and this NUMA must be a cover for an American scheme. Where are they now?'

'On the *Argo* heading back to Istanbul. I've dispatched a boat to follow her.'

'Can we destroy the NUMA ship?'

'As easily as smashing an insect, but I don't think it would be wise at this time. It might draw attention to our Black Sea venture.'

'Then we must wait.'

'I agree. After the Black Sea venture is done, then you may take your vengeance.'

'I defer to your wisdom, Mikhail.'

Razov's smile had all the warmth of an anaconda's. 'No, Boris, it is *you* who is the wise one. My expertise is business and politics, but you have the vision for the great and grand future.'

'A vision you will carry out as the lone defender against the corruption and materialism that is a cancer in our once-great country. We must show the world that our cause is right. Nothing must stand in the way of our plan to carve out decay where we find it.'

'I want you to see something,' Razov said. He punched a button on his desk. 'This is my most recent speech before the army.'

A picture appeared on the wall screen: Razov speaking in a large hall. The audience was made up of men in the uniforms of the various Russian armed services. Razov stepped onto the stage, and within minutes he had his audience in the palm of his hand. As he spoke, he seemed to grow to ten feet high, drawing on the power of his deep voice, impressive physique and his convictions to exhort the crowd:

'We must honor the warrior creed of our Cossack brothers. Our people threw off the yoke of the Ottoman Empire and defeated Napoleon. The Cossacks took Azov for Peter the Great and have defended the borders of Russia against intruders for centuries. Now, seven million strong, with your help, we will destroy the enemies within, the financiers, the criminals and the politicians who would grind our country to dust beneath their boots.'

Before long the crowd was on its feet in a frightening example of mass hysteria. They surged toward the podium with glazed eyes, arms reaching out. They wanted to be part of him. They were chanting, 'Razov . . . Razov . . . Razov . . .' He flicked off the television.

'You have learned well, Mikhail,' Boris said.

'No, Boris. You have taught me well.'

'I merely showed you how to draw upon the passions of our people.'

'This is nothing compared to what is to come. But much depends on our Black Sea work. I was talking to the salvage ship when you arrived. There are many difficulties, but they are close to their goal. I told them that their lives depended on success. I will not accept failure.'

'Do you wish me to look into the future?'

'Yes, tell me what you see.'

Boris bent his head and touched his fingers to his brow. His eyes became glassy. Speaking as if his voice were coming from a cave, he said, 'I prophesy that the day will come when you take the reins as the new tsar of Mother Russia. All our enemies will be vanquished. The United States will be the first to feel the sword of righteousness.'

'What else do you see?'

His forehead furrowed as if he were in pain, and his voice became hollow. 'Cold and blackness. A place of death under the sea.' He reached out and grabbed Razov's arm, digging his fingers into the flesh like daggers. 'There is light.' The thick lips curled into a beatific smile. 'Success is within reach.' Life returned to the stony eyes. 'The ghosts of the dead will soon bestow their blessing on our cause. They plead for you to seek revenge in their name.'

Razov had been a successful gangster and was a creature of the city. Once out of his element he was practically helpless. Razov thought back to his first meeting with Boris. He had been wandering, lost and half starved, through the bleak countryside when he came upon a stream of peasants. There were dozens of them, frail and sick, some unable to walk, carried by others. When he asked where they were going, they replied that they were going to the monastery to be cured by the 'mad one.' Having nothing else to do, he followed. He saw the crippled throw away their crutches and walk and blind people claim they could see. When he went up to Boris, the monk had gazed at him as if they had known each other forever and said, 'I have been expecting you, my son.'

Under the gaze of those remarkable eyes, Razov had poured out his story. His shock at his father's dying words. His retreat from civilization and his wanderings in the wild country around the Black Sea. Boris told him to stay after the others had left, and they talked through the night. When Razov asked where the other monks were, Boris only said, 'They were unworthy.' Razov suspected the horrible truth, but it made no difference. When he returned to civilization, the bizarre figure of the bearded monk was at his side, and he had been at his side ever since.

Eventually, other mobsters had moved into Razov's territory. At Boris's suggestion, he'd sent out word that he was abandoning his turf, and he made sure his sordid past would not come back to haunt him. First, he changed his name, then, after several assassinations, some arson fires and bombings, he had wiped out most connections to his criminal days. Using the millions stashed in Swiss bank accounts and the strong-arm methods that had served him well as a criminal, he'd bought into mines that were slipping from communist control. Soon he expanded his mining interests into the sea.

Observers noted a mysterious and profound bond between the two men. Razov consulted Boris on all crucial decisions and he rewarded Boris handsomely. The monk himself was a study in multiple personality. His stateroom on the yacht was furnished with only a cot, where he spent many hours in meditation, and he would go for long periods without washing. Sometimes, however, when the yacht was in port, he disappeared. Razov had Boris followed and learned that the monk had been spending his time in the seediest brothels. Boris seemed to be struggling with his two sides, the ascetic monk and the murderous voluptuary.

For all his madness, though, the monk was a valuable advisor, his insanity tempered by a rational intelligence. In this case, Boris was right about NUMA. It might prove a menace waiting in the wings.

8

The Black Sea

Following in the wake of the original *Argo*, the NUMA ship steamed across the Black Sea toward the Bosporus, the narrow strait that separated the Asian and European sides of Istanbul. Unlike Jason, who brought home the Golden Fleece, all that Austin had to show for his labors was a head laceration, a bedraggled television crew and a pile of unanswered questions.

The evacuation from the Russian beach had gone off without a hitch. Captain Atwood had sent a boat in to transport Austin and the television people to the *Argo*. Moving the Gooney was less trouble than anticipated; it was mostly a case of picking up the pieces. Austin didn't look forward to telling Zavala that the nifty little plane he'd designed could practically fit into a shoe box.

On the final run to the beach, Austin had spotted something floating in the water. It was the body of the Turkish helmsman, Mehmet. They'd hauled the body onto the tender and brought it back to the ship. The pitiful sight reminded Austin of the deadly game he'd been playing. One wrong roll of the dice and it would have been his body pulled from the water and wrapped in a tarpaulin.

Austin checked in with the ship's paramedic to have his cut treated, then showered and changed. He had suggested to Kaela that she meet him for dinner in the mess hall after she had a chance to rest. Austin snagged a table next to a big window that looked out over the stern deck. He was gazing out at the ship's foamy wake, trying to make sense of the skirmish on the beach, when Kaela made her entrance.

The reporter wore jeans and a faded blue chambray shirt borrowed from a female oceanographer whose figure must have been shorter and wider. What would have been practical but ill-fitting work clothes on another woman achieved an elegant sophistication draped over Kaela's slim physique. As she entered the mess, she could have been strolling down a Paris runway wearing the latest in avant-garde fashion.

She smiled at Austin and came over to the table. 'Something smells good.'

'You're in luck. The chef has decided on an Italian theme. Have a seat.'

She sat down and closed her eyes. 'Don't tell me.' She inhaled the aromas coming from the galley. 'An antipasto of truffle salad and olivi mushrooms followed by a porcini risotto.'

'Not quite.' Austin cleared his throat. 'We're having pizza. Mushroom, or pepperoni if you'd prefer *carne*.'

Kaela opened her eyes and stared at Austin. 'What happened to the four-star chef?'

Austin tried his best to look angelic, but his rugged features wouldn't cooperate. 'I confess. I exaggerated. My intentions were entirely honorable. Your spirits needed a lift back there on the beach.'

'And *you* looked like you'd pushed your face through a plate-glass window. Glad to see you're in better shape.'

'Amazing the miracles that can be performed with a needle, sutures and swabs.'

Kaela glanced over at the serving counter. 'How's the pizza?'

'Almost as good as Spago's. Especially when you have nectar like this to wash it down.' He reached under the table and produced a bottle of Brunello Chianti Classico. 'I picked up a case when we stopped in Venice.'

'You're *full* of surprises, aren't you?' Kaela said, laughing.

'Sorry the dinner is not quite as advertised, but you'll have to admit that the water-view table is as promised.'

'No argument there. The view is spectacular.' She rose and said, 'If you open the bottle, I'll get our dinner.' She grabbed a tray and stepped into the serving line. A few minutes later, she returned with two personal-sized pizzas and Caesar salads. Austin had the wine opened and poured their glasses. They hungrily attacked their dinner.

'This pizza is *incredible*,' Kaela said. She sipped the

wine with a dreamy expression on her face. Suddenly, she glanced around as if she had lost something. 'Have you seen Mickey and Dundee?'

'I meant to tell you. The boys grabbed something to eat earlier, then went up to the bridge to shoot some video. Seems they've charmed their way past Captain Atwood's gruff façade.'

'The camera tends to bring out the ham in people.'

Austin refilled their glasses. 'Tell me about your Noah's ark assignment.'

'It's the usual combination of humbug and fact that *Unbelievable Mysteries* packages for the mass TV audience. They splice old blurry images with new footage and do a dramatic voice-over. Heavy on the mysterious background music. There's usually a hint of a government cover-up and some danger to the crew. The viewers love it.'

'The danger was real this time.'

'Yes, it was,' she said thoughtfully. 'That's why I feel so bad about Captain Kemel's cousin. It was my idea to look into the old sub base.'

'Don't blame yourself. There was no way you could have known you'd be shot out of the water.'

'Still – has anyone been able to contact Captain Kemal?'

'The bridge got in touch with him a while ago. Apparently, his radio is working now. The captain gave him the bad news.'

'Poor Mehmet. I keep playing that scene over and

over again in my head. His family must be devastated.'
Austin gently tried to take Kaela's mind off a situation
she couldn't alter.

'If you're looking for Noah's ark, wouldn't you do
better poking around Mount Ararat?'

Kaela welcomed the chance to change the subject.
'No, not especially. You're familiar with the findings
of William Ryan and Walter Pitman?'

'They're the Columbia University geologists who
speculated that the Black Sea was originally a freshwater lake before the Mediterranean broke through
the Bosporus in a great flood. The people who lived
along the shore had to run for their lives.'

'Then you must know that the saga of the flood,
passed down by generations of bards, may have
inspired the tale of Noah and the ark. Which means
that the ark sailed these waters. It would be a waste
of time humping our cameras up the side of Mount
Ararat. Don't you agree?'

Austin leaned back in his chair and gazed into the
dark amber eyes. They sparkled with good-humored
intelligence.

'I'll answer that with a question of my own.'

'Let me guess. You want to know why someone
who pretends to be a serious reporter ended up on
the television equivalent of a supermarket tabloid.'

Austin added perceptiveness to the list of Kaela's
other admirable qualities. 'I've seen your show. In
the episode I watched, Big Foot had been found
living in Loch Ness with an alien love-child.'

'That must have been before *my* time, but I take your point. *U.M.* is trash television at its trashiest.'

Austin spread his hands. 'So?'

'It's a long story.'

'We've plenty of time to talk. I'll have the sommelier refill your wineglass as often as you'd like.'

'That's the best offer I've had all day.' She cradled her chin in one hand and gazed into his face. There was no timidity in her large eyes. 'I'll tell you about my background if you do the same for yourself.'

'Okay, you're on.'

She took another sip of Chianti. 'I was born in Oakland, California. I was named Katherine after my dad's mother, and Ella after Ella Fitzgerald, Mom's favorite singer. My last name was Doran. I shortened it to Kaela Dorn when I went into TV. My mother was a ballet instructor at an African-American community center and my dad was an Irish-American, long-haired, pot-smoking hippie who had come to Berkeley to protest the Vietnam War and everything else.'

'There was a lot of that in the sixties.'

She nodded. 'Dad put aside his love beads and bongos and now teaches courses in contemporary American history at Berkeley, specializing in the protest movements of the sixties and seventies. He still has his beard, but it's a lot whiter than it used to be.'

'Happens to the best of us,' Austin said, pointing to his prematurely steel gray hair.

'I was something of a rebel as a kid. Pop's fault. One day Mom came down to the corner, where I was hanging out with a gang, and dragged me into her ballet classes where she could keep an eye on me. I traded in my gangsta colors for a tutu. I wasn't a bad dancer.'

The woman sitting across from Austin seemed made for dancing. 'I would have been surprised if you were any less graceful than a Pavlova.'

'Thank you,' she said. 'I was fair, but tripping about on my toes in the *Nutcracker Suite* didn't satisfy my craving for adventure. Pop's fault, too. He bummed around Khartoum and New Delhi before he headed west to pull us out of Vietnam single-handedly. I went to Berkeley and studied English lit, then I got accepted as an intern at a local TV station that wanted to fill its minority-hiring quota. I got tired of reading gory reports about car crashes off a TelePrompTer. When I heard about the opening at *Unbelievable Mysteries*, I jumped at the chance to travel to exotic, offbeat places, and be paid pretty well for it. Okay, that's me. How about you? How did you come to be rescuing maidens in distress and their friends?'

Austin gave a condensed version of his biography, omitting his service in the CIA, stretching a fact here and there to make the pieces fit. Kaela listened intently, and if she detected his effort to massage the truth, she didn't show it.

'I'm not surprised that you like fast boats or that you collect antique dueling pistols, or even that you listen to progressive jazz. I'm more surprised to hear that you study philosophy.'

'I don't know if *study* is the right word. I like to

say I've read a few books on the subject.' He paused in thought, then said, '"One cannot conceive anything so strange and so implausible that it has not already been said by one philosopher or another." René Descartes.'

'Which means?'

'I see a lot of strange things and people in my business. It gives me comfort to know that as far as philosophy is concerned, there is nothing new under the sun. Greed, avarice, evil. And conversely, goodness, generosity, love . . . Plato once said . . .' Austin became conscious of Kaela's stare. 'Sorry. I sound like a professor.'

'I've never met a professor who swoops down out of the sky to do single-handed battle with a bunch of cutthroats.' She regarded him with leveled eyes. 'Tell me, what exactly *is* your Special Assignments Team? Somebody mentioned it to me before I came out here.'

'There's no "exactly" about it. There are four of us, each with an area of expertise. Joe Zavala is a marine engineer who designs many of our vehicles. The ultralight I flew in on was his creation. He can pilot anything under or above the sea. Paul Trout is a deep-ocean geologist with credentials from Woods Hole Oceanographic and Scripps Institute. His wife, Gamay, is a diver and marine biologist with a background in nautical archaeology.'

'Impressive. You still haven't told me what your team does.'

'Depends. In general, we handle undersea assignments that tend to be other than routine.' Austin failed to mention that those assignments often took place secretly, outside the realm of government oversight.

She snapped her fingers. 'Of course. *Now* I remember. The Christopher Columbus tomb in the Yucatán. You were involved in its discovery.'

'Somewhat. It was a NUMA project.'

'Fascinating,' Kaela said. 'I'd like to do a story on your team.'

'The NUMA Public Affairs Department would love it. Favorable publicity comes in handy when we go before Congress with our budget. Give them a jingle when you get back. I'll be glad to help.'

'Thanks, I'd appreciate that very much.'

'Now let me ask you a question. What do you intend to do with the footage your crew filmed back in Russia?'

'I'm not sure,' she said, with a furrowed brow. 'We don't have much except the dead body of a guy dressed up like a doorman at a Russian nightclub.' She broke out in laughter. 'Not that the lack of facts ever discouraged *Unbelievable Mysteries* from cooking up a story.'

'Maybe he's one of those UFO aliens you're always finding,' Austin offered.

'Not with that sword.' Kaela shuddered at the memory. 'Seriously, Kurt, what's your take on this whole thing? Who were those guys and why were they so touchy about an abandoned sub base left over from the Cold War?'

Austin shook his head. 'I can't answer those questions.'

'You must have given it some thought.'

'Of course. I don't have to be Sherlock Holmes to conclude that there's something there that someone didn't what us to see. I just don't know what it could be.'

'There's one way to find out,' Kaela said. 'Go back for a look.'

'I don't think that would be wise.' Austin ticked off the reasons on his fingers. 'We can sit here and laugh at a bunch of guys who look as if they came out of a production of *Boris Godunov*, but dumb luck is the only reason we're still alive. Second, since you don't have Russian visas you would have to enter the country illegally. Third, you don't have a way to get there.'

Kaela countered each point on her own fingers. 'I appreciate your concern, but first, we'd be more prepared than we were and would get out in a hurry at the first hint of danger. Second, lack of a visa didn't stop you from landing on Russian soil. And third, if I can't get Captain Kemal to go back, I'm sure other fishermen are willing to earn in a couple of days what it takes them a year to make otherwise.'

Austin laced his hands behind his head. 'You don't discourage easily.'

'I don't intend to stay with *Unbelievable Mysteries*

forever. A story like this could be my ticket to a big job with a major network.'

'So much for my incredible powers of persuasion,' Austin said. 'Since you appear to have your mind made up, maybe I can convince you to accompany me on a tour of Istanbul at night. Topkapi Palace is a must-see, and there are some great shops around the Sulemaniye Mosque where you can pick up some gifts for the folks back home. We can wrap up the evening with dinner on board one of the Lufer boats.'

'Another four-star chef?'

'Not quite, but the scenery is special.'

'I'm staying at the Marmara Hotel on Taksim Square.'

'I know where it is. How about seven o'clock the day we dock?'

'I'll be looking forward to it.'

Austin saw little of Kaela the rest of the trip. She was busy with her two colleagues interviewing the captain and crew or working on background for Noah. He contacted NUMA headquarters and filed a report on the Russian incident and spent the rest of the time trying to piece the Gooney back together. The *Argo* made good time, and before long they were making their passage past the villages and old forts along the Bosporus.

The two-hour passage through the Bosporus was never dull. The narrow seventeen-mile waterway is considered the world's most dangerous strait. Captain

Atwood threaded the *Argo* around tankers, ferries and passenger boats as he made the twelve course changes necessary during the final leg of the voyage. The strong current that ran from the Black Sea to the Sea of Marmara made life even more interesting. Those on board let out a collective sigh of relief as the survey ship passed the ferry terminals and cruise-ship docks to tie alongside a pier near the Galata Bridge.

From the ship, Austin watched the television crew stuff its gear into a cab. Kaela waved good-bye, and the cab headed away from the waterfront. He walked around the deck, taking in the view of the bridge guarding the mouth of the Golden Horn, and the sprawling Topkapi Palace built for Sultan Mehmet II in the 1400s. In the distance he could see the minarets of the Hagia Sophia and the Blue Mosque.

He went back to his cabin and caught up on paperwork, then showered and exchanged his shorts and sweatshirt for casual slacks and a light cotton sweater. Near dinnertime, he walked down the gang-way and made his way to the street to look for a cab. A taxi pulled up beside him. It was a vintage Chevrolet, circa 1950s. There were passengers in the car, which identified it as a *dolmus*, meaning 'stuffed' in Turkish. Unlike the regular cabs, these taxis crammed in as many passengers as they could fit.

Austin got into the backseat with two other passengers who made space between them. A heavyset man sat on a jump seat and a third passenger occupied the front seat next to the meter. Austin told the driver to take him to the Taksim Square. He had visited Istanbul several times on NUMA assignments and knew the city fairly well. When the cab went a roundabout route, Austin thought it was simply to accommodate the other passengers. But nobody got off. The cab started to head away from Taksim Square and, suspecting the driver was trying to jack up the fare, Austin leaned forward and asked him where he was going.

The driver stared silently ahead, but the man in the front seat turned around. He had a wide, brutish face that even a mother couldn't love. Austin's eyes lingered on the passenger's features for only a second before shifting to the gun in the man's hand.

'*Silence!*' the man growled.

The men sitting next to Austin pulled him back by the shoulders. A long-bladed knife pointed at his right eye. The cab accelerated at neck-snapping speed, exited from the traffic stream and plunged into a dark maze of narrow cobblestone lanes.

They headed away from the waterfront, skirting Karakoy and the police squads who monitored the official red-light district. Austin glanced longingly at the restaurant lights at the top of Galata Tower. Then the taxi was moving along the Istikal Caddesi, weaving in and out of traffic, past the nightclubs, movie theaters and unregulated brothels that lined the gaudy strip. The cab spun off the main drag and climbed a hill into Bozoglu, where all the old European embassies were housed during the Ottoman Empire, and executed a series of squealing turns.

The car stayed upright despite the protesting tires, which told Austin that the driver was a professional who knew the limits of his vehicle. There had been no attempt to blindfold Austin, and he wondered if this meant he had a one-way ticket to oblivion. As the car continued to hook left and right through the urban warren, he concluded that a blindfold was unnecessary; he didn't have a clue where he was.

The fact that they hadn't killed him offered slim solace. He knew instinctively that these men would not hesitate to use the weapons they had brandished in his face. After several minutes, during which the city lights faded to a glow, the car whipped down a darkened, garbage-strewn street and into an alley not much wider than the vehicle. Austin's companions hustled him from the taxi and stood him against a brick wall while they bound his hands behind his back with duct tape. Then they pushed him through a doorway along a dim hall and into the lobby of an old office building. Grime covered the marble floor. On one wall was a brass floor directory black with the patina of age. The smell of onions and the muffled cry of a baby indicated that the office building was being used for human habitation. Probably squatters, Austin surmised.

His escorts nudged Austin into an elevator and stood behind him. They were hulking men, as big or brawnier than Austin, who had never considered himself to be a pigmy. The space was cramped, and Austin stood with his face pressed against the cold wrought iron of the ornate gate. He guessed that the elevator must date back to the time of the sultans. He tried not to think of frayed and neglected cables as the elevator slowly jerked and rattled up to the third and last floor. The elevator was more nerve-wracking than the speeding car. The elevator cracked to a stop, and one of his escorts growled in his ear.

'Out!'

He stepped into a dark hallway. One man grabbed the back of Austin's shirt in a bunch, used it to steer him forward and brake him to an abrupt stop. A door opened, and he was maneuvered inside. There was the odor of old paper and oil from long-ago business machines. He felt pressure upon his shoulders, then the edge of a chair bumped against the back of his knees. He sat down and squinted into the darkness. A spotlight flashed on, and Austin saw sunspots as the glare hit him in the face. He blinked like a suspect being given the third degree in an old gangster movie.

A voice speaking in English came from behind the spotlight.

'Welcome, Mr Austin. Thank you for coming.'

Something about the voice sounded familiar, but he couldn't place it.

'It was an invitation I couldn't resist.'

A dry chuckle issued from the darkness. 'The years haven't changed you, have they?'

'Do I *know* you?' A memory clawed at the back of Austin's mind like a cat scratching softly at the door.

'I'm hurt that you don't remember me. I wanted to thank you in person for the lovely bouquet of flowers you sent to hasten my convalescence. I believe you signed the card with the name of John Doe.'

Austin was stunned. 'I'll be damned!' he said, with a curious mixture of delight and foreboding. 'Ivan!'

9

The spotlight snapped off and a portable table lamp came on, illuminating the face of a man in his forties. He had a broad forehead and high cheekbones and would have been handsome if not for the massive scar defacing his right cheek.

'Don't be alarmed, Mr Austin,' Petrov said. 'I'm not the Phantom of the Opera.'

Austin's mind flashed back fifteen years to the Barents Sea. He remembered the frigid waters penetrating his heated dry suit as he activated the timer on two hundred pounds of explosives. It was a miracle the Russian was still alive.

'Sorry about the booby trap, Ivan. Can't say I didn't warn you to stay clear.'

'No apology necessary. Simply a misfortune of war.' He paused, then said, 'I've wondered something for a long time. Suppose our places had been reversed. Would you have listened to a warning from me?'

After a moment's reflection, Austin said, 'I might have assumed, like you, that the warning was a diversion. I'd like to think discretion would have won over valor, but I can't say for sure. It was a long time ago.'

'Yes, it was a very long time ago.' Petrov's lips

widened in a sad smile. 'Obviously, discretion did *not* rule over *my* youthful impatience. I was impetuous in those days. Don't worry; I bear you no animosity for the fruits of my own foolishness. I would have killed you long ago if I thought you were entirely to blame. As I said, *c'est la guerre*. In a sense you are as disfigured as I am, only you can't see the scars that cover your heart. The war made hard men out of both of us.'

'I recall hearing that the Cold War is over. I have a suggestion. Why not ask your friends to give us a lift to the bar at the Palace Hotel? We can talk about old times over a drink.'

'In time, Mr Austin. In time. We have a matter of grave importance to discuss.' Petrov's voice had gained a businesslike edge, and his eyes drilled into Austin's face. 'I would like to know what you were doing at the abandoned Soviet submarine base on the Black Sea.'

'Seems I was naïve to think our brief visit went unnoticed.'

'Not at all. It's a desolate part of the coast. Under normal circumstances, you could have landed a division of Marines without detection. We've kept the area under surveillance for months, but we were caught off guard. We know from intercepted radio messages that you landed some sort of aircraft and that the NUMA ship came in to pick you up. Please tell me what you were doing on Russian territory. Take your time. I'm in no hurry.'

'I'll be glad to fill you in.' Austin squirmed in his

chair. 'It might help my memory if I weren't sitting on my wrists. How about loosening the tape?'

Petrov thought briefly, then nodded.

'I consider you a dangerous man, Mr Austin. Please don't try anything foolish.'

Petrov gave a sharp order in Russian. Someone came up from behind. Austin felt a cold blade against his wrists and the tape was severed in a single swipe.

'Now for your story, Mr Austin.'

Austin massaged the circulation back into his arms. 'I was on the NUMA survey ship *Argo*, conducting a study of wave action in the Black Sea. Three American television people were supposed to rendezvous with our ship, but they had heard about the old sub base before they sailed from Istanbul, and decided to check it out without notifying us of their change in plans. They were overdue and I went looking for them. Some men on shore murdered a Turkish fisherman who was bringing the TV people to shore, and attempted to kill them, too.'

'Tell me about these killers.'

'There were about a dozen of them, on horseback, and wearing Cossack uniforms. They even carried swords and old rifles – really old.'

'Then what happened?'

Austin laid out a detailed narrative of the fight. Petrov listened impassively, although from his experience with Austin's resourcefulness, he was not surprised at the way the battle had ended.

'An ultralight,' Petrov said, with a chuckle. 'An ingenious tactic using your flare gun.'

Austin shrugged. 'I was lucky. They were using antique weapons. Otherwise my story would not have a happy Hollywood ending.'

'You couldn't have known from the air that they were using old rifles. I assume you must have landed.'

'In a manner of speaking. Old or not, those rifles made a sieve out of my plane's wings. I crash-landed on the beach.'

'What did you see besides the weapons? Every detail, please.'

'We found the body of one of the attackers behind the sand dune.'

'He was dressed like the others?'

'That's right. Fur hat, baggy pants. I found this on one of them.' He reached into his pocket and dug out the emblem he had taken from the dead Cossack's hat.

Petrov studied the pin without expression and passed it to one of his men. 'Go on,' he said.

'After I confirmed that the TV people were okay, I called my ship in. They picked us up, and we left as soon as we were able.'

'We found no evidence of a body or weapons,' Petrov said.

'I don't know what happened to the body. Maybe his friends came back after we left, and tidied up. We took the weapons with us.'

'That's larceny, Mr Austin.'

'I prefer to call it spoils of war.'

Petrov dismissed Austin's reply with a wave of his hand. 'No matter. What of this television crew? Did they film any of this?'

'They were too busy running for their lives. They filmed the body, but without an explanation I doubt if they can do much with it.'

'I hope for their sake that you are right.'

'Let me ask you a question if I may, Ivan.'

'I'm the one asking the questions.'

'I'm aware of that, but it's the least you can do in return for the beautiful flowers I sent you.'

'I've already repaid your kind gesture with one of my own. I didn't kill you. But go ahead. I'll allow one question.'

'What the hell is this all about?'

A slight smile tweaked the ends of Petrov's lips, and he picked up the cigarette pack in front of him. Extracting a cigarette with great care, he put it between his lips, lit the end and blew the smoke from his nostrils. The strong tobacco smell filled the office and drove out the musty odor.

'What do you know about the current political situation in Russia?'

'What I read in the papers. It's no secret that your country has big problems. Your economy is shaky, organized crime and corruption are worse than Chicago under Capone, your military is underpaid and unhappy, your health care system is a mess and you've got independence movements and civil wars nibbling around your borders. But you've got an educated and energetic workforce and abundant natural resources. If you don't keep shooting yourself in the foot, you may come out okay, but it will take time.'

'A reasonably accurate summary of a complicated scenario. Ordinarily I would say you are right, that we would muddle through. Our people are used to adversity. Thrive on it, in fact. But there are forces at work that are much more powerful than anything we have talked about.'

'What sort of forces?'

'The *worst* kind. Human passions, whipped into a fiery nationalism by the winds of cynicism, dismay and hopelessness.'

'You've had nationalist movements before.'

'True, but we've managed to marginalize them, blackmail the proponents or demonize them as eccentric cranks before they could build up their cause and bring others into it. This is different. The new movement has sprung whole from the steppes of south Russia along the Black Sea where the neo-Cossacks live.'

'*Cossacks?* Like the crew I met the other day?'

'That's right. The Cossacks were originally outlaws and fugitives, nomads who drifted into south Russia and the Ukraine, where they formed a loose federation. They were known for their horsemanship, a skill that helped Peter the Great defeat the Ottoman

Turks. In time they evolved into a military class. Cossacks served as an elite cavalry for the tsars, who used them to terrorize revolutionaries, strikers and minority groups.'

'Then came the Bolshevik revolution, the tsar fell and the Cossacks ended up driving cabs in Paris,' Austin observed.

'Not all were so lucky. Some joined the Bolsheviks, others became staunch defenders of the last of Imperial Russia, even after the tsar and his family were assassinated. Stalin tried to neutralize or eliminate them, but he was only partially successful. To this day, the Cossacks are a warrior caste who believe that they embody the glories of a pure Mother Russia. There is a word for it. *Kazachestvo*. Cossackism. The idea that they are the ones chosen by a Higher Power to dominate inferior races.'

Austin was getting restless. 'The Cossacks aren't the first to think they were chosen to set the rest of the world straight. History is full of groups that have come and gone, leaving a high body count behind them.'

'True. The difference is that those groups are chapters in a history book, while the Cossacks and their blind faith are very much alive.' He leaned forward onto the desk and leveled his gaze at Austin. 'Russia has become a violent place, and violence is the life's blood of the Cossack. There has been a great revival of *Kazachestvo*. Neo-Cossacks have taken over parts of Russian territory around the Black Sea. They ignore the Moscow government, knowing that it is weak and toothless. They have formed private armies and hired out as mercenaries. Their audacity has captured the loyalty of many Russians who tired quickly of capitalism and freedom. Many in parliament and the streets yearn for a reactionary nationalism that would restore the glories of Russia. There are pure Cossack units in the Russian army with their own costumes and ranks. They have declared a New Russia around the Black Sea and are expanding into other areas, seven million strong. That pin you found is the emblem of their movement. It shows the sun in a new dawn for Russia.'

'They're still a minority, Ivan. How much damage can they do?'

'The Bolsheviks were only a minority but they knew what was in the Russian heart, that the soldiers were tired of war and the peasants wanted land.'

'The Bolsheviks had Lenin.'

'Thank you for making my point,' Petrov said, with a humorless smile. 'Absolutely correct. The revolution would have been nothing if not for a determined and ruthless leader who unified the country and squashed opponents under his thumb.' The smile vanished. 'The Cossacks have a similar leader. His name is Mikhail Razov. He is an immensely wealthy shipping and mining magnate who owns a cartel named Ataman Industries. He is dedicated to the resurrection of Great Russia. He endorses the Cossack ideals of masculinity and brute force. He has said the best way to wipe out corruption is with a machine gun. He is totally paranoid, believes that the rest of the world is out to get him.'

'Money and power are a potent formula.'

'It goes far beyond that.' Petrov lit up another cigarette. Austin was surprised to see that the match hand was trembling. 'He is advised by a monk named Boris, a man of great animal magnetism with a reputation for prophecy. He exerts an evil influence over Razov, encouraging his claim that he is a true descendant of the tsar, going back to Peter the Great.'

'I was under the impression that Tsar Nicholas was the last of the Romanov line.'

'There have always been questions.'

'Even so, I can say I'm the king of Spain, but that doesn't put me on his throne.'

'Razov says he has proof.'

'DNA?'

'I doubt if he would let anyone take a blood sample.'

'You may be onto something,' Austin conceded. 'You have a movement, a charismatic leader guided by a messianic prophet and a hereditary line. I agree that sounds like a potent formula for revolution.'

Petrov nodded solemnly. 'There is no "maybe" about it. Russia is on the verge of a neo-Cossack revival that will sweep across the country, wiping out all the gains we have made. The tsar and his family have already been canonized by the right wing in our country. And Razov is poised to take on the tsar's sacred mantle.' He smiled. 'How many politicians can claim to be descended from a saint?'

'Most of them claim to be saints. But I take your point. What's your role in this, Ivan? Are you with the KGB?'

'The KGB has been infiltrated by Razov's people. I lead a small inner group whose job is to keep watch on those who threaten Russia's stability. We report directly to the president. But I've only told you part of the story. This involves you, too, Mr Austin. Razov considers the United States to be the head of a dark worldwide conspiracy that is largely responsible for Russia's ills. He believes America is deliberately using its power around the world to keep Russia impoverished and backward. Many in parliament share his views.'

'America has a long list of enemies. It goes with being the only superpower.'

'Add Razov's name to the roster, then. But this isn't just political – he has a personal reason as well. His fiancée was accidentally killed in the Americans' bombing of Belgrade several years ago. I understand Irini was quite beautiful, and he has never gotten over her loss. So I would urge you to take him very seriously – especially as there are signs he intends to cause great harm to your country.'

'In what way?'

Petrov spread his hands. 'We don't know. We know only that he has given his scheme a name: Operation Troika.'

'Then you've wasted your time and mine. You should use diplomatic channels to take your case to higher-ups in the American government.'

'We already have. We have told them we want them to avoid any overt moves.'

'I can't picture the White House and the Pentagon ignoring a possible threat like this, not now. They've learned the hard way to take threats seriously.'

'Yes, well, they're not pleased with our position. We have told them if they respond too clumsily, they will spoil our efforts and ensure that the threat, whatever it is, will be carried out.'

'What's the connection between this threat and the sub base?'

'Come to your own conclusion. The sub pen was built for medium-range missile submarines that roamed the Black Sea, mostly to intimidate Turkish leaders who allowed the Americans to establish bases. It was abandoned after the Soviet government fell and lay undisturbed for years. Then Razov leased the facility from the government. His ships were seen coming and going. The Cossacks you encountered were camped nearby as guards.'

'Why the fancy costumes and old weapons?'

'It has something to do with the symbolism of his cause. Razov chooses to equip some of his men as if they were still cavalry for the tsar. Make no mistake. He has accumulated many modern weapons from the former Soviet Union.'

'Why haven't you moved in on these guys?'

'We were waiting and watching for the right time. Then you blundered in.'

'Sorry to spoil your stakeout. Someone was being mugged and needed help.'

'We think he intends to act against the US *before* he assumes power.'

'I can help you find out what he has in mind.'

Petrov shook his head vigorously. 'We don't need American cowboys charging in with six-guns blazing.'

'Neither do I. I'm a scientist with NUMA now.'

'You're being disingenuous. You have a reputation for bending the rules. I know about your Special Assignments Team. My office has press accounts of the NUMA team's role in the *Andrea Doria* conspiracy and the plot to take over the freshwater resources of the world.'

'We like to keep busy in our spare time.'

'Then keep busy with your ocean science.'

Austin folded his arms over his chest. 'Let me see if I understand this correctly, Ivan. You want us to count fish while your madman goes on a terror spree in our country.'

'We have every intention of stopping Razov before it gets to that. Your interference may already have spoiled any chance we have of containing him. If you don't stay out, I will consider you an enemy of the Russian people and will act accordingly.'

'Thanks for the advice.' Austin glanced at his watch. 'I hate to break off our reunion, but I'm late for dinner with a lovely young woman. So if you're through . . .'

'Yes, I'm through.' Petrov barked an order in Russian. The men guarding Austin pulled him to his feet and attempted to herd him toward the door. He stood his ground and said, 'Nice seeing you again, Ivan. Sorry for past encounters.'

'What's past is past. It's the *future* that we should both be concerned about.' Petrov's hand went to his scar. 'You know, Mr Austin, you taught me a very valuable lesson.'

'Which is?'

'Know your enemy.'

Austin was hustled down the dark hallway into the rickety elevator. Minutes later, he was in the taxi. The driver kept the car more or less under Mach 1. Before long, they pulled up at the exact point where he'd been kidnapped.

'*Out*,' said the driver.

Austin was glad to comply. He had to jump back to keep his toes from being crushed as the car sped off in a squeal of tires. He watched the taillights vanish around a corner, then walked to the *Argo*'s slip. Back aboard the ship, he called the hotel where Kaela was staying. When she didn't answer her room phone, he asked the desk if she'd left a message.

'Yes, sir, there's a message from Ms Dorn,' the desk clerk said.

'Would you read it to me, please.'

'Of course. It says, "Waited an hour. Something more important must have come up. Went to dinner with the boys. Kaela."'

Austin frowned. The message said nothing about getting together at another time. He would have to mend fences in the morning. Meanwhile, he went out on the *Argo*'s deck and paced from one end of the ship to the other, trying to remember every detail of the dialogue with Ivan. As he walked, his lips tightened in determination. Damned if he was going to ignore a threat to his country. The best way to get Austin to do something was to tell him he *couldn't* do it. He went back into his cabin and punched out a number on his cell phone.

Five thousand miles away, José 'Joe' Zavala plucked the purring cell phone from the dashboard holder of his 1961 Corvette convertible and answered with a cheery hello. Zavala had been thinking how all was right with the world. He was young, healthy and on an undemanding work project that left him plenty of free time. At his side was a lovely blond statistical analyst from the Department of Commerce. They were driving along a country road in MacLean, Virginia, on their way to a candlelight dinner at a romantic old inn. The warm air pleasantly tousled his thick black hair. After dinner it would be back to the former district library building in Arlington, where he lived, for a nightcap. Then, who knows? The possibilities were endless. This could be the start of a long relationship, *long* being a relative term in Zavala's world.

When he heard the voice of his friend and colleague,

Zavala's reaction was a happy one. A slight smile cracked the ends of his lips '*Buona sera*, Kurt, old *amigo*. How's your vacation?'

'*Over.* So is yours, I'm sorry to say.'

Zavala's smile faded and a pained expression came onto his darkly handsome features, as Austin laid out his plans for Joe's immediate future. With a mighty sigh, he replaced the phone, looked soulfully into the dreamy and compliant blue eyes of his date and said, 'I'm afraid I've got bad news. My grandmother just died.'

While Zavala tried to cushion his date's disappointment with an improvised list of outrageous promises, Paul Trout's six-foot-eight figure was bent like a praying mantis over a lab counter at the Woods Hole Oceanographic Institution in Massachusetts, examining mud samples from the deepest parts of the Atlantic Ocean. Although the work was potentially messy, Trout's white lab coat was spotless. He wore one of his trademark bright bow ties, and his light brown hair was parted down the middle and combed back at the temples.

Trout grew up in Woods Hole, where his father was a Cape Cod fisherman, and he returned to his roots whenever he got the chance. He had developed friendships with many of the scientists at the world-renowned institute and often lent them his skills as a deep-ocean geologist.

Trout's intense concentration was broken by the

sound of his name being called. Keeping his head lowered to the sample, he peered upward and saw a lab tech standing there.

'Call just came in for you, Dr Trout,' she said, handing him a phone. Trout's mind was still on the ocean bottom, and when he heard Austin's voice he assumed the head of the Special Assignments Team was at NUMA headquarters.

'Kurt, are you already back home?'

'Actually, I'm calling from Istanbul, where you'll be in twenty-four hours. I've got a job for you in the Black Sea.'

Trout blinked his hazel eyes. '*Istanbul*. The Black Sea?' His reaction was the complete opposite of Zavala's. 'I've always *wanted* to work there. My colleagues will be green with envy.'

'How soon can you leave?'

'I'm up to my ears in mud, but I can leave for Washington immediately.'

There was silence at the other end of the line as Austin pictured Trout in a pool of muck. Austin was used to Trout's Yankee eccentricities and decided he didn't want to know the details. He simply said, 'Could you pass this along to Gamay?'

'Finestkind, Cap,' Trout said, using an old fisherman's expression that spoke for itself. 'See you tomorrow.'

Twenty feet below the surface of the water east of Marathon in the Florida Keys, Trout's wife, Gamay, was chiseling away with a dive knife at a big brain coral. She broke off a small piece and put it in a mesh bag hanging from her weight belt. Gamay had donated some of her working vacation as a marine biologist to a conservation group studying the deterioration of coral growth in the Keys. The news wasn't good. The coral was worse than the year before. The growth that had not been killed outright by the poisonous run-off from south Florida was brown and discolored, totally unlike the vibrant colors to be found in the healthy reefs of the Caribbean and Red Sea.

A sharp rapping sound filled her ears. Someone was signaling from the surface. Tucking her knife back in its sheath, Gamay increased the air in her buoyancy compensator, and with a few flips of her fins, her tightly shaped body rose from the coral. She surfaced near the chartered dive boat and blinked in the bright Florida sun. The boat's skipper, a grizzled old 'conch' named Bud, after the beer he favored, was holding a ball-peen hammer he'd used to tap on the metal stern ladder.

'Harbormaster just called on the radio,' Bud yelled. 'Says your husband was trying to get in touch with you.'

Gamay swam to the ladder, handed up her tank and weight belt, then climbed aboard. She wrung the seawater out of her dark red hair and wiped her face down with a towel. She was tall, and slim for her height, and had she cared to get down to an unhealthy weight, she would have had the figure of a fashion model. She dug the coral fragment from her bag and held it up for Bud to see.

He shook his head. 'My dive business is going down the tubes if this keeps up.'

The fisherman was right. It was going to take a massive commitment from everyone, from the conchs to the Congress, to bring the reefs back to life.

'Did my husband leave a message?' she asked.

'Yeah, says to get in touch with him pronto. That someone named Kurt called. Guess your vacation is over.'

She smiled, showing the slight space between her dazzling white front teeth, and tossed the piece of coral to Bud. 'Guess it is,' she said.

IO

Washington, DC

Washington sweltered under a hot sun that combined with the humidity to transform the nation's capital into a giant steam bath. The driver of the turquoise Jeep Cherokee shook his head in wonder at the brave clusters of tourists ignoring the wilting heat. Noel Coward to the contrary, he thought, mad dogs and Englishmen weren't the *only* ones to go out in the midday sun.

Minutes later, the Jeep pulled up to the White House gate and the man at the wheel handed over a NUMA identification card with the name and photo of Admiral James Sandecker. While one guard used a mirror on a pole to check underneath the vehicle for a bomb, the other returned the ID to the driver, a trim man with flaming red hair and a Van Dyke beard.

'Good day, Admiral Sandecker,' the guard said, with a broad grin. 'Nice to see you again. It's been a few weeks. How are you today, sir?'

'I'm fine, Norman,' said Sandecker, 'You're looking well. How are Dolores and the children?'

'Thank you for asking,' the guard said, beaming with pride. 'She's great. Kids are doing well in school.

Jamie wants to work for NUMA when she gets out of college.'

'*Splendid*. Make sure she calls me directly. The agency is always on the lookout for bright young people.'

The guard let out a hearty laugh. 'It won't be for a while. She's only fourteen.' He jerked his thumb toward the White House. 'They're all in there waiting for *you*, Admiral.'

'Thank you for letting me know,' Sandecker replied. 'Please give my regards to Dolores.'

As the guard waved him through the gate, Sandecker thought how being gracious had more than its immediate rewards. By dealing warmly with guards, secretaries, receptionists and others considered low in the bureaucratic hierarchy, he had established an early-warning network all over the city. His lips compressed in a tight smile. Norman's wink and nod signaled Sandecker that his arrival had been scheduled after the others so they could confer before he arrived. He had a well-earned reputation for promptness, a habit shaped at the US Naval Academy and honed by his years of flag rank. He always arrived exactly one minute before a meeting.

A tall, dark-suited man wearing the sunglasses and granite expression that marked him as a Secret Service agent checked Sandecker's ID again, directed him into a parking space and whispered into his hand radio. He led the admiral to an entrance, where a smiling young female aide met him and escorted him down the hushed corridors to a door guarded by a lantern-jawed Marine. He opened the door and Sandecker stepped into the Cabinet Room.

Warned by the Secret Service man that Sandecker was on his way, President Dean Cooper Wallace was waiting to ambush the admiral with a handshake. The president was known as the most eager flesh-presser to occupy the White House since Lyndon Johnson.

'Great to see you, Admiral,' Wallace said. 'Thank you for coming on such short notice.' He pumped Sandecker's hand as if he were courting votes at a church fair. Sandecker managed to detach himself from the president's grip and responded with a charm offensive of his own. He went around the table and greeted each man by his first name, asking about wife, children or golf game. He had a particularly warm greeting for his friend Erwin LeGrand, the tall, lincolnesque director of the CIA.

NUMA's director was only a few inches over five feet, yet his presence filled the large chamber with the energy of a testosterone dynamo. The president sensed that Sandecker was overshadowing him. He snagged the admiral and guided him by the elbow to a seat at the long conference table.

'Got the place of honor reserved for you.'

Sandecker slipped into his seat to the president's left. Sandecker knew his placement at the president's elbow was no accident and was meant to flatter him. Despite a folksy manner that made him sound at times like the actor Andy Griffith, Wallace was a shrewd politician. As always, Vice President Sid Sparkman was seated on the president's right.

The president sat down and grinned. 'I was telling the boys here about the one that got away. Hooked a grandpappy trout as big as a whale the last time I was out west. Snapped my rod in half. Guess that ol' fellow didn't know he was dealing with the commander in chief of the USA.'

The men at the table responded to the witticism with loud laughter, the loudest coming from the vice president. Sandecker chuckled dutifully. He'd had warm relations with all those who occupied the White House during his tenure at NUMA. Whatever their political persuasion, every president he dealt with respected his power in Washington and his influence with universities and corporations around the country and world. Sandecker was not universally loved, but even his adversaries admired his hard-driving honesty.

Sandecker exchanged smiles with the vice president. Older than Wallace by several years, the vice president was the éminence grise at the White House, wielding his power out of sight of the public, covering his Machiavellian machinations and hard-knuckle style with jovial bonhomie. The former college football player was a self-made millionaire. Sandecker knew the vice president secretly held Wallace in the contempt that men who have achieved success on their own sometimes have for those who have inherited their wealth and connections.

'Hope you gentlemen don't mind if we get down to business,' said the president, who was dressed casually in a plaid shirt, navy blazer and khaki slacks. '*Air Force One* is all gassed up to take me to Montana for another crack at that trout.' He made a show of glancing at his watch. 'I'm turning the meeting over to the secretary of state to fill you in.'

A tall hawk-faced man, with his white hair so carefully coifed that it looked like a helmet, gazed around the room with piercing eyes. Nelson Tingley reminded Sandecker of what an astute observer had said about Daniel Webster, that Webster looked too good to be true. Tingley hadn't been a bad senator, but he had let his Cabinet position go to his head. The secretary saw himself playing the role of Bismarck to Wallace's Frederick the Great. In truth, he seldom got the president's ear because he had to go through Sparkman. As a consequence, he tended to grandstand when he got the chance.

'Thank you, Mr President,' he said in the sonorous voice that for years had echoed across the floor of the US Senate. 'I'm sure you gentlemen all know the severity of the situation in Russia. Within the next few weeks or possibly days, we can expect the fall of that country's legally elected president. Their economy is at an all-time low, and Russia is expected to default on its obligations around the world.'

'Tell 'em what you said about the army,' the president suggested.

'I'd be happy to, Mr President. The Russian forces

are up for grabs. The public is sick of the corruption in government and of the power of organized crime. Nationalist sentiment and antagonism toward the United States and Europe are at an all-time high. In short, Russia is a tinderbox that can be touched off at any time by the *slightest* of incidents.' He paused to let his words sink in and glanced in Sandecker's direction. Sandecker knew the secretary was famous for his filibusters and wasn't about to subject himself to a long-winded lecture. He cut the secretary off at the oratorical pass.

'I assume you're talking about the Black Sea incident involving NUMA,' Sandecker said pleasantly.

The secretary was derailed, but not discouraged. 'With all due respect, Admiral, I would hardly describe an incursion into a country's air and sea space and unauthorized invasion of its sovereign territory as an *incident*.'

'Nor would I describe it as an *invasion*, Mr Secretary. As you know, I considered the encounter important enough to submit a full report immediately to the State Department, so they would not be caught by surprise in the event the Russian government complained. But let's look at the facts, shall we?' Sandecker seemed as calm as a Buddhist at repose. 'An American television crew had its boat shot out from under it, and a Turkish fisherman whom they hired was killed. They had no choice but to swim to shore. They were about to be attacked by bandits when a NUMA engineer who had been looking for them

149

went to their aid. Later he and the television people were rescued by a NUMA ship.'

'All done without going through the proper channels,' the secretary countered.

'I'm not unaware of the incendiary situation in Russia, but I hope we aren't blowing this out of proportion. The whole incident took less than a few hours. The television crew was remiss in venturing within national waters, but there was no harm done.'

The secretary made a show of opening a folder emblazoned with the State Department emblem. 'Not according to this report from your agency. In addition to the Turkish fisherman, at least one Russian national was killed and others may have been injured in this so-called incident.'

'Has the Russian government delivered a protest through the "proper channels" you mentioned?'

The national security advisor, a man named Rogers, leaned forward. 'There has been no word from the Russians or the Turks to date.'

'Then I suggest this is a tempest in a teapot,' Sandecker said. 'If the Russians complain about a breach in their national sovereignty, I will be glad to lay out the facts, apologize personally to the Russian ambassador, whom I know quite well through NUMA's joint ventures with his country, and assure him it won't happen again.'

Secretary Tingley addressed Sandecker, but he was looking at the president when he spoke, his words dripping with acid. 'I hope you won't take this personally, Admiral, but we're not going to have a bunch of ocean groupies dictating the foreign policy of the United States.'

The tart comment was meant to be funny, but no one laughed, least of all Sandecker, who didn't take kindly to having NUMA described as 'a bunch of ocean groupies.'

Sandecker flashed a barracuda smile, but an icy coldness crept into his authoritative blue eyes as he prepared to rip Tingley to shreds.

The vice president saw what was coming and rapped his knuckles on the table. 'It seems you gentlemen have stated your case with the usual conviction. We don't want to take up any more of the president's valuable time. I'm sure the admiral considers the secretary's points well taken and that Secretary Tingley accepts NUMA's explanation and assurances.'

Tingley opened his mouth to reply, but Sandecker deftly took advantage of the exit door Sparkman had opened. 'I'm glad the secretary and I were able to settle our differences amicably,' he interjected.

The president, who was known to dislike confrontation, had been listening with a pained expression on his face. He smiled and said, 'Thank you, gentlemen. Now that that's settled, I've got a more important matter I'd like to bring up.'

'The disappearance of the *NR-1* submarine?' Sandecker said.

The president stared at Sandecker in disbelief, then burst into laughter. 'I've always heard you've got eyes in the back of your head, Admiral. How'd you hear about that? I was told the matter was top secret.' He glanced around reprovingly at his staff. 'Real grave-yard stuff.'

'Nothing mysterious about it, Mr President. Many of our people are in daily close contact with the navy, which owns the *NR-1*, and some of the men on board have worked with NUMA. Captain Logan's father is a friend and former colleague of mine. Family members who were concerned for the safety of their loved ones contacted me to ask what was being done. They assumed I was aware of the sub's project.'

'We owe you an apology,' the president said. 'We were trying to keep this matter contained until we made some progress.'

'Of course,' Sandecker said. 'Did the submersible sink?'

'We've conducted a thorough search. The sub didn't sink.'

'I don't understand. What happened to it?'

The president glanced at the CIA director. 'The people over at Langley think the *NR-1* was hijacked.'

'Has anyone contacted you to verify that theory? A request for ransom, perhaps.'

'No. No one.'

'Then why hasn't news of the sub's disappearance been made public? It might help in tracking down its whereabouts. I'm sure I don't have to remind anyone in this room that there was a crew on that sub.

152

To say nothing of the millions spent to develop her.'

The vice president took over. 'We don't think it's in the best interests of the crew to go public now,' Sparkman declared.

'It seems to me that broadcasting a worldwide alert would be in their best interests.'

'Under ordinary circumstances, yes. But this is pretty complicated, Admiral,' the president said. 'We think it will jeopardize their welfare.'

'Perhaps,' Sandecker said, without conviction. He pinioned Wallace with an unwavering gaze. 'I assume you have a plan.'

The president shifted uneasily in his chair. 'Sid, you got an answer for the admiral?'

'We're trying to be optimistic, but it is possible that all the crew are dead,' Sparkman said.

'You have evidence to support that conclusion?'

'None, but it's a strong possibility.'

'I can't accept "possibility" as a reason for sitting on our hands.'

The secretary of state had been simmering like a pot on a hot stove. At the presumed insult, he boiled over.

'We are not "sitting on our hands," Admiral. The Russian government has requested that we stay out of this for the time being. They have the contacts to chase this down. We'd stir things up, especially with nationalism riding so high. Isn't that right, Mr President?'

'Don't tell me you think the *Russians* took the sub?'

Sandecker said, ignoring the secretary and directing his question at the president.

Wallace again turned to his vice president. 'Sid, you've been on top of this since day one. Can you explain to the admiral?'

'Of course, Mr President. I'd be happy to. It relates to our earlier topic, Admiral. Shortly after the *NR-1* disappeared, we were contacted by sources within the Russian government who said they might be able to retrieve the sub and its crew. They believe its disappearance ties in with the turmoil in their country. Beyond that, I can't say for now. I can only ask your forbearance and patience.'

'I fail to follow that line of logic,' Sandecker said, boring in. 'Are you saying we should rely upon a government that could fall at any moment to protect our people? It seems to me that the Russian top brass are going to be concentrating more on saving their butts than looking for an American research submarine.'

The vice president nodded in agreement. 'Nonetheless, we have agreed to hold off. Even with their problems, the Russians are in the best position to handle something that's happened in their backyard.'

CIA Director LeGrand had been silent up to now. 'I'm afraid he's got a point, James.'

Sandecker smiled. LeGrand must have been brought in as the 'good cop' to play off 'bad cop' Tingley. The admiral could play games, too. He furrowed his brow as if he were making a tough decision.

'It appears my good friend Erwin concurs with your caution. Very well, then, I won't press the point further.'

There was heavy silence in the Cabinet Room, as if no one could believe Sandecker would give in after only a skirmish.

'Thank you, James,' President Wallace said. 'We had a chance to chat before you arrived. We know there's a big temptation, especially with your personal interest in this, to bring NUMA in.'

'You're asking me to keep NUMA at arm's length from the sub's disappearance, then.'

'For *now*, Admiral.'

'I can assure you that NUMA will not search for the *NR-1*. However, please let me know if and when we can be of help.'

'Of *course* we will, Admiral.' The president thanked everyone for coming and rose from his chair. Sandecker wished him good fishing and left the room, allowing the others to hash over the meeting, as he knew they would. An aide was waiting to escort him to a side door. As he drove through the gate a few moments later, the guard grinned. 'Hot enough for you today, sir?'

'It must be my imagination, Norman,' Sandecker said, with a grin. 'The temperature always seems to be a few degrees warmer in this part of Washington.' He gave a jaunty wave and drove out into the traffic.

*

On the way back to NUMA headquarters, Sandecker punched out a number on his cell phone. 'Rudi, please meet me in my office in ten minutes.'

Sandecker drove into the garage under the thirty-story tubular building that served as the nerve center for NUMA's worldwide operations and took the elevator to his top-floor office. He was behind the immense desk made from the hatch cover of a Confederate blockade runner when Rudi Gunn arrived carrying a briefcase.

Sandecker waved his second-in-command to a chair. Gunn, a short thin man with narrow shoulders, thinning hair and thick horn-rimmed glasses, listened intently while Sandecker described his White House meeting.

'Then we're pulling out of the search?' Gunn said.

Sandecker's eyes blazed. 'Hell, no! The fact that they put a shot across my bow doesn't mean I'm going to heave to and run up the white flag. What have you learned?'

'I went right to work on the premise we had discussed. That the only thing with the ability to hijack the *NR-1* from under the nose of its support ship would be a bigger sub. Any number of countries have submarines large enough to carry off the *NR-1*,' Gunn said. 'I asked Yaeger to run some profiles.' Hiram Yaeger was NUMA's computer whiz and head of its vast data network. 'We concentrated on the USSR because of their preference for building monster boats. My first thought was something like the Typhoon.'

Sandecker sat back in his chair and cradled his chin in one hand. 'With a length of more than five hundred feet, a Typhoon could easily piggyback our missing minisub.'

'I agree. They were designed to fire missiles from the Arctic Circle. The flat missile deck could have been converted for carrying cargo. But there was a problem when I checked further. All six Typhoons were accounted for.'

'All right. But I've never known you to give up easily, Rudi. What else do you have?'

Gunn reached into his briefcase and pulled out a folder. He handed a picture from the folder to Sandecker.

'This shows a Soviet India-class sub photographed on its way to the Pacific from the Northern Fleet.' He passed over several sheets of paper. 'These are schematic diagrams. She's a diesel-electric, nearly three hundred fifty feet long, and was designed supposedly for underwater rescue. That semirecessed area abaft the sail was fitted out to carry a couple of deep-diving minisubs. In wartime they could be used for clandestine ops with *Spetsnaz* special forces brigades. Only two India-class subs were built. They were to have been broken up after the end of the Cold War. We've been able to verify that one was indeed scrapped. We don't know the fate of the other. I think it was used to hijack the *NR-1*.'

'You sound quite sure of this, Rudi. Remember, our premise is still only a theory.'

Gunn smiled. 'May I borrow your VCR?'

'Be my guest.'

Gunn dug into his case again and pulled out a videocassette, went over to the paneled wall, opened a door to a cabinet and popped the cassette into the VCR.

'As you know, the *NR-1* had the capability to broadcast a television picture from the ocean floor,' Gunn said.

'I approved the NUMA funds myself. Great educational program. The pictures bounce off a satellite and into classrooms around the world. Teaches youngsters that the ocean is a lot more interesting than MTV. I understand the program has worked out well.'

'*Extremely* well, in this case. This picture was sent from the *NR-1* the day she disappeared.'

Gunn pressed the Play button on the remote control. The screen went fuzzy, then turned seawater green. Bright floodlights illuminated a slender black hull. There was no sound. The time and date showed in the corner.

Sandecker was sitting on the edge of his desk, arms folded. 'Looks like the bow view from the sail cam,' he said.

'That's right. Keep on watching. Right about *now . . .*'

A sharklike shadow loomed below the hull. Something much bigger than the *NR-1* had come up from below. After a few minutes, the sub began to move forward at great speed until it was obscured by bubbles. The screen went fuzzy again.

'This picture was sent from the sub via satellite at exactly the time of her disappearance. It only ran a short while, as you can see, before it was shut down.'

'Fascinating,' Sandecker said. 'Run it again, please.'

Gunn replayed the tape.

'Does the White House have a copy of this video?' Sandecker said.

'The transmission came directly to NUMA. My guess is they haven't seen it.'

'Good work, Rudi,' the admiral said. 'There's an important piece of the puzzle missing, however.' He reached into the desk humidor and pulled out two cigars – he had them personally selected and rolled for him by the owner of a Dominican Republic plantation – and held one cigar above the other. 'Assume the bottom stogie is much larger than the one on top. It comes up under the smaller boat. *Then* what?' He moved the top cigar away. 'You see what I'm getting at. There might be a problem getting the smaller sub to play piggyback.'

'It wouldn't be easy unless –'

'Unless the *NR-1* were cooperating. Which Captain Logan wouldn't do unless he were forced to.'

'Exactly my thoughts.'

Sandecker tossed Gunn a cigar and clamped the other in his teeth. They lit up and sat in the cloud of fragrant smoke.

'I understand there was a guest scientist aboard

the *NR-1*,' Sandecker said, after a moment's thought.

'That's right. I have the whole roster.'

'Go over their backgrounds with a fine-tooth comb, especially the scientist's. In the meantime, let's try to find the India-class submarine. The navy keeps track of all operational Russian submarines, but I don't want to alert anyone to the fact that NUMA is still in this.'

'I'll see if Yaeger can tap into the navy computer system.'

'Why, Rudi,' Sandecker said, studying the glowing ash on his cigar, 'what a surprising thing to hear from a navy man. First in his class at the academy, too.'

Gunn tried without success to look angelic. 'Desperate times call for desperate measures.'

'I'm glad to hear you say that. Austin called me from Istanbul. He's assembling the Special Assignments Team to take another look at that abandoned submarine base.'

'Does he think it has a connection with the *NR-1*?'

'He didn't know about the missing sub until I told him. No, apparently he's been in contact with someone, an old Russian friend, who indicated that the base may have something to do with a supposed threat against the US.'

'Terrorist activity?'

'I asked Kurt the same question. He only knows what the Russian told him, that the US is in danger. A mining magnate named Razov seems to be involved, and the old base may hold the key to what is going on. Kurt's instincts are usually sound. This threat of his is all the more reason for NUMA to get involved.'

'We can take a look at the area by satellite.'

'We still need eyes on the ground.'

'What about your promise to the president?'

'I only promised not to look for the *NR-1*. I never said anything about a Soviet sub base. Besides,' Sandecker said, with a twinkle in his eye, 'Austin is probably out of reach by now.'

'I've heard that sunspot activity has been interrupting communications.'

'We'll keep trying to establish contact, of course. The president is going fly-fishing in Montana, but I expect he'll return in a hurry if the Russian government falls.'

Gunn looked worried. 'If there really is a threat, don't you think we should tell the president?'

Sandecker walked over to the window and looked out over the Potomac. After a moment, he turned and said, 'Do you know how Sid Sparkman made his fortune?'

'Sure, he made millions in mining.'

'Correct. As did Razov.'

'Coincidence?'

'Maybe. Maybe not. There's often a worldwide good ol' boy network in certain areas of industry. It's not out of the question that they know each other. Unless we learn that the threat is imminent – I suggest we keep this conversation to ourselves for now.'

'Are you suggesting that –'

'There's a connection? I'm not prepared to go that far. *Yet.*'

Gunn pursed his lips, a grave look in his eyes. 'I hope Kurt and his team aren't getting in over their heads.'

Sandecker smiled grimly, his eyes as hard as topaz. 'It wouldn't be the first time.'

II

The Black Sea

Austin strolled along the Bosporus past the ferry terminal and sleek tour vessels until the smell of decaying fish told his nostrils he was near the working waterfront. Raucous squadrons of gulls grew more numerous as he approached the rag-tag fleet of fishing boats nuzzled up to the dock. With their paint-flaked woodwork and corroded metal, the sea-beaten rust buckets seemed to remain afloat by a miracle of levitation. Austin stopped at one exception, a solid-looking wooden boat that appeared to have undergone heroic maintenance. The black hull and white wheelhouse gleamed with many coats of paint, and the brightwork was liberally soaked with oil.

Reaching into his pocket, Austin pulled out a folded piece of notepaper and matched the scrawled word *Turgut* with the name painted in white on the stern. He smiled approvingly. He liked Captain Kemal without having met him. Turgut was a renowned sixteenth-century admiral in the reign of Süleyman the Magnificent. Anyone who would name an ancient fishing vessel after such a towering naval figure displayed a sense of history and humor.

The deck was deserted except for a man in a double-breasted black suit. He sat on a coil of thick rope mending a net spread across his knees.

Austin called out a greeting in Turkish. '*Meraba.* May I come aboard?'

The man looked up. '*Meraba,*' he said, and beckoned Austin aboard.

Austin climbed a short gangway and stepped onto the deck. The boat was about fifty feet long, with a wide beam to provide stability as a fishing platform. His eyes swept the *Turgut*, taking in the extraordinary efforts that had been made to maintain a vessel that looked as if it went back to the Ottoman Empire itself. He went over to the seated man and said, 'I'm looking for Captain Kemal.'

'I'm Kemal,' the man said. His fingers flew over the mesh without missing a loop.

The captain was a slightly built man in his fifties. His face was narrow, his olive skin burnished to a reddish glow by sun and wind. He wore a woven skullcap over dark brown hair going to gray, and he was clean-shaven except for a toothbrush mustache that seemed to be held in place by the curve of his prominent nose. The soft wail of Turkish music came from a portable radio at his feet.

'My name is Kurt Austin. I'm with the National Underwater and Marine Agency. I was on the NUMA ship *Argo* when we found your cousin Mehmet's body.'

Kemal nodded solemnly and put the net aside. 'Mehmet's funeral was this morning,' he said in well-spoken English. He plucked at his sleeve to show that he was wearing his best and only suit.

'They told me on the *Argo*. I hope I'm not intruding by coming by so soon.'

The captain shook his head and indicated a nearby waist-high stack of netting.

'Sit, please, Mr Austin.'

'You speak English very well.'

'Thank you. When I was younger, I worked as a cook for the American air base near Ankara.' He smiled, displaying a brilliant gold tooth. 'The pay was good, I worked very hard and saved the money to buy this boat.'

'I noticed you named it after a great admiral.'

Kemal raised a bushy eyebrow, impressed. 'Turgut was a big hero to my people.'

'I know. I read a biography about him.'

The captain studied Kurt with deep-set liquid brown eyes. 'Thank your NUMA people for me. It would be very hard for Mehmet's family if they did not have his body to bury.'

'I'll be sure to tell Captain Atwood and the *Argo*'s crew of your appreciation. Miss Dorn mentioned your name.'

The captain smiled. 'The beautiful television woman came by last night. She said Mehmet's widow will be well provided for. It will not bring Mehmet back, but it is more than he could have earned in his whole life.' He shook his head in wonder. 'God is great.'

'I called the hotel earlier, and they told me Miss Dorn had checked out.'

'She has gone to Paris. She wants to hire my boat again, but must get permission from her bosses.'

Austin received the news of Kaela's departure with mixed feelings. He regretted not having had the chance to get to know Kaela better, but the lovely TV reporter would have been a distraction.

'What else did Miss Dorn say?'

'She told me what happened to Mehmet. She said men on horses shot at the TV people and killed my cousin.' He frowned. 'They are very bad men. Mehmet never hurt anyone.'

'Yes, they are. *Very* bad men.'

'She told me how you shot at them with your little plane. How many did you kill?'

'I'm not sure. There was one body.'

'*Good.* Do you know who these people are who killed him?'

'No, but I intend to find out.'

Kemal raised his eyebrows. 'You are going *back* to that place?'

'If I can find a boat to take me there.'

'But you have the big NUMA ship.'

'It wouldn't be a good idea to use a government vessel.' Austin glanced around at the *Turgut*. 'I need something that won't attract attention.'

The light of understanding dawned in the dark eyes. 'Something like a fishing boat maybe?'

Austin smiled. 'Yes, something very *much* like a fishing boat.'

The captain studied Austin's face, then got up and went into the wheelhouse. He reappeared with a large bottle and two chipped coffee mugs. He uncorked the bottle, poured liberal quantities into the mugs and handed one to Austin.

'To Mehmet,' he said, raising his drink high in toast.

They clinked the mugs and Kemal took a generous swallow, gulping the strong drink down as if it were water.

Austin knew from the licorice smell that the mug held the potent Turkish firewater known as *raki*. Although he did not ordinarily drink alcohol before the sun appeared over the yardarm, he didn't want to be impolite. He took a tentative sip and let the fiery liquor trickle down his throat, thinking that this is what it must be like to swallow broken glass.

Kemel took another healthy swig, and to Austin's relief set his mug aside.

He affixed Austin with a leveled gaze. 'Why would you want to go back there? You could be shot, too.'

'That's a possibility, but it wouldn't have to happen. Last time we had no warning or weapons. This time we will.'

Kemal pondered the answer. Austin was glad to see that the captain was not someone who made rash decisions. His coolness could come in handy.

The Turk stared into his cup. 'I feel responsible for Mehmet. I let him go with the TV people so he could make some extra money.'

'No one could have predicted he would be shot.'

'Of course, you are right. I fished there many times with no trouble.'

'Would you ever go back?'

'Not for pay, no.'

Austin was disappointed but not surprised. 'I understand, Captain. It could be very dangerous, no matter how well-prepared we are.'

'Fah!' Kemel spat off to his side. 'I am not afraid. I said I would not go there for *pay*. I owe you a favor for killing that pig.' He dismissed Austin's protest with a wave of his hand. 'The *Turgut* is at your disposal,' he said as grandly as if he were turning over the wheel of the *QE2*.

'You're not obligated to me in any way.'

The captain thrust his chin forward. Speaking in measured tones to make sure there was no mistaking his intentions, he said, 'The men who killed my cousin are the ones who must be made to pay. I am not a stranger to these affairs. As a young man, I was a smuggler. I was never caught.' He thumped the deck with his heel and flashed his fourteen-karat grin. 'Twin diesels,' he said proudly. 'Thirty knots cruising speed. When do you wish to go?'

'I'm expecting three other people from the United States today. I have to round up some equipment as well. How about tomorrow morning?'

'The boat will be fueled up and ready at dawn.'

'What about crew?' Austin said. 'I don't want to place anyone in danger after what happened to Mehmet.'

'Thank you. I will keep two crewmen, my most trusted. I will warn them about the danger, so they can make a choice. I know what they will say. They are cousins to Mehmet, too.'

They shook hands on the deal. Austin said he would be there with the sun. He left before Kemal wanted to seal the agreement with another cup of *raki*. His head was spinning on the walk back to the *Argo*, though by the time he returned to the NUMA ship, the fresh air off the Bosporus had cleared away most of the alcoholic vapors. He went up to the bridge to see Captain Atwood, who was poring over some charts.

'How's the television star?' he asked.

'You've obviously heard about what a natural I am before the cameras,' Atwood replied. 'Okay, I admit it,' he said, with a sheepish grin. 'I had a good time filming with those crazy characters. My guess is that they'll edit out my pretty mug in favor of the lovely Miss Dorn.'

'Would you blame them?'

'Hell no! Not in a hundred years. I'm surprised you didn't make a move on the lady. Losing your touch?'

'My heart belongs only to NUMA,' Austin said, placing his hand on his chest. 'Which brings up why

I'm here. I'm going to need some help, no questions asked.'

The captain cocked his head. He had known Austin a long time and never knew the man to leave business of any sort unfinished.

'We'll do what we can, as long as it doesn't involve putting the *Argo* or its crew in jeopardy.'

'It won't. All I need is the loan of some gear.'

Austin summarized his wish list and asked that the equipment be delivered to the *Turgut*. None of it would be a problem, the captain said. While Atwood ordered up the requested gear, Austin went to his cabin and plugged in his laptop computer. He called up a commercial satellite-imaging company off the Internet and requested photos of a location on the Russian coast of the Black Sea. He examined the photos closely, but wasn't surprised when nothing unusual popped out at him. The Soviets would not be advertising their secret base.

He punched out a number on his Globalstar phone. It was still early back in the States, but he knew from his days of working with the CIA that Sam Leahy would be in his office.

'How's the weather at Langley?' Austin said, when Leahy's brass-lunged voice came on the phone.

There was a pause. 'You've got the wrong number, pal. If you're looking for a goddamn weather report, call the National Underwater and Marine Agency. Hell, I hear the smart alecks at NUMA know everything there *is* to know.'

'*Almost* everything, Sam. That's why I'm calling for your help.'

'I knew you'd come crawling back to the Company. Great hearing from you. How have you been, you old sea dog?'

'I'm fine. They still have you tied to a desk?'

'Not for long. Retirement is in six months. Then it's running fishing charters on the Chesapeake. I could use a first mate if you ever get tired of the Washington rat race.'

'Sounds tempting. Put me down for a charter at the very least. Right now I could use some information. What do you know about Soviet sub bases?'

'Broad subject. Anything in particular you'd like to know?'

'Yes. How were they physically constructed?'

'To begin with, they were *big*. They had to be large enough to accommodate the babies like the Typhoon, with a length of five hundred fifty-seven feet. The beam alone was seventy-five feet. Those monsters were armed with twenty nukes a piece. The Soviets wanted them protected from a nuclear attack, so they built the pens deep. They learned from the German U-boat pen construction that held up pretty well under Allied bombing. Basically, they'd blast a tunnel out of a hillside and line it with several yards of reinforced granite.'

'Do you have any data on the *where* and *how* of these bases?'

'I can get it.'

Austin heard an unspoken conditional in the answer. 'It would really be a help if you could dig out what you can.'

'No problem. Lots of that stuff has been declassified anyhow. But I'll hold you to that promise to do a charter.'

Austin was relieved. He'd expected Leahy to say he would have to run the request through his higher-ups. 'You provide the bait and I'll bring the beer.'

Austin gave Leahy his e-mail address, thanked him again and hung up. He worked out some logistical problems on his computer, then he went out to check on the preparations for his trip with Captain Kemal. The equipment he'd asked for was stacked in boxes on the deck and ready to go. A truck was on its way to run the equipment to the *Turgut*. Austin had done all he could until he heard from the Special Assignments Team. He didn't have to wait long. As he was taking an equipment inventory, his phone buzzed. It was Joe Zavala calling.

'We're at the airport,' Zavala said.

'What took you so long?'

Zavala sighed loudly. 'That's gratitude for you. You yanked me out of the arms of the most beautiful woman on the planet.'

'Every woman you've ever been involved with was the most beautiful woman on the planet.'

'What can I say? I am a fortunate man.'

'One day you'll thank me for rescuing you from the bonds of matrimony.'

'*Matrimony!* A sobering thought. Don't even *joke* about it.'

'We can talk about your love life later. How soon will you be at the *Argo*?'

'Gamay is nailing down a cab and Paul is humping the luggage out to the curb. We'll be there sooner than you can spell *Constantinople*.'

Within the hour, Zavala and the Trouts arrived at the hotel. After a brief reunion, Zavala said, 'Not that it matters, but we were wondering if you could give us a hint why we raced halfway across the world at warp speed.'

'I missed your smiling faces?'

'Right,' Zavala said. 'That's why you asked me to bring along your shooting iron and my own metal delivery system.'

'I'll admit I had an ulterior motive, but I'm not lying when I say it's good to see you.'

Austin glanced around at the other members of the Special Assignments Team and grinned with pleasure at their eager expressions. Then he began to outline his plan.

12

Rocky Point, Maine

The image on the oversized computer monitor looked like the profile of a very tall tortoise. Leroy Jenkins clicked the computer mouse until the shell flattened as if it had been run over by an eighteen-wheeler. Jenkins made some computations from the numbers on the screen, then exploded with the blue-lightning curses he usually reserved for a tangled lobster pot line. He turned away from the computer and swiveled his chair so he was facing a big picture window. From its position high on the hill, the tall white clapboard house offered an unequaled view of the harbor and the sea beyond.

The harbor swarmed with activity. Front-end loaders scooped scattered debris into a waiting line of dump trucks. Forklifts normally used to hoist boats onto multistory racks for winter storage were plucking battered wrecks from the parking lot and lining them up where their owners could claim them: Cranes had been brought in to pick remnants of the motel off the breakwaters.

Jenkins's boat was tied up at the town pier with the others lucky enough to have been out of the way when the big wave struck. Jenkins rubbed his eyes and turned back to the computer to enter some new numbers. After a few minutes, he shook his head in frustration. He had gone through the modeling process dozens of times, feeding in different combinations of data, and his findings still didn't make sense. Jenkins was grateful when the doorbell rang. He went out into the hallway and yelled down the stairs, 'Come in.'

The door opened and Charlie Howes stepped inside. 'Not bothering you, am I?' the police chief said.

'Hell no, Charlie. Come on up. I was just fiddling around on the computer.'

The chief climbed to the second-floor office. 'You've done a nice job with the house,' he said, glancing around at the well-ordered space with its neatly arranged filing cabinets and bookcases.

'Thanks, Charlie. Wish I could claim credit.' He picked up a framed photograph of a handsome middle-aged woman who was smiling directly at the camera from a sailboat cockpit. 'Mary knew that I'd need more than lobstering to keep my brain from fossilizing. Setting up my office in the attic space was her idea. You know how she was. She could make a silk purse out of a sow's ear.'

'She didn't do a bad job of filing down some of *your* rough edges.'

Jenkins laughed. 'I consider that a *miracle*, given the material she had to work with.' He glanced out the window again. 'Looks like they're making progress down there.'

'Getting the harbor cleared out real fast. There was some worry about oil spills from the fuel tanks, but the environmental people from the state got it under control. I needed a break from the press people. Started getting in the way anyhow, with all the insurance guys showing up.' He jerked his head toward the computer. 'See you've been workin'. Got things figured out yet?'

'Been trying. Pull up a seat and take a look. I could use your detective's intuition.'

Despite the chief's folksy language and country ways, he was no bumpkin. Howes had a master's degree in criminal science from the state university. He replied with a skeptical snort, dragged a stool next to Jenkins's chair and squinted into the computer monitor.

'What's that thing that looks like a pregnant snake?'

Jenkins raised an eyebrow. 'Rorschach would have a field day with you. What do you know about *tsunamis*?'

'I know I never want to see one again!'

'That's a good start. Let me don my professor's hat, and I'll give you a crash course.' He wrote out the words *tsu* and *nami* on a pad of paper. 'These words represent the Japanese characters for "harbor" and "wave." An international conference adopted the term in 1963 to avoid confusion.'

'I always heard them called tidal waves.'

'That was the popular term, but it isn't accurate. Tides come from gravitational forces such as the moon, sun and planets. Even we scientists were wrong. We called them seismic sea waves, which implies that earthquakes generate all *tsunamis*. A quake is only *one* cause.'

'You think a *quake* caused that mess out there?'

'Yes. No. Maybe.' He grinned at the chief's befuddled reaction and ripped a sheet of paper off the pad. 'Here's the real culprit.' He held the paper horizontally. 'Make believe this is the ocean bottom.' He pushed the ends in so that the middle of the paper humped up. 'A quake occurs when tectonic plates bump together and deform the seafloor. This hump pushes up the column of water all the way to the surface. The water tries to regain its equilibrium.'

'You're losing me.'

Jenkins thought for a moment. 'It's like Joe Johnson, the town drunk, staggering home after a night on the town. Reason he zigzags is because the booze has affected his equilibrium. He has to keep catching himself from going off in the wrong direction. Sometimes he can't stop and slams into a wall and knocks himself out.' He frowned. 'Okay, it's a rough analogy.'

'I get the picture.'

'Think of Joe as that column of water and the wall as the Maine coast. Only difference is the wall gets the worst of it, not Joe.'

'How come every wave isn't a potential tidal wa – I mean *tsunami*?'

'I knew your policeman's logic would come into play. *Two* reasons. Time and distance. The time between waves hitting the beach is five to twenty seconds. With a *tsunami*, that time can be ten minutes to two hours. The distance between waves is called the wavelength. Beach waves can be three hundred to six hundred feet apart. With a *tsunami*, you're talking three hundred miles – plus.'

'I've seen some pretty destructive beach waves.'

'So have I. But even an ordinary wave crashing on the beach only has a short life and a speed of ten to twenty miles per hour. Your *tsunami* has had hundreds of miles and hours to build up its energy. The deeper the water, the faster the wave. That's why a *tsunami* can hit six hundred miles per hour as it crosses the ocean, even though ships don't feel it and you can't see it from the air. Let me give you an example. In 1960, an offshore quake near Chile sent a wave across the Pacific. The wave was no more than three feet high. Twenty-two hours later, when the wave hit the coast of Japan, it was twenty feet high and killed two hundred people. The wave bounced around the Pacific for days, causing damage wherever it touched.'

'If it's only a ripple in the ocean, how'd you figure this was going to be a big one?'

'I was lobstering out on the ledge where it's comparatively shallow. The wave slowed down when it hit the shallows and started to peak. It was moving slower, but all the energy it built up was still there. That energy has to go somewhere. When the wave approaches shore, the mousy little sea grows up into a monster. Sometimes it builds up into a great towering wave. It might be a bunch of series of breaking waves, or a bore, like a bunch of steps with a steep breaking front. It might suck out the water and spit it back out.'

'That's what happened with us. Like someone pulled the plug out of the harbor.'

Jenkins nodded. '*Tsunamis* are fascinating and very adaptive critters. Reefs, bays, entrances to rivers, can affect the damage, the slope of the beach. The waves can crest to one hundred feet or more, but mostly they just *surge*. All depends on what's in the way. They can wrap around a headland and cause damage on the opposite side of an island. When they get squeezed, they become really dangerous, because you've got all that intensity built up in a small space.' He pointed out the window at a river that fed into the harbor. The high banks were littered with debris. 'They can even go up rivers, as they did here.'

'Good thing the condos Jack Schrager built on the banks of the river weren't occupied, or there would be a lot of dead people floating around in that harbor instead of scraps of wood. Damned lucky you saw those waves and recognized their threat.'

'*More* than lucky.' Jenkins clicked his computer mouse and pulled up a map of the world with arrows pointing to various countries. 'In the decade starting in 1990, *tsunamis* killed more than four hundred people and caused billions of dollars in damage.' He tapped the screen. 'This one in Papua New Guinea was a real horror. The wave was forty-five feet tall when it hit along nineteen miles of coast. A few minutes later, there were more than two thousand people dead.'

He switched over to a simulation. 'This is an animation of a quake-generated wave attacking a Japanese village back in 1923. You see a lot of big waves in the Pacific. It's surrounded by the "rim of fire," all those tectonic plates that shift every so often.'

'Hate to be so parochial, but we're talking the *Atlantic*, not the Pacific, and the coast of Maine, not Japan. I've lived here all my life and I've yet to hear about a quake.'

'You've probably had more minor tremors than you know of, but I agree, that's why I started thinking about other causes. *Tsunamis* caused by landslides are less common. Then you've got volcanic eruptions and large meteorites.'

'Not too many volcanoes around here that I know of.'

'Be grateful. The Krakatoa volcano created waves one hundred feet high and killed thousands back in 1883. If an asteroid five miles across landed in the mid-Atlantic, it would create a wave high enough to swamp the upper east coast of the US. New York would be wiped off the map.'

'That leaves landslide.'

'It's what we call a *slump*. Here – let me show you.' Jenkins pulled up another map on the monitor. 'This is Izmit Bay in Turkey. They had a slump-generated wave there that caused extensive damage.'

'What caused the slump?'

'An earthquake.' Jenkins chuckled. 'I know, it's like asking which came first, the chicken or the egg? In general, a slump is caused by a quake. That's the problem with our Rocky Point ripple. There was a slump, but no quake.'

'Are you sure?'

'Absolutely. I've talked to the folks at the Weston Observatory in Massachusetts. They keep tabs on all seismic disturbances in the area. They picked up some rumbles that indicated a slump, but no quake preceding it, as I'd expect. I heard a tremendous underwater boom shortly before I saw things happening. There was apparently a movement of ocean bottom east of Maine, but without the normal crash of tectonic plates. I've talked to *tsunami* experts all around the country. Nobody has heard of such a thing.'

'Then we're stumped.'

'Not exactly.' Jenkins brought the wave profile back onto the computer screen. 'I've put together a simulation of our wave. It's pretty crude. Even with the best information, wave calculations can be complicated. You've got to factor in stuff like velocity, wave height and destructive force. Then you've got all the coastal features that cause a wave to deflect or diffract. You've got to calculate the effects of backwash from following waves.'

'Sounds impossible.'

'It nearly is. But not totally. A few years ago, scientists used computer-based mathematical modeling techniques to solve the demise of the civilization on Crete. Look, this is a map chart of the Maine coast. That's the harbor. The hardest hit was several miles from here, where some fishermen saw waves breaking over Newcomb's Rocks.'

The chief whistled. 'Those cliffs must be fifty feet high.'

Jenkins nodded and indicated the chart on the screen. An arrow pointed toward the land. 'The main wave force was just to the north of here, so even with my warning, things could have been worse here at the cove. I don't even know if this house would have been safe.'

The chief went pale. 'That would have been the whole town.'

Jenkins leaned forward and peered at the computer. 'This is amazing. Look at how straight it came in. Almost like a child creating a wave in a bathtub.'

The chief tapped the screen. 'Is this where it started?'

'Yeah. It's only an estimate built on circumstantial evidence.'

'I took a course in accident reconstruction. It's amazing what you can tell about speed and impact from skid marks and broken headlights.'

'I'm pretty confident that it originated about a hundred and fifty miles to the east.'

'What are you going to do now?'

Jenkins's shoulders ached from tension. 'First I'm going to brew up some tea. Then we're going to have us a slam-bang game of chess.'

13

The Black Sea

As the fishing boat *Turgut* approached the Russian coast, Austin swept the deserted shoreline through the lenses of his Fujinon gyro-stabilized binoculars, alert to any feature out of sync with its surroundings. The barren coast seemed peaceful. Wind and tide had scrubbed the sand clean of footprints. Green tufts of new growth sprouted in the fire-blackened patches of dune grass. It was hard to imagine the deadly game he had played over this tranquil setting only days before.

The beach was about a mile wide, flanked by two headlands like the arms of a sofa. Except for the cliff sculpted by wind and sea into the sharp profile of an old man, the shoreline was unremarkable. A misty curtain hung over the dunes. Austin remembered that the land hidden behind the grassy ridge sloped down to the abandoned buildings, then flattened out in a scraggly plain edged by woods, gradually rising to low rolling hills.

A smell like burning rope assaulted Austin's nostrils. Wrinkling his nose, he lowered the Stabiscope and turned to see Captain Kemal. The captain removed the twisted black cigar from between his tobacco-stained teeth and jabbed it toward the shore.

'How does it look, Mr Austin?'

'As quiet as a grave, Captain.'

'I don't think I like it quiet like *that*.' He exhaled twin streams of smoke through his crooked nose. 'When I smuggled, I never liked a beach that was calm like this. Not even birds flying. You sure you want to go there now?'

'Unfortunately, we don't have much choice. I was hoping the fog would burn off, though.'

Kemal squinted toward shore. 'Another hour. Two, maybe.'

'That's too long. We'll move soon.'

The captain waved his cigar in the air, discharging a shower of sparks. 'The men are ready when you say.'

Austin nodded, thinking about the conversation he'd had with Kemal on the trip from Istanbul. Austin had asked the captain if he knew the Russian sailor who'd sold Kaela Dorn the map that led her to the sub base.

'His name is Valentin,' the captain had replied, with no hesitation. 'The other fishermen use him when they need an extra hand. Miss Dorn paid him too much money for this big "secret,"' he said, with a sad shake of his head. 'All the fishermen know about the submarines.'

'People *knew* there was a base here?'

'Sure.' Kemal's thin lips had widened in a knowing

grin. 'Fishermen know *every*thing. We watch the weather, the water, birds, other boats.' He tapped the corner of an eye with his forefinger. 'If you don't keep a lookout, you're going to be in trouble.'

Kemal's revelation was no surprise to Austin. He often worked with fishermen on NUMA assignments and found them to be keen observers of conditions under, on and above the sea. A fisherman had to be a combination biologist, meteorologist, mechanic and mariner. Their livelihood, their very lives, depended on their store of practical knowledge. As a former smuggler, Kemal would have been more vigilant than the average fisherman.

'How long did you fish these waters?' Austin asked.

'*Many* years. In the old days, you would see many boats from all over. Turkish, Russian, sometimes even Bulgarian. The fishing is good. Big schools of bonito come in close to feed. Nobody bothers us. Then one day the Russians come with patrol boats and men with machine guns. They tell the fishermen this is a science station. They will kill anyone who gets too close. Some fishermen didn't believe them and got shot, so the rest of us stayed away. We work offshore, where nobody bothers us. Sometimes the fishermen see periscopes. Once a big black fin came up near my boat.'

'A submarine conning tower?'

'He wanted to look, I guess,' Kemal said, with a nod. 'Then Russia falls apart. The submarines stop coming. Everyone says the Russian navy is broke.

One day I take a chance. I follow a school of fish in close.' He held an invisible steering wheel in his hand to demonstrate. 'I'm ready to run if they come. But nobody stops me. Since then I fish here with no trouble.' He shrugged. 'When the television people want to go in with Mehmet, I think it's no big deal.'

'Did you ever go ashore and look around?'

'No. What's there was not my business. That was before Mehmet got shot.' He spat over the side. 'Now it *is* my business.'

Kemal's story meshed with the report Austin's friend Leahy had sent him. According to the CIA files, construction on the base started in the 1950s. A U-2 plane photographed the site on an overflight. The US kept close tabs on the growing complex. The Turkish counterpart of the CIA confirmed the reports of submarine traffic. US listening posts determined that the base was under the command of the Black Sea Fleet at Sevastopol. The scientific station was built to do ocean research that would help the fleet do its job.

Military activity slowed after the Cold War. The cash-strapped new Russian republic shut the base down, much as obsolete army installations were closed in the US. The scientific station was abandoned. The CIA could have saved millions in surveillance expense by talking to Kemal and his friends. Unfortunately, the one point on which the Turk was wrong, his belief that the base was deserted, had cost his cousin's life.

When the *Turgut* was less than a mile from shore, Austin asked the captain to drop anchor. Kemal yelled an order to his crew, and a minute later the boat coasted to a stop and vibrated with the rattle of the anchor chain. As the anchor splashed into the sea, Kemal excused himself and went off to supervise the setting of the trawls.

Zavala appeared from the other side of the boat, where he had been getting their scuba gear ready for a dive.

Austin eyed the twisted stub of the cheroot clenched between Zavala's teeth. 'I see you've been raiding the captain's humidor.'

'He insisted. I didn't want to hurt his feelings.' Zavala removed the stogie from his mouth and held it at arm's length. 'I think they make these things out of old tires, but I'm sort of getting used to the taste,' he said with a shrug. 'Gear's all set to go.'

Austin followed Zavala to the port side, where the wheelhouse hid them from prying eyes on the mainland. Neatly laid out on the narrow deck were two rows of double air tanks, weight belts, hoods, gloves, boots and fins and two black Viking Pro dry suits manufactured to NATO specifications. Sunlight glinted off the yellow fiberglass housings of two Torpedo 2000 driver propulsion vehicles. Mounted in tandem, the dual rocket-shaped battery-powered vehicles had a top speed of five miles an hour and a running time of an hour.

They shimmied into their dive suits, helped each

other on with their air tanks and did a buddy equipment inspection. Then they waddled to the rail with the shuffling walk divers use out of water and stood at the edge of the deck.

'Any questions before we plunge in?' Austin said.

Zavala flicked the black cigar stub over the side. 'Plan the dive and dive the plan. Get in. Take a look. Get out. Stay flexible. Improvise when necessary.'

Zavala's succinct summation could have applied to any mission Austin led. Austin was a staunch believer in simplicity of execution because the more elements in a plan, the greater the chance for a screwup. He knew from experience that it was impossible to anticipate every situation when the details were sparse. His muscular body was marked with scars that were stark reminders that even the most carefully laid scheme could unravel in the face of the unexpected. As insurance, though, they carried guns and extra ammunition in their chest packs. They also had communications equipment, although it would be of limited value. They were invading the soil of a foreign country. If he and Zavala encountered trouble, they were on their own.

'You forgot one thing,' Austin said.

Zavala looked behind him. 'Cover your ass?'

'CYA is *always* a good idea. But what I was thinking was this: We're not *Mission Impossible*. We're not the Suicide Squadron. We're simply a couple of nosy guys who want to come back, preferably with our skin in one piece.'

'That suits me fine,' Zavala said. 'I'm very attached to my skin.'

Austin winced at Zavala's joke and gave the captain the thumb's-up sign. He held on to his mask and chest pack so they wouldn't fly up, and jumped fins first into the dark blue sea, sinking several feet before his automatic buoyancy control lifted him back to the surface. Zavala bobbed up a few feet away. As they floated in the mild swell, they made sure their regulators were working, then Austin signaled Kemal.

The captain lowered the bright yellow Torpedo 2000s down to the water. The crewmen were setting trawls on the land side. From shore, the *Turgut* looked like any other fishing boat harvesting the sea. Austin reminded Kemal to keep his radio on and to leave quickly at the first sign of trouble. He didn't want more funerals in the captain's family.

Kemal gave him a smile that showed he had no intention of following Austin's advice and wished them good luck in Turkish and in English. Austin bit down on his regulator mouthpiece, folded his body in a surface dive and with a flip of his fins disappeared below the surface. Zavala was only a moment behind. At twenty feet, they hovered and tested their voice-activated Divelink wireless underwater communications systems system.

'Ready to invade Russia?' Austin asked.

'Can't wait!' Zavala said, sounding like Donald Duck in Austin's earphones. 'Russia has some of the most beautiful women in the world. Green eyes, high cheekbones, lush lips –'

'Keep a lid on your raging libido, José. This isn't Club Med we're going to. When we get home, you can order a Russian bride over the Internet.'

'Thanks for dashing cold water on my lustful thoughts.'

'Speaking of cold water, we've got about a mile of the stuff ahead of us, so I suggest we get moving.'

Austin checked his wrist compass and jerked his thumb toward shore. They flicked on the switches of their propulsion vehicles, the battery-powered motors hummed into life, and the Torpedo 2000s surged ahead, smoothly pulling the divers through the pale green water. Their approach sent schools of fish flying off to either side, making it evident why Kemal and his fellow fishermen had risked their necks to work these waters.

Near the surf line, the water became turbid from floating particles of vegetation kicked up by the crashing waves. Austin angled the Torpedo 2000 down to the sandy sea bottom, with Zavala a few feet behind him.

'Any idea what we're looking for?' Zavala said, squinting toward the gravelly banking that rose sharply from the sea floor to meet the beach.

'A neon sign saying, THIS IS IT would help. But I'll settle for something that looks like a big garage door.'

Zavala switched on his powerful Phantom dive light and played the bull's-eye across the slope.

'I don't even see a doorknob.'

'We're wasting our time here. They wouldn't build on the beach. They'd want solid rock over their heads. Let's check out the cliffs. I'll take the one to the right.'

Zavala waved, and with the ease of a natural pilot he put his propulsion vehicle in a graceful turn and shot off, quickly disappearing into the murk. Austin headed in the opposite direction. A moment later, the voice of a singing duck filled Austin's earphones as Zavala rendered an off-tune version of 'Guantanamera.'

Austin moved parallel to the undersea embankment until the sand and gravel gave over to solid rock. Zavala's quacking became fainter as they expanded their range. Austin was grateful for this development, but he didn't want too much space separating them. He saw nothing that resembled an entrance, and was about to tell Zavala to head back, but Joe broke off his serenade with a loud 'Whoa!'

'Say again?'

'*Got* something, Kurt,' he said excitedly.

Austin wheeled the Torpedo 2000 around in a tight arc. He glided past the beach and homed in on a silvery pinpoint that blinked like a firefly on a summer night. Zavala was hovering at midwater and flashing his light as a homing beacon. When Austin got closer, Zavala adjusted his light to flood pattern and pointed the beam toward the face of the undersea wall that rose to become the chin of Imam's Point.

Austin was looking at a huge pile of rubble that resembled a landslide one might see in a mountain valley. The sea bottom below the slide was littered with hundreds of chunks of rock and concrete obviously flung there with great force, most likely by an explosion.

'Not exactly what I'd call a welcome mat,' Austin said.

With short fluttering fin strokes, he swam up the face of the rubble pile. If this was the entrance to the pen, no submarines would be using it soon. He swam back and forth searching for an opening, but the blockage was complete.

Zavala floated up beside him. 'So much for my dreams of beautiful Russian women.'

Austin scanned the rubble, then swam over to a slab about six feet tall and half as wide that stood like a giant gravestone in a more or less vertical position. A pair of steel rods protruded from the top, like antennae on an insect.

'If we could topple this slab, maybe we could start a slide that would open up this mess.'

'Not a bad idea. Too bad we forgot to pack dynamite.'

'We may not need it. Remember what Archimedes said?'

'Sure, he's the guy who runs the Greek restaurant down the street. He said "Eat here or to go?"'

'I'm talking about the *other* Archimedes.'

'Oh, *that* one. He said, "Eureka!"'

'He also said, "Give me a place to stand and I will move the earth."'

Zavala stared at the steel rods. 'Archimedes was into levers and fulcrums, as I recall.'

'Eureka,' Austin said, swimming up the rock slide until he was above the slab. He squeezed in between the concrete and the cliff, braced his back against the wall and placed his feet on one of the rods. Zavala took a position beside Austin with his feet on the other rod.

'Let's see if we can move a small piece of the world,' Austin said. 'On *three*.'

They pushed against the rods and the slab tilted a few inches before settling back into place. The air tanks got in the way, so they adjusted them and tried again. The slab tipped precariously this time. For a moment, it seemed as if the block would go over, but despite their shoving and grunting, it rocked back into place.

Zavala suggested that they push higher for more leverage. They slid their feet to the ends of the rods, planted their backs and tried again. This time the slab went over so fast that they almost tumbled down with it. It crashed in slow motion off a big boulder, breaking in half, then bounced a few more times before landing in a muddy cloud. Several other chunks followed it down in a secondary landslide.

'Crude but effective,' Austin said, as he drifted down the face of the pile and stopped in front of a newly created opening in the rubble. He probed the hole with his light, then tried to squeeze through only to have his air tanks get in the way. He removed the tanks. Keeping the regulator in his mouth, he backed into the opening feet first and pulled his tanks in after him. Zavala followed using the same procedure.

They were wedged in a tight space between the pile of boulders and two massive steel blast doors. The armored doors were sealed, but near the top of one was a shadow where the force of the explosion had peeled back a corner like a page in a book. The gap was big enough for them and their tanks. They slipped through the hole and flashed their lights around. The beams faded into nothingness except for a grayish reflection over their heads. They swam up several feet until their tanks scraped against concrete. Swimming a few feet below the ceiling, they proceeded through the murky water.

After a few minutes, the ceiling disappeared and they swam up until their heads emerged into the open. They were in complete darkness. Austin removed the regulator from his mouth and took a tentative breath. The air was musty but breathable. They switched on their lights and saw that they were near the edge of a man-made pool. They swam to a ladder, pulled themselves up on the side of the pool and flashed their lights around, probing the perimeter of the rectangular basin.

'Hel-lo,' Austin murmured. 'Someone left their rubber ducky in the bathtub.'

His light outlined the contours of a submarine on the far side of the pool.

They stacked their scuba gear in neat piles for quick retrieval and stripped down to their lightweight black insulated liners. They were traveling light, taking only their weapons, extra ammunition and lights and, in Austin's case, a belt radio. He tried to call Kemal, but the thick concrete walls made radio contact impossible. Setting off to explore the high-ceilinged chamber, they followed a set of narrow-gauge tracks that ran around the pool's perimeter, making their way past fuel pumps and conduits for water and electricity.

Gantries and cranes hung from the ceiling to service heavy loads. Sideways-traversing machinery could move a sub to the dry side for maintenance. Austin and Zavala went around the pool to where the submarine lay in dry dock. The sub was between three hundred and four hundred feet long, Austin estimated. They climbed aboard and explored the sub from end to end. The deck behind the conning tower was of an unusual design, long and flat and recessed. They climbed the sail and opened the entry hatch. The stale smell of food, unwashed bodies and fuel issued from the opening.

As the expert on underwater vehicles, Zavala volunteered to go inside the sub while Austin stood watch. A short while later, Zavala emerged.

'Nobody home,' he said, his voice echoing in the great chamber.

'Nothing?'

'I didn't say that.' Zavala handed Austin a navy baseball cap. 'I found this in a bunk room.'

Austin examined the white lettering on the front of the cap. *NR-1*. 'This raises more questions than it answers.'

'The boat itself is less of a mystery,' Zavala said. 'It's a diesel, built for a specialized purpose. No torpedoes. She's probably pretty fast on the surface, from the looks of her, and those hydroplanes on the sail would give her good maneuverability under water. The deck is modified to carry something. Cargo. Submersibles maybe.'

'Something like the *NR-1*?'

'Easily. But why block off the entrance doors to the pen?'

'They don't need this baby anymore. What better way to hide the evidence? Let's see if we can find the owner of this cap,' he said, tucking the cap inside his suit.

Satisfied that the sub could yield no further clues, they walked the rest of the way around the pool until they came back to their dive gear. Railroad tracks led to a set of double steel doors about twelve feet high. Next to the doors was an entryway to allow passage without having to open and close the big doors. Zavala tried the handle.

'It's unlocked,' he said. 'We're in luck.'

'Don't be too sure about that. This may be a case of the spider welcoming the flies.'

'No problem,' Zavala said, fitting the holster to the butt of his Heckler and Koch .9-mm VP70M to form a shoulder stock, giving the pistol the capability of firing three-round bursts. 'I brought spider repellent.'

Austin slipped his own brand of pesticide out of its leather holster. His Ruger Redhawk, custom-built by the Bowen Classic Arms Company, was a heavy-duty revolver chambered for the .50 special cartridge. His hand was filled with grips made of snake wood, a rare South American wood. The fat barrel was only four inches long, but the gun packed a deadly wallop.

They opened the door and stepped into a chamber half the size of the sub pen. A railroad spur extended from the main chamber. Sitting on the tracks were a half-dozen car-sized freight carriers powered by propane. The tracks ran down the center of the room, with tributaries branching out on both sides to a series of arched portals that allowed entrance into side chambers.

Entering the nearest room, they found shelves filled with spare parts. The other storerooms contained tools, firefighting equipment and workshops. One room, separated from the others by a heavy steel blast door, contained demolition charges and small arms.

They returned to the main chamber and walked over to an elevator. Next to the elevator was a door that led to a stairwell. The smell of cooked cabbage drifted from above. They climbed the stairs to the next landing and saw light coming from beneath a door that led off the landing.

Austin put his ear up to the door and listened. Hearing nothing, he cracked the door a few inches. Then he gently pushed the door open and stepped through, motioning for Zavala to follow. They were in a corridor lit by lights recessed in the ceiling. It was wide enough for four people to walk abreast. The passageway echoed the poured-concrete, bomb-shelter motif of the lower level.

Several doors opened off one side. The first led to a cold-storage room stocked with meats and vegetables. The cold room was connected to food lockers provisioned with canned goods and groceries. Next to the pantry were a large kitchen and bakery. They moved from the kitchen into the adjacent mess hall, which was furnished with long benches and tables. The smell of cooked food was strong.

Austin went over to a table, brushed some crumbs off the top and dabbed his finger into a circle of water.

'Keep a sharp eye out,' he said. 'Some of the regular customers may still be around.'

A door led from the mess hall to another passage-way and a deserted dormitory fitted out with fifty bunks. The beds were unmade and the footlockers were empty. Next to the dormitory was a small game room with a few tables and chairs. Austin walked over to a chessboard, studied the pieces for a moment, then moved a black knight to a different square.

'Checkmate,' he said.

With Austin in the lead, they headed back to the main corridor and climbed the stairs to the next floor. In contrast to the spartan barracks, the floors were covered with thick wall-to-wall carpeting and the walls were paneled in dark wood. They explored half a dozen offices and conference rooms. On the walls were a few yellowed charts, but the desks were cleaned out and the filing cabinets were empty.

'This must have been the command post for the submarine base,' Austin said.

Zavala glanced around the haunted precincts. 'It's been awhile since they did any commanding. Spooky. Maybe we should call Ghostbusters.'

Austin grunted. 'The guys who shot me out of the air a few days ago weren't made out of ectoplasm.'

From the command post, they went back to the main passageway, poked into several rooms, each with two beds, that could have been officers' quarters, and followed another connector that led to a large and luxurious suite. The polished oak floors were covered with finely woven oriental rugs. The ornate furniture was made from heavy dark wood. The décor was a blend of Byzantine and Middle Eastern, with a liberal use of red cloth and gold fringe.

Zavala looked at the painting of a voluptuous woman, one of several that decorated the walls. 'Remind me when I get home to redo my place in harem modern.'

Austin was having a problem imagining a bulldogjowled Soviet sub commander in these decadent surroundings. 'It looks like someone's idea of a Victorian bordello.'

Despite their bantering, both men were uneasy. Austin recalled the violence that had greeted his first visit to these shores. The quiet gave him the jitters. They explored the rest of the suite, eventually coming to a thick wooden door built with rivets and ornamental straps as if it guarded the portal to a medieval keep. Carved in the door was a large stylized letter *R*.

Zavala examined the antique keyhole, then he reached into his pack and pulled out a soft leather case that he unfolded to display an array of lock picks that would have gotten him arrested in most states. He selected a particularly large pick.

'The basic skeleton key should do the job.' He ran his fingers over the door carving and strong steel hinges. 'There must be something valuable on the other side. I'm surprised they didn't use a better lock.' Bending to his task, he inserted the pick in the keyhole, jiggled the tool, then turned it. The lock had been well-lubricated and the deadbolt opened with a loud *clunk*.

Austin put his ear up against the dark wood. Hearing nothing, he tried the ornamental knob. He paused, wondering if hidden cameras had watched them every step of the way into the labyrinth. A gang of cutthroats could be lurking on the other side of the door. The thought of a bullet or dagger in the eye made him squeamish. His lips tightened in a grim smile. Being shot or stabbed in the heart would leave him just as dead as a poke in the eye.

Austin couldn't remember who'd said the best defense is a good offense, but he had always considered it good advice. He cocked his Bowen, motioned to Zavala to back him up, then turned the knob, threw the door open and stepped inside.

14

The dented black Lada taxi clattered down the dirt road, with every bolt in its ancient chassis rattling in protest. The potholed ruts led through thick pines and ended at an encampment of rustic chalets clustered near the Black Sea. The cab bounced on its worn shock absorbers even after Paul and Gamay Trout extricated themselves from the cramped backseat like clowns in a circus skit. They removed their duffel bags from the roof rack and paid the driver. The cab drove off in a cloud of dust, and the door to a nearby chalet flew open with a bang. A bearlike man charged out, roaring in a voice that practically shook the cones off the trees.

'*Trout!* I can't believe you're here.' He wrapped Paul in a bear hug. 'How good to see you, my friend!' He pounded Trout on the back.

'Go-od to see you-oo, Vlad,' Trout replied, in between the breath-stealing thumps. 'Thi-is is my wife, Gamay-may. Gamay, meet Professor Vladimir Orlov.'

Orlov extended a ham-sized hand and attempted to click the heels of his rubber sandals together. 'A pleasure to meet you, Gamay. Your husband often talked about his brilliant and lovely wife as we drank beer at the Captain Kidd.'

'No less than he talked about you, Professor Orlov. Paul has often said how much he enjoyed your time together at Woods Hole.'

'We have many fond memories, your husband and I.' He turned to Paul. 'She is as beautiful and charming as I imagined. You are a lucky man.'

'Thank you. And you will be pleased to know that your barstool awaits your return.'

'Then it is only a question of *when*. Tell me how things are at the Oceanographic?'

'I was there only a few days ago. I try to get back home in between NUMA assignments. Woods Hole hasn't changed since the year you spent there.'

'I envy you. As a pauper nation, Russia is stingy with money for pure scientific research. Even a well-thought-of institution such as Rostov State University must beg for funding. We're fortunate that the government allows the university to use this place as a fieldwork center.'

Gamay looked around at the rustic cottages and the water sparkling through the trees. 'It's *wonderful*! Reminds me of the old cottage colonies on the Great Lakes where I grew up.'

'The Soviet navy used it as a getaway for middle-level officers and their wives. There's a tennis court, but the macadam looks like the face of the moon. We've brought in students and they have done a good job fixing up the chalets. It's perfect for seminars or retreats like this one where we academics simply come to *think*.' He grabbed the duffel bags. 'Come, I'll show you where you're staying.'

Orlov led the way along a soft pine-needle path to a chalet that gleamed with new green-and-white trim. He climbed onto the porch, dropped the bags and held the door open for the Trouts. The one-room cottage had up-and-down bunks for four people, a rough-hewn table in the middle, a sink with a pump and a gas camp stove on the other side. Orlov went to the sink and pumped the handle.

'The water is pure and cold. Be sure to save some in this coffee can to prime the pump. There's a shower outside. The WC is just behind the house. It's a bit primitive, I'm afraid.'

Gamay looked around the room. 'Looks quite cozy to me.'

Paul said, 'We invited ourselves, Professor. We should be grateful we're not sleeping in a tent.'

'*Nonsense!* I'll have no more such talk. You'll probably want to unpack and get into something more comfortable.' The professor was wearing baggy black shorts and a red tank top. 'As you see, we're very informal. When you're ready, follow the path back to the main clearing. I'll be waiting with some refreshment.'

After Orlov left, they filled the sink and washed up. Gamay traded her stylish cotton slacks and sweater for blue shorts and a T-shirt from the Scripps Oceanographic Institute, where she'd first met Paul, who was studying there. Paul was wearing an L.L. Bean nonwrinkle navy blazer and tan slacks and one of the wildly colored bow ties he favored. He put on new tan shorts, navy polo shirt and Teva sandals. Then they strolled back through the pines to the main clearing.

Orlov sat at a picnic table in the shade of an arbor. He was talking to a middle-aged couple he introduced as Natasha and Leo Arbikov, both physicists. They spoke little English but communicated with sunny smiles. Orlov said that there were a number of other academicians and students from various fields scattered about in the woods working on experiments or simply reading. From an oversized cooler, he produced plastic containers of fresh fruit, caviar, smoked fish, cold borscht, a jug of water and a bottle of vodka. The Trouts sampled the food, but drank water, putting off the hard stuff until later. Orlov had no such hesitation, drinking his vodka with apparently little effect.

'It helps my concentration,' he said with good cheer, washing down a mouthful of caviar. He gave Trout another teeth-rattling pound on the back. 'This is so incredible to see you, my friend. I'm glad you called to say you would be in the neighborhood.'

'It's wonderful to see you again, Vlad, although it was a little difficult getting through to you.'

'We're connected to the outside by a single telephone. That's the beauty of this place. It's the Lost World. Only *we* are the dinosaurs.' He roared with laughter at his own joke. 'We are paid practically nothing, but we can pursue our work with little in the way of expenses.' He lifted the bottle, smacked his lips and poured himself another two fingers of vodka. 'Enough about me. Tell me what brought you to the Black Sea.'

'You've heard of the NUMA research vessel, *Argo*?'

'Oh, yes. I've been on her, in fact. A few years ago. She's a wonderful ship. I would expect nothing less from NUMA.'

Paul nodded in agreement. 'Gamay and I are doing some research in connection with the *Argo*'s most recent survey. I remembered you were at the university and thought I'd give you a call to let you know we were in the neighborhood.'

Austin had asked the Trouts to look into Ataman Industries while he and Zavala checked out the submarine base. Ataman's headquarters were in the port city of Novorossiysk, on the northeast corner of the Black Sea. Trout immediately thought of Orlov, who had been a visiting professor at the Woods Hole Oceanographic Institution, because he remembered that the professor taught at the university in Rostov near Novorossiysk. When he'd called Orlov, the professor said he would never forgive Paul if he and Gamay didn't come to visit him.

'You had no problem getting here?' the professor inquired.

'Not at all. We were lucky to catch a commercial flight to Novorossiysk on short notice. The university arranged for a cab to pick us up at the airport, and here we are.' He looked around at the bucolic setting. 'Let me get my bearings. We're between Rostov and Novorossiysk?'

'That's right. Novorossiysk is the port for the oil fields in the Caucasus. It's also a Hero City full of large ugly monuments commemorating the heroic resistance of the people during the Great Patriotic War.' Orlov turned to Gamay. 'Paul has lauded your skills as a marine biologist. What sort of work have you been doing?'

'Before coming to the Black Sea, I was in the Florida Keys looking at coral damage from industrial runoff.'

Orlov gave a shake of his head. 'It seems that we Russians are not the only environmental barbarians. I am involved in a study of Black Sea pollution. What about you, Paul?'

'I was at Woods Hole doing some consulting work on a study of ocean mining. I think one of the ocean mining concerns I read about is in Novorossiysk, as a matter of fact.'

Guile was not one of Trout's strong suits. He had a blunt Yankee openness and felt uncomfortable skirting the truth, especially with an old friend. Trout figured that if he threw out a few conversational seeds, one of them would sprout. This seed fell on fertile soil.

'Ocean mining? You must mean Ataman Industries.'

'Sounds familiar. I'm sure I read about it somewhere.'

'I'd be surprised if you hadn't. Ataman is *huge*. They started as a land-mining conglomerate, but they saw the potential under the sea and now their fleet ranges all over the world.'

'Smart move, with the worldwide demand for fuel.'

'Yes, that is true, but less commonly known is that Ataman has been in the forefront in devising ways to extract methane hydrate from the sea bottom.'

'I don't remember any mention of that in the corporate literature.'

'Ataman tends to be secretive. Russian capitalism is still in its Wild West phase. We don't have all the disclosure laws your country does. I doubt if they'd make that much difference, anyway. With the thousands employed by Ataman, it's very difficult to keep a secret. Ataman has built an entire fleet of monstrous ships that will be used in the extraction of fire ice.'

'*Fire ice?*' Gamay said.

'It's a term someone came up with for methane hydrate, a compound of methane gas,' Paul explained. 'Pockets of the stuff are trapped under the sea bottom all over the world. Looks like icy snow, only it's flammable.'

Orlov chimed in. 'Everyone knows that Soviet scientists claim to have invented everything, from the electric lightbulb to the computer, but in this case I must give them credit. The first natural deposits were found in Siberia, where it was known as marsh gas.

Some American scientists picked up on the work of our glorious scientists and discovered hydrates under the ocean.'

'Off the South Carolina coast, as I recall,' Trout said. 'Woods Hole did some dives with the deep-water submersible *Alvin* and found the plumes escaping from the sediment along faults in the ocean floor.'

'What are the commercial applications?' Gamay said.

Orlov started to pour himself more vodka, thought better of it and pushed the bottle aside. 'The potential is enormous. The deposits around the world possibly hold more energy than all the other fossilized fuels combined.'

'You see it as a *replacement* for oil and gas, then?'

'No less than *Scientific American* called it the "fuel of the future." It could be worth trillions, which is why so many people are interested in its extraction. The technical problems are formidable, though. The substance is unstable and quickly decomposes once it is removed from conditions of extreme depth and pressure. But whoever controls the process may control the future energy supply of the world. Ataman is in the forefront of the exploration and research,' Orlov said. His wide brow wrinkled in a worried furrow. 'Which is not good.'

'Why not?' Paul asked.

'Ataman is owned in its entirety by an ambitious businessman named Mikhail Razov.'

'He must be fabulously wealthy,' Gamay said.

'It goes *beyond* riches. Razov is a complex man. While he keeps his business dealings shrouded in secret, his public persona looms quite large in Russia. He has been outspoken in his criticism of the way things are being run in Moscow, and has gained a substantial cult following.'

'A tycoon with political ambitions is not unusual, even in the United States,' Gamay said. 'We've often elected rich men as governors, senators, presidents.'

'Well, God help us if we put someone like Razov in power. He's a nationalist zealot who talks only of restoring the good old days.'

'I thought communism was dead.'

'Oh, it *is*, only to be replaced by another form of oligarchy. Razov believes Russia achieved its greatest glories under the rule of the tsars: Peter the Great, Ivan the Terrible. He's not clear on the specifics, which is what frightens many people. He says only that he wants to see the spirit of the old empire embodied in the New Russia.'

'Guys like him come and go,' Paul said.

'I hope so, but this time I'm not so sure. He has a magnetic quality, and his simplistic message has struck a chord in my poor country.'

'Is Ataman a city or region?' Gamay asked.

Orlov smiled. 'It's a Russian term for a Cossack chieftain. Razov is a Cossack by birth, so I suppose he fancies himself as the company's chief. He spends most of his time on a magnificent yacht. It's called the *Kazachestvo*. Loosely translated, it stands for

Cossackism, the whole bloody chest-thumping exercise. You should see it! A floating palace a few miles from here.' Orlov displayed his gold teeth. 'But *enough* of politics. We have more pleasant things to talk about. First, I must excuse myself. I have some unavoidable work I must attend to. It will take only an hour or two, then I will be completely free. In the meantime, you might like to sun yourself on the beach.'

'I'm sure we can find something to do.'

'*Splendid.*' He got up, shook hands with Trout and embraced Gamay. 'I will see you back here later this afternoon and we will talk all night.' The middle-aged couple also took their leave and the Trouts were left alone. Paul suggested that they inspect the beach.

The deep blue sea was a short walk from the camp. A lone swimmer was paddling around about a hundred feet out. The beach was stony and not conducive to sun bathing, and the metal beach chairs were as hot as grills to the touch. While Gamay looked for a place to stretch out, Paul walked down the beach. He came back a few minutes later.

'I found something interesting,' he said, and led the way around a bend, where a powerboat was drawn up on shore. The white paint was peeling on the wooden hull, but the boat looked sound enough. The outboard motor was a Yamaha in good condition and there was gas in the tank.

Gamay read her husband's mind. 'Are you thinking of taking a spin?'

Trout shrugged and glanced off at a young man of college age who was coming out of the water. 'Let's ask this guy if it's okay.'

They went over to the swimmer, who had come to shore and was toweling himself dry. When they said hello, the young man smiled. 'You're the Americans?'

Paul nodded and introduced himself and Gamay.

'My name is Yuri Orlov,' the Russian said. 'You know my father. I'm a student at the university.' He spoke English with an American accent.

They shook hands all around. Yuri was tall and gangling, about twenty years old, with a shock of straw-colored hair over his forehead and big blue eyes magnified by horn-rimmed glasses.

'We were wondering if it would be possible to take a spin in the boat,' Paul said.

'No problem,' Yuri said, beaming. 'Anything for friends of my father.'

He pushed the boat out to where the water was deeper and gave the cord a pull. The motor coughed, but didn't start. 'This motor has an attitude,' he said in apology. He rubbed his hands together, then adjusted the fuel mixture and tried again. This time, the motor sputtered and snarled before smoothing out. The Trouts got in the boat and Yuri gave it a push, jumped aboard and pointed the boat out to sea.

15

Austin's eyes took a few seconds to adjust to the dimness. The pungent fragrance of incense evoked the image of an ancient Byzantine chapel in a monastery he had visited high on a hill at Mystra, overlooking the Greek city of Sparti. Gaslight flickered in brass lanterns of ornate gold and stained glass that were set into sconces in rough plaster walls covered with brilliantly painted icons. The vaulted ceiling was reinforced with thick wooden ribs. A high-backed chair faced an altar at the far end of the room.

They moved in for a closer look. The altar was draped with a dark purple cloth stitched in gold with the letter *R*. On top of the altar was a smoking incense burner. Set in the wall above the altar was a lamp whose yellow light illuminated a large black-and-white photograph in an ornate gold frame.

Seven people were pictured in the photograph. From the facial resemblance they shared, the two adults and five young people appeared to be posing for a family portrait. Standing on the left side was a bearded man wearing a military-style visored cap and a ceremonial military uniform trimmed with fancy piping. Medals adorned his chest.

A thin, pale-faced young boy in a sailor suit stood

in front of the man. Next to the boy were three girls in their teens and another girl slightly younger, all gathered around a seated middle-aged woman. The children's features combined their father's wide forehead and the broad face of their mother. In the foreground was a low column like those used for museum display. Resting on top of it was a magnificent crown.

The crown was massive and obviously not designed to be worn for very long. It was heavily encrusted with rubies, diamonds and emeralds. Even in the black-and-white photograph, the gemstones crowding the surface glittered as if they were on fire. A two-headed gold eagle surmounted the globe.

'That little bauble must be worth something,' Zavala said. He leaned closer and studied the somber faces. 'They look so unhappy.'

'They could have had a premonition of what awaited them,' Austin said. He ran his hand over the embroidered altar cover. '*R* as in Romanov.' He glanced around the funereal chamber. 'This is a shrine to the memory of Tsar Nicholas II and his family. The boy in the picture would have been in line to wear that crown if he and his family hadn't been murdered.'

Austin plunked into the chair facing the altar, and, as he leaned back, a deep chorus of male voices poured from hidden speakers. The religious chanting welled throughout the chamber and echoed off the walls. Austin shot out of the chair like a jack-in-the-box, his revolver at the ready. The haunting music stopped.

Zavala saw the look of alarm on his partner's face and stifled a laugh. 'A bit jumpy, my friend?'

'Cute,' Austin said. He pressed his hand against the back of the chair and the chanting resumed. It stopped when he removed his hand. 'A pressure-activated switch turns on the tunes. It gives a whole new meaning to the term "musical chair." Care to try it?'

'No, thanks. My musical taste runs more to salsa.'

'Remind me to rig a Barcalounger up to my collection of progressive jazz.' Austin glanced at the door. 'We're done here. Even a rat wouldn't be dumb enough to be caught in a trap like this.'

They left the somber confines of the Romanov shrine and returned to the staircase they had climbed from the submarine pen. They went up another level and found themselves in a barracks similar to the one below. Whereas the lower dormitory was neat, here blankets were bunched on the dirty mattresses as if thrown there in a hurry. Cigarette butts and plastic cups littered the floor. There was the stale smell of sweat and rotting food.

'*Phew!*' Zavala said.

Austin wrinkled his nose. 'Look on the bright side; we won't need bloodhounds to pick up the trail.'

They followed a wide corridor that slanted upward like the ramp in an underground parking garage. After a few minutes, fresh air blew against their faces, replacing the foul odor emanating from the barracks. Natural light coming from a bend in the passageway began to fill in the spaces between the puddles of illumination from overhead bulbs spaced in the ceiling.

The passageway ended in a steel door that had been left ajar. A short ramp led to the interior of what appeared to be a warehouse or garage. The concrete floor was stained with oil and spotted with the droppings of small animals. Austin picked an old, yellowed copy of *Pravda* out of a pile of rubbish. The beetle-browed face of Leonid Brezhnev glowered from the front page.

Austin tossed the newspaper aside and went over to a window. Not a shard of glass remained in the metal frame, giving him an unimpeded view of several nearby steel structures. The warehouse was part of the complex of abandoned buildings Austin had first seen from the air. The corrugated exteriors were streaked with rust, and the seams on the walls and roofs had buckled with age. Concrete walks linking the complex were overgrown with tall grass.

Zavala caught Austin's attention with a sharp whistle. He was looking out from the opposite side of the warehouse. Working his way around the rubbish, Austin crossed over and peered through the window. The warehouse sat on a rise overlooking a large weed-grown field that was roughly rectangular in shape and depressed a few feet, like a giant soap dish. The rusty framework of a soccer goal jutted from the grass at one end. Austin guessed that the area had once been an athletic field used for R&R by visiting submarine crews.

Now, horsemen were strung out along the perimeter of the field on three sides. Only the side nearest the warehouse and the other buildings was open. Austin recognized the gray tunics and black pants worn by the gang of Cossacks that had shot him out of the sky. There were at least three times as many riders, now all facing into the field.

'You never told me this was a polo club,' Zavala said, in a bad imitation of a British accent.

'I wanted to surprise you,' Austin said, focusing on a frightened-looking group of people huddled in the center of the field. 'We're in time for the last chukker. Follow me and I'll introduce you to the chaps I met the last time I was here.'

Austin and Zavala slipped out of the warehouse, dropped to their hands and knees and wriggled snake-style until they came to the edge of the field where the grass thinned out. Austin pushed aside the grass for a better look as three horsemen broke away from the others, one from each side. With a series of bloodcurdling yells, the Cossacks galloped toward the huddled people, then broke off their charge at the last second and circled like Apaches attacking a wagon train. With each pass, they came closer. The horses kicked up fountains of dirt and the riders leaned out of their saddles and brought their whips down in slashing blows.

Austin quickly figured out the one-sided rules of the game. The Cossacks were trying to break the group apart so they could run them to ground individually. The field had been left unguarded on one side to tempt someone to make a break for freedom. But the strategy wasn't working. With each charge, their prey bunched closer together, like zebras being stalked by hungry lions.

Yelping loudly, the riders galloped back to the edge of the field and took their place in line again. Austin expected another attack, maybe with more riders. Instead, a lone horseman broke from the ranks and put his mount into a trot as if he were out for a Sunday ride.

Austin shielded the binocular lenses with his hands to prevent the sun from reflecting. The rider was dressed in the familiar mud-colored belted tunic, baggy black pants and boots and fur hat, although the day was warm. Cartridge belts crossed his chest. He rode a big dark gray horse with wide flanks and shoulders like a draft animal.

Austin studied the man's long, unkempt red beard and let out an evil chuckle. The last time he'd seen the giant Cossack was over the barrel of a flare gun. 'Well, well, we meet again.'

'Is that clean-cut chap a friend of yours?' Zavala said.

'More a passing acquaintance. We had a glancing encounter not too long ago.'

Taking his time, the Cossack put his mount into a

parade strut and circled the field, showing off for the other horsemen, who cheered him on. Then he drew his saber, raised it high and let out a hoarse yell. Digging his spurs into his mount, he charged toward the center of the field like a bowling ball rolling down on tenpins. At the last second, he brought the horse to a skidding stop and pulled back on the reins. The big horse reared up on its hind legs and pawed the air.

The people huddled in the field scrambled to avoid the flailing hooves and to escape the crushing weight of the giant animal. In the confusion, one man tripped and fell, and became separated from the others. He got up and tried to regain the relative safety of the pack, but the Cossack saw the opening and wedged his horse between. The man feinted to the right and made a dash to the left. The Cossack anticipated the move and herded the man like a cowpoke culling out a steer for branding. Seeing no alternative, the man sprinted for the unguarded side of the field.

The runner's face was set in a determined expression, even though he must have known his two legs were no match for the horse's four. The Cossack made no move to give chase and continued to put his strutting mount through its paces for the benefit of his comrades. Not until the runner was halfway to the edge of the field did the rider wheel his horse around. He spurred his horse into a trot, then into a ground-eating canter. Raising his sword again, he urged his mount into a full gallop.

Alerted by the pounding hoofbeats, the runner thrust his chest out like a sprinter at the finish line and pumped his arms to wring out the last ounce of speed. No use. As the horse thundered by him, the Cossack leaned over to one side and the sword swept down in a killing blow to the neck. The runner's legs crumbled and he slammed face-first into the ground. Austin swore with helpless anger. The cowardly attack had come too fast for him to react. The Cossack laughed at his own cleverness and wheeled his mount around, then rode leisurely back to the center of the field, daring someone else to make a run for it.

Austin brought the Bowen up and sighted on the Cossack's broad back. He was squeezing the trigger when he caught movement out of the corner of his eye. To Austin's amazement, the figure slumped on the ground began to stir. The runner got onto his hands and knees and staggered to his feet. The Cossack had only toyed with his prey, using the flat of his sword so as to extend the game.

The Cossacks began shouting. Redbeard pretended that he didn't understand, then turned and went through a great show of being surprised. He waved his arms as if he were nonplussed at his victim rising from the dead – then once more he gave chase. The runner was almost to the edge of the field. Austin knew that the Cossack would never let his prey reach the buildings, where it would be difficult to get at him. The next sword blow would be lethal.

Zavala had lost his patience. 'Game's over,' he snarled. Bringing his Heckler and Koch up in the classic prone shooting position, he sighted on the Cossack's chest.

Austin put his hand on the barrel and said, 'No.' Then he stood up.

When the runner saw Austin spring from the earth, his sweat-streaked face fell in dismay. Seeing his escape route cut off, he jammed his heels in and came to a skidding stop. Redbeard saw Austin at the same time. He reined in his horse, leaned forward on the pommel and stared at the broad-shouldered man with the strange pale hair. Austin could see the hate burning in the red-rimmed eyes. The horse snorted and nervously pawed the ground. Losing interest in the runner, the Cossack sat up in his saddle and put his horse into a pirouette. Then he made a false charge, only to retreat when Austin showed no sign of yielding ground.

Austin had been standing with his hands behind his back like a child hiding cookies. He brought his left hand out and beckoned. The horseman's puzzled frown turned into a gap-toothed grin. He *liked* this new game. He edged his mount closer, still wary.

Austin beckoned again with more animation. Emboldened, the horseman came nearer. Austin smiled like Davy Crockett grinning down a grizzly. The horseman let out a roar and goaded his mount forward.

Still smiling, Austin waited until he couldn't miss,

then in a smooth fluid motion he brought the Bowen from behind his back. Holding the heavy revolver in both hands, he sighted on the X made by the Cossack's crossed cartridge belts.

'Here's one for Mehmet,' he said, squeezing the trigger.

The revolver barked once. The heavy bullet smashed into the rider's sternum and splintered his rib cage, sending fragments of bone into his heart. The Cossack was dead even before his hands lost their grip on the reins. The horse continued toward Austin like a runaway cement mixer, its eyes rolling in panic. Austin cursed himself for not getting down to business and firing sooner.

Spooked by the human standing in its way, and with no signal coming from the slack reins, the animal veered off. Its rock-hard haunch swung around, slammed into Austin with the force of a battering ram and knocked him off his feet. He flew through the air, and crashed to the turf with a teeth-rattling shock, landing on his left side. When he stopped rolling, he tried to stand but only made it up onto one knee. He was covered with dust and wet on one side from horse sweat. Zavala was by Austin's side, helping him to his feet. As Austin's blurred vision cleared, he expected to see the Cossacks bearing down on them.

Instead, the world seemed frozen in time and place.

Stunned by their leader's fall, the horsemen sat in their saddles like statues in a park. The people on the field were equally immobilized. Austin spat out a mouthful of dirt. Slowly and deliberately, he walked over to where his gun had landed and picked it up. He yelled at the runner and told him to go for the warehouse. The order shocked the man into action. He started to run.

It was if a power switch had been thrown.

Seeing their friend break for safety, the men in the field bolted after him in a disorganized mob. Austin and Zavala yelled encouragement and pointed to the warehouse. With their leader dead and their prey escaping, the Cossacks yelled as one, poured into the soccer field and advanced at a gallop, sabers held high, toward Austin and Zavala. The two men stood there in awe at the fearful beauty of a Cossack charge.

'Wow!' Zavala shouted over the thunder of hooves. 'It's like being in an old Western.'

'Let's hope it isn't a remake of Custer's Last Stand,' Austin said, with a thin smile.

Austin brought his Bowen up and fired. The lead rider pitched from his saddle. Zavala's H and K stuttered, and another horseman crashed to the ground. The riders advanced without slackening their pace, well aware they held the advantage in numbers and momentum. The guns fired simultaneously and two more men flew from their saddles.

The Cossacks were bold but not suicidal. First one, then another, leaned out of his saddle and hung from his horse's neck so he no longer offered an easy target. As Austin and Zavala adjusted to the new strategy, one horse came to a sudden stop, dropped to the ground and rolled onto its side.

Austin thought the animal had stumbled. Then he saw that the rider was firing at them, using his mount as a protective barricade. Other riders followed suit. Those Cossacks still in their saddles split up, coming in from both sides in a pincer movement. Austin and Zavala hit the ground and dug in. Bullets flew over their heads like angry bees.

'Automatic weapons!' Zavala yelped. 'You said these guys carried blunderbusses and pigstickers.'

'How would I know they'd stop off at a gun show?'

'What ever happened to background checks?'

Austin's reply was drowned out by the stutter of automatic-arms fire. He and Zavala let off a couple of rounds more for show than effect, then pulled back from the rise and crawled toward the warehouse. The Cossacks peppered the ridge with gunfire. Thinking their prey was dead, they climbed onto their horses and took up the charge where they had left off.

From the shelter of the warehouse, Austin and Zavala aimed through the windows and two more riders toppled from their mounts. Seeing that their foe was still alive, the Cossacks called off the attack and galloped to the center of the field to regroup.

Taking advantage of the momentary battle lull, Austin turned from the window and surveyed the men who had taken refuge. Austin couldn't remember when he'd seen a more bedraggled-looking bunch. Their tan jumpsuits were wrinkled and begrimed, and their hollow-eyed faces bristled with whiskers. The first runner, who had felt the direct wrath of the Cossack leader, came over to speak with Austin. His uniform was torn at the knees and elbows and covered with dust. Yet he kept his chin as high as if he were wearing newly pressed dress whites on parade.

The young man gave Austin a crisp salute. 'Ensign Steven Kreisman of the US Navy submarine *NR-1.*'

Austin reached under his belt, where he had tucked the cap Zavala found on the Russian submarine. 'Maybe you can get this back to its owner,' he said, handing the cap over.

'It's the captain's. Where did you get this?' Kreisman said, looking at the cap as if he were seeing it for the first time.

'My partner found it in a Russian sub.'

'Who *are* you guys?' Kreisman said, losing his aplomb.

'I'm Kurt Austin and that's my partner Joe Zavala at the window. We're with the National Underwater and Marine Agency.'

The ensign's jaw dropped down to his Adam's apple. With their battle-hardened eyes and smoking guns, the two who had rescued him and his crew looked more like commandos than ocean scientists.

'I didn't know NUMA had its own SWAT team,' he said with wonder.

'We don't. Are you okay?'

'I feel as if I've been run over by a bulldozer, but other than that I'm fine,' he said, rubbing his neck where the saber had whacked him. 'I won't be wearing a tie for a while. This may sound like a dumb question, Mr Austin, but what are you and your friend doing here?'

'Your turn first. Last I heard, your sub was diving for relics on the bottom of the Aegean.'

The young man's shoulders sagged slightly. 'It's a long story,' he said, with weariness.

'We don't have much time. See if you can tell me what happened in thirty seconds.'

Kreisman chuckled at Austin's audacity. 'I'll do my best.'

He took a deep breath and delivered a condensed version of events.

'A guest scientist we had on board, a guy named Pulaski, pulled a gun on us and hijacked the *NR-1*. We were transported on the back of a giant submarine. This whole thing is so *unbelievable*.' He paused, expecting a skeptical reaction. Seeing none in Austin's attentive eyes, he continued. 'They transferred the crew to a salvage ship. They made us work on an old sunken freighter. Tricky retrieval stuff using the manipulators. Then the big sub brought us here. They kept the captain and pilot with the *NR-1*. We were held prisoner underground. When they brought us up today, we thought we were going back to the *NR-1*. Instead they herded us onto that field. The guards who'd been watching us disappeared, and

227

those cowboys with the fur hats started trying to break us up.' He rubbed his neck again. 'Who *are* those SOBs?'

Zavala was signaling to Austin. 'Sorry,' he said. 'Our thirty seconds appears to be up.'

He went to the window, and Zavala handed him the binoculars. 'The members of the polo club are having an argument,' he said lazily.

Austin peered through the binoculars at the Cossacks, who were still gathered in the field. Some riders had dismounted and were waving their arms in the air.

Lowering the glasses, Austin said, 'They could be exchanging borscht recipes, but my guess is that they're adding our names to the guest list for a slice-and-dice party.'

Zavala looked as if he had a stomachache. 'You have a way with words. How can we decline the invitation without hurting their feelings?'

Scratching his chin in thought, Austin said, 'We've got a couple of options. We can run for the beach and swim out to sea, hoping our fur-hatted friends won't have settled their differences. Or we can hole up below.'

'I'm sure you see the same problems I do,' Zavala said. 'If they catch us in the open, we're sitting ducks. If we go back down to the sub pen, we've only got dive gear for two people.'

Austin nodded. 'I suggest that we go with a double. You and the crew run for the beach. I'll stay here, and if the riders move in I'll draw them into the sub base, where they'll be at a disadvantage on foot. I'll escape the way we came. Like a fish slipping through a hole in a net.'

'Your chances would be better if we were watching each other's back.'

'Someone has to cover for the sub crew. They look pretty beat-up.'

Ensign Kreisman had edged closer. 'Excuse me for eavesdropping. I went through SEAL training when I joined the navy. I washed out, but I still know the drill. I can take the men out of here.'

Austin sized up the determined set of Kreisman's jaw and decided he would be wasting time arguing with the young navy man. 'Okay, it's your show. Run for the beach and start swimming. A fishing boat will pick you up. We'll stay here and cover you as long as we can. I'd urge you to get going. Joe will ride shotgun part of the way.'

If the ensign wondered how Austin had arranged for an at-sea pickup, he didn't show it. He snapped his arm in a crisp salute and rounded up his comrades. Then they climbed out of the back of the warehouse through a window. While Zavala escorted the crew to the beach, Austin kept watch. The Cossacks still seemed disorganized. He got on his hand radio and called Captain Kemal.

'You are all right?' the captain said. 'We heard guns shooting.'

'We're okay. Please listen carefully, Captain. In a

few minutes, you will see men swimming out to sea. Go in as close to the beach as you safely can and pick them up.'

'What about you and Joe?'

'We'll come out the way we went in. Anchor offshore and watch for us.' He clicked off. Something had caught his eye.

Austin was outside the warehouse when Zavala returned a few minutes later. 'I went as far as the dune. They should be in the water by now.'

'Kemal's been alerted for a pickup.' He pointed to the sky, where the sun glinted off metal. 'What do you make of that?' The object grew from a pinpoint to the size of a flying insect, and they could hear the beat of rotors.

'You didn't tell me the Cossacks had an air force.'

Austin peered through his binoculars at the helicopter speeding their way. 'Oh hell –' Lombardo hung out of the open door holding a video camera. 'That sawed-off little idiot.'

As Zavala took the glasses for his own look, the helicopter spun around so that the other side came into view. He studied the figure in the doorway, then lowered the glasses and gave Austin a strange look.

'You need your eyes examined, my friend.' He handed the binoculars back.

This time when Austin looked, he swore even more loudly. Kaela's dusky face, framed by windblown dark hair, was clearly visible. The helicopter was practically over the field. Chastened by their earlier encounter, the TV crew must have instructed the pilot to stay a prudent distance from the ground. They couldn't have known that the horsemen had substituted modern automatic weapons for their antique rifles. The Cossacks saw the helicopter and lost no time targeting the aircraft in a withering fire. Within seconds, the engine began to throw off oily dark smoke. The helicopter shuddered like a bird buffeted in a strong wind, then it dropped from the sky.

The rotors had slowed to a point where individual blades were visible, but the spin was enough to create a parachute effect. The chopper came down like a falling leaf. The impact with the ground was hard enough to crumple the landing gear, but the fuselage remained intact. Seconds after the helicopter hit, Kaela, Lombardo, Dundee and another man spilled out like dice from a shaker.

The Cossacks saw the stunned crew and pilot, and their frustration and anger erupted like a long-dormant volcano. They swung into their saddles and charged down on the hapless foursome at a mad gallop. Austin's blood went cold. The Cossacks were seconds away from their targets. There was no time to save the crew. He sprinted toward them anyhow, pistol in hand. He was still a hundred yards away when the Cossacks started to pop out of their saddles like grain being harvested by a giant, invisible scythe.

The charge that seemed so inevitable faltered, fell apart, then stopped completely. The horsemen milled around in confusion. More Cossacks dropped from their saddles.

Austin saw movement at the edge of the woods bordering the field. Men clad in black uniforms were emerging from the trees. They advanced slowly and deliberately toward the horsemen, weapons at their shoulders, firing as they walked. Seeing themselves overmatched, the Cossacks rode off in panic toward the distant woods.

The men in black moved relentlessly after the retreating horsemen. Except for one. He broke off from the others and came toward where Austin and Zavala stood. He was limping, Austin noticed. As the man drew closer, Zavala automatically raised his gun. Austin put his hand on the barrel and gently pushed the weapon down.

Petrov stopped a few yards away. The pale scar on his face stood out in vivid relief against his sunburned skin.

'Hello, Mr Austin. A pleasure to see you again.'

'Hello, Ivan. You have no idea *how* nice it is to see you.'

'I think I do,' Petrov said, with a careless laugh. 'You and your friend must join me for a shot of vodka. We can talk about old times and new beginnings.'

Austin turned to Zavala and nodded. With Petrov leading the way, the three men made their way to the soccer field.

16

With his tall gangling physique and questing intelligence, Yuri Orlov reminded Paul Trout of himself as a kid hanging around the ocean scientists at the Woods Hole Oceanographic Institution. The way Yuri stood in the stern with one hand on the tiller, the Russian student could have been any of the skiff fishermen Trout knew on Cape Cod. All the youth needed to complete the picture was a Red Sox baseball cap and a big black Labrador retriever.

Yuri had taken immediate control of the boat, steering it a few hundred feet offshore, then stopping and letting the motor idle.

'Thank you so much for allowing me to go with you, Dr Paul and Dr Gamay. It's really an honor to be in the company of two such famous scientists. I envy you working for NUMA. My father told me all about his experiences in the States.'

The Trouts smiled, even though the young man had upset their plan to sneak off on a scouting expedition. He brimmed with youthful enthusiasm, and the big blue eyes danced with excitement behind the thick glasses.

'Your father often talked about his family back in Russia,' Paul said. 'I remember him showing me pictures of you and your mother. You were younger then, so I didn't recognize you today.'

'Some people say I look more like my mother.'

Trout nodded in agreement. During Professor Orlov's stay in Woods Hole, the Russian had countered bouts of homesickness by whipping family snapshots from his billfold and proudly passing them around. Trout remembered being struck by the contrast between the bearlike professor and Svetlana, his tall, willowy wife.

'I enjoyed working with your father. He's a brilliant man, as well as personable. I hope we can work together again someday.'

Yuri lit up like a bulb. 'Next time the professor goes to the States, he has promised to take me with him.'

Trout smiled at Yuri's use of the proper title before his father's name. 'You should have no problem. Your English is excellent.'

'Thank you. My parents used to have American exchange students stay with us.' He pointed in the opposite direction from the one the Trouts wanted to take. 'It's pretty nice along the coast here. Are you bird-watchers?'

Gamay saw their mission going astray. 'Actually, Yuri,' she said sweetly, 'we were hoping to go to Novorossiysk.'

A look of amused amazement crossed Yuri's young face. '*Novorossiysk?* Are you sure? The coast the other way is much prettier.'

Paul picked up on Gamay's cue. 'We do a lot of bird-watching in the Virginia countryside, but as an ocean geologist I'm more interested in deep-sea mining. I understand one of the largest ocean mining companies in the world has its headquarters in Novorossiysk.'

'Sure. You're talking about Ataman Industries. They're *huge*. I'm doing my grad work in ecological mining, and I may apply for a job there myself when I get out of school.'

'Then you'll understand why I'd be interested in taking a look at their facilities.'

'Absolutely. Too bad I didn't know earlier. Maybe we could have set up a tour with them. You can't get a good idea of the scale of their operation from the water.' Yuri grinned with relief. 'I like birds, too, but not that much.'

Gamay said, 'I'm a marine biologist. Fish and plants are my game, but I think it would be interesting to go to Novorossiysk.'

'That settles it, then,' Paul said.

Yuri goosed the throttle and brought the boat around in a big, lazy turn. He stayed about a quarter of a mile offshore on a course roughly parallel to the coast. After a while, the woods began to thin out, giving way to coastal plain and high, rolling hills. The beach was replaced by extensive reed-grown marshes and meandering creeks.

Paul and Gamay sat side by side on the center seat as the powerboat plowed through the sun-sparkled sea. The boat was around eighteen feet long and built like a tank, with overlapping planks and a thick prow. Yuri kept up a running narrative as he pointed out landmarks. The Trouts nodded with appreciation, although the snarl of the motor and the *shush-shush* of the hull drowned out most of Yuri's words.

Any misgivings the Trouts had about Yuri were quickly dispelled. He turned out to be a godsend. He knew how to keep the touchy motor supplied with the proper mixture of air and fuel, and was intimately acquainted with the countryside. They would have had trouble navigating the busy port on their own. Finding Ataman would have been almost impossible without a guide. As they got farther into Zemes Bay, the city's importance as a major Russian seaport became apparent. Ship traffic in both directions was nonstop. The parade included every type of commercial vessel imaginable: cargo ships, tankers, ocean-going tugs, passenger ships and ferries.

Yuri kept a respectful distance from the big ships and their boat-swamping wakes. The shoreline became more built-up. High-rise buildings, smoking chimneys and grain elevators could be seen through the industrial haze that hung over the port. Yuri slowed the boat down to a fast walk.

'The city is very historic,' Yuri said. 'You can't go ten feet without tripping over a monument. The Russian Revolution ended here, when Allied ships evacuated the White Army in 1920. It's also one of the biggest ports in Russia. Oil is piped here from the wells in the northern Caucasus. That's the Shesharis Oil Harbor over there.'

Paul had been studying the dark hue of the water. 'It's a deepwater port, judging from the size of those ships.'

'Novorossiysk doesn't freeze up in the winter. This is the major port for cargo moving between Russia and the Mediterranean and the rest of Europe, and it's also more or less convenient to Asia, the Persian Gulf and Africa. The port facilities are state-of-the-art. There are actually five parts to the harbor: three dry cargo handling areas, the oil harbor and the passenger terminal. You came in through the airport, so you know it's got connections all over the world.'

'I can see why Ataman would have its headquarters here,' Gamay noted, as she scanned the bustling bay.

'I'll show you.'

Yuri kicked the boat's speed up and angled the bow in toward a wide indentation on the shore. Six long concrete piers extended from land. Several ships were tied up at the wharves. Rising behind the piers was a sprawling complex of industrial buildings, gantry cranes, big straddle carriers and cargo derricks. Forklift trucks and tractors moved along the piers like oversized insects.

'Which part is Ataman's?' Gamay asked.

Yuri grinned and swept his hand in a wide arc. '*All* of it.'

Gamay whistled in astonishment. 'I can't believe the

size of this place. It's bigger than some major ports.'

'Ataman has its own fleet of tugboats, fuel and water supplies and tanks for bilge and waste removal,' Yuri said. 'See those giant cranes over there? That's Ataman's shipyard. They build all their own vessels. That way they can control design and cost.' He furrowed his brow and looked around as if he had lost something. 'That's funny, Ataman's port is practically empty.'

Paul exchanged a puzzled glance with his wife. 'It doesn't look empty to *me*. Look at all that activity. I can see five ships of considerable size pulled up to the dock.'

'Those are Ataman's *small* ships. I wanted to show you their ocean drilling rigs. They look like they could drill through to the other side of the world. Each one is like a city in itself.'

'Maybe they're all at sea working.'

'Maybe,' he said, with skepticism in his voice. 'But I don't think so. Ataman has so many ships, a few are always being outfitted. Even with all those wharves, they don't have space to take care of their whole fleet at the same time.' He scanned the shoreline until he saw what he was looking for. 'I can show you something almost as interesting.'

Yuri kept the boat on the same heading until they were past the main wharves, then he steered in toward a smaller pier. A luxurious yacht four hundred feet long was tied up at the dock. The gleaming white hull was set off by black trim. The superstructure was unusually sleek and streamlined. The hull was shaped in a deep V to cut through the waves. The wide rear of the boat was concave.

'Wow!' Yuri said. 'I've heard of this baby, but it's the first time I've seen it.'

'Quite a luxury yacht,' Paul said with appreciation.

'It belongs to Razov, the head guy at Ataman. They say he lives on the boat and runs his business from it.' Yuri gave the tiller a wiggle. Gamay pressed the shutter release and banged off several shots. 'Can we go around to the other side?' Gamay said.

Yuri replied with a pull on the tiller that brought them around behind the boat. Gamay lifted the camera up to her eye again and started to press the control button that would give her a wide-angle shot, when she detected movement on the deck. A figure had come into view. She extended the zoom to its full 200 mm range. 'Dear God!' she said with a gasp.

'What is it?' Paul said.

She handed the camera over. 'Take a look.'

Paul peered through the viewfinder and scanned the deck, but saw no one.

'Deck's deserted now. What did you see?'

Gamay didn't spook easily, but she couldn't suppress a shudder. 'A tall man with long black hair and a beard. He was staring straight at me. It was one of the most frightening faces I've ever seen.'

A Jeeplike vehicle was racing toward the wharf along an access road, and Trout's instincts were aroused. He looked through the camera lens as the vehicle drove onto the boat dock. Speaking calmly, he said, 'We've got company. Time to go.'

The vehicle screeched to a stop. Six uniformed men carrying weapons jumped out, dashed along the wharf, raced toward the gangplank and climbed onto the ship. Yuri had hesitated, but when he saw the armed men, he twisted the throttle as far as it would go, and headed out to the bay.

The bow lifted and the boat got on plane, making a respectable speed despite its heavy construction. Flashes of small-arms fire could be seen on the yacht's fantail. The bullets stitched a line of small fountains in the water. Paul yelled at the others to get down. A round hit the boat and took a chip out of the transom, but seconds later they were out of range. The danger wasn't over, though. Another vehicle had followed the first, and the men who piled out headed for the dock, where some powerboats were tied up.

Yuri pointed the boat out into the busy channel, crossing behind a cargo ship that was making its way out of the bay. The small boat leaped like a dolphin as it crossed the wake, but it rode the waves out comfortably. Yuri brought the boat around to the other side of the ship, using the cargo vessel as a screen. When they were safely beyond the Ataman complex, he peeled the boat away and they followed the coast back toward the camp. At one point, Paul suggested that they pull into a creek. They waited ten minutes, but no one followed.

Yuri's face was flushed with excitement. 'Man, that

was fun. I've heard a lot of businesses have their own armies to protect them from the Russian Mafia, but this is the first time I've ever seen them.'

Paul felt guilty about putting the son of his old colleague in harm's way. He and Gamay owed Yuri an explanation, but too much knowledge could be just as dangerous. Communicating with her eyes, Gamay silently sent a message saying that she knew what to do.

'Yuri, we've got a favor to ask,' she said. 'We'd like you to say nothing about what happened back there to anyone.'

'I guess your visit to my father wasn't entirely social,' Yuri said.

Gamay nodded. 'We've been asked by NUMA to check out Ataman Industries. They're suspected of being involved in some shady business. We had planned to do so from a safe distance. We never dreamed that they would be, well, so *touchy.*'

'It was like something out of James Bond!' Yuri had a broad smile on his face.

'Except that this isn't fiction. It's very real.'

Gamay's calming tone got through to Yuri far more effectively than any bombast Paul might have been able to summon up.

Yuri tried to look serious. 'I'll be quiet, but it's going to be hard not to tell my friends.' He sighed. 'They wouldn't believe me anyhow.'

Paul said, 'We'll fill you in as soon as we know what this is all about. We can assure you that you'll be one of the first to know. Deal?' He stretched his hand forward.

'It's a deal,' Yuri said, pleased to be in on the conspiracy. They shook hands all around.

The sun had dropped toward the horizon, and shadows were gathering as they saw the lights of the camp glimmering on shore. They all breathed a sigh of relief as the boat drew nearer the beach. They would have been less assured if they knew that a birdlike speck in the sky high above them was a helicopter equipped with high-powered optics.

Professor Orlov was waiting on the beach. He waded into the water and pulled the boat into shore. 'Hello, my friends. I see that you've met my son, Yuri.'

'He was kind enough to take us on a sightseeing tour,' Gamay said. She slipped over the side and used her body to hide the hole gouged out by the bullet. 'We had a nice talk about now and the future.'

'The *now* is that you go back to your cottage and get ready for dinner. The future is a wonderful meal and talking about old times. Our accommodations are primitive, but we feed ourselves well.' He patted his expansive stomach.

The professor ushered the Trouts back to the main clearing and instructed them to return in a half hour with their appetites. Then he hustled off with his son. As he walked away, Yuri looked back over his shoulder and winked. The silent message was clear. Their secret was safe with him.

Paul and Gamay returned to their cottage and showered away the salt and sweat from their nautical adventure. Gamay changed into designer jeans that emphasized her long legs, a blazer and lilac camisole. Paul had not left his fastidious sartorial habits behind. He wore loose tan slacks with a Gatsby-style pale green shirt and a violet bow tie.

Some of the other inhabitants of the camp were assembled at or around the picnic table. The Trouts were greeted by the middle-aged couple they had met earlier, a tall intense-looking physicist who resembled the writer Alexander Solzhenitsyn and a young married couple, both engineering students at the university in Rostov. The table was set with an embroidered tablecloth and colorful china. Japanese lanterns lent a festive air to the gathering.

Orlov broke into a beaming smile when he saw the Trouts approach. 'Ah, my American guests. You look lovely, Gamay, and you are handsome as usual, Paul. A new bow tie? You must have an endless supply of cravats.'

'I'm afraid my addiction is starting to get expensive. You don't know anyone who makes cheap throwaway bow ties, do you?'

The professor roared with laughter and translated for the others. Then he directed the Trouts to the seating that had been saved for them, rubbed his hands in anticipation, and went into his cottage to start the meal moving. Dinner was salmon-filled *pirogi*, basically Russian turnovers, served with rice and a clear borscht. The professor also had a case of the famous Russian champagne that was made in nearby Abrau-Dyurso. Even without vodka and a common language, dinner was loud and friendly and extended late into the evening. It was nearly midnight when the Trouts pushed themselves away from the table and begged to be allowed to go back to their cottage.

'The party is just starting!' Orlov bellowed. His face was red from alcohol and sweaty after serenading the other diners with an energetic rendition of a bawdy Russian folk song.

'Please don't stop on our account,' Paul said. 'We've had a long day, and it's starting to catch up with us.'

'Of course, you must be very tired. I've been a poor host, making you sit here and listen to my attempts to sing.'

Paul patted his stomach. 'You've been a great host. But I'm a little older than I was when we used to drink the night away at the Captain Kidd.'

'You're obviously out of training, my friend. One week here and we would have you back in shape.' He hugged both Trouts. 'But I understand. Would you like Yuri to escort you?'

'Thank you, Professor. We'll find our way,' Gamay said. 'See you in the morning.'

Orlov let them go after another round of hugs and kisses. As they made their way along the path toward the single light glowing on the porch of their cottage, the Trouts could hear Orlov belting out a spirited but hardly recognizable rendition, in Russian, of 'What Should We Do With the Drunken Sailor?'

'I don't envy Vlad for the hangover he's going to have,' Gamay said.

'There's no party animal like a Russian party animal.'

They laughed as they climbed onto the porch. They weren't exaggerating their exhaustion. They brushed their teeth, stripped down to their underwear and slipped beneath the cool sheets. Within minutes, both were asleep. Gamay was the lighter sleeper. Later that night, she sat up in bed and listened. Something had awakened her. The sound of voices. High-pitched and excited. She poked Paul out of his slumber.

'What's going on?' he mumbled, his voice thick with sleep.

'*Listen.* It sounds like . . . children playing.'

But just then a loud shriek of unmistakable terror echoed through the woods outside.

'*That* was no kid,' Paul said, vaulting from the bed. He scooped his slacks off a chair and jumped into them, nearly falling on his face. Gamay was one second behind, pulling her shorts over her slim hips and throwing a T-shirt over her head. They burst out onto the porch, where they could see a reddish glow through the trees. The smell of smoke hung heavily in the air.

'One of the camps is on fire!' Paul said.

They ran along the path in bare feet and almost

mowed down Yuri, who was running in the opposite direction.

'What's going on?' Paul said.

'Don't talk,' Yuri replied breathlessly. 'We must hide. This way.'

The Trouts glanced at the fire, then followed Yuri's lead. He moved fast in a long, loping gait. When they were deep in the pines, he took Gamay by the arm, pulled her onto the soft cover of pine needles and motioned for Paul to duck down. They could hear branches and twigs snapping and rough voices. Paul started to get up to look, but Yuri pulled him back down. After a few minutes, the crashing stopped. Yuri spoke from the darkness.

'I was asleep in my father's camp,' he said, his voice hoarse from tension. 'Men came in the night.'

'Who were they?'

'I don't know. They had their faces covered. They dragged us out of bed. They wanted to know where the redheaded woman and the man were. My father said that you had left to go home. They didn't believe him. They beat him. He yelled in English for me to warn you. While they were busy, I ran to tell you.'

'How many were there?'

'A dozen, maybe. I don't know. It was dark. They must have come by water. Our camp is right by the driveway, and we would have heard someone come in.'

'We've got to get back to your father.'

'I know a way,' Yuri said. 'Come.'

Paul grabbed onto the back of Yuri's shorts and Gamay held on to her husband's other hand as they made their way through the woods, taking a circuitous path. The smoke thickened. Soon they could see the source of the smoke: the professor's cottage. They stepped out of the woods into the clearing, where students were spraying the cottage with hoses apparently powered by a generator. They couldn't save the building, but their efforts kept the fire from spreading to the adjacent woods and cottages. The older people were huddled in a group. Yuri spoke in Russian to the tall physicist, then turned to the Trouts.

'He says the men are gone. He saw them leave in a boat.'

The group parted to reveal Orlov lying on the ground, his face covered with blood. Gamay was on her knees in an instant, put her ear close to the professor's mouth and felt for a pulse in his neck. Then she examined his arms and legs.

'Can we get him somewhere where he'll be more comfortable?' she asked.

The professor was lifted onto the picnic table and covered with the tablecloth. At Gamay's request, a pot of warm water and towels were produced. She gently sponged the blood away from the professor's face and balding scalp.

'The bleeding seems to have stopped,' she said. 'It's coming from the head, so it's worse than it looks.

He's also bleeding from the mouth, but I don't think it's internal.'

Paul's jaw hardened at the plight of his old colleague. 'Someone used him for a punching bag.'

The professor stirred and mumbled some words in Russian. Yuri leaned close for a second, then grinned. 'He says he needs a glass of vodka.'

Glowing embers were coming down on them from the fire and the smoke made it hard to breathe, so Paul suggested that they move the professor to a more sheltered location. Trout and three other men carried him to the cottage farthest from the fire. They laid him out on a bed, covered his body with blankets and brought him a glass of vodka.

'Sorry this isn't champagne,' Gamay said, offering him a sip as she tilted his head up.

The vodka dribbled down his chin, but he swallowed enough of the potent liquor to bring color back to his cheeks. Paul dragged a chair over. 'Do you feel like talking?'

'Keep the vodka coming and I'll talk all night long,' Orlov said. 'How's my cottage?'

'The fire brigade couldn't save it, but they kept the fire from spreading,' Yuri said.

A satisfied smile crossed the professor's swollen lips. 'One of the first things I organized here was a fire company. We draw water directly from the sea.'

'Please tell us what happened,' Gamay said, as she dabbed the professor's forehead with a damp washcloth.

'We were sleeping,' he said, talking slowly. 'Some men came into the cottage. We never lock the doors out here. They wanted to know where the people in the boat were. I didn't know what they were talking about at first, then I realized they wanted you. So naturally I said I didn't know. They beat me until I was unconscious.'

'I ran off to warn the Trouts,' Yuri said. 'I didn't want to leave you. They came looking for us. We hid in the woods until they were gone.'

Orlov reached out and put his hand on Yuri's shoulder. 'You did the right thing.'

He motioned for more vodka. The drink seemed to clear his mind, and the scientific analysis of cause and effect came into play.

Looking Paul directly in the eye, he said, 'Well, my friend, it seems you and Gamay made some interesting friends in the short time you have been here. On your little sightseeing trip, perhaps?'

'I'm truly sorry. I'm afraid we're responsible for this mess,' Paul said. 'It was entirely unanticipated. We made your son a partner in crime, too.'

Paul told Orlov that NUMA was investigating Ataman and related the events surrounding their boat trip.

'*Ataman?*' Orlov said. 'In a way, I can't say I'm surprised at their violent reaction. Huge cartels tend to act as if they are above the law.'

Gamay said, 'There was a strange man on the yacht. He had a thin face, long black hair and a beard. Was that Razov?'

'It doesn't sound like him. Probably his friend, the mad monk.'

'Pardon me?'

'His name is Boris. I don't even know if he has a last name. He is said to be Razov's éminence grise, his mentor. Few people have seen him. You're very lucky.'

'I don't know if I'd call it lucky,' Gamay said. 'I'm sure he saw us, too.'

'He's probably the one who called out the hounds,' Paul said.

Orlov groaned. 'That's where we are in Russia today. Thugs advised by mad monks. I can't believe Razov has become such a powerful political figure in our country.'

'I was wondering,' Paul said. 'How did they know where to find us? I'm pretty sure Yuri lost them.'

'Maybe the bigger question is what they intended to do *after* they found us.' Gamay turned to the professor and his son. 'We're profoundly sorry for what happened. Please tell us how we can make it up to you.'

'Perhaps a little help in rebuilding my cottage,' Orlov said, after some thought.

'That goes without saying,' Paul said. 'Anything else?'

Orlov furrowed his brow. 'One more thing,' he said, his face lighting up. 'As you know, Yuri is intent on visiting the United States.'

'Consider it done, with the condition that you come along.'

The professor could barely control his pleasure. 'You drive a hard bargain, my friend.'

'I'm a tough old Yankee, and don't you forget it. I think we should be on our way the first thing in the morning.'

'I'm sorry you have to leave so soon. Are you sure?'

'It might be best for everyone if we go.'

They talked until the professor's weariness caught up with him and he drifted off to sleep. The Trouts and Yuri split the rest of the night into shifts, so at least one person would stand watch while the others caught some sleep in the bunk beds. The morning dawned without incident, and after a quick breakfast of coffee and rolls, the Trouts said their good-byes, vowing to get together in a few months, and squeezed into the same taxi that had dropped them off.

As the Lada bumped down the road, Gamay looked out the back window at the charred remains of the cottage. Smoke still hung in the air. 'We'll have a lot to tell Kurt when we get back,' she said.

Paul's eyes blinked with amusement. 'If I know Kurt, he'll have even more to tell *us*.'

17

The man Austin knew only as Ivan gazed around in wonder at the shrine to the Romanovs. Austin had just given him a demonstration of the chanting chair. 'This is really quite extraordinary,' he said, letting his eyes wander around the room. 'You have made quite a find.'

Austin responded with a lopsided grin. 'Then all is forgiven for coming in with six-guns blazing?'

'On the contrary. It's exactly what I *wanted* to happen.'

'You're a strange man, Ivan,' Austin said, with a shake of his head.

'That may be, but in this case my actions were purely logical.' He spread his forefinger and thumb apart. 'Don't forget that I have a dossier this thick on you, as well as my personal experience with your methods. I knew warning you off would be the surest way to bring you here.'

'Why be so Machiavellian? Why not simply invite me to your party? I'm an agreeable guy.'

'You're not naïve in these matters. If I had said back in Istanbul that I needed your help, what would you have replied, given the stormy history of our relationship?'

'I don't know,' Austin said with a shrug.

'*I* do. You might have regarded it as a trap, an ingenious way of getting back at you for *this* souvenir of past encounters.' He touched the scar on his cheek.

'The Russians are famous for their chess skills. And you must admit revenge can be a potent motivator.'

'I've learned to control my passions and exploit those of others to defeat them. There's another reason I held back. I suspect that if I had asked for your help, you would have gone to your higher-ups. Your government would have discouraged this mission.'

'What makes you so sure of that?'

'Some of your countrymen are supporting the dark forces gathering in Russia.'

Austin raised an eyebrow. 'Anyone I know?'

'Probably, but I doubt if you'd believe me, so I'll keep my thoughts to myself for now.'

'How can you be sure that I *didn't* act with official permission?'

'I consider it highly unlikely that your government would tolerate a clandestine invasion of a foreign country.'

'Last time I looked, NUMA was *part* of the government.'

'You're not the *only* one I have kept tabs on, Mr Austin. I have files on everyone of any consequence in NUMA, from your partner Joe Zavala right up to Admiral Sandecker. We both know that the good admiral would *never* allow a rogue operation.' The

Russian smiled. 'Unless it was under his control, of course.'

'Sounds as if you've done your homework,' Austin admitted.

'Knowing the inner workings of NUMA was vital in order to make your agency a part of the equation.'

'I don't understand. Why involve NUMA?'

'The intelligence services in both our countries have been infiltrated by the enemy. Those fighting men you saw today have all served with me for years. But even a tightly knit force can be compromised by a single person. NUMA's integrity is above reproach. On a more practical side, I need NUMA's global capacity for communications and transport, your incredible intelligence and research facilities.'

'Thanks for the endorsement, but I don't know if I can help. I'm only one person out of thousands at the agency.'

'Please don't be disingenuous, Mr Austin. You could never have undertaken this mission if it were not for the tacit approval of Admiral Sandecker and Rudi Gunn.'

Austin was impressed with Ivan's knowledge of how things worked at NUMA. 'Even if I admitted you were right on that score, I still don't have the power to give you everything you want.'

'When the threat to your country becomes apparent, you'll feel different. We *need* each other.'

'That's another problem. You still haven't told me what this threat is.'

'Only because I don't know.'

'Yet you're still convinced it's real.'

'Oh yes, Mr Austin. Knowing the players in this drama, I'd say it's *very* real.'

Austin still didn't know how much to believe Ivan, but there was no mistaking the Russian's seriousness. 'Maybe one of the Cossacks could tell us something.'

Petrov's lips tightened in a smile. 'We both should have thought about that earlier. Their leader was the big man with the red beard. Dead men tell no tales, unfortunately.'

'Sorry, but it couldn't be helped under the circumstances. I'm curious. How long were you and your boys hiding in the woods?'

'Since dawn. We landed a few miles up the coast and made our way overland at night. I saw the fishing boat arrive and suspected you were on it. We didn't know you had landed and were quite surprised to see you pop up out of nowhere. Congratulations on a successful infiltration.'

Austin ignored the compliment. 'Then you saw that the submarine crew was in trouble?'

'We observed the men being rounded up and marched to the field. To answer your unspoken question, yes, we would have intervened. My men were readying for the attack. Then you and your friend arrived and our intervention hardly seemed necessary. From the damage you inflicted, I thought a platoon of US Marines had landed. It's doubtful how much the Cossacks could have told us. They are nothing more than bandit scum whose sole function was to guard this complex.' Petrov walked over to the altar and touched the photograph above it. 'The last of the tsars,' he said.

'That's quite a headpiece,' Austin said, pointing to the jeweled crown in the picture.

'Whoever wears the crown of Ivan the Terrible will rule Russia,' Petrov said. Seeing Austin's perplexed expression, he smiled. 'An old Russian proverb. Don't look for hidden auguries in the words; they mean what they say. Whoever is strong enough to keep all that weight on his head, and brutish and terrible enough to possess the crown, will find those same qualities of use in ruling this land.'

'Where's the crown now?'

'It disappeared with a great deal of the tsar's other treasure that went missing after the revolution. When the White government came into Yekaterinburg, where the tsar was probably murdered, they found a list of items belonging to the imperial family. Some items were recovered, but it is generally conceded that the list represented only a portion of the items the family had with them in exile. The most valuable items, the crown included, have never been found.'

'Was there a list of the missing treasure?'

'The Soviets made such a list, but it has never turned up. It's assumed that the KGB had the list before the overthrow of communism. I've made inquiries that lead me to believe the list is still in existence, but its whereabouts is a mystery.'

'How did you know about the crown without the list?'

'I've seen this and other photos of it. It's made in two parts, representing the east and west empires. The double-headed eagle was the crest of the Romanovs. The orb the eagle surmounts is a symbol of earthly power.'

'It must be worth a fortune.'

'The crown's value can't be measured in dollars or rubles. This crown and the other treasure came from the sweat and toil of the Russian serfs, who saw the tsar as godlike. The tsar was the richest man in the world. He had revenue from the crown lands, a million square miles, including gold and silver mines, and owned incredible riches. Our sovereigns had an almost barbaric taste for the glitter of gold and gems. *Tsar* is Russian for "Caesar." Emirs and shahs laid gifts of incredible value at his feet.'

'The family in the photo doesn't look as if it's enjoying all that wealth.'

'They knew the crown was more of a curse than a blessing. It was reserved for the frail head of the young boy, Alexander, although it's doubtful he would have lived long enough to take his father's place. He had hemophilia, uncontrollable bleeding, you know? A real problem among European royalty – all those intermarriages. Anyway, other relatives would have stepped in to claim the throne.'

'Any idea who built this shrine?'

'I thought it might be Razov at first. I could see

him sitting here, imagining that he will someday become the ruler of Russia. But the decadent trappings of the apartment in the main complex puzzle me. Razov is almost ascetic in his convictions. The monk, on the other hand, is said to be debauched. It's odd how much he resembles Rasputin in his depraved lifestyle. My guess is that Boris spent more time here than Razov. Razov would like to bring back the past. In his madness, Boris *lives* it.'

'That's quite a role reversal.'

'Perhaps, but one thing is certain: They both must be stopped,' Petrov said, his eyes boring into Austin's. 'And you must help me.'

Austin was still skeptical. 'I'll think about it, Ivan. Right now I need some fresh air.'

Petrov gripped Austin by the arm. 'Maybe your own countryman can persuade you. You remember the words of the great American patriot-philosopher Thomas Paine. He said he was not defending a few acres of ground, but a *cause*.'

Austin knew the dossier Petrov had on him would have mentioned the volumes of philosophy that lined his bookshelves.

'What is *your* cause, Ivan?'

'Perhaps it's the same as yours.'

'Don't take this the wrong way, but I can't see you waving the flag for motherhood, apple pie and the American way.'

'I did my share of waving the hammer and sickle as a Young Pioneer marching in the May Day parades.

There are deeper issues here. Don't let our past get in the way. Judge me by the present, so that both our countries will have a future.'

Austin saw a slight softening in Petrov's rock-hard eyes. Maybe the man was human after all. 'Guess we're stuck with each other, whether we like it or not.'

'Then you'll work with me?'

'I can't speak for NUMA, but I'll do what I can,' Austin said, extending his hand. 'C'mon, partner, I've got something else that will interest you.' He led the way down through the labyrinth to the submarine pen. Petrov recognized the sub immediately.

'It's an India class,' he said. 'It was designed to carry submersibles for use by special-operations forces.'

'Any idea how it got here?'

'There's a booming market in the world for Soviet armaments.'

'This isn't exactly a box of AK-47s.'

'My country has always done things on a grand scale. For the right price, you could probably buy a battleship. As you know, the Soviet Union launched dozens of huge subs during the Cold War. Many have been mothballed or otherwise decommissioned. But given the sad state of our armed forces, anything is possible. This could be an important lead. I can't imagine anyone making a purchase this big without somebody knowing about it. I'll run a discreet check. Tell me about these men from your *NR-1* submarine. What did they have to say?'

'I talked to one of them. The sub was hijacked by someone posing as a scientist, transported on the back of that submarine and made to work salvaging cargo from an old freighter. The fact that they're still holding the captain and pilot indicates that they have more work planned for the *NR-1*.' Austin rapped the stone floor with his heel. 'Maybe you can look into the ownership of this place.'

'I already have. The property is still owned by the Russian government. About two years ago, it was leased to a private corporation. They said they wanted to establish a fish-processing plant here.'

'From what I've seen, the leaseholder was more interested in what was *under* the ground than on top of it. Any leads on the corporation?'

'Yes. We got a break there. It was a straw for Ataman.'

Austin nodded. 'Why does that not surprise me? I should get back above. Joe will wonder what happened to us.'

They followed the network of corridors and stairs that took them back to the surface. It was a relief to break out into the sunshine and fresh air. To Austin's surprise, the soccer field was clear of carnage.

Petrov sensed the question on Austin's lips. 'Before we went below, I ordered my men to drag the dead into the woods and bury them.'

'That was considerate of you.'

'There was nothing considerate about it. I wanted nothing left that could be seen from the air.' They walked across the field toward the downed helicopter. 'I've taken care of the dead,' he said, glancing toward the helicopter. 'I will leave it up to you to deal with the living.'

It was a wonder that the chopper had been able to land as softly as it had. The Cossacks had shot high, and the upper cockpit and engine housing were riddled with bullet holes. Kaela sat on the ground nearby with her legs crossed, writing in a shorthand notebook. Austin put on his most winning smile. Kaela felt his shadow and looked up.

'Small world,' he said, with his best show of teeth enamel.

Kaela skewered Austin with a hard stare.

Undaunted, Austin plunked onto the ground beside her. 'Nice of you to go to all this trouble just so we'd have the opportunity to reschedule our dinner date.'

'*You're* the one who didn't show up back there in Istanbul.'

'True. Which is why I'm glad I have the chance to apologize and see if I can make it up to you over cocktails.'

She raised an eyebrow. 'Apologize for standing me up or for stealing Captain Kemal?'

Kaela was no pushover for the Austin charm offensive. This was going to be more complicated than he thought.

'Okay. Let's deal with this in tiny steps. First, I

apologize for missing the dinner date. I was unexpectedly tied up and couldn't make it. As for Captain Kemal, you'll have to admit you made a mistake by not holding him with some sort of retainer while you went off to Paris.'

'Please spare me the lecture. I never thought you would *steal* him after you warned me to stay away from this place because it was too dangerous and an infringement of Russian territory.'

'You'll have to admit I was right about the danger,' he said, glancing at the wreckage of the helicopter.

Kaela took a deep breath and slowly let it out. 'I'll grant you the obvious. But I'll bet nobody gave you or your NUMA friend an invitation to drop by for tea.'

'That's correct, but it doesn't make it right.'

'You sound like my mother,' she said with mock disgust. 'Your apology for missing dinner is accepted. Luckily, my producers bankrolled enough money to lease a helicopter, so I wouldn't have hired Captain Kemal anyhow. You still owe me, though.'

Austin noticed the twinkle in the amber eyes and realized she had been setting him up, using his guilt as leverage.

'You're playing me like a fish, aren't you?'

Kaela threw her head back and laughed. 'I'm certainly *trying* to. You deserve to be jerked around after trying to put me off with that phony shark smile and the "small world" routine. Real smooth character! Next thing you'd be asking me what my astrological sign was. Well, it's Capricorn, in case you're interested.'

'I didn't mean to make it sound like a singles bar. My sign is Pisces, by the way.'

'Pisces? That's fitting for a NUMA guy.' She put her notebook aside. 'I'd advise you to stay out of singles bars. With that corny line, you'd go home alone every night.'

Austin decided he really *liked* this woman. She was tough and feminine at the same time, had a sharp sense of humor and plenty of intelligence. And the qualities he admired were gift wrapped in a lovely package.

'Okay, now that I've snapped up the hook, I'll let you reel me in. But only to a point! What does your devious little soul want from me?'

'The *truth*, for starters. Why are you here, for instance? And who are the tough guys in the black suits? And why are the people around here so damned unfriendly?'

'Is this for a story?'

'Maybe. But I want to know mostly because I want to know. Curiosity is the best tool of a good reporter.'

Austin was no fan of mendacity, but he didn't want to involve Kaela and her gang in something that could bite them. They had been lucky twice so far. Their third encounter with the bad guys could be a strikeout.

'You're not the only one who's curious. After my first run-in with those guys on horses, I wanted to

263

know more. I also felt I had to do something for Kemal's cousin Mehmet.'

'Is there a submarine base here?'

'Yes. Quite extensive, as a matter of fact.'

'I *knew* it. I want to get inside.'

'Okay by me, but you may have problems with that gentleman over there.' Ivan was making his way across the field from the woods, where he had been inspecting his men's work.

'Who is he?'

'His name is Ivan. He's the boss man.'

'Military?'

'Why don't you ask him yourself?'

Kaela grabbed her notebook and sprang to her feet. 'I think I will.' She strode toward the Russian and intercepted him. Austin watched with interest as she used her body language to send a tantalizing message. She was wading in with a full feminine court press, standing first on one leg, then the other, hip out, touching Ivan lightly on the chest, flashing him her incredible smile.

Ivan stood there with his arms crossed like a granite statue, resisting the full assault. When she was done, he spoke a few words. Kaela's shoulders suddenly squared, she leaned forward and stuck her jaw into his face, then she wheeled and strode purposefully back to Austin.

'What a stubborn little man,' she fumed. 'He said that the sub base is the property of the Russian government and is off-limits to the public. He *suggests* that I make arrangements with you to leave here as quickly as possible or suffer the consequences.' She grinned. 'Well, we can still run the story. I've got film.'

She marched over to the helicopter wreckage with a determined step and talked with Lombardo and Dundee, who had been poking around in the wreckage. Their conversation was animated, and grew more so when he showed her the jumble of metal and plastic that was what was left of the video camera. Kaela slowly walked back to Austin.

'It looks as if we'll have to bum a ride with you,' she said, without enthusiasm.

Austin saw Joe Zavala making his way toward them from the direction of the beach, where he'd been checking visually and on the radio to see if the *NR-1* crew had made it to the fishing boat. He excused himself and took Zavala aside.

Zavala said, 'They all made it to Kemal's boat.'

'Good news, but we've got a problem. Kaela and her guys need a ride, and I don't want them anywhere near the *NR-1* crew.'

Zavala cast an admiring glance toward the TV reporter. 'Then you'll be happy to know the *Argo* was keeping an eye on us and monitoring radio transmissions. I just talked to Captain Atwood. They've sent a boat in to transfer the navy to the survey ship. Kemal's boat is free and clear.'

Austin let out a nasty chuckle. 'Would you send a message to the *Argo* and ask them to pick *us* up, too?

Then call Captain Kemal, tell him that we will be transferring to the *Argo* and ask if he wouldn't mind taking on a few passengers in our place.'

'Aye, aye, sir,' Zavala said with a snappy salute.

While Joe was calling the fishing boat, Austin went over to tell Kaela and her friends that first-class transportation had been arranged.

18

The trip from Novorossiysk to Istanbul was an aviation nightmare. Unspecified mechanical problems delayed the flight on the ground. The Trouts sat in the hot and crowded cabin for an hour before being switched to another plane. The passengers who sampled the mystery meat served for the in-flight meal paid a price for their daring when the plane encountered turbulence. Adding to everyone's misery, only one toilet was operable.

Paul and Gamay thought their suffering had ended after the white-knuckle flight, but the taxi driver who picked them up at the airport drove as if he had a death wish. When Paul asked him to slow down, he punched the gas pedal.

'I think something got lost in the translation,' Gamay said over the squeal of tires.

'Must be my New England accent,' Paul said.

'Don't worry about it,' Gamay said, with a determined set to her jaw. 'After what we've been through on this trip, *nothing*, not even death, will stand between me and a hot shower, a Bombay Sapphire gin martini and a long nap.'

The cab narrowly missed the doorman, who stepped back like a matador playing a bull, and screeched to a jarring stop in front of the Marmara Istanbul Hotel on Taksim Square. They exited the cab as if they were in a twin ejection seat, paid off the smiling cabby and made their way across the spacious lobby to the check-in desk.

The desk clerk was a dapper man whose slicked-down hair and razor-trimmed mustache made him resemble Hercule Poirot. He saw the Trouts approach and flashed a high-wattage smile. 'Welcome back, Drs Trout. I hope you had a pleasant journey exploring Ephesus.' When they'd left the hotel for Novo-rossiysk, the Trouts had announced with great fanfare that they were going to visit the ancient ruins on the coast of Asia Minor.

'Thank you, yes, the Temple of Artemis was *fascinating*,' Gamay gushed with the proper amount of awe. The clerk smiled and handed Paul an envelope along with the room key. 'This message came for you earlier today.'

Paul opened the envelope, unfolded the paper inside and handed it to Gamay. She read the single sentence neatly printed on hotel stationery: 'Call me soonest. A.'

A telephone number followed the brief message.

'Duty calls,' Paul said.

Gamay rolled her eyes. 'Sometimes duty calls at the worst damn time!' She snatched the key from his hand and headed for the elevator.

Back in their room, Paul suggested that Gamay take the first shower while he called Austin. She snapped up the offer without hesitation and left a trail of clothes leading to the bathroom. Concluding that a palliative was in order, Paul called room service and asked to have a shaker of extra-dry martinis sent up. The tray arrived about the same time the shower stopped running. Paul poured a glass and knocked on the bathroom door. It opened in a cloud of steam, and a hand reached out for the martini. He poured himself a drink, propping his long legs up on a footstool, took a grateful sip and pronounced the cocktail tolerable for Istanbul. Fortified for the task ahead, he dialed the number on Austin's note.

'We're back in Istanbul,' Trout said, when Kurt's voice came on the line. 'Got your note.'

'Good. How was your trip?'

'Informative and full of surprises.' Trout gave Austin a summary.

'From your description of Razov's yacht, it sounds like a FastShip. Probably powered by gas turbines that can kick it up to speeds twice that of comparable boats. Smart. Razov can move his center of operations anywhere on the globe within days. I'm glad no one was hurt, but it's too bad about the professor's cottage. As soon as we hang up, I'll start the ball rolling on an official NUMA invitation to Orlov and his son.'

'They'll be thrilled. How did your excursion go?'

'Like you and Gamay, we got a warm reception, but I wouldn't advise it for a Cook's Tour. I'll fill you in when we meet.'

'Can't wait to hear the details.'

'You'll get your chance sooner than you think. I'm on the *Argo*, and I could use the immediate services of a deep-ocean geologist and a marine biologist who will work cheap.'

'Unfortunately, I know where you can find a couple of poor wastrels who fit that description exactly.'

'I knew I could count on you. I've made arrangements for transportation. How soon will you be ready to travel?'

'We arrived at the hotel a few minutes ago, so we won't even have to pack.' Paul glanced at the bathroom door and smiled. Gamay was singing an off-key version of 'Gonna Wash That Man Right Out of My Hair.' 'Do we have time to finish our martinis?'

'Oh hell, Paul, have *two*. You'll be sharing space with a VIP from the States. You've got a couple of hours before he flies in.'

'Wonderful! We get to ride with a six-chinned Senator Claghorn with a comb-over.'

Austin chuckled. '*Incredible*, Paul. You must be psychic. How'd you know it was the good senator?'

'Lucky guess. I'll break the news to Gamay. We'll see you tonight.'

Paul jotted down the travel time and place. As he hung up, Gamay came out of the bathroom with a towel wrapped around her slim body, another turban-style on her head and a half-empty martini glass in her hand. The shower and drink had mellowed her mood. When he told her they would have to hit the road again, Gamay even greeted the news with a smile, saying that she missed Kurt and Joe.

Paul took his turn in the shower, and Gamay sent down to room service for lamb shish kebab and pilaf. The food arrived as they were starting on their second martini. After dinner, they changed their clothes, and with full stomachs, clean bodies and refreshed spirits, they took another cab to the airport. The cab driver had no kamikaze yearnings and except for the usual heavy traffic, the trip was uneventful.

As Austin instructed, they asked to be dropped off away from the main airport terminal at a section used by small private airlines. They made their way to a hangar whose floodlights gleamed off the turquoise paint of a midsized helicopter. The letters NUMA were painted in black on the side. The rotor turned slowly as the engines warmed up. The pilot stood on the tarmac talking to someone. Even though the man's back was turned, the Trouts immediately recognized the narrow shoulders and hips and thinning hair of NUMA's deputy director. Rudi Gunn turned, greeted them with a wide grin and jerked his thumb toward the open door of the aircraft.

'Need a lift?'

Gamay turned to Paul. 'So *this* is the six-chinned senator with the major comb-over that you were telling me about?'

Trout did a classic double-take. 'For God's sakes, Rudi, why didn't you tell us you were the bigwig VIP?'

'Didn't want to spoil your fun. Admiral Sandecker thought I should be in the neighborhood in case the situation got complicated. I've been in Athens representing NUMA at a conference on nautical archaeology. It was only a short hop here via executive jet. The helicopter flew in from a project in the eastern Aegean. Sandecker figured it was time for me to jump in with both feet after Kurt called him with news of the "package" he had to deliver.'

'Package?' Paul said.

'I'll tell you everything I know on the way. Shall we?'

They climbed into the chopper and took their seats in the spacious cabin. The engines revved up, and minutes later the Sikorsky S-76C lifted rapidly into the sky. The sprawling lights of Istanbul straddling the Bosporus on two continents spread below them like a sequined tapestry. Powered by its twin Arriel engines, the helicopter headed north at a cruising speed of one hundred seventy-five miles per hour.

The pilot's voice came over their earphones in a lazy, slightly western Chuck Yeager drawl.

'Hi, folks. My name is Mike. Make yourselves comfortable. Should be plenty of room to stretch. They designed this chopper for oil-rig support, so it's pretty much of a flying bus. We can take twelve passengers. You're lucky to be going on this leg. We expect to be pretty crowded on the return trip. There's a thermos of hot coffee up near the bulkhead. Help yourselves. Please let me know if you need anything. Otherwise, sit back and enjoy the flight.'

Gunn poured the coffee and passed the steaming cups around. 'Good to see you both. Sorry your sabbaticals were cut short. Officially speaking, you're still on leave, I'm sitting in an auditorium at the Greek National Archaeological Museum, and this meeting is not taking place.'

'What's been going on, Rudi?' Paul said. 'We've only heard bits and pieces.'

'I'm not sure what the total picture looks like, but here's what we *do* know. Several days ago, Admiral Sandecker was invited to a White House meeting with the president and his advisors. The White House was worried about the deteriorating political situation in Russia. Some of the president's men scolded Sandecker for allowing Kurt to violate Russian sovereign territory at the abandoned Soviet submarine base. They were worried that it would give Russian opposition forces ammunition to use against the government, which is already fighting for its life. The admiral apologized, said it was an accident and offered to talk directly to the Russians. His offer was rejected. Then he asked what the White House was doing about the *NR-1*. Strangely, the president and his people had forgotten to tell Sandecker the sub was missing.'

Paul grinned and said, 'Assuming the admiral wouldn't know was pretty dumb on their part.'

Gamay shook her head. 'It's unbelievable that the *NR-1* could vanish with no trace, as if it had been swallowed by a sea monster.'

'You're not far off the mark. The *NR-1* was hijacked and transported on the deck of a submarine.'

'That's more far-fetched than the sea monster theory,' Gamay said.

'We were trying to figure things out, when Kurt called and said a source had told him that a mining tycoon named Mikhail Razov is behind the political unrest in Russia. According to the White House, there's a tie between the *NR-1*'s disappearance and the mess in Moscow. In addition, Razov's company, Ataman Enterprises, has leased the sub base from the Russian government.'

Gamay said, 'That's why Kurt asked us to look into Razov's operation at Novorossiysk.'

'You think the *NR-1* was taken to this old sub base?' Paul said.

'We thought that was a possibility. But we were more worried about something else Kurt's source said, that Razov was connected to a plot against the United States.'

'What sort of plot?' Paul asked.

'We don't know. Sandecker considered the tip serious. When Kurt said he was assembling the Special Assignments Team and planned to go back to the base, the admiral gave his unofficial blessing. Kurt must have mentioned that his mission was, uh, unofficial.'

'He put it quite colorfully,' Gamay said, laughingly.

'I won't even ask,' said Rudi, imagining Austin's report. 'The White House *specifically* warned Admiral

Sandecker to stay clear of the *NR-1* investigation. I'm sure it won't surprise you to know he managed to get around that warning by a technicality. He agreed not to search for the sub, but said nothing about the sub base.'

'I'm shocked, *shocked*,' Gamay said with mock horror, echoing *Casablanca*.

'Me, too,' said Paul. 'Who would have thought such a thing?'

'Your sarcasm is dutifully noted and ignored. But you get the point. We had to keep the admiral insulated to give him room to maneuver.'

'Risky,' Paul said. 'The whole thing could blow up in NUMA's face.'

'Sandecker was well aware of that possibility, but the gods who watch over the Black Sea were in a benevolent mood.'

'You look like the cat who swallowed the canary,' Gamay said, noting Gunn's enigmatic smile. 'Apparently, Kurt has some good news.'

'*Very* good. He and Joe found the *NR-1*'s crew – the package I mentioned. They were being held captive at the Russian base. They're on the *Argo* now.'

'That's great, but I don't understand,' Paul said, furrowing his brow. 'The *Russians* were holding them prisoner?'

'It's more complicated than that, from what I gather. The captain and pilot are still missing, along with the sub itself. Kurt wanted us all to be at the crew's debriefing.'

'Finding these guys is quite a coup for NUMA and the admiral,' Paul observed.

'Unfortunately, we can't claim credit for the rescue. I'm not sure how it will be announced, since no one has ever told the public of the hijacking. The top brass has been keeping the sub's hijacking a secret.'

'Hard to keep a secret in Washington,' Paul said. 'The story is bound to get out.'

'I agree. We've notified the navy that we found the sub's crew, but we've deliberately been short on details. We won't be able to get away with that strategy forever. Which is why this brainstorming session with the crew is so important. We've *got* to get to the bottom of this. Why don't we help ourselves to more coffee while you fill me in on your encounter with Ataman?'

Gamay volunteered to refill their coffee mugs. 'I'll let Paul do the play-by-play and I'll add the color,' she said.

Gunn listened to their story without interrupting. From experience, they knew that Gunn would absorb every detail; his analytical skills were legendary. He had been the first in his class at the US Naval Academy, had formerly held the rank of commander and before he became second-in-command to Sandecker, had overseen logistics and oceanographic projects for NUMA.

Gunn peppered them with questions after they finished their tale. He was particularly interested in Boris, the 'mad monk,' and in Yuri's comment about the absence of the big drilling ships. Ataman's violent reaction was simple to explain. Razov had something to hide and didn't like people snooping around. But Boris and the missing drilling ships didn't fit into any equation he could formulate. He sat back in his seat, adjusted the horn-rimmed glasses on his hawkish nose and tented his fingers, much as Sherlock Holmes would have looked, absorbed by a puzzle. All he needed to complete the picture was a pipe and a deerstalker's cap.

The pilot's voice broke Gunn's concentration. 'We're coming up on the *Argo*, folks. If you look off to the right, you'll see the ship.'

The *Argo* had switched on every light in greeting and looked like a giant floating Christmas tree against the inky darkness of the sea. The helicopter hovered over the ship and slowly descended onto the large, blinking *X* that marked the landing pad. The touchdown was nearly perfect, marked by a slight thump of the wheels on the deck. The rotors spun to a stop, and the copilot came back to open the door. The passengers thanked the crew for a smooth flight and descended the boarding steps, eyes blinking against the brilliant floodlights that turned the night into day.

Austin's broad shoulders and pale hair were easy to spot among the crowd that had gathered to greet the arrivals. He strode over, shook hands with Gunn and put his arms around the Trouts.

'Hope you had time for your martinis,' Austin said.

Gamay smiled and pecked his cheek. 'We squeezed in two drinks apiece, thank you.'

'Sorry to drag you out here so soon after your Novorossiysk trip.' He guided them to the mess hall and brought them three tinkling glasses of fresh-squeezed lemonade. 'Joe's baby-sitting the crew in the conference room. We're meeting with them in fifteen minutes to hear their story. The crew is anxious to get home, and I've asked them to give us an hour while the chopper fuels up.'

Gunn puckered his lips in amusement as Austin filled them in on the crew's rescue. 'I don't mean to demean the dangers you described, Kurt, but it sounds like a Pink Panther movie, with all those people running around.'

'I was thinking more of the Keystone Kops,' Austin said. 'Someday I'll look back and chuckle over the whole crazy episode.' He brushed his head lightly with his fingers. 'But if my hair could have gotten any whiter, it would have.'

'I'm intrigued by this Russian you call Ivan,' Gunn said. 'How do you know him?'

'Our paths crossed when I was working for the CIA.'

'Is he a friend or foe?'

'I'd call him a friend for the moment. I suspect that he'll do pretty much what he thinks is in the best interests of Russia. He is devious and shrewd – and he didn't survive all those purges in Russian intelligence by being a choirboy.'

'That's quite a resumé. Despite his checkered background, you think we should trust him?'

'For now. And for one very good reason.'

'What's that?' Gunn said.

'He's all we've got.'

19

The soggy bunch Captain Kemal had rescued from the sea and transferred to the *Argo* was gone. In their place was a happy band of submariners who could laugh about their ordeal, which was what they were doing when Austin and the others arrived at the conference room.

After boarding the *Argo*, the *NR-1* crew had been checked out by the ship's medical technician, filled with extraordinary meals from the galley and given the loan of NUMA work coveralls. Except for scratches and bruises, the men in the conference room showed few visible effects from their ordeal. Sitting at the metal table that occupied center place were Captain Atwood, Ensign Kreisman and Joe Zavala. Joe smiled broadly when he saw his NUMA colleagues come through the door. He rose and went over to shake hands with Gunn and Trout. Ever the ladies' man, he gave Gamay a kiss on the cheek.

After a quick round of introductions, Austin announced, to claps and whistles, 'In a few hours you'll be back in Istanbul, where a jet is waiting to fly you home. Your relatives have been notified that you're safe.' More applause. 'You must be anxious to be on your way, but I've got a favor to ask. We've only heard parts of your remarkable story. While the chopper is fueling up for the return trip, I'm hoping you can tell us what happened from start to finish.'

Ensign Kreisman stood and said, 'It's the least we can do. I'm sure I speak for the crew when I say thanks to you and Joe for getting us out of that place in one piece.'

'Remind us to bring a Bradley fighting vehicle the next time,' Austin said. He waited for the laughter to die down. 'If you don't mind, Ensign, I'll play Perry Mason. I think it will go faster that way.'

'No problem, sir.'

'Good. Why don't you start from the beginning?'

Kreisman took a position in front of a wall chart that showed the eastern Aegean. 'Our mission was to dive on underwater archaeological sites off the Turkish coast. *Here.*' He tapped the map. 'In addition to our regular crew under the command of Captain Logan, we carried a guest scientist who called himself Dr Josef Pulaski, supposedly from MIT.'

Gunn raised his hand. 'Point of information. After we learned the sub was hijacked, we went over the roster and found Pulaski's name. When we checked with MIT, they said they'd never heard of him.'

'Too bad we didn't check *before* he came on board,' the ensign said, with a shake of his head. 'In any event, the mission was an unqualified success. We retrieved some artifacts with our manipulator capacity. We were preparing to surface, when Pulaski pulled a gun. Most of the crew was aft of the control room and didn't see it happen. The captain informed us over the intercom. He ordered us to stay put or Pulaski would shoot us. The sub went up a few hundred feet and hovered.'

'For how long?' Austin said.

'About twenty-five minutes. Then a huge shadow appeared in the monitors. It looked like a whale or shark coming up under the sub, and then there was a horrendous clang. The sub shook so hard, anyone who wasn't holding on was thrown to the floor. Next we heard a scraping and clawing, as if big metal beetles were crawling around on the outside of the hull. Divers. We could see them on the monitors. One clown even waved at the camera! Next thing we knew, the divers were gone and we were flying through the ocean.'

'Where were the captain and pilot and the other scientist during all of this?' Austin asked.

'In the control room.'

'Did the captain say anything more?'

'Yes, sir. He said to send coffee and sandwiches forward.'

'What was the support ship doing at this time?'

'We heard them calling on the radio until Pulaski ordered all communications shut down. I assume they tracked us until we were out of range.'

'How long did you travel underwater?' Austin asked.

'A matter of hours. When we surfaced, it was as dark as Hades. Not a light to be seen anywhere. Then armed men came down the hatch into the *NR-1*.'

'Russians?'

'We couldn't tell, although I think they were carrying AK-47s. They were wearing cami and acted like professional soldiers. Not like those jerks on horseback that you saved us from. They kept their mouths shut. Pulaski did all the talking. He told us to get out of the *NR-1*. We climbed out onto the deck of a big sub.'

'Any idea on the sub's length?' Gunn said.

Kreisman looked around the room. 'Anyone want to take a stab at a guess?'

Another seaman spoke up. 'I served on a boomer when I first joined the navy. Judging from its beam, around thirty feet, I'd estimate this baby was as long as a Los Angeles class. About three hundred sixty feet.'

'The *NR-1* is only one hundred fifty feet long. They could easily piggyback you with more than two hundred feet to spare,' Austin said.

The sailor nodded. 'That sub was bigger than our support vessel.'

Austin glanced around the room. 'Anyone see markings?'

Nobody responded. 'Too dark and no moon,' Kreisman explained.

'So they moved you into the big sub?'

'Correct. They locked us in a bunk room. Not enough beds for all of us, so we took turns sleeping. They brought food from time to time. We submerged for twenty-four hours. When we surfaced again, it was night. The ocean was different from the Aegean. The air didn't have the saltiness we'd been used to. More like one of the Great Lakes.'

'Tell them about the ship sounds we heard before that,' one of the submariners said.

'Sorry, I forgot about that. It was awhile before we surfaced. The bunk room was as quiet as a grave. Some of the guys in the bunks said they could hear the sound of ship engines through the bulkheads. We all put our ears up to the hull and listened. It was true.'

'You were in an area of heavy ship traffic?'

'That's what we figured. Eventually, the noise died out. Several hours later, we came up next to a surface ship. It must have been waiting for us. They hustled us onto the ship and into another bunk room. That was our home sweet home for three days.'

'They kept you there all that time?' Gunn said.

'Hell, no! Early the next morning, we were assembled on the deck. Guys with guns kept us covered, and the big sub was nowhere to be seen. Pulaski was there. He gave us that creepy smile of his. "Good morning, gentlemen,"' Kreisman imitated Pulaski's accent. '"In return for this delightful cruise, we are going to ask that you do a little job for us." He said we would be salvaging material from an old ship. Pulaski and another thug were going with us. So we piled into the *NR-1* alongside the ship, which was acting as our tender, and down we went.'

'How deep?'

'Four hundred feet plus. No big deal for the *NR-1*.

We noticed the water buoyancy was different. We needed less ballast to bring us down. The sea bottom was mud for the most part, sloping before it abruptly dropped off into the deep. The wreck sat on the bank of an underwater canyon or valley that ran at right angles to the cliff face.'

'Was there a name on the ship's hull?'

'None that we could see. The vessel was covered with seaweed and barnacles. The bow was more up-and-down than raked, like those pictures you see of the *Titanic*.' He used his hand to demonstrate.

'What was its position on the bottom?'

'The ship sat on the slope, leaning over at a sharp angle. It looked as if a good shove would tip it over. We saw a big hole in the starboard side.'

'Could you see inside the hole?'

'It was filled in with rubble. We only stayed there a minute. They were more interested in the other side. They had fitted out the manipulator arm with a cutting torch. We touched down on the slanting deck. It was pretty dicey putting the sub down at an angle. We had the feeling the ship could roll over at any time. Then they told us to cut a hole in the super-structure.'

'Not in the hold?' Austin said with surprise. 'That's where the cargo would be.'

'You'd think so, but we weren't in a position to argue. We made an opening around ten by ten feet. It wasn't too hard – the metal was old and rusted. We had to be careful, though. It was like a surgical operation. One nudge and the ship would drop off into the deep; we were all aware of that. We could see the old bunks and mattresses. Pulaski and his buddy got real agitated. They started to jabber over some diagrams of the wreck that they had with them.'

'In Russian.'

'Sounded like it. Apparently, they'd had us cut through the wrong spot. We tried two more times before they found what they wanted. It was a fairly big cabin filled with metal boxes the size of those old steamer trunks you see in antique shops.'

'How many boxes?'

'About a dozen, jumbled every which way. Pulaski told us to grab them with the *NR-1*'s manipulator arm. We had a tough time moving them. They were obviously heavy and strained the manipulator to capacity. We pulled the boxes to the opening and called the surface ship and told them to lower some lines with hooks on the ends of them. We attached the lines, stood off and let the ship winch the stuff up with its superior lifting power.'

Austin, who had been trained in deepwater salvage, nodded. 'Exactly the way I would have handled it.'

'Captain Logan's idea.' Kreisman smirked with embarrassment. 'We were like the British soldiers in that movie, *Bridge on the River Kwai*. We really got into it. Professional pride, I guess.'

'Don't feel bad. They probably would have killed you if you hadn't done the job.'

'That's what the captain said. We worked round-the-clock shifts. There were a few of the hitches you'd expect with a job that complicated, but we got all the stuff they wanted off the ship.'

'Did you see what was in the steamer trunks?'

'That was a funny thing. They shoved us around the corner, but we could hear them prying the boxes open with a crowbar. They sounded pretty excited. Then there was this silence, and next we heard them yelling. It sounded like an argument. Then Pulaski appeared and started shouting at us in Russian, like whatever happened was our fault. He looked real angry, but I think he was a little scared.' Kreisman glanced around the room and got nods of agreement from the other crewmen.

'No indication what the dustup was all about?'

He shook his head. 'They put us below, and when they brought us on deck again it was night. The monster sub was back. There was a ship nearby, too. We couldn't see in the dark, but it sounded like a big one. They loaded us aboard the sub, except for the captain and pilot – same first-class accommodations. We traveled underwater, a shorter time than before. When we were allowed out, we were in a place as big as an airplane hangar.'

'That would be the sub pen. What happened to the *NR-1*?'

'We don't know. It was still tied up alongside the salvage vessel when we left. The captain and pilot are okay, I hope,' he said with consternation. 'Why would they keep us prisoner and let them go?'

'They may have further work for the *NR-1* or simply want hostages. What happened next?'

'They put us in yet *another* bunk room. A real dump. We were there a couple of days. Bored as hell. The only excitement was what sounded like a big explosion from somewhere below.'

'They were sealing the entrance to the sub pen.'

'Why would they do that?'

'The base had been discovered, and they wanted to make sure no one would find the evidence. The big sub used in the hijack had served its purpose. I wouldn't be surprised if they planned to plug the surface entrance later. Maybe with you inside. What was the guard situation?'

'Same bunch who kept an eye on us on the salvage ship. Military types with automatic weapons. They gave us black bread and water, and locked us in. Next thing we know, these guys with the funny hats and the baggy pants showed up. The first guards were Girl Scouts compared to this gang. They beat up a couple of the guys just for chuckles, dragged us outside and herded us into that big field. You know the rest.'

Austin looked around the room. 'Any questions?'

'Did you get a glimpse of your GPS position when you were on the *NR-1*?' Gunn asked.

'They kept us away from the positioning gauges, then turned them off later so we couldn't see.'

'Damn shame,' Gunn said.

Laughter rippled around the room.

'Are we missing a joke?' Gunn said.

A slim blond-haired crewman in his midtwenties stood and identified himself as Seaman Ted McCormack. He passed a sheet of paper toward the table. 'These are the GPS coordinates for the wreck.'

'How can you be sure?' Gunn said, reading the figures.

McCormack held out his arm and displayed what looked like an overgrown digital wristwatch. 'My wife gave this to me. We got married just before I shipped out. She's got a chart back home so when I called her she could mark exactly where I was.'

'We used to kid Mac about being on a short leash,' Kreisman said. 'Not anymore.'

'When we were hijacked, I slid this thing up my arm and kept it covered under my sleeve,' McCormack said. 'They never frisked us. Figured we were harmless, I guess.'

The ProTek GPS watch was a miracle of miniaturization, said by its manufacturer to be the world's smallest GPS device. It could give the wearer his position anywhere on the planet within a few yards.

Austin grinned. 'Let's hear it for love.' He looked around the room. 'Now, to quote the immortal words of Porky Pig, "That's all, folks." Thanks for your help. And *bon voyage*.'

The *NR-1* crew rose to their feet as one and stampeded out of the conference room like thirsty steers who'd smelled water. Austin turned to the NUMA team.

Paul flipped open his laptop computer and connected it to the modem that would allow files to be projected on a large screen at one end of the room. Gamay stood next to the projection screen with a laser pointer. Paul tapped a few keys, and a map of the kidney-shaped Black Sea and the surrounding land appeared.

'Welcome to the Black Sea, one of the most fascinating bodies of water in the world,' Gamay said, outlining the shores with the bright red dot. 'It's roughly six hundred thirty miles from east to west and three hundred thirty from north to south. It's only one hundred forty-four miles here at the "waist," where the Crimea sticks out. Despite its relatively small size, it's got a big bad reputation. The Greeks called it *Axenos*, which means "inhospitable." The medieval Turks were less diplomatic. They named it Karadenez. The "Sea of Death."'

'Catchy,' Zavala said. 'It has a certain poetic quality.'

'I can definitely see the chamber of commerce using that in a *New York Times* ad,' Austin agreed.

Gamay rolled her eyes. 'Are you two *ever* serious?'

'We try not to be,' Austin said. 'Sorry to interrupt, teacher. Please go on.'

'*Thank* you. Despite the bad press, the Black Sea gets a lot of visitors. Jason came this way in the original *Argo* to look for the Golden Fleece. The sea has been an important trade route and fishing ground for thousands of years. During the Ice Age, it was a big freshwater lake. Then around 6000 BC a natural land dam broke and the waters of the Mediterranean burst through. The sea level rose hundreds of feet.'

'Noah's Flood,' Austin said.

'Some people think so. The people who lived around the lake fled for their lives.' Gamay smiled. 'I can't say whether they did it on an ark. The salt water effectively smothered the lake. River nutrients pouring into the sea have only made the situation worse.' She signaled to Paul, who projected a profile of the sea onto the screen.

'This gives you an idea of the incredible depth. A continental shelf that's probably the remnant of the old shoreline runs around the perimeter. It's the widest off the Ukraine, then it plunges down for seven thousand feet. The thin layer near the top is rich with life. But below the five-hundred-fifty-foot mark, there is no oxygen and the sea is lifeless. It's the biggest body of dead water in the world. Even worse, the depths are loaded with hydrogen sulfide. One breath of the stuff can kill you. If that mass of poison ever rose to the surface, it would release a cloud that would kill every living thing in and around the sea.'

'The Turks weren't kidding about the sea of death,' Zavala said.

Paul projected a map that had a dotted line running around the inner edge of the sea. 'Kreisman said the ship was found around the four-hundred-foot level. That would put it at the edge of the continental shelf. Any deeper and the ship wouldn't be there. Wooden vessels are perfectly preserved in the depths, because there is no oxygen to sustain wood-boring worms, but the chemicals eat away at metal.'

'The ship would have been reduced to its basic molecules,' Austin said.

'That's right. That gorge he talked about is probably an extended riverbed. The continental shelf is smooth and gradually dips seaward, pretty much like the ensign's description. The decay from all those organisms has formed pockets of methane gas. Presumably, a diver could be insulated from that type of thing, but there might still be some danger in diving in a poisonous environment.'

Gunn had been absorbing the discussion. He rose from his seat and borrowed the laser pointer.

'Let's see what we've got. The *NR-1* was hijacked here.' He ran the red dot from the Aegean through the Bosporus. 'This is where they heard sounds of ship traffic. He moved the pointer along the edge of the continental shelf. 'Here's our mystery ship, according to the GPS.'

Using his cursor, Paul drew an *X* at the location Gunn indicated.

'Someone went to a great deal of trouble to salvage that ship,' Austin said. 'Maybe it holds the key to unraveling this whole mess.'

Gunn turned to the captain. 'How soon can we haul anchor and get moving?'

Atwood had kept silent throughout the ensign's presentation and the NUMA team's discussion. He smiled and said, 'You people have been so engrossed in the Black Sea, you didn't notice me calling the bridge. We're on our way. Should be on-site in the morning.'

The faint vibration of the engines came through the deck under their feet. Gunn got up. 'I'm going to hit the sack. Tomorrow could be a long day.'

Austin got directions to his cabin, then told Joe that he'd catch up with him later. When Austin was alone, he sat at the table and stared at the lines and squiggles of the Black Sea map projected on the screen as if they were letters of an unknown language whose secret could be unlocked by a Rosetta Stone. His eye fastened on the X that marked the position of the mystery ship.

He sorted through the events that had brought him to this place on a NUMA vessel in pursuit of *what*? He felt like someone making his way through a snake pit, trying to pick out the nonpoisonous snakes from the vipers. He snapped off the lights and left the conference room. As he made his way to his cabin, he had a depressing thought. Maybe they were *all* poisonous.

20

The gray dawn light streaming through the cabin porthole woke Austin up. He glanced over at Zavala, who was in the next bunk, no doubt lost in a dreamworld of red Corvettes and beautiful blond statisticians. He envied his partner's ability to drop off to sleep, snooze soundly through the night and wake up fresh and ready for action. Austin's own slumber had been fitful, disturbed by churning thoughts, as if his brain were searching for answers hidden in the maze of his subconscious.

Levering himself out of bed, Austin went over to the sink and splashed cold water on his face. He dressed quickly, pulling on jeans, a heavy sweatshirt and a windbreaker, and stepped out of the cabin. A cool morning breeze from off the water smacked him in the face and blew away the lingering shreds of sleep. The sun's eyebrow was starting to peek over the eastern horizon, its soft rays bathing the clouds in a reddish gold light.

With the *Argo* steaming at fifteen knots, Austin hung over the railing and stared out at the opaque surface of the sea, listening to the soothing hiss of the waves against the hull. Seabirds skimmed the foam like windblown confetti. It was hard to believe that a few hundred feet below was the most lifeless place on the planet. The Black Sea was a big puddle of dead water, but Austin knew that an abyss with far more reason to be feared was the remorseless evil that lurked in the depths of the human mind. Austin shivered, not entirely from the cold, and headed back into the ship.

As he stepped through the door into the warmth of the mess hall, the mouth-watering bouquet of coffee, fried eggs and bacon provided an antidote for his morbid mood, and his spirits improved. Except for the blue sea visible through the windows, the ship's dining area could have been a small-town breakfast hangout where the locals have coffee mugs with their names on them. Sleepy-eyed crew members coming off the night watch occupied a few tables.

Austin grabbed a coffee to go. On his way to the bridge, he encountered the Trouts, who had come down for breakfast earlier and taken a tour of the ship. Together they climbed up to the wheelhouse, where the wraparound windows gave a wide view of the bow and deck.

Rudi Gunn, an early riser going back to his navy days, stood near a bank of instruments and monitors, talking to Captain Atwood. He smiled broadly when he saw his colleagues. 'Good morning, everyone. I was about to go looking for you. The captain was going over his plans for the wreck site.'

'Looking forward to hearing them,' Austin said. 'How soon will we be on-site?'

Atwood pointed to a circular gray screen with

white concentric circles etched into the glass. Specks of gray indicated the GPS readings from an antenna that picked up information from the network of twenty-four satellites orbiting the earth at a height of eleven thousand miles. A digital readout next to the screen displayed current latitude and longitude. The system could place the ship within thirty to forty-five feet of its target.

'We should be on-site in about fifteen minutes if the navigational coordinates from the sub sailor's Dick Tracy wristwatch are on the mark.'

'You weren't joking when you said we'd be there first thing this morning,' Austin said.

'The *Argo* may look like a workhorse, but she's got racing genes in her blood.'

'What are your plans for the initial survey?'

'We'll map out the general area with side-scan sonar using our new UUV, then take a closer look. The crew is down on the deck getting things ready.' The Unmanned Untethered Vehicle, or UUV, was one of the hottest developments in undersea exploration.

Paul asked to see a chart. The captain pushed aside a blue curtain that divided the wheelhouse from the smaller chart room. A map of the Black Sea was spread out on the table. 'We're here,' Atwood said, putting his finger on a spot off the western shore of the Black Sea.

Trout's tall form bent over the chart. 'We're over

the edge of a shallow underwater shelf that wraps around the shoreline past Romania and the Danube delta, the Bosporus and around to Crimea in the north.' He turned to his wife. 'Gamay can fill us in on the biological and archaeological angles.'

Gamay took over. 'The shelf Paul talked about is an incredibly productive fishery. It's home to salmon, beluga sturgeon, turbot. You'll find dolphins here and bonito, although the stocks are down. Some say the Turks have overfished the sea, but they say it's European Union pollution coming from the Danube. What's not in dispute is the fact that below a fluctuating depth of around four hundred fifty feet, there is no life. Ninety percent of the sea is sterile. With the fish population down, huge red tides and jellyfish infestations have come in. People are concerned enough to actually start doing something.'

'That's how NUMA came to be involved,' Captain Atwood said. 'We were collecting information for a joint Russian-Turkish project.'

'I was wondering why you didn't have representatives from either country aboard,' Paul said.

'On earlier trips the government observers spent most of their time telling the ships where they *couldn't* conduct surveys. Admiral Sandecker insisted on carte blanche when NUMA was asked to lend a hand. Which meant no observers on this preliminary survey. Between his prestige and their desperation, he was able to hold his own.'

'These countries have a good reason to be desperate,' Gamay said. 'The pollution is creating the conditions for a "turnover." If the dead water rises to the top, everything in the sea and around the rim could be wiped out.'

'There's nothing like the threat of extinction to get people off their butts,' Gunn remarked.

'That would do it for me,' Austin said.

Trout drew his finger along the map. 'The bottom here will be covered with black mud over clay that marks the change of the ancient lake to a sea. When you get beyond the edge of the shelf, we find deep submarine canyons carved into the steep shelf slope. Ten thousand years ago, the sea level was a thousand feet lower than it is now. The Flood theory suggests that sixty thousand square miles were inundated by the waters of the Mediterranean.'

'Which made anyone with a boat very popular,' Austin said.

Gamay said, 'This deals directly with our situation. As Paul explained last night, ship worms can't survive in the deep water, so wooden wrecks will be perfectly preserved for thousands of years. And steel ships will disintegrate.'

A crewman called the captain into the wheelhouse. Atwood excused himself. A minute later, he returned, his face wreathed in a wide grin.

'We're on target. Our mystery ship should be right below our radio antenna.'

Gunn said, 'Remind me to send a bouquet of

flowers to the young woman who gave her sailor boy a GPS watch.'

Austin looked out at the sea stretching to the horizon and thought of the wasted time that could have been spent in a fruitless search for the ship. 'I've got a better idea,' Austin said. 'Let's send her a whole greenhouse.'

Zavala arrived and they went down to the starboard deck, where sunlight gleamed off the metal skin of a small torpedo that rested in an aluminum rack. The tall man disconnecting a computer modem attached to the device was Mark Murphy, the *Argo*'s expert in remote-operated undersea vehicles.

Murphy was a nonconformist who scorned the NUMA work coveralls for his own uniform: faded jean cutoffs, chamois shirt worn over a T-shirt, scuffed work boots and a short-billed baseball cap. Both his cap and T-shirt had the word *Argonaut* printed on them. He was in his early fifties, and a thick salt-and-pepper beard covered his chin, but his ruddy sunburned face glowed with boyish enthusiasm.

He saw Zavala gazing at the torpedo and said, 'Be my guest.'

'Thanks.' Zavala ran his fingertips lightly over the wide stripes of green, yellow and black painted on the metal skin. 'Sexy,' he said with a low whistle. '*Very* sexy.'

'You'll have to excuse my friend,' Austin said. 'He hasn't had shore leave for at least twenty-four hours.'

'I understand perfectly,' Murphy replied. 'This

baby is *hot*. Wait'll you see the way she performs.'

Austin was amused but not surprised to hear the two men fawn over the device. Zavala was a brilliant marine engineer who had designed or directed construction of many underwater vehicles. Murphy was the *Argo*'s expert in their use. To them, the clean lines of the compact object cradled in its aluminum rack were as sensual as the curves of the female body.

Austin could understand their passion. The UUV was only 62 inches long, 7.5 inches in diameter and weighed a mere eighty pounds. But the bantam-sized device represented the cutting edge of undersea exploration, a vehicle that could operate almost independently of its shipboard controllers. This model was developed by the Woods Hole Oceanographic Institution, which had dubbed it SAHRV, for Semi-Autonomous Hydrographic Reconnaissance Vehicle.

'We're about ready to launch,' Murphy said. 'We've dropped two separate transducers over the side, one at each corner of the survey area. That sets up the navigational net. The vehicle talks constantly with the transducers that tell it where it is at all times. The data she picks up will be recorded on a hard drive and downloaded later.'

'Why not telemeter the information directly back to the ship?' Austin asked.

'We could, but the data would take too long to make it through the water. I've told the vehicle to survey ten one-hundred-foot lanes at high resolution for a start. She'll run at five point five knots around ninety feet off the bottom. The collision avoidance sonar will make sure she goes over or around any big obstacles.'

Murphy reached over and pressed a magnetic switch on the side of the vehicle. The battery-powered stainless steel propeller whirred softly. With the help of another crewman, Murphy gently lowered the rack into the water.

The *Argo* bristled with an amazing array of winches and cranes to handle the variety of electronic eyes and ears and hands, manned and unmanned submersibles the scientists on board dropped into the ocean. One crane, so powerful it could lift a house, also had weak links that would deliberately break under undue stress – that was to prevent them from sinking in case the ship hooked onto an undersea mountain.

Most of the heavy equipment was lowered through the moon pool, a center section of the *Argo*'s hull that opened to the sea through huge sliding doors. With the UUV, however, it was only a matter of lowering it over the side. The propeller grabbed water and the vehicle took off like a fish released from a hook. It headed away from the ship and arced into a preprogrammed thirty-foot circle when it hit open sea.

'She'll go around four times to calibrate the compass,' Murphy explained. 'The vehicle is talking to the navigational net now, getting its bearings through triangulation.' As they watched, the vehicle made a final circle and disappeared below the surface. 'She's heading off to do her first lane.'

'What do we do now?' Austin said.

Murphy gave them his big-toothed grin. 'We go have some coffee and doughnuts.'

The undersea vehicle moved back and forth above the ocean floor in a lawn-mowing pattern, its path on the ocean floor displayed on the computer screen. When its task was finished, the UUV homed in on a third transducer like a puppy who'd heard the word *bone*. The vehicle nosed up to the side of the ship, where it was snagged in a special pickup rack and lifted back on deck. Murphy hooked up a modem and transferred all the data from the dripping vehicle to his laptop computer. Then he disconnected the computer.

Tucking the laptop under his arm, Murphy led the way to the conference room, where he set the laptop down on a table and connected it to a large-screen monitor. The computer's SeaSone software began to generate high-resolution sonar images in slow motion onto the screen, and the pictures of the seafloor as recorded by the UUV flowed down from the top of the monitor like twin waterfalls. Latitude, longitude and position were displayed to the right of the screen. Murphy adjusted the screen's color control to a yellow-brown that was easy on the eyes.

The seafloor was largely unmarked. Occasionally, a boulder showed up or dark and light patches indicated differences in sediment. Halfway through its fourth track, the sonar caught two straight lines joined at an angle. All eyes were focused on the monitor as the vehicle finished the track, turned and came back. Murphy froze the picture.

'Bingo!' he said.

The unmistakable image of a ship stood out in sharp relief. With a click of the computer mouse, Murphy zoomed in the picture. The darks and lights became doors, hatches and portholes. The computer compiled the ship's measurements. 'She's two hundred fifty feet long,' Murphy said.

Austin pointed to a shadow on the hull. 'Can you zoom in on that section?'

Murphy obliged with a click of the mouse, and the section Austin had noticed appeared as a small box to one side of the screen. The scientist played around with the resolution until the hole in the side of the hull near the waterline was clearly visible.

He ran off a full-color copy of the survey area, showing the target hits, and spread it out on a table. 'She's at four hundred fifty feet,' he said. 'Here's where the three-hundred-foot bottom begins to fall away into a canyon. The ship is on the slope, just past the lip of the cut. We're lucky. A few hundred feet farther and the wreck would have been lost forever from metal deterioration.'

'Good job, Murphy,' Captain Atwood said. Turning to the others, he said, 'I've got a crew ready to launch an ROV from the moon pool.' A robotic vehicle. They all moved to a small room that contained the control consoles for vehicles operating out of the moon pool. Gesturing toward a computer console, the captain said to Gunn, 'Would you care to handle the controls, Commander?'

Gunn's academic demeanor cloaked a personality that enjoyed action, and he had been chafing in his role as a bystander since boarding the ship. He was an experienced hand at running an ROV and needed no prodding. 'I'd like that very much. Thank you, Captain.'

'Whenever you're ready.'

Gunn sat behind the control console and familiarized himself with the instruments and the feel of the joystick that controlled the ROV. Then he grinned and rubbed his hands together. 'Drop 'er in.'

The captain unclipped a small radio from his belt and gave a command. A moment later, the screen flickered to life and projected a view of the cavernous moon pool through the video camera in the nose of the ROV. The camera seemed to flood as the ROV was lowered into the pool. A diver wearing a wet suit came into view as he uncoupled the line attached to the lifting crane. Then he was gone, replaced by a cloud of bubbles and the deepening blue of the sea, as the ROV sank slowly beneath the open bottom of the ship.

A thousand-foot Kevlar-jacketed tether connected the Benthos Stingray ROV to the ship. The tether transmitted Gunn's commands to the operating system and relayed the video picture back to the screen. The *Argo* carried larger and more powerful ROVs, but after hearing the *NR-1* story, the captain had thought they would need a smaller vehicle that could be maneuvered into tight spaces. The vehicle was the size and shape of a large suitcase. Although the ROV was relatively small, it carried video and digital cameras and a manipulator arm.

Moving the joystick with a skilled hand, Gunn angled the ROV into a long dive. The vehicle used the navigational net established for the UUV to find its way directly to the target. Color faded from the water, as each descending fathom took the ROV farther from the dappled surface light. Gunn switched on the twin 150-watt quartz halogen lights, but even their powerful beams were swallowed by the thickening gloom.

The ROV smoothly descended to three hundred feet, then leveled out a few yards above the ocean floor. The vehicle bucked a slight bottom current that kept its speed under a knot as it moved forward above the black mud. Then the bottom dropped away and the ROV soared over the lip of the undersea canyon so suddenly that everyone in the room felt a slight wave of queasiness. Gunn nosed the ROV downward, keeping the vehicle parallel to the sharp slope. The ROV's side-scan sonar painted the target on a separate monitor until it was close enough for visual inspection. Gunn goosed the vertical thrusters, and the vehicle rose slowly above the vessel.

The ship lay at an angle on the sloping side of the canyon, the bottom section of hull embedded in mud. The ROV descended several yards and moved alongside the hulk at main-deck level, past a row of portholes, including some that were still open. Barnacles covered most of the ship and heightened its spectral aspect. Reddish patches of antifouling paint peeked out here and there. The wooden wheelhouse had disintegrated and the decks had rotted away. The lifeboat davits were empty, and wire shrouds hung with seaweed. A pile of rusty debris was all that remained of the collapsed funnel.

The ship was a metal cadaver, useless except for the schools of fish that nosed through passageways where humans had once walked. To Austin, who watched the screen with an expression of fascination on his bronzed features, this sad and lifeless hunk of rusty metal was a living thing. Although there were no hands to close the hatches forced open by the pressure of escaping air, Austin could almost hear the creak of the booms and the throbbing engine as the ship plowed through the seas. In his mind's eye, he pictured the helmsman standing with feet braced on a wooden grating, hands on the wheel while crewmen went about their business on deck or fought the inevitable boredom of shipboard life.

Austin asked Gunn to steer the ROV around to the stern. As Ensign Kreisman described it, the hull was covered with growth that hid the ship's markings. Gunn poked the vehicle into several nooks and crannies, hoping to come across a manufacturer's metal plate, but they found nothing.

Austin turned to Gamay. 'What's our resident nautical archaeologist have to say about this old gal?'

Gamay pinched her chin in thought as she stared at the ghostly images on the glowing screen.

'My specialty was Greek and Roman wooden ships, and if you asked me to ID a bireme or a trireme I might be of more help. I'll venture a few guesses, though.' The camera was moving along the midships section, where the rusty steel plating had buckled and was clear of barnacles. 'Those are riveted steel plates. By the 1940s, shipbuilders had switched to welding. The booms indicate that she's probably a cargo ship. She's an old-timer, judging from her lines, maybe built in the late eighteen-hundreds or around the turn of the century.'

Austin asked Gunn to move the ROV around to the damaged side. The ship leaned downhill, and from this angle it looked as if it could come crashing over at any second. Gunn brought the ROV straight in until the hole filled almost the entire screen. The lights probing the ship's innards picked out twisted pipes and steel columns.

'Damage assessment, Rudi?' Austin said.

'From the way those edges are curled, I'd say a projectile hit the engine room. Too high for a torpedo. Probably a shell from a big gun.'

'Who would sink a harmless old freighter?' Zavala asked.

'Maybe someone who thought she wasn't so harmless,' Austin said. 'Let's check out the cabin section that Ensign Kreisman told us about.'

Gunn tweaked the controls, and the ROV rose abovedecks. It was clear from the grin on his face that Rudi was having a ball. He brought the vehicle around, taking care not to catch the tether in the foremast or booms. The ROV moved past the bridge, then stopped and hovered in front of a dark rectangular opening. Unlike the ragged cavity in the hull, the edges of the hole were relatively even from the cutting torch. Gunn brought the ROV to within a few feet of the opening. The lights picked out the framework of a bunk and the remnants of a metal chair and desk that lay in a tumbled heap.

'Can we go inside?' Austin asked.

'I'm getting a side current that could make things tricky, but I'll see what I can do.' Gunn maneuvered the vehicle left and right, then when it was directly centered, he put it through the hole as easily as a seamstress threading a needle. The ROV was capable of turning within its own radius, and Gunn executed a three-hundred-sixty-degree turn. The camera captured slimy gray piles of debris. Gunn probed a corner with the ROV's manipulator, stirring up a powdery cloud of rust. Then the ROV got tangled and wouldn't move. Gunn waited for the dust to settle and wriggled the ROV until it broke free of the overhead wire that had snagged a projection of its protective shielding.

'What do you think?' Gunn said, turning to Austin.

'I think anything of value has been removed. We'll have to piece together the story from the ship itself, not what's in it.' He pointed to a wall shelf. 'What's that?'

Austin's sharp eye had caught a dark, squarish object. Gunn used the manipulator to clear away a pile of amorphous grayish-brown trash and made several fruitless attempts to grab the object. It kept slipping away like a prize in a penny-arcade game. Gunn set his jaw in determination and pushed the object into a corner where he could get a firm grasp on it, then he backed the ROV out of the cabin and moved the manipulator to put the prize directly in front of the lights. The claw clutched a small, flat box.

'I'm bringing her up,' he said. He reversed the ROV's direction and sent the vehicle scuttling back to the *Argo*. Minutes later, the lights of the moon pool appeared on the screen. The captain ordered the ROV's handlers to stabilize the artifact in seawater and send it to the vehicle control room. Soon a technician arrived, carrying a white plastic bucket. Gamay, whose background in nautical archaeology made her the most experienced conservator on board, asked for a soft brush. She removed the box from the bucket and gently placed it on the floor. Then, with soft strokes, she brushed a thumbnail patch of the black patina to reveal the gleam of metal.

'It's made of silver,' she said, and continued to

work until fifty percent of the top was cleaned. The metal was embossed with a double-headed eagle. Gamay examined the clasp. 'I might be able to get this open, but I don't dare because I could destroy what's inside when it hits air. It may need intense conservation.' She glanced at the captain.

'The *Argo* is primarily set up for biological and geological survey,' Atwood said. 'There's another NUMA ship called the *Sea Hunter* doing archaeological work not far from here. They might be able to help.'

'I'm sure they can. I did some research on the *Sea Hunter* a couple of years ago,' Austin said. 'She's the sister ship of the *Argo*, isn't she?'

'That's right. The two vessels are almost identical.'

'We should get this box there soon,' Gamay said. 'I'll stabilize it in seawater as best I can.' She glanced with longing at the box. 'Damn! Now I'm *really* curious about the contents.'

'How about running it through the X-ray machine in the infirmary?' Austin suggested. 'That might partially satisfy your curiosity.'

Gamay carefully replaced the box in the bucket, and the technician carried it off. 'You're brilliant,' she said.

'You may not think so after you hear my next idea,' Austin replied. He outlined his plan.

'Worth a try,' Atwood said, and clicked on his hand radio. Before long the screen flickered into life and the moon pool appeared again. The ROV was being put back into the water. The dive was a repeat of the first, with the diver, bubbling foam and dark water.

Gunn put the ROV on a direct trajectory to the wreck. Before long, the vehicle was coming from behind the ship. Gunn worked the joystick, and the mechanical arm unfolded and extended to where it could clearly be seen in the glare of the halogen lights. Watching Gamay clean the artifact had given Austin the idea. Clasped in the metal claw was a metal-bristled brush used in preparing the *Argo*'s hull for painting.

The ROV made several attempts to clear away the barnacles. Newton's law of action-causing-reaction kicked in, and the brushing pushed the ROV away from the hull. The ship did not want to give up its identity without a fight. After forty-five minutes, they had succeeded in clearing away a patch about a foot in diameter. A portion of a letter embossed in white was visible. It could have been an *O* or any of several other letters.

'So much for brilliant ideas,' Austin said.

Gunn was equally frustrated. His forehead glistened with beads of perspiration. He'd been trying to counteract the push by revving up the ROV's thrusters. At one point, he lost control and the ROV slammed into the hull. A layer of gunk a couple of feet across dropped off to reveal an *S*.

'There's concretion under the marine growth,'

Gamay said. 'That's why you can't brush the stuff away.'

'Can you bang off another chunk?' Austin asked. He turned to the captain. 'With your permission, of course.'

Atwood shrugged. 'Hell, I'm as curious about this old hulk as you are. If it takes a few dents in a piece of NUMA equipment to do the job, let's do it.'

His face flushed as he remembered that NUMA's second-in-command was sitting at the controls. But Gunn had no compunctions. He gritted his teeth and rammed the ship again and again, as if he were trying to break down a castle door. Pieces of thin brittle concretion began to flake off, to reveal more letters. After one sharp jab, a huge piece of the covering dropped off to reveal the ship's name in Cyrillic letters.

Austin studied the letters illuminated in the glare of the ROV's lights and shook his head.

'My Russian is rusty, but the name of the ship seems to be *Odessa Star.*'

'Doesn't ring a bell,' Atwood said. 'Have you ever heard of her?'

'Nope,' Austin said. 'But I'll bet I know somebody who *has.*'

22

Washington, DC

St Julian Perlmutter had spent most of his day researching a twin-hulled Civil War ironclad for the Smithsonian Institute, and the work had made him hungry. But then, practically *everything* made Perlmutter hungry. An ordinary human faced with this state of affairs would have satisfied his needs by slapping a wad of cold cuts between two slabs of bread. Not so Perlmutter. He indulged his addiction for German cooking with a plate of pig's knuckles and sauerkraut, paired with a light-bodied Reisling Kabinett plucked from his four-thousand-bottle wine cellar. He dined using silver and china from the French liner *Normandie*. He was sublimely happy. The mood persisted even when his telephone gave off a ring like a ship's bell.

He patted his mouth and thick gray beard with a monogrammed linen napkin, and reached with a plump hand for the phone. 'St Julian Perlmutter here,' he said pleasantly. 'State your business in a brief manner.'

'I'm sorry. I must have the wrong number,' the voice on the phone said. 'The gentleman I'm trying to reach would never answer the phone so politely.'

'Ah *ha!*' Perlmutter's voice ratcheted up the decibel scale to a supersonic boom. 'You *should* be sorry, Kurt. What happened to *imam?*'

'Can't say I know anyone by that name. Have you tried Istanbul missing persons?'

'Don't toy with me over such an important matter, you impertinent young snit,' Perlmutter boomed, his sky blue eyes twinkling in the ruddy face. 'You know perfectly well you promised to get me an authentic recipe for *imam bayidi.* Translated loosely as "the imam fainted," because the old boy was overcome with delight when he tasted the dish. You *did* remember, didn't you?'

Austin kept on Perlmutter's good side by searching out authentic recipes on his travels around the world. 'Of *course* I remembered. I've been trying to persuade one of the finest chefs in Istanbul to part with his recipe and will send it to you forthwith. I wouldn't want you to waste away to nothing.'

Perlmutter roared with laughter, the belly laugh amplified by the nearly four hundred pounds of flesh adhering to his sturdy frame. 'There's not much danger of *that* happening. Are you still in Turkey?'

'In the neighborhood. I'm on a NUMA ship in the Black Sea.'

'Still on your vacation cruise?'

'Vacation's over. I'm back at work and need a favor. Could you dig up something on an old cargo ship named the *Odessa Star*? It went down in the

Black Sea, but I don't know when. That's all I can tell you for now.'

'Tracking down your ship should be no problem, not with such a helpful description,' Perlmutter responded with dry humor. 'Please tell me what you *do* know about it.' Perlmutter jotted down the sparse information Austin was able to give. 'I'll do my best, although I may be weak with hunger, a condition easily remedied by the receipt of a certain Turkish recipe.'

Austin again assured Perlmutter that the recipe was in the pipeline, and hung up. He felt guilty for shading the truth somewhat. With all that was going on, he had forgotten Perlmutter's request. He turned to Captain Atwood. 'Does anybody in the galley know anything about Turkish cooking?'

While Austin tried to track down the *imam*, thousands of miles away in his N Street carriage house behind two vine-encrusted Georgetown town houses, Perlmutter was grinning with pleasure. Despite his bluster, he enjoyed a challenge. The Smithsonian would have to wait, although the concept of an obscure twin-hulled ironclad was intriguing. He glanced around the huge combination living room, bedroom and study at the stacks of books occupying every square inch. Although the space looked like a librarian's nightmare, Perlmutter's apartment contained the finest collection of historical ship literature ever assembled.

Perlmutter had read every volume he owned at

least twice. His encyclopedic mind had absorbed a numbing number of facts, each connected like the links of a Web site to related caches. He could pluck a book from a dusty pile, run his finger down the spine and remember practically every page.

He knitted his brow in thought; something was eluding him, lurking in a shadowed corner of his mind beyond the periphery of consciousness. He was sure he'd heard of the *Odessa Star* before Austin mentioned it. He would find it in five minutes or not at all. He dug through his piles of books and periodicals, mumbling under his breath. Damned if he could remember. Must be getting old. He rummaged for an hour before giving up. He picked a card out of his telephone number file and dialed the international code for London and a number.

A moment later, a clipped British accent answered, 'Guildhall Library.'

Perlmutter gave his name and asked for an assistant cataloger he had dealt with on previous calls. Like many English institutions, the Guildhall Library had been around for centuries. The original library dated back to 1423 and was acknowledged worldwide for a history collection that went back to the eleventh century.

The library also had the finest collection of wine and food books in the United Kingdom, a fact that had not escaped Perlmutter's attention. But it was the Guildhall's extensive maritime records that Perlmutter often drew upon in his research.

England's naval tradition, and the wide reach of the British Empire colonies and trade, made the collection a treasure trove of information about practically every seagirt country in the world.

The cataloguer, a pleasant young woman named Elizabeth Bosworth, came on the line. 'Julian. How nice to hear from you again.'

'Thank you, Elizabeth. All goes well with you, I trust.'

'Very well, thank you. I've been quite busy indexing agreements of colonial registered vessels dating back to the seventeen hundreds.'

'I hope I'm not calling at a bad time.'

'Of *course* not, Julian. The material is fascinating, but the work does get a bit tedious at times. What can I do for you?'

'I'm trying to track down some information on an old cargo ship named the *Odessa Star* and wondered if you could tickle the Lloyd's file for me.'

The Guildhall Library held all the shipping records for the giant international marine insurance underwriter prior to 1985. Lloyd's of London had been established in 1811 to provide a universal system of 'intelligence and superintendence' in all the principal ports of the world. To accomplish this goal, Lloyd's had set up a network of agents. By the turn of the century, the agency had more than four hundred agents and five hundred subagents scattered around the globe. Their reports on marine casualties, shipowners, shipping movements and voyages were contained in the library's files, where they were accessible to historians like Perlmutter.

'I'd be happy to look into it for you,' Bosworth replied. Her enthusiasm was due only in part to the generous contributions, far and above the usual research fee, that Perlmutter consistently made to the library. She shared his love of sea history and admired his book collection. More than once, she had gone to him with queries of her own.

Apologizing for providing so little information, Perlmutter relayed the facts outlined by Austin. Bosworth said she would get back to him as soon as she could. Perlmutter hung up and returned to his research for the Smithsonian. With bulldog perseverance, he unearthed a rough sketch of the Confederate twin-hulled ironclad and was typing out a report on his computer when the phone rang. It was Bosworth.

'Julian, I've found some references to the *Odessa Star*. I'll fax them to you.'

'Thank you so much, Elizabeth. In return, the next time I'm in town I'll take you to lunch at Simpson's on the Strand.'

'It's a date,' she said. 'You know where to find me.'

They said their goodbyes and, a minute later, the fax buzzed and spat out several sheets of paper. Perlmutter examined the top sheet. It was the report of the Lloyd's agent in Novorossiysk, a Mr A. Zubrin. It was dated April of 1917.

'This is to report that the *Odessa Star*, freighter of

ten thousand tons, carrying a cargo of coal from Caucasus, enroute from Odessa to Constantinople 1917, February, did not arrive at its destination and is presumed lost. Have confirmed such with G. Bozdag, Lloyd's agent, Constantinople. No report of ship at any Black Sea port. Vessel owned by Fauchet, Ltd., of Marseilles, France, which has put in a claim. Last survey, June 1916, showed ship in desperate need of repair. Please advise as to claim.'

The other papers included a three-way correspondence among the agent, the central office in London and the French owners. The French were insisting on full payment of the claim. Lloyd's resisted, citing the perilous condition of the ship, but eventually settled for a third, most of it the value of the cargo.

Perlmutter turned to a ceiling-to-floor bookcase and extracted a thick volume whose burgundy cloth cover was worn with use. He leafed through the registry of French shipping companies. Fauchet had gone out of business in 1922. Perlmutter grunted. Small wonder, the way they neglected their ships. He replaced the registry and picked up another document Bosworth had sent him. It was a copy of a book review from the *London Times* dating to the thirties. The headline read: VETERAN SEA CAPTAIN REVEALS SECRETS OF THE BLACK SEA. He put the review aside and turned to the note from Bosworth.

'Dear Julian. Hope this material is of help. I found a reference to your mystery ship in a summary of archival material bequeathed to the library by the estate of Lord Dodson, who served for many years in the Foreign Office. It was a manuscript containing Dodson's memoirs, but it seems to have been withdrawn by the family. There was also mention of the *Odessa Star* in a book called *Life on the Black Sea*. We have a copy here and I can FedEx it to you if you wish.'

Perlmutter put the note down and went over to a shelf crammed to the gills with volumes of every size and description. He ran his pudgy fingers along a row of books and pulled out a small, slim volume with a leather cover handsomely embossed in gold leaf.

'Hah!' Perlmutter exclaimed in triumph. If he could have danced, he would have done a two-step. No longer worried about his temporary lapse of memory, he scribbled a note on a piece of paper and inserted it in the fax machine. 'No need to send book. Have it in my collection. Thanks.' As the message flew across the Atlantic, Perlmutter settled into a comfortable chair with a tumbler of iced hibiscus tea, a plate of crackers and white truffle paste by his side, and began to read.

A Russian ship captain named Popov had written the book in 1936. The captain had an eye for detail and a sense of humor, and Perlmutter found himself smiling frequently as Popov related his adventures with waterspouts and storms, leaky vessels, pirates and bandits, thievish merchants, knavish bureaucrats and mutinous crews.

The most poignant chapter was one entitled 'The

Little Mermaid.' Popov had been the skipper of a freighter carrying a cargo of lumber across the Black Sea. One night the lookout saw the flash of lights in the distance and heard what sounded like distant thunder, although the sky was clear. Thinking someone might be in trouble, Popov investigated.

'When my ship arrived several minutes later, we encountered an oil slick, and a cloud of black greasy smoke hung on the water. There was debris floating everywhere and, more horrifying, burned and mutilated bodies. Despite my entreaties, my crew refused to recover the corpses, saying they were bad luck, and dead and gone in any case. I called for Stop engines and we listened. All was silent. Then came what sounded like the cry of a seabird. I enlisted my loyal first mate and launched a boat. We made our way through the sad flotsam toward the sound. Imagine our surprise when the lamplight fell upon the golden tresses of a young girl. She was clinging to a wooden crate and, had we arrived minutes later, would have frozen to death in the frigid black water. We pulled her into the boat and cleaned the oil from her face. My mate exclaimed: "Why, she looks like a mermaid!" My crewmen, seeing our lovely burden, put aside their rebellious emotions and ministered to the girl. When she recovered, she proved herself to be quite well-spoken. She conversed easily in French with one of our crew. She said she had been traveling with her family on a ship called the *Odessa Star*. Although she recalled the ship's name, she could not remember her own but thought it might be Maria. Of her life before the ship went down and the circumstances of its sinking, she could remember nothing. The tough old salts aboard my ship could not have been more tender in their regard and called her "the little mermaid."'

The captain reported the incident when he got back to port, but strangely he told the authorities nothing about the girl. His omission was explained in the epilogue.

'Some of my dear readers may have wondered what became of the little mermaid. Now that many years have passed, I feel free to reveal the truth. When I found the girl floating barely alive on the billows, I had been married five years. In all that time, my lovely young wife had been unable to conceive a child. Upon my return to the Caucasus, we adopted Maria as our own. She was a joy to both of us before my wife died, and became a lovely young woman who, in time, married and had children of her own. Now, in my retirement, I feel that it is time to reveal to the world the precious gift the sea gave to me after years of inflicting so many hardships.'

Perlmutter put the book down and picked up the *Times* review. The reviewer had been critical of the writing, but intrigued by the story of the mermaid, which he described at great length. Perlmutter guessed that some sharp-eyed Lloyd's operative had seen the reference to the *Odessa Star* and attached it to the claim file on the missing ship.

The captain's account had been so fascinating Perlmutter had forgotten his snack. He remedied the situation quickly by slathering twenty dollars' worth of truffle onto a cracker. Back once more in the present, Perlmutter stared out the window as he savored the delicate earthy taste. Then he remembered Bosworth's comment about Lord Dodson. He read her note again and wondered why the Dodson family would have pulled the archives from the library.

Despite his ungainly bulk, Perlmutter was very much a man of action. He picked up the phone and dialed a couple of acquaintances in London. Within minutes, he learned that Lord Dodson's grandson, himself a lord, was alive and living in the Cotswolds. Perlmutter got a phone number, although his source made him swear under pain of eating at Burger King not to reveal where he had gotten it. Perlmutter called and identified himself to the man who answered the phone.

'This is Lord Dodson. You say you're a marine historian?' He sounded bemused but pleasant, speaking in the clipped accent of the British upper class.

'That's correct. I came across a reference to your grandfather's memoirs while doing some research on a ship called the *Odessa Star*. The library apparently relinquished the material at the request of your family. I wonder when the material might be going back to Guildhall.'

There was a silence on the other end. Then Dodson said, 'Never! I mean, some of the material is much too personal in nature. You must understand that, Mr Perlman.' He sounded flustered.

'The name is Perl*mutter*, if you don't mind, Lord Dodson. Surely the historical material could be made separate from the personal.'

'I'm sorry, Mr Perlmutter', Dodson said, getting his voice under control. 'It's all part and parcel. It would do *no* one any good and cause a great deal of painful embarrassment if this material were made public.'

'Forgive me for being obtuse, but I understand that he willed *all* the material to the library to be put in the archives.'

'Yes, that's true. But you have to understand my grandfather. He was a man of towering rectitude.' Catching the unintentional comparison to his own character, Dodson said, 'What I mean was that he was naïve in many ways.'

'He couldn't have been too naïve to hold a high post in the Foreign Office.'

Dodson laughed nervously. 'You Americans can be *damnably* persistent. Look Mr Perlmutter, I don't wish to be rude, but I must terminate this conversation. Thank you for your interest. Good-bye.'

The phone went dead. Perlmutter stared at it for a moment and shook his head. *Strange.* Why would the old boy be so upset at an innocent query? What secret could be so painful after so many years? Well, he had done his best. He punched out the number Austin had given him. He would let others determine why the *Odessa Star* could upset someone more than eighty years after the ship had gone to her grave in the Black Sea.

23

Moscow, Russia

The nightclub was a short walk from Gorky Park, in a narrow alley that had once been a rat-infested flophouse for vodka-soaked human derelicts who used trash-can covers as their pillows. The drunks had been displaced by swarms of young people who looked as if they had stepped off a UFO. The crowds gathered each night outside a blue door lit by a single lamp. The unmarked door was the entrance to a Moscow night spot so trendy it didn't even have a name.

The enterprising young Muscovite who'd founded the club had seen the potential in bringing together Moscow's crass nouveau riche and the tackiest of Western pop culture. He'd modeled his venture on Club 54, the defunct but exclusive New York dive that had made international headlines before it drowned in a sea of tax woes and illegal drugs. The club was located in a cavernous space that had once housed a state-run sweatshop where underpaid workers toiled making ripoffs of American jeans. Clubgoers who were allowed inside found frenetic dance music, stroboscopic lighting and designer drugs supplied by the Russian Mafia, which had taken over the club after the original owner died of acute lead poisoning.

Petrov stood at the edge of the crowd, watching. The hopeful patrons wore bizarre costumes to attract the attention of the burly doorman in black leather who stood between them and drug-induced ecstasy. Petrov stared at the crowd in wonder for a moment, then shouldered his way between a young woman dressed in a translucent plastic halter and shorts and her male companion, who wore an aluminum foil bikini. The doorman glared at the approaching stranger like a bull mastiff watching a cat move in on its food dish. Petrov stopped short of the entrance and handed the doorman a folded sheet of paper.

He read the note with small, suspicious eyes, pocketed the hundred-dollar bill inside, then called another guard to take his place. He disappeared through the blue door and returned with a stocky middle-aged man dressed in the uniform of a Soviet naval officer, complete with high-peaked cap. The officer's chest was covered with more medals than anyone could have earned in several lifetimes. The guard pointed out Petrov. The man in uniform scanned the faces, scowling. Recognition flickered in his heavy-lidded eyes and he waved Petrov inside.

The full impact of the pulsating music almost knocked Petrov over. Out on the huge dance floor, a mass of bodies writhed as one to the monotonous rave beat from dozens of speakers that looked as if they had been used at Woodstock. He was grateful when the naval officer led him down a passageway into a storage room and closed the door so that the sound was a muffled throb.

'I come here sometimes to get away from that racket,' the naval officer said. The commanding voice Petrov remembered had become gravelly, and there was the stale smell of vodka on the man's breath. His thick lips curled in a smile. 'I thought you were dead, *tovarich.*'

'It's a miracle I'm *not* dead, Admiral,' Petrov said, eyeing the uniform from head to toe. 'Some things are worse than death.'

The admiral's smile vanished. 'You don't have to tell me how low I have fallen. I still have eyes. But no lower than someone who would amuse himself at the expense of an old comrade.'

'I agree, but I am not here for amusement. I came to ask your help and to offer mine.'

The admiral let out with a wet laugh. 'What help can *I* give you? I am nothing but a clown. The human garbage that runs this place keeps me around to entertain their patrons and remind them of the bad old days. Well, they were not bad for everyone.'

'True, my friend. Nor were they *good* for everyone,' Petrov said, bringing his hand up to the scar that disfigured his face.

'In the old days, we were *feared* and *respected.*'

'By our enemies,' Petrov said. 'Yet we were de-spised by our government, who quickly forgot our sacrifices when they no longer needed us for their dirty work. Your once-proud navy is a joke. Heroes like you are reduced to *this*.'

The admiral's shoulders sagged under the gaudy epaulets. Petrov realized he had gone too far.

'I'm sorry, Admiral.'

The admiral pulled a pack of Marlboros from a pocket and offered one to Petrov, who declined. 'Yes, I believe you are sorry. So are we all.' He stuck a cigarette in his mouth and lit up. 'Well, enough talk about the past. What's done is done. Are you sure you don't want a whore? Not all my job is for show. I get a commission and an employee discount. Capitalism is truly a wonderful thing.'

Petrov smiled as he recalled the razor-sharp wit from the days when he and the admiral had served on secret missions together. With the changes in government, the admiral's outspoken criticisms had not been well received by the new generation of thin-skinned bureaucrats. Petrov had survived by allowing himself to sink, undetected, into the governmental morass. The admiral had attempted to stand above the fray, and his demise mirrored that of his beloved navy.

'Later, maybe. But for now, I need information about a certain naval property.'

The admiral's eyes narrowed behind their thick folds. 'That covers a wide range.'

Petrov said one word: 'India.'

'The *submarine*? Well, well. What is your interest?'

'It's better if you don't know, Admiral.'

'You mean there is some risk involved here? Well, that must be worth something.'

'I'm prepared to pay for the information.'

The naval officer frowned, and a sad look came into his eyes. '*Listen* to me. I have become no better than the prostitutes who get their customers to buy them glasses of fake champagne.' He sighed. 'As for your questions, I'll do my best to answer them.'

'Thank you, Admiral. I once saw an India-class sub at its base, but never went aboard one. I understand it was designed to carry on operations similar to mine.'

'*Integration* is a swearword in the armed forces anywhere in the world. Ask the Americans how much money they've wasted in duplication because the army, navy, air force and marines wanted to have their own versions of virtually the same weapons systems. It was the same with us. The Soviet navy had no desire to share its assets with anyone else, especially a group like yours, which was beyond its control.' He smiled. 'Beyond *anyone's* control.'

'Supposedly, the sub was designed for underwater rescue.'

'Now there's a fairy tale! How many submarine crews were rescued by this thing? I'll tell you.' He curled his thumb and forefinger in a circle. '*Zero.* It certainly had the capacity to dive on a sunken sub. The India class could carry two deep submergence recovery vehicles in wells abaft the sail. They could fit onto the rescue hatch of a downed sub, but they weren't there to pull some poor sailor from the bottom of the sea. They were designed for clandestine intelligence gathering and to carry *Spetsnaz*.'

'Special forces?'

'Sure. When we did some snooping off Sweden, the subs carried armored tracked amphibious vehicles. They could crawl along the sea bottom like big bugs. It was a sweet ship, the India. Fast and very maneuverable.'

'The public literature said two were built?'

'That's correct. We had one in the northern fleet and another in the southern. Sometimes one would join the other for special operations.'

'What happened to them?'

'We lost the Cold War and they were withdrawn from service. They were scheduled for demolition.'

'So they were scrapped?'

The admiral grinned. 'Yes, of course.'

Petrov replied with a hike of an eyebrow.

'On paper, anyhow,' the admiral said. 'You know, everyone is worried about our nuclear bombs getting in some madman's hands. But while there's been all that talk, we've sold half our conventional weaponry, which can be as deadly under the proper circumstances. Nobody says anything about that.'

'*I'm* saying something. Where did the India-class subs go?'

'One *was* scrapped. The other was sold to a private buyer.'

'Do you know his name?'

'Of course, but what difference does it make? He represented a group that was obviously a straw for someone else. There could be many layers in between the buyer and the person who forked over the money.'

'But you have a suspicion about who bought it?'

'I'm pretty sure it stayed within the country. The buyer was an outfit called Volga Industries. They had an office in Moscow, but who knows where their parent companies were? Nobody really cared. They paid in cash.'

Petrov shook his head. 'How could someone so easily remove a war machine three hundred and fifty feet long?'

'It's done all the time. All you need is some hard-up officers in the military who haven't been paid in a year. We've got lots of them living on promises. Then you have the collusion of government maggots and it's done. The worst are the former communists.'

'Like us?'

'Tripe! We waved the red flag, but we were never ideological. I know you didn't believe that bull. We did it because it was exciting and somebody else was paying the bill.'

'I'll need some names.'

'How could I forget? The scum who were making millions selling all this war material asked if I wanted a piece. I said no, that it wasn't right to sell the people's property for personal gain. Next thing I know, I was out of the navy on my ass. Nobody would hire me. So here I am.'

The admiral was wandering into a bitter swamp. 'The *names*, please, Admiral.'

'Sorry,' he said, composing himself. 'The years haven't been easy. There were five principals in the deal.' He rattled off the names.

'I know all of them,' Petrov said. 'They were petty functionaries in the party who have flourished by picking the bones of the Soviet Union.'

'What can I say, my friend? Well, is that enough? It's all I've got. The people who come here don't talk about military secrets. Anyway, it was good to see you. My employers expect me to make the rounds of the tables every few minutes. So excuse me, I must get back to work.'

'Maybe not,' Petrov said. He reached into his suit pocket and extracted a brown envelope. 'If you could make a wish, what would it be?'

'Aside from making my wife alive again and persuading my children that it is worth their time to talk to me?' He thought about it for a moment. 'I would like to move to the United States. To Florida. I would sit in the sun and talk only to those I wanted to talk to.'

'What a coincidence,' Petrov said. 'Within this envelope is a one-way plane ticket to Fort Lauderdale, leaving tomorrow, a passport and visa, and the immigration paperwork that will ensure your stay there.

There is also some money to live on and the name of a gentleman who is looking for an investor to buy into his fishing company. He especially wants someone who has experience on the sea. It would be a much smaller fleet than you have been used to.'

A defeated expression came onto the admiral's face. 'Please don't toy with me. We were once comrades.'

'We still are,' Petrov said, handing over the envelope. 'Consider this a delayed payment from your country for past services.'

The admiral took the envelope and examined the contents. When he looked up, tears brimmed in his eyes.

'How did you know?'

'About Florida? Word gets around. It was not hard to find out.'

'I don't know how I can repay you.'

'You already have. Now I must be on my way, and you have to inform your employers of your wish to end your services here.'

'Inform them? I'll leave as soon as I can change my clothes.'

'That might be a good idea, considering the amount of cash you're carrying. Oh, I forgot. One thing.'

The admiral froze, wondering if strings were attached after all. 'What's that?'

'Don't forget to use sunscreen when you're out on the water,' Petrov said.

The admiral threw his arms around Petrov and embraced him in a bone-cracking bear hug. Then he tossed his cap across the room. His jacket, with medals clattering, followed.

Petrov slipped away. He allowed himself a rare smile as he stepped through the outside door. He shook hands with the doorman, passing along another hundred-dollar bill. He was feeling generous tonight. The doorman shoved his way through the crowd to make a path for Petrov, who quickly limped through the alley and disappeared into the night.

24

The Black Sea

The call from Captain Atwood came in as the
NUMA helicopter sped across the Black Sea toward
the Turkish mainland. Austin had been jotting down
his thoughts in a notebook when he heard the familiar
voice crackle in his earphones.

'Kurt, are you there? Come in, please,' Captain
Atwood urged.

'Miss me already, Captain?' Austin said. 'I'm truly
touched.'

'I'll admit things are a lot quieter here since you
left, but that's not why I'm calling. I've tried to get
in touch with the *Sea Hunter* and still can't raise her.'

'When was the last time you talked to her?'

'I called last night to say you'd be on your way in
the morning. Everything was okay. Then I tried again
after you took off, to let them know you were in the
air. No answer. We've been calling at regular intervals.
I called again a few minutes ago. Still no reply.'

'That's odd,' Austin said, glancing down at the
watertight bucket sitting on the floor at his feet.
Inside the bucket, soaking in seawater, was the silver
jewelry box plucked from the *Odessa Star*. At Gamay's

suggestion, the *Argo* had called the *Sea Hunter* and asked if a conservator could take a look at the box and its contents. The *Sea Hunter*'s captain said the ship had finished its project in the Black Sea and was on its way to Istanbul, where he would be happy to hook up with Austin.

'It's more than odd; it's crazy. What the hell do you make of it?'

Austin went down a mental checklist of possible reasons for the ship's silence, but none of them held water. All NUMA vessels carried the latest in communications, and their systems were redundant several times over. They kept in constant contact with other ships.

He felt as if someone were walking on his grave. 'I don't know, Captain. Have you called NUMA headquarters to see if anyone there has heard from the ship?'

'Yes. They said the *Sea Hunter* called in yesterday, saying they had found some significant Bronze Age relics and were heading into port.'

'Hold on, Captain,' Austin said. He hailed the pilot over the intercom. 'How far can we fly on our current fuel supply?'

'We're coming up on the Turkish mainland now. We're carrying a light load, so we can go another forty-five minutes or so before we drop out of the sky. Planning a side trip?'

'Maybe.' Austin looked over at Rudi Gunn, who had been listening to the exchange with Captain

Atwood. Gunn nodded slightly, like someone bidding at an auction. *Do what has to be done.* Austin got back to Captain Atwood and said they would try to find the *Sea Hunter.* Then he relayed the ship's last known position to the pilot. The chopper banked and headed off at a tangent.

Zavala sat up and his eyes snapped open. He had been plugged into a Walkman, completely absorbed in a Latin American CD. Zavala was an experienced pilot who flew by the seat of his pants like an old barnstormer. Sensing the course change, he removed his earphones and peered out the window, a quizzical expression on his face.

'We're making a detour,' Austin said, explaining the situation. Then he called the *Argo* and asked the captain to advise the Trouts of the change in plan. Paul and Gamay had stayed aboard the ship to map out the sea bottom in the area of the sunken cargo vessel and planned to return to port with the ship in a few days.

Austin closed his eyes and tried to picture the *Sea Hunter* as he remembered her from two years before, when he had sailed on the research vessel during a survey in the Caribbean. He visualized the vessel as if he were looking at a computer-rendered image. It was a relatively easy task because it was practically identical to the *Argo*, having been built at the same shipyard in Bath, Maine. The two-hundred-foot-long hull was painted the familiar turquoise hue, like all NUMA research vessels. An A-frame hung over the stern, a hydraulic crane towered over the raised deck behind the bridge and there was a smaller boom on the starboard side. A single tapering funnel stuck out through the roof of the cream-colored bridge superstructure and a tall radio mast rose like a flagpole from the bow.

His mental camera floated from the aft deck into the ship, through the winch-operation station, the main lab, library and mess hall. Below this deck would be scientific stores, the lower lab and crew and scientists' accommodations. The ship normally traveled with a crew of twelve and room for a dozen scientists. In the wheelhouse, he could picture the *Hunter*'s good-natured skipper, Captain Lloyd Brewer, a highly competent sailor-scientist who would not have ignored a call from another NUMA vessel.

The pilot flew a dead-reckoning course, following a line between the ship's last-known position and her destination. Austin took a post on one side of the helicopter, and Zavala pressed his nose against a window on the other. Gunn went up to the cockpit to scan the sea ahead. They saw fishing boats, commercial vessels and cruise ships. Sightings thinned as they moved away from the more heavily traveled traffic lanes.

Austin checked his watch and called the pilot on the intercom. 'How are we doing?'

'We'll have to turn back pretty soon.'

'Can you give us five more minutes?' Austin pleaded.

A pause. 'I'll give you ten, but one second more and we learn to walk on water.'

Austin asked the pilot to do his best and squinted into the glare, thinking about the line from the old sailors' prayer: *Oh Lord, Thy sea is so great and my boat so small.* Zavala's voice broke into his reverie. 'Kurt. Check this out at two o'clock.'

Austin shifted to the opposite side of the cabin and followed Zavala's finger with his eyes. A large, dark object was silhouetted against the sea's surface a couple of miles away. The pilot had picked up Zavala's alert and pointed the chopper's sharp nose at the object. Soon the full light of the sun fell upon a blue-green hull and the letters NUMA painted in black amidships.

'It's the *Sea Hunter*,' Austin said, recognizing the ship's features.

'I don't see a wake,' Gunn observed from the cockpit. 'She seems to be dead in the water.'

The helicopter angled down until the water was a sparkling blur. They soared over the ship's mast, then wheeled around and hovered. Upturned faces and hand waves would have greeted a normal flyover. Nothing stirred, except for the desultory flutter of the ship's flags. The pilot moved the helicopter forward until it was directly over the ship. He tilted the aircraft first one way, then the other, so those on board could look straight down. Powered by the twin turbos, the rotors made a horrendous racket.

'We're making enough noise up here to wake King

Neptune,' Gunn said. 'I don't see one damned person. No anchors over the side. She looks like she's drifting.'

'Can you try them on the radio?' Austin said.

'I'll give it a shot.'

The pilot reported no answer from the ship. 'Wish I could set this bird down for you,' the pilot said. 'Deck is too cluttered with junk.'

A research vessel was basically a floating platform that allowed scientists to drop various ocean-probing instruments or submersibles over the side. Dozens of different research projects might be in progress. The decks were designed for flexibility, with cleats and bolt eyes where equipment could be fastened down with cable or chain. Sometimes ship containers were brought aboard to use as extra lab space. The *Argo*'s deck was relatively uncluttered, allowing use of the helicopter pad. But the *Sea Hunter* had installed labs on the space normally used for chopper landings.

Austin scanned the deck and focused on a cargo container. 'How low can you get us?' he said.

'Maybe thirty or forty feet. Any lower and the rotor might hit a mast. It could be tricky.'

'Does this aircraft have a winch hoist?'

'Sure. We use it on short hops for carrying stuff that's too big to fit in the chopper.'

Zavala was listening intently to the discussion. From long experience with his partner's thought processes, Joe knew exactly what Austin had in mind. Zavala reached over and grabbed his rucksack from the adjoining seat. Austin told the pilot what they planned to do, then he checked the load in the Bowen, stuck it in his rucksack and slung the pack over his shoulder.

The copilot came back from the cockpit and opened the side door, bringing a blast of sea air into the cabin. Gunn helped the copilot uncoil cable from a winch drum and feed it through the doorway. Austin sat in the doorway with legs dangling. When the chopper was as low as it was going to be, he grabbed onto the cable and swung his body out of the helicopter. He slid down the cable, wedged one foot in the hook on the end and hung on as the cable swung back and forth like a twisting pendulum, buffeted by the powerful downdraft from the rotors.

From his perch, the pilot could not see Austin and relied on the copilot, who was crouched at the open door where he shouted directions. The chopper inched lower. The deck whirled under Austin's feet. The main hydraulic crane took up a major portion of the aft deck, along with coils of chain and rope, orange plastic containers holding various instruments, cartons, bollards and air vents.

Hanging on to the twisting cable with one hand, Austin pointed to the nearest cargo container and jabbed the air with his finger. The chopper moved several feet until it was directly over the container. Austin gave a thumbs-down signal. Released from its drum by the slow-turning winch, the cable unwound until the container was barely a yard below Austin's feet. Waiting for the right moment, he decided it wasn't going to come. He dropped onto the metal roof and rolled over a couple of times to absorb the shock and to avoid being bashed in the head by the hook swinging wildly inches above his head.

The cable was winched up, and Austin scrambled to his feet and waved to the faces peering down at him to show he was all right. Zavala lost no time exiting the helicopter. He dropped to the roof of the cargo container, but his timing was wrong and he would have fallen off if Austin hadn't grabbed his arm and pulled him back. Seeing them both on board, the pilot headed off. Watching the aircraft as it sped toward the horizon, Austin prayed that the fuel supply would hold out.

As the chopper receded to the size of a mosquito, Austin and Zavala dabbed antiseptic from their first-aid kit onto hands rubbed raw by the cable. From their elevated perch, they had a good view of the ship, and from what they could see the vessel was completely deserted.

They climbed down to the deck and Austin suggested that they move forward on each side of the boat, keeping their weapons at the ready. Austin took the starboard deck and Zavala the port. They advanced cautiously, guns in hand. The only sound was the snap of pennants and flags in the warm breeze. They came out onto the foredeck at the same time.

Zavala's face wore an expression of astonishment.

'*Nothing*, Kurt. It's like the *Mary Celeste*,' he said, referring to the famous old sailing ship that had been found adrift with no one on board. 'Did you find anything?'

Austin gestured for Zavala to follow and led the way back along the starboard deck. He knelt next to a dark streak on the metal deck between the railing and a doorway into the ship. Austin gingerly touched the sticky stain and sniffed the coppery odor on his finger.

'I hope that isn't what I think it is,' Zavala said.

'If you said blood, you'd be right. Someone dragged a body, maybe more than one from the looks of it, across the deck and threw the corpse overboard. There's more blood on the rail.'

With a heavy heart, Austin took the lead and stepped through the door out of the hot sun into the cool interior of the ship. Moving methodically, he and Zavala checked out the mess hall, library and the main lab, then climbed to the upper lab and the bridge. The farther into the ship they got, the more apparent it became that the *Sea Hunter* had been transformed into a charnel house. Everywhere they looked they saw spatters or puddles of blood. Austin's jaw grew rock hard. He had known many of the crew and scientists on board.

By the time they got to the wheelhouse, their nerves were as taut as piano strings. The floor was littered with charts and paper and broken glass from the windows. Austin picked up the radio microphone that had been ripped from its connection. The mike would have been of little use, since the communications console was riddled with bullet holes.

'Now we know why they didn't answer their calls,' he said.

Zavala murmured softly in Spanish. 'It looks like the Manson gang was here.'

'We'd better check the ship's quarters,' Austin said.

They made their way down two levels in the tomb-like silence and worked their way through the accommodations for the crew, officers and the scientists, finding more evidence of violence but no one alive, finally stopping outside a door marked STORES.

Austin pushed the door open, slipped his hand around the jamb and flicked on the lights. Cardboard cartons stacked several levels high were arranged in a rectangle on wooden palettes with a narrow aisle running around the outside. In one corner of the room was a service elevator used to haul supplies up to the galley.

Austin heard a soft muffled sound, and his finger tightened on the trigger. He signaled to Zavala to take one side of the room while he took the other. Zavala nodded and started off, moving as silently as a ghost. Austin edged along the other wall, then peered around a stack of canned-tomato cartons. The noise was repeated, louder now, sounding more animal than human. Zavala peered around the far corner, then they both stepped into the clear. Austin put his finger to his lips and pointed toward a narrow cleft between stacked boxes. A low moan issued from the alcove.

Austin waved Zavala off. Holding his gun in front of him with both hands, he stepped forward, and swung the Bowen around, pointing it between the boxes. He let out a robust curse, thinking how close he had come to shooting the young woman who cowered in the tight space.

She was a pitiful sight. Her dark curly hair hung over her face, her red-rimmed eyes brimmed with tears, her nose was wet and runny. She had crammed herself into a space less than two feet wide, her legs tight together, her arms around her knees. Her clenched fists were white-knuckled. When she saw Austin, a toneless ululating sound escaped her lips.

'Nunununu.'

Austin realized the woman was repeating the word 'no' again and again. He holstered his gun and squatted down so their faces were level.

'It's okay,' he said. 'We're from NUMA. Do you understand?'

She stared at Austin and mouthed the word *NUMA*.

'That's right. I'm Kurt Austin.' Joe had come up behind him. 'This is Joe Zavala. We're from the *Argo*. We tried to call your ship on the radio. Can you tell us what happened?'

She replied with a vigorous shake of her head.

'Maybe we should go on deck where there's fresh air,' Zavala suggested.

She shook her head again. This wasn't going to be easy. The woman was wedged tightly in her space and they would hurt her, and maybe themselves, if they tried to pull her out by force. She was in a state of shock.

Austin extended his hand palm up. She stared at it for a minute, then reached out and brushed his fingers as if she wanted to make sure he was real. The physical contact seemed to bring her back into the world.

'I was on this ship two years ago. I know Captain Brewer very well,' Austin said.

She studied his face for a moment, and the flame of recognition flickered in her eyes. 'I saw you at NUMA headquarters once.'

'That's possible. What department did you work in?'

She shook her head. 'I'm not with NUMA. My name is Jan Montague. I teach at the University of Texas. I'm a guest scientist.'

'Do you want to come out, Jan? It can't be too comfortable in there.'

She made a face. 'I'm beginning to feel like a sardine.'

The flash of humor was a good sign. Austin helped Jan from the alcove and turned her over to Zavala, who asked if she was hurt.

'No, thank you. I can walk on my own.' She took a few steps and had to reach out for Joe's arm for support.

They climbed up to the aft deck. Even the fresh air and sun couldn't dispel the black cloud that hung over the ship. Jan sat on a coil of line, blinking her eyes in the sunlight. Zavala offered her a flask of tequila he carried in his pack for what he said were medicinal purposes. The liquor brought color back to her cheeks, and signs of life returned to the impassive eyes. Austin waited patiently for her to speak.

She stared out at the water in silence. Finally, she said, 'They came out of the sea.'

'Who did?'

'The killers. They came at dawn. Most people were in bed.'

'What kind of boat did they come on?'

'I don't know. They were just . . . here. I never saw a boat.' Once the plug was pulled, the story poured out. 'I was sleeping, and they came into my room and pulled me out. They were dressed in strange uniforms, baggy pants and boots. They killed my roommate, shot her without warning. I could hear gunfire all over the ship.'

'Did they tell you who they were?'

'They didn't say a word. They just went about their business as if they were killing cattle in a slaughterhouse. Only one of them talked.'

'Tell me about him.'

She reached out with trembling hands and took another swig of tequila. 'He was tall, very tall, and skinny, almost emaciated. He was pale, as if he never saw the sun, and had a long beard and hair all matted as if he never combed it.' She wrinkled her nose in disgust. 'He smelled, too, as if he hadn't taken a bath in months.'

'How was he dressed?'

'All in black, like some kind of priest. But the worst thing were those eyes.' She shuddered. 'They were too big for his face, round and staring. I don't think he blinked. They were like fish eyes. Dead with no emotion in them.'

'You said he spoke to you.'

'I must have passed out. When I awoke, I was lying on my bunk. He was bending over me. His breath was so foul, it was all I could do not to vomit. The ship was quiet. There was only that voice, soft like the hissing of a snake. Almost hypnotic. He said he had killed everyone on the ship except me. They were leaving me alive to deliver a message.' Her body convulsed into choking sobs, but her anger helped her pull herself together and she continued. 'He wanted NUMA to know that this was revenge for killing his Guardians and violating the "sacred precincts." He said he wanted Kurt Austin.'

'You're sure he called me by name?'

'I wouldn't make a mistake about something like that. I said that you weren't here. They knew you were on the *Argo*. I told him this wasn't the *Argo*. He had one of his men check. When he learned he was on the wrong ship, he flew into a rage. He said to tell NUMA and the US that this was a small taste of the destruction that was yet to come.'

'Is there anything else?'

'That's all I remember.' She stared dumbly.

Austin thanked her and went over to where his pack was lying on the deck. He pulled out his Globalstar phone. Within seconds, he was talking to Gunn.

'Are you still in the air?'

'Just barely. We're running on fumes, but we'll make it. Are you and Joe okay?'

'We're fine.'

Gunn sensed from Austin's tone that there was more behind the terse reply. 'What's the situation on the *Hunter*?'

'I'd rather not say over the phone, but it's about as bad as it can get.'

Gunn said, 'Help is on its way. I talked to Sandecker, and he called his friends in the navy. They're grateful for getting the *NR-1*'s crew back. When he said you needed some assistance, they broke a cruiser off from NATO exercises in the area.'

'I wouldn't mind an aircraft carrier at this point, but a cruiser will be fine.'

'The ship will be there within two hours. Anything else you need?'

Austin's eyes hardened and a razor-sharp edge came into his voice. 'Yeah. I'd like about five minutes with a certain bug-eyed freak.'

25

The navy put an armed party aboard the *Sea Hunter*, but nothing could be done until an investigation team arrived. Austin needed no forensic expert to tell him the murderous sequence of events that had transpired aboard the unsuspecting ship. The attackers had arrived by sea, silently stolen onto the vessel, then made their way through the ship and systematically slaughtered everyone on her except for the one witness they purposely left alive. A maniac who talked of revenge had led the attack.

The message left with the sole survivor made it clear that the raid was payback. Austin called NUMA headquarters and asked that a warning be issued to all the agency's vessels, especially those in the Mediterranean area. He felt responsible despite Zavala's argument that no one could have anticipated the savage attack on the *Sea Hunter*. He could barely keep his anger under control. Zavala recognized the cold, distant expression on Austin's face, and he knew the contest between Austin and the killers had become intensely personal. If he hadn't seen what Boris and his minions had done on the NUMA ship, he might have felt sorry for them.

The trip back to Istanbul on the navy cruiser was

uneventful. Austin and Zavala arrived at their Istanbul hotel in the wee hours of the morning. An overnight FedEx packet from the States awaited Austin at the front desk. He took it up to his room and smiled as he read the note inside the envelope: 'Herewith is enclosed information on the *Odessa Star*. Will forward more as unearthed. Haven't you *forgotten* you owe me something? P.' Austin called the hotel concierge and said a large tip would be forthcoming if he could dig up a recipe for *imam bayidi* and forward it to Perlmutter. Then he scanned the material on the *Odessa Star*.

The Lloyd's record was enlightening, but Austin didn't know what to make of the story of the little mermaid and filed it in the back of his mind. Perlmutter's description of the strange conversation with Dodson caught his attention. *Curious*. Why would the English lord hang up on Perlmutter? For an old derelict, the *Odessa Star* elicited strong reactions. At the mere mention of the vessel, Dodson had rolled down a curtain of silence.

Austin picked up the phone and called Zavala's room.

'Cool your jets, my friend. I'm almost packed,' Zavala said.

'I'm happy to hear that. How would you like to take a slight detour through England? I need you to talk to someone. I'd do it myself, but Rudi and I have to get back to Washington to fill Sandecker in.' Austin was also aware of his own impatience and sometimes intimidating physical presence and reasoned that the soft-spoken Zavala might fare better with a reluctant source.

'No problem. I may look up a lady friend in Chelsea – '

'She'll be devastated when she learns you won't have time for socializing. This won't wait,' he said, his voice serious. 'I'm bringing you something I'd like you to read.'

Austin went next door to Zavala's room. While Zavala dove into the material from Perlmutter, Austin called the concierge again and asked him to find a seat for Joe on the next flight to London. The concierge said he had finished faxing the recipe to Perlmutter and would do his best. Austin knew there were at least two ways of getting things done in Istanbul, the official route and the unofficial way, which relied on a network of family and friends and the leverage of IOUs for old favors. The concierge was apparently well connected because he found the last seat on a plane leaving within two hours.

Zavala finished reading the material. After conferring with Austin, he got on the phone and called Dodson. Identifying himself as a researcher for NUMA, he said he would be in London the following day and asked to talk to Dodson about his family's historical involvement in Britain's naval history and service to the Crown. It was a thinly veiled excuse that wouldn't get past a kindergarten teacher, but if Dodson suspected the subterfuge, he didn't let on.

He said he would be available all day and gave directions to his house.

As the British Airways jet began the final approach to Heathrow Airport, Zavala looked off toward London with longing in his soulful eyes. He wondered if the auburn-haired journalist he had dated still lived in Chelsea and thought how nice it would be to catch up on old times over tandoori at a favorite Indian restaurant on Oxford Street. With Herculean resolve, he pushed the thought from his mind. Prying an old family secret out of a reluctant British aristocrat would be hard enough without feminine distractions.

Zavala breezed through customs, picked up his rental car and headed for the Cotswolds, the historic Gloucestershire countryside a few hours' drive from London. He hoped none of the bean counters back at NUMA would have a heart attack when they saw the bill for renting a Jaguar convertible. Zavala rationalized that the small luxury helped compensate for the dent NUMA was putting in his love life. At this rate, he ruminated grimly, he'd be joining a monastery.

Turning off the main highway, he drove briskly along meandering narrow roads, some no wider than cow paths, doing his best to stay to the left. The picturesque landscape looked like pictures from a calendar. The rolling hills and pastures were almost unnatural in their greenness. Sturdy houses of honey-brown stone clustered in the villages and dotted the unspoiled countryside.

Lord Dodson lived in a tiny hamlet that looked like a village in one of those British mysteries, the ones in which everyone is suspected of the vicar's murder. Dodson's house stood off by itself on a winding lane slightly wider than the car. Zavala followed a gravel drive hemmed in by hedgerows and pulled up next to a vintage Morris Minor pickup truck. The truck was parked in front of a substantial two-story structure of warm brown stone and dark tile roof. The cottage was nothing like the manor Zavala had imagined an English lord would live in. A stone wall ringed the house, enclosing colorful flower gardens. A man dressed in patched cotton slacks and a faded work shirt was knee-deep in blossoms.

Assuming the man was the gardener, Zavala got out of the car and said, 'Excuse me. I'm looking for Sir Nigel Dodson.'

A white stubble covered the man's chin. He removed his soiled cotton work gloves and extended his hand in a firm grip. 'I'm Dodson,' he said, to Zavala's surprise. 'You must be the American gentleman who called yesterday.'

Zavala hoped Dodson didn't see his embarrassment. After hearing the upper-class accent on the phone, Zavala had pictured a craggy-chinned Englishman in tweeds with a bushy upturned mustache decorating a stiff upper lip. Dodson was actually a small, slim, balding man. He was probably in his seventies, but he looked as fit as a man twenty years his junior.

'Are those orchids?' Zavala asked. His family's adobe house in Santa Fe was surrounded by flower beds.

'That's right. These are frog orchids. Spotted here, pyramidal there.' Dodson raised an eyebrow in a hint that his own stereotype of Americans had been shattered. 'I'm surprised you recognized them. They don't look like those big meaty plants everybody thinks about when you mention orchids.'

'My father was crazy about flowers. Some of those blossoms looked familiar.'

'Well, I'll have to show you around after we're done. Now, you must be thirsty after your trip, Mr Zavala. You said you were in Istanbul? Haven't been there in years. Fascinating city.' He invited Zavala to follow him around behind the house to an expansive flagstone patio. Dodson called in through the open French doors to his housekeeper, a stout ruddy-faced woman named Jenna. She eyed Zavala as if he were an insect her employer had picked off one of his orchids and brought them tall glasses of iced tea. They sat under an oriental pergola laced with ivy. The broad lawn, as well manicured as a golf course, sloped down to a slow-flowing river and extensive marshes. A boat was tied up at a small dock.

Dodson sipped his tea and gazed out at the vista. 'Paradise. Sheer *paradise*.' His piercing blue eyes turned to his guest. 'Well, Mr Zavala. Has this something to do with the telephone call I received a few days ago from Mr Perlmutter?'

'Indirectly.'

'*Hmm.* I've made some inquiries. It seems Mr Perlmutter is highly respected in marine-history circles. How may I help you?'

'Perlmutter was doing some research for NUMA when he came across a reference to your grandfather. He was puzzled about why you were reluctant to talk about Lord Dodson's papers. And so am I.'

'I'm afraid I was abrupt with Mr Perlmutter. Please offer him my apology if you see him. His query caught me off-guard.' He paused and let his eyes sweep over the roof of his cottage. 'Do you have any idea how old this house is?'

Zavala studied the weathered stones and massive chimneys. 'I'll take a stab at it,' he said with a smile. '*Old*?'

'I see you're a man of caution. I like that. Yes, it *is* very old. This village dates back to the Iron Age. The original Dodson manor, beyond those trees where you can't see it, goes back to the seventeenth century. I have no children to pass the property along to and couldn't afford to maintain the old ark in any case, so I turned it over to the National Trust and retained this cottage. It rests on a foundation placed here at the time of Augustus Caesar; I could show you the Roman numerals carved in the cellar stones. The house itself is one of four that have occupied the site for over two thousand years. The present structure dates back to the fourteen hundreds, just about the time your country was being discovered.'

'I'm not sure I understand what this has to do with my question.'

Dodson leaned forward like an Oxford don instructing a dim student. 'This country doesn't think in terms of decades or even centuries, as in America, but in *millennia*. Eighty years is a mere tick of the clock. There are powerful families who could still be embarrassed by the revelations in my grandfather's papers.'

Zavala nodded. 'I respect your wishes and won't press you, but is there anything that you *can* tell me?'

Dodson's eyes twinkled with merriment. 'I'm prepared to tell you *everything* you want to know, young man.'

'Pardon?' Zavala had hoped to excavate a few nuggets and hadn't expected Dodson to offer him the whole gold mine.

'After Mr Perlmutter called, I gave this matter a great deal of thought. In my grandfather's will, he left his papers to Guildhall, to be made available to the public at the end of the century. Even *I* had never seen them. They were in my father's possession and became my responsibility after his death. They were being held by the law firm that handled my grandfather's will, and I didn't get around to actually reading them until they were at the library. I pulled them back after I came across my grandfather's narrative explaining his part in all this. Now, however, I've decided to honor his wishes, despite the consequences. *Damn* the torpedoes. Full speed ahead.'

'Admiral Farragut at the battle of Mobile Bay.'

'You're something of a naval historian yourself.'

'It's hard not to be in my business.'

'Which brings up a question of my own. Exactly what *is* NUMA's interest in this matter?'

'One of our survey ships found the wreck of an old freighter named the *Odessa Star* in the Black Sea.'

Dodson sat back in his chair and shook his head. 'The *Odessa Star*. So *that's* what happened to her. Father thought she was caught in one of the dreadful storms that can plague those bloody waters.'

'Not exactly. She was sunk by gunfire.'

Dodson couldn't have looked more startled if Zavala had thrown the glass of iced tea in his face. He composed himself. 'Excuse me. I'll give you some material to read.' He disappeared into the house and came back with what looked like a thick manuscript. 'I'm going into the village to pick up some heirloom plantings for my garden. You should have plenty of time to absorb this. We can talk about it on my return. Jenna will keep you well supplied with tea or something stronger if you wish. Just ring this little bell.'

Zavala watched Dodson's battered truck jounce down the driveway. He was surprised Dodson had entrusted the manuscript to a complete stranger. On second thought, Jenna looked capable of restraining him if he made one step toward his rental car with packet in hand. He untied the thick black ribbon that bound the pages of lined pale yellow paper and riffled through the manuscript. The letters were gracefully executed by someone who had studied penmanship, but the strokes were thick and wild, slanting forward, as if the writer was in a great hurry. Attached was evidently an English translation of the transcript.

The first page contained a short paragraph: *'This is the journal of Major Peter Yakelev, captain in the tsar's Royal Cossacks Guard. I swear to God on my oath as an officer that all I'm about to tell you is true.'* Zavala turned a page. *'Odessa, 1918. As I sit in my humble room writing with fingers crippled by frostbite, I think of all I have endured in the past weeks. Bolshevik treachery, unspeakable cold and starvation have killed most of my* sontia, *the band of loyal Cossacks originally one hundred strong, only a handful of brave men remain. But the history of this valiant band will be written in blood, as saviors of Mother Russia, guardians of the flame of Peter the Great. Our own privations are nothing compared to those suffered by the gracious lady and her four daughters who, by the grace of God, have come into our care. God save the tsar! Within hours we leave our country forever and will set sail across the sea to Constantinople. This is the end of one story and the beginning of another . . . .'*

Zavala became totally engrossed in the pages. The captain tended toward rhetorical flourishes, but he told a compelling story that took Zavala away from the sunlight playing on the English countryside to the bleak Russian winter. Blizzards howled across the steppes, death lurked in the dark forest, and treachery lay in wait in the humblest shack. He almost shivered with cold as he read of the hardships the captain and his men endured as they traveled through a dangerous and unforgiving land toward the sea. A shadow fell across the pages. Zavala looked up and saw Dodson standing there, a bemused smile on his face.

'Fascinating, isn't it?'

Zavala rubbed his eyes, then checked his watch. Two hours had passed. 'It's *incredible*. What does it all mean?'

The Englishman picked up the bell and rang it. 'Teatime.'

The housekeeper brought out a steaming teapot and a tray of cucumber sandwiches and scones. Dodson poured their cups full, then leaned back in his chair and tented his fingers.

'My grandfather was undersecretary in King George's Foreign Office in 1917. He and the king had been drinking and womanizing companions in their youth. He was well acquainted with all the royal heads of Europe, including Tsar Nicholas, who was George's cousin. Nicholas was a short, slight man, although his ancestors had been a race of giants, and his limitations went beyond the physical. My father used to say that Nick wasn't a bad sort but a bit of a dim bulb.'

'That description could fit half the political leaders in the world today.'

'No argument there. Nicholas was even more inept than most, totally unsuited by intelligence and temperament for the job. Yet he had absolute authority over a hundred and thirty million people. He was entitled to the revenue from a million square miles of Crown lands and gold mines. Technically speaking, he was the richest man in the world. He owned eight magnificent palaces and was worth an estimated eight to ten billion dollars. In addition, he was the head of the church and, in the eyes of the peasantry, one step removed from God.'

'That would have been a crushing responsibility for anyone.'

'Quite so. He couldn't govern worth a damn, hated being tsar except for the chance to play soldier, and would have preferred living out his days in an English country house like this one. Unfortunately, it wasn't to be.'

'The Russian Revolution came along.'

'Precisely. You probably know much of what I'm about to say, but let me pull it all together for you. The conservatives in his court wanted him out even before the revolution. They worried that Russia's battering in World War I would trigger an uprising, and they hated the mad monk Rasputin because he had his hooks into the tsarina. There were demonstrations, food shortages, rampant inflation, strikes, refugees and anger over the millions of young Russians killed in this senseless war. Like the autocrat he was, Nicholas overreacted to the protests, his troops turned against him and he abdicated after being told it was in the best interests of the country. The

Provisional Government arrested him, and he and his family were kept prisoner in their palace outside Saint Petersburg. The Provisional Government was overthrown by the well-organized Bolsheviks under Lenin, and Russia began its long, tragic experiment with Marxism.'

'So Lenin and the communists inherited the tsar and his family.'

'That's a good way of putting it. Lenin had the royal family and some servants and retainers moved to a mansion in Ekaterinburg, a gold-mining center in the Urals. And there, in July of 1918, they were supposedly all shot and bayoneted. Lenin was under pressure from his hard-liners, who wanted the entire family eliminated, and his people were talking to the Germans, who insisted on the safety of the women, but regarded the death of the tsar as an internal Russian affair. Lenin ordered the limited killings, then shifted the blame from his people to leftist revolutionaries. The story was generally accepted.'

'What was your father's role at the time?'

'The king had ordered him to keep a close watch on events. King George and the tsar were cousins, after all. My father dispatched a trusted Russian-speaking agent named Albert Grimley to determine what had happened. You might say Grimley was the James Bond of his day. He arrived in Ekaterinburg shortly after the White Army chased the communists out and talked to the army officer investigating the murders. He found bullet holes and blood – but no bodies. The officer confided to Grimley that at most only *two* of the Romanovs had been murdered: the tsar and his son, who was heir to the throne. The officer's superiors suppressed his findings.'

'Why would they do that?'

'The Whites were commanded by a reactionary monarchist general on a divine mission to save Russia from ruin. He wanted the public to *believe* that the Bolsheviks murdered women and children. The family were more valuable to his cause as martyrs than as living people.'

'What happened to the women?'

'It's all in Grimley's report. He suggested that the Bolsheviks moved the tsarina and the four girls before the male Romanovs were disposed of. The communists were in military trouble, and Lenin may have wanted the family as bargaining chips in case he got himself into a hash. Some researchers think the tsarina and her daughters were taken to a city called Perm, and stayed there until Perm came under attack by the Whites. Witnesses say the family was moved out with treasure and gold bullion that the communists had accumulated, and they and their treasure supposedly vanished from the official record on a train trip to Moscow. The Soviets clamped the lid down on all further information. It would have tarnished Lenin's halo if it got out that he was dealing with the Germans over the fate of the Romanovs.'

'What happened to the Romanov treasure?'

'Only a small fraction of it was ever found.'

'Your father reported his agent's findings to the king?'

'He filed a report saying that the mother and girls were probably alive and asked for help in putting together a rescue scheme. King George washed his hands of the affair, although he and Nicholas were related. Remember that the hated kaiser was cousin to George and Nicholas as well. Family loyalty only went so far among the royals. The king was afraid that he'd stir up the British left if he gave the women asylum. The tsarina was German by birth, and Germany was the enemy.'

'So no attempt was made to rescue them.'

'A rescue scheme was hatched by some Englishmen, but it didn't go anywhere because the family was moved. There were a couple of attempts by Cossacks, supported by Germans who wanted a restoration of Russia's imperial house. The kaiser may have felt guilty about inflicting Lenin on the tsar to take pressure off the Eastern Front. The most interesting plot was a scheme to kidnap the family and spirit them through German-occupied Ukraine, then across the Black Sea in a neutral ship.'

'Why did it fail?'

'It *didn't*, actually.'

'They were rescued?'

'Yes, but not by the Germans. The Cossacks didn't trust Germany. Somewhere along the way, possibly during that trek to Moscow, the intrepid band of Cossacks who had failed to save them once before managed to kidnap the family and fought their way to the Black Sea.'

Zavala picked up the manuscript. 'Major Yakelev?'

Dodson smiled. 'The Cossack officer must have been extremely resourceful and determined. Yakelev is vague about exactly how the women came under his protection. He was saving that for when he got out of Russia. The journal was to be published when the Romanovs made their appearance in Europe. This manuscript was to go to Europe by a neutral ship and would garner them the instant sympathy of the world. It came into the possession of my grandfather, and when the family failed to arrive, he kept it for want of anything better to do.'

'Do you have any idea who might have sunk the ship?'

'This is where it gets dicey,' Dodson said, with a frown. 'Especially in light of what you said about the ship having been sunk by gunfire.' He took a deep breath. 'As my father recounts it in his papers, the family were to be taken secretly to Turkey, where a German U-boat would be waiting to spirit them out of the country. Turkey was allied with Germany. Britain was told of the plan and agreed not to attack the U-boat on its way to Europe.'

'That was generous of the British.'

Dodson guffawed. 'Oh, they were a wily bunch in the good old days. Their generosity was based on the assumption that the family would be captured by the Bolsheviks.'

'That was quite a gamble.'

'Not really. England *told* Lenin and his thugs that the family were escaping on the *Odessa Star*.'

'Your grandfather *knew* of this?'

'He argued strenuously against it, but was overruled.'

'By whom?'

'By King George.'

Zavala's eyes narrowed. 'I see why you were reluctant to make this information public. Some people might not like learning that the king was a traitorous informant and accessory to a multiple murder.'

'I don't know if I'd go so far as to identify the king as a criminal, though what he did was morally reprehensible. It was naïveté on his part, but George never dreamed that Lenin would be so ruthless as to order them assassinated. My father said the king assumed the women would be kept in a convent. The Bolsheviks may have given the impression that no harm would come to them.'

They sat in silence for a few moments, alone with their thoughts, listening to the trill of the birds.

Zavala shook his head in puzzlement.

'There's something I don't get. A few years ago, the Russians dug up some bones that were supposedly identified as those of the Romanov family.'

'The Soviet government was masterful at fabricating evidence. I would assume that they passed along that skill to their successors. There may be some truth to the story of the tsar's bones, but even so, the remains of the boy, Alexis, and his sister the Grand Duchess Maria were never found.'

'Maria?'

'Yes, she was the second youngest. Why?'

Zavala went out to his car and returned with the Perlmutter file. He leafed through the contents and pulled out the book excerpt on the little mermaid, which he handed to Dodson. The Englishman donned a pair of wire-rimmed reading glasses. As he pored over the file, his expression grew grave.

'Astounding! If this is accurate, the Romanov line *didn't* die out! Maria, or Marie as she's called here, went on to marry and have children.'

'That's my take on it.'

'Do you know what this *means*? Somewhere there may be a legitimate heir to the tsar's throne.' He ran his fingers through his hair. 'My God, what a catastrophe!'

'I'm not sure I understand.'

Dodson composed himself. 'Russia is in the midst of great turmoil. It is still seeking its identity. Beneath this bubbling cauldron is a fire of nationalism. Those who would go back to the days of Peter the Great and the tsars have touched a yearning in the Russian people, but all they have had to sell is a memory of a forgotten time. With an actual heir to the tsar, their cause would have focus. It is a country that still controls weapons of mass destruction and a major share of the world's natural resources. It will not be safe for the world if Russia lapses into a civil war and follows the lead of the worst kind of demagogue. British complicity in the plot against the tsar will stir up all those paranoid feelings against the West.' He affixed Zavala with a steely gaze. 'Tell your superiors that they must be discreet. Otherwise no one may be able to control the consequences.'

Zavala was bowled over by the emotional reaction from this reserved Englishman. 'Yes, of course, I'll tell them what you said.'

But Dodson seemed to have forgotten that Zavala was even there. 'The tsar is dead,' he murmured. 'Long live the tsar.'

26

Washington, DC

Leroy Jenkins caught his breath as he stepped from the wilting Washington heat into the cool interior of the thirty-story green glass tower overlooking the Potomac. The exterior of the tall tubular building was impressive enough, but nothing could have prepared him for his first glimpse inside NUMA headquarters. He craned his neck to gaze up to the top of the atrium lobby, then swept his eyes around the tumbling waterfalls and aquaria filled with exotic fish, taking in the huge globe of the world that rose from the center of the sea-green marble floor.

Smiling like a child in a toy shop, he started across the giant lobby, threading his way among the gaggles of tourists who trailed behind impeccably uniformed guides. An attractive woman in her twenties, one of several receptionists at a long information desk, saw Jenkins approach and beamed him in with a pleasant smile.

'May I help you?'

Jenkins was struck dumb. On the flight from Portland, he'd rehearsed what he would say when he got to NUMA. Now his tongue seemed glued to the roof of his mouth. He was overcome by awe at being in the heart of the biggest ocean science agency in the world. He felt like Fred Flintstone visiting the Jetsons. As an oceanographer, he had long contemplated a trip to the Holy Grail of ocean science, but his teaching duties had intervened and later he was consumed by his wife's illness. Now, he'd reached the point where he didn't like to leave Maine, because, as he joked, his gills would close up if he ventured too far from the sea.

The air seemed to crackle with electrical energy. Every nontourist in view clutched a laptop computer. No one carried anything remotely resembling the battered tan briefcase in his sweaty hand. Jenkins was uncomfortably aware of his wrinkled khaki pants, his worn Hush Puppies and the faded blue chambray work shirt, damp from the heat. He removed the tan fisherman's cap and wiped the sweat off his forehead with a red bandanna, immediately regretting the move because it made him look even more like a hick. He stuffed the bandanna back into his pocket.

'Someone in particular you'd like to see?'

'Yes, but I'm not sure who it might be.' Jenkins offered a weak grin. 'Sorry to be so vague.'

The receptionist was familiar with the symptoms. 'You're not the first person who's been vague. This place can be a bit overwhelming. Let's see what we can work out. Could you tell me your name?'

'Sure, it's Roy Jenkins. *Dr* Leroy Jenkins, I mean. I taught oceanography at the University of Maine before I retired a few years ago.'

'That narrows it down. Would you like to speak to someone in the oceanography division, Dr Jenkins?'

Hearing the title before his name gave him courage. He said, 'I'm not sure. I've some questions of a specialized nature.'

'Why don't we start in oceanography and go from there?'

The young woman picked up the phone, pressed a button and spoke a few words. 'Go right up, Dr Jenkins. The receptionist on the ninth floor is expecting you.' She flashed her fabulous smile again and directed her eyes to the next person in line.

Jenkins made his way toward the ranks of elevators off to one side of the lobby. Still wondering if he had come all this way to make a fool of himself in front of some young Ph.D. with a pocket protector and a condescending attitude, he stepped into an elevator and pushed a button. Too late now, he thought as the elevator whisked him skyward.

On the tenth floor of the NUMA building, Hiram Yaeger sat in front of a horseshoe-shaped console and stared at an immense computer monitor that looked as if it were suspended in space. Displayed on the screen was the image of a narrow-faced man with beetling brows bent over a chessboard. Yaeger watched the man move the white rook two spaces. He studied the board a moment and said, 'Bishop to queen five. Check and checkmate.'

The man on the screen nodded and tipped his

king over with a forefinger. In a thick accent, he said, 'Thank you for the game, Hiram. We must play again.' The screen went blank except for a pale green afterglow.

The middle-aged man sitting next to Yaeger said, 'Very impressive. Victor Karpov isn't exactly a slouch.'

'I cheated, Hank. When I programmed all of Karpov's games into Max's data banks, I set up an array of responses based on Bobby Fischer's strategy. Fischer simply overrode any dumb move I made.'

'It all sounds like magic to me,' Hank Reed replied. 'Speaking of vanishing acts, I wonder where our pastrami sandwiches are.' He licked his lips. 'I think I'd work for NUMA even if they didn't pay me, just so I could use the cafeteria.'

Yaeger nodded in agreement. 'Let's get back to work. If the delivery guy doesn't arrive in five minutes, I'll call again.'

'Sounds good,' Hank said. 'Did Austin ever say why he wanted this stuff?'

Yaeger chuckled knowingly. 'Kurt's the ultimate poker player. He never shows his cards until he lays down his hand.'

Austin had called Yaeger earlier in the day with a cheery 'Good morning.' Getting right to the point, he'd said, 'I need some help from Max. Is she in a good mood?'

'Max is always in a good mood, Kurt. As long as I ply her with electronic cocktails, she'll do anything

I ask.' In a stage whisper, he said, 'She thinks I want her for her *mind* and not her body.'

'I didn't know Max *had* a body.'

'She has her *pick* of bodies. Mae West. Betty Grable. Marilyn Monroe. Jennifer Lopez. Whatever I program in.'

'Please soften her up with a few drinks and ask her to dig up what she can on the subject of methane hydrates.'

Austin had been thinking about methane hydrates since the Trouts had told him Ataman Industries was attempting to mine them from the ocean floor.

'I'll have a package for you later today, if that's okay.'

'Fine. I'll be pretty much tied up with Admiral Sandecker this morning.'

Yaeger made no attempt to ask when Austin wanted the information. If Austin wanted it, it was important. And if it was important, he wanted it *immediately.*

People who met Yaeger for the first time sometimes found it difficult to reconcile the scruffy-Levis-and-T-shirt look with his reputation as a computer whiz. It only took a few minutes of watching him at work to see why Admiral Sandecker had made him the head of NUMA's oceans data center. From his console, he had access to vast resources of data on ocean technology and history and every related bit of information on and under the seas.

Finding his way through the massive amount of

data at his command required a deft hand. Yaeger knew that if Max searched out every mention of methane hydrates recorded, he would drown in the digital deluge. He needed someone to point the way. Hank Reed immediately came to mind.

Reed was in his lab when Yaeger called. 'Hi, Hank. I could use your geochemical expertise. Any chance you could break away from your Bunsen burners for a few minutes?'

'Don't tell me NUMA's resident computer whiz needs the help of a mere human being. What's wrong, did your know-it-all machine blow a fuse?'

'Nope. Max truly *does* know it all, which is why I need someone on the slow side to bird-dog the data. Tell you what, I'll buy lunch.'

'Flattery and food. An irresistible combination. I'll be right up.'

Reed walked into the data center wearing a warm smile. Despite their playful insults, they were the best of friends, bound by their eccentricities. With his graying ponytail and wire-rimmed granny glasses, Yaeger looked like he belonged in the cast of *Hair*. Dr Henry Reed had a round cherub's face and a high thatch of wheat-colored hair that added a few inches to his five-foot height and looked like it could have been combed with a pitchfork. The thick round glasses perched on his small nose gave him the expression of a benign owl. He took the chair Yaeger offered and rubbed his pudgy hands together.

'Plunk your magic twanger, Froggy.'

Yaeger looked over the tops of his granny glasses. 'Huh?'

'It's from an old program, I can't remember which it was. Froggy was a – Never mind. You probably never even heard of radio.'

Yaeger grinned. 'Sure I have. My grandmother told me about it. Television without pictures.' He leaned back in his chair with his hands behind his head and said, 'Max, say hello to my pal, Dr Reed.'

A feminine voice purred through the speakers placed strategically around the room.

'Hello, Dr Reed. How nice to see you again . . .'

As the doors hissed shut behind him, Roy Jenkins thought it strange that he was the only one getting off the elevator. He looked at the numerals on the wall and swore to himself. He'd become the absentminded professor he had always scorned. The receptionist had said the ninth floor. Preoccupied with his thoughts, he had pushed the button for the *tenth*.

Instead of the standard office architecture of hallways, cubicles and offices, a vast glass-enclosed area took up the entire floor. Jenkins should have turned back to the elevator, but scientific curiosity got the best of him. He walked past banks of blinking computers, glancing from left to right, listening to the electronic whisperings. He could have landed on an alien planet peopled only by machines.

With some relief he came upon the two men behind the large glowing console at the center of the computer complex. They were looking at a large screen that seemed to hang by invisible wires, and was dominated by the image of a woman in vivid color. She had topaz brown eyes, auburn hair and the bottom of the monitor barely hid her ample cleavage.

The woman was talking, but even more odd, one of the men, who wore his long hair in a ponytail, was talking back to her. Thinking he had stumbled into a showing of a very private nature, Jenkins was about to back out, but the other man, who sported a hairdo like a wheat plant gone to seed, saw him and grinned.

'At last, our pastrami sandwiches,' he said.

'Pardon me?'

Reed saw that Jenkins was carrying a briefcase instead of a white paper bag, studied Jenkins's weathered and tanned face and then took in the workshirt and cap.

'Guess you're not from the cafeteria,' he said sadly.

'My name is Leroy Jenkins. I'm sorry to bother you. I got off at the wrong floor and sort of wandered in here.' He looked around. 'What *is* this place?'

'NUMA's computer center,' said the ponytailed man. He had a boyish, clean-shaven face with a narrow nose and gray eyes. 'Max can answer just about any question you throw her way.'

'Max?'

Yaeger gestured to the screen. 'I'm Hiram Yaeger. This is Hank Reed. That lovely lady up there is a holographic illusion. Her voice is a feminine version of my own. I used my own face originally, but I got tired of looking at myself and dreamed up a pretty woman, my own wife.'

Max smiled. 'Thank you for the compliment, Hiram.'

'You're welcome. Max is smart as well as beautiful. Ask her any question you'd like. Max, this is Mr Jenkins.'

The image smiled and said, 'Pleased to meet you, Mr Jenkins.'

I've been in the wilds of Maine for too long, Jenkins thought. 'Actually, it's *Dr* Jenkins. I'm an oceanologist.' He drew a breath in. 'I'm afraid my questions are rather complicated. They've got to do with methane hydrates.'

Yaeger and Reed looked at each other, then at Jenkins.

Max said, with a sigh that was more than human, 'Is it really necessary to repeat myself?'

'Nothing personal, Dr Jenkins. Max has been working on the same subject for the last hour or so,' Yaeger said. He punched out the cafeteria number on the phone and turned to Jenkins. 'We'd like you to join us for lunch.'

Reed leaned forward. 'I recommend the pastrami. It's an existential experience.'

The sandwich was as tasty as promised. Jenkins realized that with the exception of the bag of peanuts he'd had on the plane, his stomach was empty. He took a swig of root beer to wash his lunch down and looked at the other men, who were waiting expectantly.

'This is going to sound crazy,' he said.

'*Crazy* is our middle name,' Yaeger said. Reed nodded his head in agreement. Although the two men looked like an overaged hippie and a munchkin with a Don King hairdo, they appeared very bright. More important, they were interested in hearing his story.

'Don't say I didn't warn you,' he said. 'Okay,' he began, 'I retired from teaching college a few years ago and bought a lobster boat in Rocky Point, my hometown.'

'Aha! A fisherman,' Reed said. 'I knew it.'

Jenkins smiled, then resumed. 'You probably read about the *tsunami* that hit there not too long ago.'

'Yes, it was an awful tragedy,' Reed said.

'It could have been worse.' Jenkins explained his role in warning the town.

'Lucky you were there,' Yaeger said. 'Something puzzles me, though. First time I've heard of something like that happening. New England isn't at the edge of a major fault like Japan or California.'

'The only comparable precedent I found was the big wave caused by the Grand Banks earthquake in 1929. The quake's epicenter was under the ocean on the continental slope south of Newfoundland and east of Nova Scotia. The tremor was felt in Canada and New England, but the source was two hundred and fifty miles from the nearest land, so damage was negligible. Roads were blocked by landslides, chimneys broken and dishes rattled. Otherwise, the shock had little impact. The biggest effect was on the sea.'

'In what way?' Reed said.

'There were two ships near the epicenter. The vibrations were so violent they thought they'd lost a propeller or hit an uncharted wreck or sandbar. The quake created a great wave that struck the south coast of Newfoundland three hours later, running up into rivers and inlets in the little fishing villages along sixty miles of coastline. The worst damage was at a wedge-shaped bay on the Burin Peninsula. The *tsunami* rose to thirty feet at the apex of the bay, damaged docks and buildings and killed more than twenty-five people.'

'Very similar to what happened at Rocky Point.'

'Almost a mirror image. The fatality and injury rate was lower in my town, thank goodness. There was another important similarity. Both waves seem to have been caused by huge underwater slides. There was no doubt that an earthquake caused the Grand Banks disaster. The oceanic cables were broken in dozens of places.' He paused. 'Here's where they were different: The Rocky Point slide seems to have been caused *without* a quake.'

'Interesting. Were there any seismic readings?'

'I checked with the Weston Observatory outside of Boston. The Grand Banks quake had a magnitude of 7.2. So we know something of that magnitude will cause a *tsunami*. The Rocky Point readings were more muddled.' He paused. 'There was a shock, but it didn't fit the classic pattern for a quake.'

'Let me see if I'm clear on this. Are you really saying the Rocky Point slump was *not* from an earthquake?'

'I think that can be fairly well established. What I *can't* say is what actually caused the landslide.'

Yaeger looked over the tops of his granny glasses. 'Which came first, the chicken or the egg?'

'Something like that. I had read about the methane-hydrate deposits found off the continental slope and wondered if instability in those pockets of gas could have caused the slump.'

'It's certainly possible,' Reed said. 'There are huge pockets of the stuff off both coasts. We've found major deposits off of Oregon and New Jersey, for instance. You've heard of the Blake Ridge?'

'Sure. It's an undersea promontory a couple of hundred miles southeast of the US.'

'Off the North Carolina coast, to be exact. The ridge is loaded with methane hydrate. Some people think the ridge is a "pressure cooker." Surveys have found craters pockmarking the ocean floor where the stuff has melted and seeped out, releasing methane gas.'

Jenkins scratched his head. 'I'm sorry to say I don't know a lot about hydrates. I try to keep up through the professional journals since leaving the university, but what with the lobstering and so on, I never seem to have enough time.'

'It's a comparatively new area. You're familiar with the chemical composition of hydrate?'

'It's made up of natural gas molecules trapped in ice.'

'That's right. Someone dubbed it "fire ice." It was discovered in the nineteenth century, but our knowledge has been pretty sketchy. The first natural deposits were found under the permafrost in Siberia and North America – they called it marsh gas – then in the 1970s, a couple of scientists from Columbia University found pockets under the seafloor when they were doing seismological studies at the Blake Ridge. In the 1980s, the Woods Hole submersible *Alvin* found stone undersea chimneys formed by escaping methane. I was on the first big survey back in the mid-1990s. That's when we discovered the deposits in the Blake Ridge. They're only a fraction of what's out there. The potential is vast.'

'Where are the major deposits?'

'Mostly along the lower slopes of the world's continental shelves, where the seabed drops from four hundred feet or so into the abyss several miles deep. There are major pockets off both US coasts. As I said, you can find them in Costa Rica, Japan, India, and under the arctic permafrost. The sheer size of the deposits is astounding. The most recent estimates are ten thousand gigatons. That's *double* the total amount of all known reserves of coal, oil and natural gas.'

Jenkins let out a low whistle. 'Waiting there to be tapped when we suck our petroleum reserves dry.'

'I wish it were so easy,' Reed said with a sigh. 'A few technical problems have to be ironed out before extraction is practical.'

'Is it dangerous to drill?'

'The first time a ship drilled into a pocket was in 1970. Nothing happened, but drillers were afraid for years afterward that they'd get blown out of the water. Eventually, a few experimental bores showed that research drilling was safe. Getting hydrates to the surface to heat your home or run your SUV is another question. The environment is extremely hostile in the deep water where hydrates are found, and the stuff simply fizzes when we bring it up. The deposits may be another few hundred feet below the seafloor.'

'That sounds like a tough neighborhood for rigs to operate in.'

'*Absolutely*. A number of countries and companies are working on the problem, though. One method is pumping steam or water down the drill hole. This melts the hydrate and releases methane. Then you pump the methane to the surface of the seafloor through another drill hole. Next comes the question of what you do with it. When you remove the hydrate, the seafloor destabilizes.'

'There goes your expensive pipeline.'

'A good possibility. Which is why engineers have come up with a scheme to put a production facility on the seafloor. You pump the hydrate out and combine it with water. The mix goes into big tanks shaped like dirigibles. Submarines would tow them to the shallows, where the hydrates would be safely broken down into fuel and water.'

'With any of those methods, it sounds like mining hydrates is going to be like walking on eggshells.'

'Even *more* difficult. Now back to your original question.'

'About hydrates as a source of earthquakes and big waves.'

'It's highly possible. There is evidence that the natural melting has destabilized seafloor slopes. They've found massive submarine landslides off the US East Coast, Alaska and other countries. The Russians found unstable hydrate fields off Norway. They think one of the biggest releases ever recorded caused the Storrega submarine landslide: Eight thousand years ago, more than a thousand cubic miles of sediments slid for miles down the slope of the Norwegian continental slope.'

'I'm acquainted with Storrega,' Jenkins said.

'Then you'd know that the huge mud slide caused unimaginable *tsunamis*. The Grand Banks and Rocky Point would have been bathtub waves by comparison.'

Jenkins nodded. 'What about man-made landslides. Possible?'

'I'd say they're plausible, sure. A drilling platform could inadvertently cause a deposit to collapse, triggering a landslide.'

Jenkins held his breath, then released it. 'Inadvertently, yes. But could something like that be triggered deliberately?'

The tone grabbed their attention. Reed said, 'What are you saying, Dr Jenkins?'

Jenkins squirmed in his chair. 'It's been driving me crazy. My gut instinct has been in conflict with my scientific training, which says gather all the evidence before coming to a conclusion, especially one as wild as this.'

Reed scratched his chin. 'Maybe, but as a scientist, I'm like you – I can't make that leap from conjecture to conclusion without a bridge of facts.'

Yaeger got into the discussion. 'Poetically said, Doc. Let's see if Max can help us. Were you eavesdropping, my love?'

The auburn-haired image of a woman reappeared. 'It's hard not to listen in when I have six supersensitive microphones. Where would you like me to take you?'

Yaeger turned to the two scientists. 'Gentlemen, it's all yours.'

Reed had been giving it some thought. 'Max, please give us an idea of the undersea methane-hydrate deposits along the US coasts.'

The face vanished and they were looking at a three-dimensional rendering of the sea bottom to the east and west of the United States, complete with mountains and canyons. Pulsating patches of crimson appeared in the shimmering blue sea off the Atlantic and Pacific coasts.

'Now let's isolate this to the East Coast.'

The shoreline between Maine and the Florida Keys appeared.

'Good. Please zero in on Maine and show us the continental shelf.'

They were looking at the long irregular coastline of the Pine Tree state stretching from Canada to New Hampshire. A wavy line appeared off the coast, running through the red patches of hydrates.

'If I may,' Jenkins interjected, 'could you highlight Rocky Point?'

A cornflower blue bull's-eye indicated Jenkins's hometown. A close-up aerial view of the town showing its bay and river appeared in the lower right-hand corner of the screen.

'Not bad,' Jenkins said, noting the extra touch.

'Thank you,' purred a disembodied voice.

Jenkins gave Max his boat's position when he had first seen the nascent *tsunami*. A silhouette of a fishing boat appeared in the holographic sea.

'Now we need a diagram showing the major undersea faults.'

A spidery network of white lines appeared.

The boat appeared to be in between Rocky Point and a major fault due east of the town.

Yaeger said, 'That was great, Max. While you're in profile mode, let's go back to the continental shelf at the epicenter of the shock.'

Displayed on the screen was a cross-section of the ocean floor showing a wavy line representing the ocean's surface and a lower one that was the sea bottom. The continental shelf dropped off sharply. At the edge of the shelf was a thick fault that angled down. The fault intersected a variegated line that represented the methane-hydrate deposit under the limestone crust.

'There's our trouble spot. Show us what happens when methane hydrates are released.'

A methane plume rose from the ocean floor. The sea bottom along the slope of the continental shelf collapsed. A depression occurred in the water surface where the landslide occurred. The surface of the water cratered above the slide. The water tried to stabilize, creating a bump that moved along the ocean surface.

'There's the genesis of the big wave,' Reed said.

'Let me try something,' Yaeger said. 'You heard what Dr Jenkins said about the Richter scale reading at that location. Please give us a simulation of what happened.'

Ripples that represented waves began to travel out from the area immediately around the slide. Max zoomed in on the wave heading for Rocky Point. When the moving arc was close to shore, the close-up of Rocky Point enlarged to fill the whole screen. The wave could be seen rolling into the harbor, onto the shore and up the river.

Without being asked, Max split the screen showing the side view displaying the profile of the wave. The *tsunami* grew as it approached land, morphed into a giant watery claw, and crashed down on the sleepy harbor. There was silence in the room as Max repeated the scene again and again in fast and slow motion.

Yaeger swiveled in his chair and said, 'Comments, gentlemen?'

'We've established effect,' Jenkins said. 'The big question is whether the cause was man-made.'

'It's happened before,' Reed said. 'Remember what I said about a drill platform's collapsing after accidentally releasing a plume.'

'Max, I know you've worked hard, but I wonder if you could do me a favor.'

'Of course, Dr Jenkins.'

'Thank you. Go back to your map of the East Coast and show us weak spots similar to those off Maine.'

The map appeared again with pulsating bull's-eyes of varying sizes. The biggest were off the New England coast, New Jersey, Washington, Charleston and Miami.

'Max, please simulate what would happen if the continental shelf collapsed at the major intersections with methane-hydrate deposits.'

Within an instant, waves rippled out from the larger epicenters, reaching a height of thirty feet, hitting the coast and flowing into bays and up rivers and far onto land.

Reed's eyes blinked rapidly behind the thick lenses. 'Good-bye Boston, New York, Washington, Charleston and Miami.'

'Meth is death,' Yaeger said softly. Seeing the puzzled faces of the older men, he explained, 'It's an old hippie saying, meant to warn people of the dangers of using methamphetamines to get high.'

Reed said, 'This is worse than any drug, my friend.'

Jenkins cleared his throat. 'There was something I didn't mention.' He told them about the encounter with the huge ship the same day as the Rocky Point *tsunami*.

'It sounds as if you think the ship had something to do with the landslide and the *tsunami*,' Yaeger said.

Jenkins nodded.

'Were there any markings on it?'

'Yes, as a matter of fact. The ship was registered in Liberia, as a lot of them are, and the name on the hull was *Ataman Explorer I*. I checked the dictionary. It means the head man of a bunch of Cossacks.'

'*Ataman?* Are you sure?'

'Yes, does the name ring a bell?'

'Possibly. How long are you in Washington, Dr Jenkins?' Yaeger asked.

'I don't know. As long as I have to be I guess. Why?'

Yaeger rose from his chair. 'I've got a couple of people I want you to meet.'

27

The sunlight streaming through the tinted floor-to-ceiling window washed the sharp features of Admiral James Sandecker in a sea-green patina that made his face look like a bronze bust of Father Neptune. From his office on the top floor of NUMA headquarters, he had an unparalleled view of official Washington. He stood at the window, in thought, his authoritative blue eyes sweeping the city, taking in the White House, the tall spire of the Washington Monument and the dome of the Capitol, as if he were a hawk searching for its prey.

Austin had spent most of the morning filling Sandecker in on the events in the Black Sea. The admiral had been fascinated by the description of the sub pen, and intrigued at the meeting with Petrov and the *Odessa Star* link to Lord Dodson, whom he had met. Occasionally, he asked a question to clarify or offer a theory of his own. But he listened in stony silence, tugging at his precisely trimmed red Van Dyke beard, when Austin told him about the massacre aboard the *Sea Hunter*. At the end of the grisly narrative, he rose from his desk without a word and walked over to gaze out the window.

After a few moments, he turned to Austin and

Gunn, who sat in leather chairs in front of the desk, and said, 'In all my days as a navy commander, I never lost a ship *or* its crew. Damned if I'm about to start now. This son of a bitch and his friend Razov are not going to get away with the massacre of an entire NUMA crew.'

The temperature in the room seemed to drop twenty degrees.

Sandecker came over and settled behind his desk. 'How is Ms Montague, the young lady who survived the attack?'

'She's tough,' Austin said. 'She insisted on staying aboard the ship while the replacement crew brings the *Sea Hunter* back to port.'

'Make sure I see the young lady on her return.'

'I'll do that,' Austin said. 'What's the latest from the CIA?'

Sandecker reached into the humidor on his desk, pulled out a cigar and lit it. 'The CIA is barking up the wrong tree, the FBI is skeptical, and the armed forces aren't much good unless you point them in the right direction and give them marching orders. The secretary of state doesn't return my phone calls.'

'What about the White House?'

'The president is sympathetic and concerned, of course. But I can't help thinking there is a bit of glee among some of his Cabinet, a hint that the massacre was justified retribution for sticking our nose in where it doesn't belong. They are angry that NUMA rescued the *NR-1* crew.'

'What *difference* does it make who rescued the crew, as long as it was rescued?' Austin said in frustration.

Sandecker puffed out a plume of smoke that temporarily enveloped his head in a purple cloud. 'I assume that was a rhetorical question, because you're much too savvy in the ways of this city. You know that gratitude simply does not exist inside the Beltway. We've stolen their thunder, and they resent that.'

Gunn sighed. 'That's pretty much the scuttlebutt I've heard. There's even criticism behind our back that our "bungling" is the reason that the captain and pilot are still missing with the sub.'

'Nice of us to provide an excuse for the incompetence of other agencies,' Sandecker said. 'But I'm afraid it means NUMA is on its own when it comes to the *Sea Hunter* business. Any lead on this man, Boris?'

'He's a will-o'-the-wisp,' Austin said. 'Our best chance is to concentrate on Razov. At last report, his yacht had left the Black Sea and we're trying to track it down.'

'We're going to have to do better,' Sandecker said.

Sandecker's intercom beeped softly, and the voice of his secretary came on.

'I know you're in conference, Admiral, but Mr Yaeger is here with two other gentlemen and he says it's urgent that they see you.'

'Send them in, please,' Sandecker said. A moment later, the office door opened and Yaeger came in, followed by the diminutive Dr Reed and a stranger. Sandecker had spent too much time on the water not to recognize Jenkins as a fisherman, especially after they shook hands and he felt the barnacle-hard calluses.

He greeted them warmly and told the men to pull up chairs. 'Well, Hiram, what brings you out of your sanctum sanctorum?'

'I think Dr Jenkins can explain it better than I can.'

Jenkins was nervous at being in the presence of the legendary director of NUMA. But once he started to talk, he hit his stride. When Jenkins finished his saga, Reed gave his opinion as a geochemist. Finally, Yaeger pitched in, passing around printouts of the diagrams Max had projected onto the screen. Sandecker sat back in his chair, tenting his fingers, his eyes alert to every nuance.

When they were through with their presentation, he tapped his intercom. 'Please see if Dr Wilkins can come up from the Geology Department.'

Dr Elwood Wilkins arrived a few minutes later. He was a slim, reserved midwesterner who looked like one of those movie character actors who always played the kindly pharmacist or family doctor. Sandecker pulled over another chair close to his desk. He passed Wilkins the printouts and gave the geologist a few minutes to study them. Wilkins finished reading the material and looked up.

Sandecker answered the question in the scientist's eyes. 'These gentlemen have suggested that it is possible for the edge of the continental shelf along the East Coast to cave in, creating destructive *tsunamis*. While I value their opinion, it never hurts to hear from a disinterested observer. What do you think?'

Wilkins smiled. 'Oh, I don't think there's any danger of the Atlantic City Boardwalk being washed into the sea.'

Sandecker raised an eyebrow.

'*But,*' Wilkins added, 'there is new research which indicates that what they suggest is not at all far-fetched. The rock under the overlying layer of the continental shelf is quite waterlogged. If the pressure exerted by the sea bottom reached a critical state, the water would squeeze out. It's as if you stepped on a balloon. The blowout could cause landslides that deform the water and send giant waves toward the shore. Some of my colleagues at Penn State University have run computer models demonstrating that the possibility is very real.'

'These slides would have to be triggered by a quake?' Sandecker said.

'A quake could do it, most certainly.'

'Could it happen on the East Coast?' Gunn asked.

Wilkins tapped the sheaf of printouts in his hand. 'This material pretty much spells it out. The continental shelf runs the full length of the coast. In several places along its slope are big cracks and craters where the potential for landslides is greater.'

'Could a slide be caused by something other than a quake?' Gunn said.

'It could happen *spontaneously*. I'm sorry I can't be more specific. This is a whole new area of science.'

'I was thinking of a release of methane hydrate.'

'Why not? If the hydrate layer is destabilized, sure, the whole shooting match could come tumbling down and set off your giant waves.'

Sandecker could see Wilkins's lips about to form a question. He cut the discussion short. 'Thank you, Doctor. You've been a great help, as always.' He ushered Wilkins to the door, patted him on the back and thanked him again. Returning to the others, he said, 'I hope you weren't insulted at my bringing Dr Wilkins in. I wanted to hear from an independent source.'

'From what we heard,' Gunn said, 'I'd say there's a pretty good case here that Razov has discovered how to cause a *tsunami*. The wave that struck the Maine coast was a dry run, if you'll excuse the expression. If we're correct in our assumption, he's somehow capable of causing enormous destruction.'

'The *Ataman Explorer* is the key,' Austin said. 'We've got to find her.'

'We'll have to do more,' Sandecker said with quiet urgency. 'We've got to get *aboard* that ship!'

28

Rocky Point, Maine

Before the big wave had hit, Rocky Point had been the quintessential rock-ribbed Maine town, its picturesque harbor and neat clapboard-and-shingle houses appearing in countless calendars. The tidy Main Street could have come from a Frank Capra movie. But as Jenkins's boat moved out of the harbor, Austin gazed back toward land and thought that the town now looked like one of those pictures where the viewer was challenged to detect the mistakes. *Plenty* was wrong with *this* picture.

The waterfront lobster restaurants, the fish pier and the controversial motel were gone, and all that was left were pilings that jutted from the water like bad teeth. Spherical Day-Glo warning buoys bobbed on the water to mark sunken wrecks. Cranes clawed away at the wreckage of boats on shore. Debris of every kind swirled in the *Kestrel*'s wake.

Had Austin been of a more poetical bent, he would have said that the big wave had stolen the town's soul. 'What a *mess*,' was the best he could come up with.

'Coulda been worse,' said Police Chief Charlie

Howes, who stood next to Austin in the boat's stern.

'Yeah, if hit by a nuclear missile,' Austin said, with a shake of his head.

'Yep,' Howes replied, not letting an outlander outdo his Maine talent for brevity of speech.

Austin had been introduced to the chief a few hours earlier. A NUMA executive corporate jet had whisked Austin to the Portland Airport. Jenkins had called ahead to Chief Howes, and he was waiting at the airport in a police cruiser to drive Austin to Rocky Point.

After the meeting with Sandecker, Austin had gone to his office with the satellite photos of the *Ataman Explorer* and studied them under a high-powered magnifying glass. Even though the pictures had been shot from thousands of feet up, they were sharp and detailed. He could easily read the ship's name on the hull and see people on deck.

Austin was immediately struck by the ship's resemblance to the *Glomar Explorer*, the six-hundred-foot-long salvage vessel Howard Hughes had built in the 1970s on secret contract to the CIA to retrieve a sunken Soviet submarine. Tall derricks and cranes similar to those on the *Glomar* extended off the deck like waterborne oil rigs.

Austin examined the ship from stem to stern, paying particular attention to the deck area around the derricks. He made a few sketches on a pad of paper and sat back in his chair, a smug smile on his face. He had figured out a way to get onto the *Ataman*

Explorer. It was a long shot and depended on how close he could get to it. The vessel would run for cover at the first sight of a NUMA ship. He thought about the problem for a few minutes, recalling his Black Sea experience with Captain Kemal, then picked up his phone, called Yaeger and asked where Jenkins was.

'Doc Reed is giving him the NUMA VIP tour. He's offered to put Jenkins up for the night before he catches a plane back to Maine tomorrow.'

'See if you can track them down and give me a call.'

Austin's phone rang a few minutes later. Austin outlined his plan to Jenkins, making no effort to soft pedal its possible dangers. Jenkins didn't hesitate for a second. When Austin was through describing his wild scheme, Jenkins said, 'I'll do anything you can think of to get back at the bums who ruined my town.'

Austin told Jenkins to enjoy his tour while he made a few phone calls. The first call was to the NUMA transportation section to see if fast transportation was available. The second was to the Trouts' Georgetown town house. Gamay had left a message saying she and Paul were home from Istanbul and were standing by for orders. Austin got Paul on the phone and brought him up to date.

In the meantime, Jenkins started calling those local fishermen whose boats were still afloat and asked if they would like to do a job. At Austin's suggestion, Jenkins told the fishermen that NUMA needed their boats for a deep-ocean species study. As a bonus, the substantial sums they were being paid would be matched by no-strings grants to get their port back into shape without going through the usual government red tape.

Jenkins had no trouble recruiting fishermen, and when the *Kestrel* left port shortly after dawn, six other lobster boats and trawlers trailed behind him single-file. Charlie Howes had insisted on going along, and Jenkins was glad to have him. The chief had trapped lobsters for a living before joining the police department and hadn't lost his sea sense.

The fishing fleet passed the rock-ribbed promontory that gave the town its name, and entered the open ocean. The sea was a bright bottle green. Only a few whispery cirrus clouds marred the azure sky, and the breeze was a gentle westerly. The line of boats plodded east, then south, climbing the rolling swells and sliding down the other sides in an easy rhythm. Periodically, Gamay called from NUMA headquarters with the *Ataman Explorer*'s position as seen by satellite.

Austin penciled the positions on a chart of the Gulf of Maine, the expansive stretch of water between the long Maine coast and the curving arm of Cape Cod. The ship seemed to be moving in a big, lazy circle. Austin guessed it was in a holding pattern. Gamay used a simple code so anyone listening would think they were hearing fishermen's chatter. Jenkins and Howes politely ignored Gamay's butchering of the

Maine dialect. But when the voice that came over the speaker said, 'Catching some good haaadik and floundah soweast of my last set, ayup' they could remain silent no longer.

'*Ayup?*' Jenkins cringed. 'Did she say, "ayup"?'

Howes shook his head. 'I've lived Down East my whole life, and I've *never* heard anyone say "ayup." Wouldn't know what it means.'

Trout suppressed a smile. Mumbling an apology, he explained that Gamay had seen too many episodes of *Murder, She Wrote*, which had been set in the Hollywood version of a Maine town. Jenkins cut him off. With clear excitement in his voice, he pointed to a large blip on the radar screen. 'There she is. No doubt about it.'

Austin, who was leaning over his shoulder, looked at the target to the southeast. 'Ayup,' he said.

Jenkins gunned the throttle, picking up speed. The other boats did the same. It was more than a matter of impatience. Jenkins wasn't lulled by the playfulness of the sea. He had been studying the fetch, the distance between waves, with an experienced eye, assessing the situation as a fisherman and a scientist. 'We've got some weather coming in,' he said.

Austin said, 'I've been listening to the NOAA report on the radio.'

'I don't need the squawking of a computer-generated voice to tell me there's a storm on the way,' Jenkins said, with a grin. 'You just have to know how to read the signs.'

Since leaving port, Jenkins had watched the clouds gather and thicken and the sea spectrum shift to an oily gray. The breeze had moved a couple of compass points to the east. 'If we get our work here done quickly, we can get back to port ahead of the storm. Problem is that if the sea and the wind kick up, it could be dangerous hauling back on our net.'

'I understand,' Austin said. 'Paul and I will get ready.'

'Might be a good idea,' Chief Howes said, his easygoing voice gaining an uncharacteristic tautness. 'We've got company.'

The chief was pointing at a huge, dark shape that loomed from the gathering fog. As the amorphous mass grew closer, it lost its spectral aspect, and the lines that had been softened by the vaporous mists hardened into the silhouette of a very large ship. The vessel was completely black, from the waterline to the top of the single funnel protruding from the high superstructure. Derricks and cranes bristled from the deck like the quills on a porcupine. The dull, light-absorbing paint made the ship hard to see and gave it an evil, brooding aspect that wasn't lost on the other fishermen.

The radio crackled with excited voices. One fisherman said, 'Jeez, Roy, what's that thing? Looks like a floating hearse.'

'*Hearse*,' said another voice. 'Looks like the whole damned funeral parlor.'

Austin smiled at the chatter. Anyone listening to

the comments would know they hadn't been rehearsed. Jenkins warned his fellow fishermen to keep a sharp eye out so they wouldn't be run down. They didn't have to be told and gave the monster ship a wide berth. Austin estimated the ship's speed at around ten knots.

The *Ataman Explorer* seemed to slow as it came nearer. A dot detached itself from the deck. The speck grew larger, buzzing like a hornet stirred from its nest. Moments later, the black helicopter flew low over the fishing fleet. Jenkins and Howes gave the aircraft a friendly wave. The chopper circled the fishing fleet a few times, then headed back to the ship.

From inside the pilothouse, where he and Trout were donning their scuba gear, Austin watched the departing aircraft with calm eyes.

'Guess we passed inspection,' Austin said.

'That was a lot friendlier than the reception Gamay and I got when we poked around Ataman's property in Novorossiysk.'

'You can thank Jenkins for that. It was his idea to have lots of witnesses so Ataman would stay on the straight and narrow.'

Austin was glad that he had listened to Jenkins when he'd asked if he'd be willing to offer his services. Jenkins pointed out that there was safety in numbers. Since the vessel was sitting in prime fishing grounds, it was not all that suspicious for boats to be trawling in the area. In fact, Austin could see a half dozen fishing boats tending their nets on the way out.

Austin had based his plan on the successful infiltration of the sub base from Captain Kemal's fishing boat. Penetrating the sub pens had been easy compared with what he had in mind now. Unlike the scruffy Cossacks, who were more interested in playing people polo than standing guard, watchful and well-armed sentries would be manning the Ataman vessel.

Then Austin caught the break he was looking for. The ship plowed to a stop and floated dead in the water. Jenkins ran his boat as a trawler when he wasn't going after lobsters, and it was fitted out with a drumlike stern hauler to handle the net. With the help of the chief, he got the net in the water. Then the *Kestrel* got under way again and made a sweep by one side of the ship, a hundred yards off. The maneuver gave those on the ship a chance to inspect the fishing boat at close range. What they didn't see were the two divers hanging off the opposite side of the boat.

After traveling about halfway along the length of the ship, Jenkins cut the *Kestrel*'s engine to an idle and went out onto the deck. He and Howes tinkered with the hauler, as if there was a problem. During the pause, Austin and Trout dropped into the water and dove under the boat. They wanted to get deep and out of the way of the net.

It was agreed that Jenkins would make a sweep by one side of the ship, then trawl for a couple of miles before turning back and returning on the other side.

That gave them an hour to get on board the ship and back. They would keep in touch with Jenkins using their underwater communicators to talk to a hydrophone Trout had hung into the water before they went over the side.

They swam deeper, moving their legs in a steady flutter that ate up the distance. They could hear the muffled grumble of the fishing boat engine as Jenkins got under way again and dove to thirty-five feet, where the visibility was still fair. With powerful scissors kicks, they covered the distance to the ship in a short time.

The gigantic hull emerged from the murk like the body of an enormous whale asleep on the surface. Austin signaled Trout to go deeper. When they were directly under the massive keel, they looked up and snapped their lights on. It was hard not to be unnerved by thousands of tons of black steel floating above their heads.

'Now I know how a bug feels just before someone steps on it,' Trout said, gazing up at the massive hulk.

'I was thinking the same thing, but I didn't want to make you nervous.'

'Too late. Where do you want to start?'

'If I interpreted the satellite photos correctly, we should find what we're looking for at midships.'

They swam slowly upward until the ship's barnacle-encrusted bottom entirely filled the lenses of their face masks. In the beam of his light, Austin saw what he was looking for, a rubber-edged seam that ran across from one side of the flat-bottomed hull to the other. 'Bingo!' he said.

When Austin had first looked at the satellite pictures, he'd noticed an open area around one of the derricks that rose from the deck. Someone had carelessly left off a tarp that covered the opening and he could see down into a black void. He was sure he was looking into a 'moon pool,' a docking space similar to that on the *Argo* and other NUMA ships.

Austin knew from experience that odds favored the pool's gates being closed. It was standard operating procedure, otherwise the drag from the open sea would slow the ship down. But he remembered that some NUMA ships had a smaller pool used for launching ROVs. He saw what he was looking for on the port side, forward of the larger moon pool, an indented rectangle about twelve feet square. When they swam close, they saw that the gates of the ROV launch well were shut tight.

Austin unclipped the Oxy-Arc cutting torch from his belt and uncoiled the hose. Trout produced the oxygen tank he had been carrying and coupled it to the hose. From his belt bag, Austin pulled out two small powerful magnets with hand grips on them. He attached the magnets to the hull, then he and Trout slipped plastic shades over their masks to shield their eyes from the bright flame. While Austin held on to the magnet with one hand, Trout lit the torch. Even with the protection of the eyeshades, it was like looking at the sun.

Austin began to cut, hoping that the pool cover was thinner than the actual hull. Although the ship wasn't moving, water churned around its great bulk and created eddies of current that pulled at Austin's body. With Trout's help, he had been able to stay more or less in one place, but a particularly violent current twisted him completely around. He had to let go of the magnet and when he made a grab with the other hand in reflex, he dropped the torch.

Trout was having similar problems, only he lost the oxygen tank. They managed to grab onto the magnets and whipped their eyeshades off in time to see the tank and the torch, still lit, plunge out of sight into the depths.

Every sailor's curse Austin had learned in years at sea crackled in Trout's earphones. After exhausting his repertoire of curses, he said, 'I couldn't hold on to the torch.'

'You may have noticed that I lost the tank. I didn't realize you knew so many cusswords.'

Austin managed a chuckle. 'Zavala taught me the ones in Spanish. Sorry for dragging you all this way for nothing.'

'If I weren't under a giant ship in the middle of the Atlantic Ocean, Gamay would have me wall-papering our townhouse. Got any backup plans?'

'Maybe if we knock, they'll open the doors. Or we swim to the surface, look for a ladder hanging down and climb aboard.'

'Hardly practical.'

'You asked if I had backup ideas. You didn't say they had to be practical.'

Austin was about to give the word to head back when Trout let out a yell of surprise and jabbed his forefinger straight down.

Paul's sharp fisherman's eye had seen faint lights rising from the darkness below. The hazy glow reminded Austin of the luminescent fish William Beebe had found on his half-mile dive in a bathysphere. The oncoming object grew larger. They hurried out of its path until they were off to one side of the ship. They turned around and saw a small submarine ascend until it was about a hundred feet beneath the hull of the Ataman ship. The sub was clearly outlined by its running lights.

'I'll be darned,' Trout said, recognizing the distinctive silhouette. 'It's the *NR-1*. What's she doing here?'

'More important, where's she going next?' Austin's nimble mind had already sprinted several steps ahead. 'Let's go for a boat ride.'

Austin angled his body downward and swam behind the hovering sub. He had once made a dive on the *NR-1* and knew a camera was mounted forward of the conning tower. He and Trout grabbed onto the stair rungs built into the sail and hung on. Within seconds, a thin glowing line of yellow light appeared above. The moon pool gates were being retracted.

Trout looked up, the illumination from above

reflected in his mask lens. 'I think I saw this on *The X-Files* when the aliens abducted a human.'

'It's always nice to meet new friends,' Austin said, his eyes glued to the line as it widened into a long narrow rectangle, then a square of blazing light.

The sub's vertical thrusters whirred, and the *NR-1* rose slowly into the ship. Austin and Trout slid off the deck before the sub surfaced inside the pool. They swam toward a dark area between the circles of illumination cast by the lights inside the ship. At the edge of the pool, they cautiously poked their heads from the water. From the safety of the shadows, Austin took measure. The pool was about two hundred feet long and half as wide. Steel mesh catwalks accessed by short flights of open stairs ran along both sides.

Men in coveralls leaned over the railings and watched the *NR-1* emerge from the water. Then the loud grinding of gears filled the enormous chamber as the pool doors closed. Heavy-duty hoists fitted with steel hooks descended from the ceiling. A door opened in the side of the chamber, and several divers dressed in dry suits jumped into the water. They slid wide yokes under the front and back of the sub. The yokes were attached to the hooks, and powerful winches lifted the sub like the chain falls that were used to yank car engines out.

The hydraulic gates slid shut, sealing the chamber from the sea, and with a mighty grumble, invisible pumps began to suck water from the pool. The powerful pumps cleared the pool in minutes. Then the winches lowered the sub. Crews of men flowed down the stairs onto the slimy floor of the pool. While some men swept the deck clear of seaweed and flopping fish, others attached cables to the *NR-1* and braced it with timbers so it wouldn't shift with the ship's movement. The whoosh of ventilators brought fresh air into the space.

Austin and Trout had scrambled up a ladder when the pumping started, and now they hung above the deck. The weight of their scuba equipment pulled at their arms and fingers. While they huddled in the shadows, below them in the glare of lights men leaned a ladder against the sub. The hatch opened in the conning tower, and a man with a white beard climbed out. He had a revolver holster on his belt and matched the description Ensign Kreisman had given of Pulaski, the phony scientist who'd pulled a gun on the *NR-1*.

Two more men came out. Austin recognized Captain Logan and the pilot of the *NR-1* from pictures he'd been shown. Four more men emerged. They had tough, impassive faces and carried heavy-duty firearms that identified them as guards. The *NR-1* men were ushered up the stairs and disappeared from view. Hauling bags of sea debris, the last of the cleaning crew followed. The lights went out except for a glow above their heads.

'What now?' Trout said.

'We've got two choices. Up or down.'

Trout looked at the darkness below them and then grabbed the rung above his head and started to climb. The scuba gear seemed to get heavier the higher they got. Luckily, they had to climb less than twenty feet before they reached a narrow landing. With a mighty grunt, Trout pulled himself up and over the rail and slipped off his tanks and weight belt. He gave Austin a hand and they both sat there, catching their breath.

While he sat with his back to the bulkhead, Austin retrieved his Bowen from a watertight pack. Trout carried a SIG-Sauer .9 mm pistol of Swiss design. They walked to where the short landing joined a catwalk at a right angle. The catwalk ran into a well-lit passageway. Seeing that it was deserted, they kept on the move. They came upon a large alcove that sheltered a shiny, white, domed structure with small portholes on its side. They recognized the white dome immediately as a decompression chamber.

After making sure no one was using the chamber, they went back for their scuba gear and stashed it inside. Then they slipped out of their dry suits and stowed them with the tanks. A short distance from the decompression chamber, they found a locker room. Hanging from a thick rod and still dripping with seawater were the suits worn by the divers who had tied down the *NR-1*. Austin was more interested in the neatly folded sets of coveralls stashed on shelves near the lockers. They pulled the coveralls on over their suit liners.

At six feet eight and 270 pounds, Trout wasn't easy to fit. The legs of his uniform came down to his ankles, and his arms protruded from his sleeves.

'How do I look?' Trout said.

'Like a very tall scarecrow. Aside from that, you should fool anyone we meet for at least ten seconds.'

He scrunched down. 'How's this?'

'Now you look like Quasimodo.'

'That hair of yours isn't exactly inconspicuous. Let's hope anyone we meet is legally blind. What's next?'

Austin plucked a cap from a pile, tossed it to Trout and jammed another on his head. He pulled the visor down over his head and said: 'We go for a stroll.'

29

Austin stopped at an intersection and glanced up and down the corridors like a bewildered tourist. 'Damn,' he said. 'I think we're lost.'

'We should have left a trail of bread crumbs,' Trout said wistfully.

'This isn't exactly a gingerbread house and we're not Hansel and – Whoops.' Austin jerked his thumb at a door off to the left. His ear had picked up the click of a knob turning.

Trout stepped back, but Austin grabbed his arm. 'Too late,' he whispered. 'Look as if we belong here.' He bent his head over a clipboard he'd liberated from the divers' room and kept one hand close to the gun concealed under his uniform. Trout got down on one knee, untied his shoelace and began to tie it.

The door opened, and two men came out. Austin glanced up from his clipboard, gave them a friendly smile and checked them out for weapons. The men differed from each other in physique, but both wore glasses and their faces had a studious look. They were deep in conversation and only glanced at the NUMA men before they disappeared down a corridor.

Austin watched them go and said, 'You can stand now. Those two looked like techies. We've got a major problem. It could take days to search this ship properly. The longer we're here, the greater the chance someone will see through our highly imaginative disguises.'

Trout stood and rubbed his knee. 'To say nothing of the toll to be exerted on my aging joints. What do we do now?'

Austin stared off past Trout's shoulder, and a smile replaced the frown on his lips. 'For starters, I'd suggest that you look behind you.'

Trout grinned when he saw the diagram on the wall. It was a map showing the ship's layout as seen from above and in profile. 'We're apparently not the only ones who need help finding their way around this little houseboat.'

Austin examined the map closely and tapped a red dot that indicated their intersection. 'We're coming up on a restricted area. Let's see what they're trying to hide. If it's restricted, there may be less chance of bumping into Razov's thug brigade.'

Austin's words had barely faded when they heard rough male voices approaching. Without hesitation, Austin stepped over to the door from which the scientists had emerged, and tried the knob. The door was unlocked. He gestured for Trout to follow him. The room was dark, but he could smell chemicals and guessed it was a lab. He quietly closed the door, leaving it open a crack. Within seconds, a pair of stocky guards, each carrying an automatic weapon, passed by and disappeared down the passageway. He flicked on a wall light long enough to see that they were, indeed, in a laboratory of some sort. Then he checked once more, saw the way was clear, and they cautiously slipped back into the corridor.

He pointed to the passageway on the right. Ever alert, they set off along the corridor until a door blocked their way. Austin used his rusty language skills from his CIA days to translate the Cyrillic letters printed on the outside. AUTHORIZED PERSONNEL ONLY. He tried the door. Locked. He reached into his pack and came out with a set of burglary lock picks, another holdover from his time with the Company. With Trout keeping watch, Austin tried several picks before coming up with the right one. He turned the knob, and they stepped inside.

With its horseshoe-shaped console, the room resembled the control area of Yeager's computer center, although it was a fraction of the size. Instead of facing out onto a voice-activated hologram stage like Max, beyond the console was a large screen controlled by a keyboard, archaic relics that Yaeger would have disdained.

Trout walked over and examined the set-up. It was fairly sophisticated. Although he was considered a computer whiz in his own right, specializing in the modeling of deep ocean bottom phenomena, Trout was not in the same league as Yaeger.

'Well?' Austin said.

Trout shrugged and said, 'I'll give it a try.' He settled his long form into a swivel chair. Like a concert pianist looking for a lost chord, he let his fingers play over the keyboard without touching the keys. After first asking Austin to translate the Cyrillic, he took a deep breath and pushed the key that said *Enter*. The fish school screensaver that had been swimming across the screen disappeared, and in its place was an icon of a sunburst. 'So far, so good,' he said. 'I didn't set off any alarms that I know of.'

Austin, who was leaning over Trout's shoulder looking at the monitor, gave him a back pat of encouragement.

Trout bent to his task. He clicked on the icon, which was replaced by a number of options. For several minutes, he pecked away at the keys, muttering under his breath. Then he sat back and folded his arms. 'I need a password to get in.'

'That could be anything,' Austin said with frustration.

Trout nodded sadly. 'We have to think Russian. Anything you've come across that might work?'

Taking a stab at it, Austin told him to try *Cossack*. When that didn't work, he tried *Ataman*. Nothing. One more false try, and the computer would freeze up on them. He was about to give up when he recalled his first conversation with Petrov back in Istanbul. 'Try *Troika*.' Trout let out a triumphant, 'Yes!' Then his shoulders sagged as the screen filled with lines of words. 'This is the Russian equivalent of gobbledygook.' He worked on it a few more minutes. Beads of perspiration appeared on his forehead. He sat back in the chair and threw his hands up in the air.

'Sorry, Kurt, this is beyond my skills.' He shook his head. 'What I need is a teenage hacker.'

Austin only had to think about Trout's request for an instant. 'Hold on. I can get you the next best thing.'

He produced his Globalstar phone and punched out a number. When Yaeger's voice came on, Austin said, 'Good morning, Hiram. I can't get into details because we're short on time, but Paul needs help.'

He handed the phone to Trout. Before long, the two men were into a deep discussion of firewalls, packet filters, application, Trojan horses, gateway circuits, tunnels and decoys. He gave the phone back to Austin.

'Let's see if I can explain the problem,' Yaeger said. 'Think of the computer as a room. You go into the room, but it's dark, so you can't see what's written on the blackboard. So you flick the switch, which is what Paul has done, but the blackboard is still unreadable because it's in a language you can't understand.'

'Where does that leave us?'

'Nowhere, I'm afraid. I wish Max and I were there to take a crack at the puzzle.'

Austin replied with a grunt, then looked at the phone. 'The solution may be at hand. You tell me if it's possible.'

He explained what he was thinking and Yaeger said it was doable, given the right equipment. Austin returned the phone to Trout, who got up and began to go through drawers in the console and other cabinets in the room. He found some cables that he spliced together, and then plugged one end into the computer's entry port. 'It's not the greatest modem in the world, but I'll try to attach it to the phone now.' He removed the back of the phone and ran the other end of the cable inside. Then he dialed a number.

The computer screen went squirrelly for a second. Letters and numbers streamed by in a blur. The screen went blank. Then a message appeared: 'We're wired. Starting to download. Hiram and Max.'

Austin glanced at his watch as he paced back and forth, wondering how long it would take Yaeger to do his job. The minutes ticked by. He feared that they would have to leave before the job was done. But after ten minutes, a big yellow smiley face wearing granny glasses that looked suspiciously like Yaeger's appeared. 'Hack job done. Hiram and Max.'

They quickly disconnected the makeshift modem and replaced the parts. Austin stuck his head out the door to see if the way was clear. The corridor was deserted. Moving with haste they made their way back to the ship diagram and selected a shorter route to the moon pool. So far their luck had held out and they'd seen no one. Austin was puzzled at the lack of personnel, but wasn't about to argue with good fortune. They were hurrying along a passageway, when they passed a door and heard voices speaking in English. The accents were unmistakably American. Austin tried the door and found it locked. Again, he resorted to his lock picks.

The door opened onto a cabin with two bunks. Lounging on the bunks, with bored expressions on their faces, were Captain Logan and the pilot from the *NR-1*. Their conversation stopped in midsentence, and they stared at the newcomers with unbridled hostility, assuming they were guards who had come to make their life miserable.

Logan turned to the pilot and said, 'Where are they getting these guys?'

'The tall one looks like he should be scaring crows in a field,' the pilot said.

'That suit on the shorter guy sure didn't come from Armani,' Logan said, with a chuckle.

'Armani was closed, Captain Logan. We had to borrow our wardrobe from the ship's crew.'

Suspicion clouded Logan's eyes. 'Who the hell are *you*?'

'That gentleman imitating a scarecrow is my colleague, Paul Trout. My name is Kurt Austin, but you can call me "Shorty."'

The captain sprang from his bunk. 'Damnit, you're *Americans*!'

'Told you our disguises wouldn't hold up,' Austin said to Trout. He turned back to Logan. 'Guilty as charged, Captain. Paul and I are with the NUMA Special Assignments Team.'

The captain looked toward the door. 'We didn't hear

any fighting. Have your guys taken over the ship?'

Austin and Trout exchanged amused glances. 'Sorry to disappoint you. Delta Force was busy, so we came alone,' Austin said.

'I don't understand. How –?'

Austin cut him off. 'We'll explain after we get you off this ship.'

He motioned to Trout, who opened the door slightly to see if it was safe to exit. Again the hallway was clear. With Trout leading the way and Austin taking up the rear, they moved along a corridor toward the stairway as if they were escorting the submariners.

The strategy came in handy a moment later when they encountered a lone guard walking in their direction, his weapon shouldered. Austin guessed from the man's casual demeanor that he was on his way back to his quarters. The guard's eyes flicked toward Trout and his brow wrinkled as he tried to figure out why he didn't recognize a shipmate of Trout's imposing height. The captain stopped when he saw the guard, unsure of what to do.

Austin could have taken the guard out, but he preferred that the visit to the ship go unnoticed, if possible. He hooked his foot around Logan's ankle and gave him a shove. The captain went down on his hands and knees. The guard's puzzlement changed to amusement, and he roared with laughter and said something in Russian. He laughed again when Austin kicked the captain lightly in the rear end.

Austin shrugged and replied with an innocent look.

Still laughing, the guard continued along the hall until he was out of sight. Austin reached down and helped Logan up.

'Sorry, Captain,' he said, with obvious embarrassment. 'He was getting a fix on Paul, and I had to divert his attention.'

Logan dusted off the seat of his pants. 'I've had my command hijacked, my crew kidnapped, and been forced by these seagoing thugs to use a US Navy vessel for their purposes,' he said with a grin. 'I'll suffer whatever it takes to get off this ship.'

Trout stopped and examined another wall diagram. 'It looks as if the moon pool hold is divided into a smaller and larger section. I'd advise going in the smaller end to avoid crew quarters here.'

Austin told him to lead the way. With long, loping strides, Trout led them along a series of passageways until they came to an unlocked door. On the other side was a catwalk that ran along the wall of a high-ceiling chamber about a third the size of the moon pool.

'What the hell is *that* thing?' the captain said.

He was looking at a huge cylindrical object suspended from the ceiling. It was at least four feet across and fifty feet long. The bottom end was cone shaped and several projections were clustered around the top, where a complex set of cables and hoses snaked into the ceiling.

'Looks like an ICBM,' the pilot said, 'only it's pointing the wrong way.'

'That's not *all* that's wrong with it,' Trout said. 'Those are *thrusters* around the top, not fins.'

Austin was as fascinated as the others, but time was short. 'Take a good look at it now, gentlemen, and we'll compare notes later.'

They continued along the walkway through another door and found themselves outside the changing room, where they found dry suits that fit the navy men. Austin and Trout carefully folded their borrowed coveralls and replaced them on the shelves. Then they all moved on to the decompression chamber. The dive gear was undisturbed. They descended a short stairway that led to a room with the smaller moon pool. Set into the deck was a depressed twelve-by-twelve-foot-square section outlining the pool that was used for launching ROVs. Trout studied the controls on the wall, then hit a button and the floor of the shallow well slid back. Water lapped over the top of the well and a damp, briny chill filled the room.

The pilot looked into the dark square of ocean and gulped. 'You're kidding.'

'Sorry it isn't a hot tub,' Austin said. 'But unless you can figure a way to open the main floodgates so we can use the *NR-1*, this is the only way off the ship.'

'Hell, this should be no different from the escape training tank at Groton,' the captain said with bravado, although his face was pale.

'We don't have any spare air tanks, so we'll buddy-breathe. It's about a hundred-yard swim to our pickup. The open hatch probably sets off an alarm up in the wheelhouse, so we don't have much time.'

Despite his bluster, the captain didn't look enthusiastic about the prospect ahead, but he gritted his teeth, pulled the hood down and the face mask over his eyes. 'Let's go before I change my mind,' he growled.

Austin handed the pilot the auxiliary air hose, called the octopus. Trout did the same with the captain. When all were ready, Austin linked arms with the pilot, stepped to the edge of the pool and jumped in.

They sank in a cloud of bubbles until their buoyancy overcame their downward momentum. The bubbles quickly cleared, and Austin saw Trout's light waving in the gloom from several feet away. Austin started swimming. The submariners' kicking technique was uneven and the Siamese-twin arrangement was awkward, but they managed to claw their way out from under the ship's massive bulk.

Austin felt himself rising and falling. Sea conditions must be deteriorating. Austin's compass was useless so close to the huge metal mass of the Ataman ship. He relied on dead reckoning to move them in the general direction of the rendezvous.

When Austin gauged they were a hundred yards from the ship, he stopped and signaled for the others to do the same. While they hovered thirty feet below the surface, he undid a small self-inflating buoy from his belt and looped a nylon line tied to the buoy over his wrist. He released the buoy and let it rise to the surface, where the miniature transponder it carried would start broadcasting their location.

The next few minutes were excruciating. Despite their suits, the cold numbed the exposed areas around their hands and masks. The *NR-1* men were courageous, but being held prisoner had sapped their strength and they were simply out of shape from spending long idle hours in their cabin. Austin wondered what they would do if the *Kestrel* failed to show up. He was savoring the bleak possibilities when Jenkins's voice came through his earphones.

'Got a lock on your position marker. You boys okay?'

'We're fine. We picked up a couple of hitchhikers, and they're turning six shades of blue from the cold.'

'On my way.'

Austin signaled to the others to get ready. The *NR-1* men responded with okay hand signals, but the slowness of their movements indicated that they were becoming fatigued. For the plan to work, they would need energy. All four men looked up as they heard the muffled grumble of an engine. The noise grew louder until it was right overhead.

Austin jerked his thumb up. Then he and Trout rose, pulling their exhausted companions with them. Austin kept his free arm extended straight above his head until his fingers closed on the moving net being towed behind the slow-moving *Kestrel*. The others all managed to grab onto the cod end, the tapering pocket where the fish are actually caught.

When Austin saw that everyone had a grip on the net, he shouted to Jenkins. 'All aboard!'

The boat's speed picked up and they felt as if their arms were being pulled out of their sockets. But after the initial shock, the ride smoothed out and they were flying through the water. The water pressure tried to brush them off, but they held on gamely until they were well away from the ship. Jenkins hove to.

'Hauling back,' he said in warning.

Austin and Trout got a firm grip on their charges as the net pulled them to the surface. Their troubles weren't over, however. They were tossed around in the heaving seas and hampered by their scuba gear, until, finally, they jettisoned their air tanks and belts. Without the awkward weight, they could work with the waves rather than fight them.

Jenkins was leaning over the stern controlling the hauler, the big metal drum that the net was wound upon when not in the water. The net had drawn Austin and the pilot within a few feet of safety, but the boat pitched and yawed violently and the seas lifted them one second, dropped them the next. Choking fumes from the exhaust rose from the water. To make matters worse, Austin's right arm had become entangled in the net.

Jenkins saw their predicament, and the narrow blade of a razor-sharp filleting knife flashed dangerously close to Austin's biceps. With his arm free, he reached up to Jenkins, who grabbed his wrist in an iron grip. Working the hauler with the other hand, he pulled Austin, then the pilot, closer.

'Damn funny-looking fish we're catching these days,' he yelled over the rumble of the engine.

Howes was manning the helm and doing his best to keep the boat steady. 'Those fellas are a bit small,' he shouted back. 'Maybe we should throw them back.'

'Not on your life,' Austin said, as he got one leg over the transom and practically fell into the boat.

Jenkins helped the pilot on board. With three of them working, they got Trout and Logan onto the boat in short order. The submariners staggered drunkenly across the pitching deck into the wheelhouse. The net had caught several hundred pounds of fish; and the weight threatened to drag the ship down. Jenkins hated to lose the fish and let the net loose in the sea where it might catch on a propeller, but he had no choice. He cut the lines and watched the net drift off into the foamy sea. Then he took over the helm and gunned the boat through the white-capped seas that splashed over the bow.

Howes helped the others out of their dry suits, then passed around blankets and a bottle of Irish whiskey. Austin peered through the spume, but the black ship had disappeared. There was also no sign of the fishing boats that had accompanied them on the way out. He asked where the other boats were.

'Things got dicey out here, so I sent them home,' Jenkins yelled over the grinding roar of the engine. 'We should get back to port before the storm hits. Sit back and enjoy the ride.'

'I wonder what our former hosts will say when they discover us gone,' Logan said with a wolfish smile.

'I'm hoping that they'll think you tried to escape and were drowned.'

'Thanks for coming to our rescue. My only regret is that we couldn't leave the way we came, on the *NR-1*.'

'The important part was getting you out in one piece.'

Trout passed the whiskey bottle to Austin. 'Here's to a job well done.'

Austin raised the bottle to his lips and took a sip. The fiery liquid overwhelmed the salty taste in his mouth and warmed his stomach. He stared out past their heaving wake, thinking about the huge projectile they had seen on the ship.

'Unfortunately,' he said, 'the real work may have just begun.'

Hiram Yaeger toiled late into the night. He had moved away from his usual place at the grand console and sat in a corner of the vast computer center, his face lit up by a single screen. He was typing commands into a keyboard, and Max didn't like it.

HIRAM, WHY AREN'T WE USING THE HOLOGRAM?

THIS IS A SIMPLE ACCESS PROBLEM, MAX. WE DON'T
NEED THE BELLS AND WHISTLES. IT'S BACK TO
BASICS.

I FEEL PRACTICALLY NAKED SITTING OUT HERE IN
A PLAIN PLASTIC CABINET.

YOU'RE STILL BEAUTIFUL IN MY EYES.

FLATTERY WILL GET YOU EVERYWHERE. THE
PROBLEM, PLEASE.

Yaeger had been working for hours to carve away the useless and misleading data in the files Austin and Trout had transmitted from the Ataman ship. He'd run into countless dead ends and had had to cut through more layers than an onion. Finally, he had distilled his findings into a series of commands that would cut through the dross. He typed them out one at a time and waited. Before long, words written in Cyrillic appeared. He entered a command to use translation software.

Yaeger scratched his head, mystified at the image on the screen. It was a menu.

As he was watching, the menu disappeared and in its place was a message from Max.

MAY I TAKE YOUR ORDER, SIR?

WHAT'S THIS ALL ABOUT?

I COULD TELL YOU BETTER IF WE USED THE
HOLOGRAM.

Yaeger blinked. Max was trying to bribe him. He rotated his shoulder blades to relieve the stress of working, breathed a weary sigh and brought his fingers back to the keyboard.

30

Washington, DC

The NUMA executive jet was one of dozens of planes coming into Washington National Airport. Unlike the regularly scheduled arrivals that followed the buglike ground vehicles to their respective terminals, the turquoise plane taxied to a restricted section on the south end of the airport not far from an old airplane hangar with a rounded roof. The engines whined to a stop and a trio of dark blue Suburban SUVs emerged from the shadows with darkened headlights, and lined up alongside the plane.

Two Marine guards and a man dressed in civilian clothes got out of the lead vehicle. While the guards took their place at the foot of the gangway, standing stiffly at attention, the third man, who carried a black satchel, strode quickly up the gangway and rapped on the door. It opened a second later, and Austin stuck his head out.

'I'm Captain Morris, a doctor from the naval hospital,' the man said. 'I've come to check out our people.' He looked past Austin and saw the unconscious forms of the captain and the pilot slumped in their seats. 'Dear God! Are they dead?'

'Yeah, dead *drunk*,' Austin said. 'We celebrated their homecoming on the trip from Portland and they had a little too much of the bubbly. Those strapping young Marines down there might want to assist your men off the plane.'

Captain Morris called the Marines, and they managed to help the *NR-1* men down the gangway to the tarmac. The cool night air revived Captain Logan and the pilot. They gave Austin and Trout an emotional and slurred thank-you, staggered to the middle vehicle and were whisked off into the night in a squeal of tires, leaving Austin and Trout breathing in their engine exhausts.

The taillights were barely out of sight when a figure stepped from the shadows and a familiar and unmistakable voice said, 'That's gratitude for you. The least the navy could have done was call a cab to run you home.'

Austin glanced at the departing SUVs. 'The navy doesn't like fly-by-night operations like us showing up their expensive intelligence services and aircraft carriers.'

'They'll get over it,' Admiral Sandecker said, with amusement. 'Can I offer you a lift?'

'Best offer I've had all night.'

Austin and Trout got into the Jeep Cherokee parked nearby. Sandecker deplored limousines, or any of the trappings of power for that matter, and preferred to drive a four-wheel drive from NUMA's agency pool. The pilot and copilot finished buttoning down the plane and Sandecker gave them rides home.

Austin had called Sandecker from Maine to tell him about the mission. As he drove onto the George Washington Memorial Parkway, Sandecker said, 'I said it before, but you boys deserve a medal for getting aboard that ship.'

'It was getting *off* the ship that I preferred, although I may give up fishing forever now that I've seen a trawl from a cod's point of view,' Trout said with his understated New England humor.

Sandecker chuckled. 'You're reasonably certain no one on board the Ataman ship will suspect the navy men were spirited away?'

'A few crewmen might remember seeing us and put two and two together with the missing dry suits and the open moon pool. I doubt they'd think anyone was crazy enough to do what we did, and get away with it.'

'I agree. They will report the missing navy men to Razov, but they'll assume they drowned or died from hypothermia. Even if they suspect an intrusion, I doubt whether they'd tell Razov, for fear of their lives.'

'He might learn the truth when the navy announces that all the *NR-1* crew have been rescued.'

'I've asked the Navy Department to keep a lid on the announcement, which they were glad to do. The crew members will be reunited with their families and whisked off to a seaside retreat for some R & R.'

'That will buy us some time.'

432

'We'll need every minute. Get a good night's sleep, both of you, and we'll have a meeting first thing in the morning.'

Sandecker drove Trout to his Georgetown town house and gave Austin a lift to Fairfax. Austin dropped his overnight bag inside the door and went into the den-study, a spacious room with dark wood colonial furniture and walls lined with shelves for his books and progressive jazz collection.

The red light was blinking on his telephone answering machine. He clicked through the messages and was happy to hear that Joe Zavala was back from England. Austin grabbed a tall can of Speckled Hen ale from his refrigerator and settled into a black leather chair with his phone. Joe answered on the first ring. They talked at length. Zavala filled him in on his interview with Lord Dodson, and Austin gave a summary of Jenkins's visit to NUMA and the successful mission to the Ataman ship.

After he hung up, Austin walked out onto the deck and drew a deep breath of river air into his lungs. The exercise cleared his head, and he began to think about the drama that had played out on the Black Sea decades ago. With the passage of time, the people who had struggled for their lives had no more substance than the lights glowing like fireflies along the Maryland shore. Yet the long-ago echoes of their voices were still being heard more than eighty years later.

According to Zavala's report, the empress and her

daughters were traveling on the *Odessa Star* with some of the royal treasure when the ship was attacked and sunk. Razov probably had the treasure now. Austin was uncertain why a man who already had more money than Croesus would go through so much trouble to dive for treasure. Greed knows no bounds, he concluded.

More important was the fact that the Grand Duchess Maria had escaped. Lord Dodson was worried about political turmoil if and when the news got out. Austin frowned at the tacit approval of the British Crown in the sordid tale. The story might embarrass some families, but all those involved were long dead. Mendacity by those in high office was no longer the scandal it once had been. Austin was more concerned about how the story connected to Ataman and the supposed plot against the United States.

Austin glanced at his watch. He hadn't realized the lateness of the hour or how worn-out he was. He crawled up to his bedroom in the turret of the old Victorian boathouse, crashed into bed and was asleep within minutes.

Austin was up at dawn, dressed in T-shirt, shorts and baseball cap, put a pot of Jamaican coffee on to brew and went downstairs to where his twenty-three-foot Mass Aero racing scull was stored under the house. He was lifting the forty-pound scull off its rack in preparation for a morning row on the Potomac, when he heard the telephone ring. Irritated at having his routine interrupted, he sprinted up the stairs to the main level and snatched the phone from its cradle.

'We've *got* it,' Yaeger said, his voice scratchy from weariness. 'That is to say, Max and I *almost* got it.'

'Should I be happy or sad?'

'Maybe both,' Yaeger said. 'I had Max working on the file all night. She did a hell of a job. Click on your computer, and I'll show you what I've got.'

Austin did as he was told and called up the e-mail and the attachment Yaeger had forwarded. The image that came up showed a document with several lines of Russian written in graceful script, the words bounded by fancy scrollwork.

'What is it?'

'It's a menu,' Yaeger said. 'The first one is the appetizer, Beluga caviar. The rest is a list of courses for something like a Russian banquet. Perlmutter would love it. Sounds quite tasty after this morning's snack of sugar-glazed doughnuts and weak coffee.'

'I'll buy you a full-course breakfast later, but are you saying that after all we went through to get this stuff, the best we can come up with is *caviar*?'

'Yes and no. The menu is really a set of files encrypted with steganography. It means "covered writing." It's a way of hiding messages in pictures. Uses a special software. Man, whoever set up security is real good. Even Max hit the wall on this one. I wrote a new program that unravels the puzzle. Watch.'

A gray dialog box appeared.

'What is that?'

'It's asking for the password.'

'What about the password we used to get into the ship's computer?'

'*Troika* was only good so far as it went. It got me to this point. Now I need another one.'

Austin groaned. 'So we're right back to where we started.'

'Yes and no. I've got Max running through possible words or combinations. She'll come up with an answer . . . but it could be days.'

'We may not have days,' Austin said.

'Then I've got another idea that may help you. The files indicate that there is a master control somewhere other than on your mystery ship. Find that, and we can find your password.'

Austin's head was swimming, as it did after any conversation with Yaeger. 'Let me think about it. I'll get back to you.'

Austin went back downstairs and shoved his racing scull into the water. Easing into the narrow craft, he warmed up for ten minutes under quarter pressure, gradually working his rate to twenty-eight strokes a minute, his eyes glued to the dial of the Stroke-Coach over his toes. The strokes merged with an unbroken rhythm that sent the light shell scudding smoothly over the river's misty surface like flowing quicksilver.

Austin rowed without gloves so he could feel the river with each dip of the oars. He wanted to sweat out the white-hot anger he felt over the *Sea Hunter* so that the heat would not consume him. He slipped into a meditative state and felt his rage ebb, although it didn't go away entirely. After rowing for a time, he turned in a wide circle and headed back. Before long, the scull was gliding up to the ramp of the boathouse. He threw his sweaty clothes in a hamper, took a long shower and shaved, and dressed in a tan sports jacket, navy blue polo shirt and light slacks.

A sound sleep and an energetic row had given him perspective. He brushed aside the distractions that had been pulling his mind apart in a hundred different directions and concentrated on the prime force behind all he had experienced. *Razov*. He had to find Razov. Everything else would flow from there. He picked up the phone and called Rudi Gunn, who had never shaken his old navy habits and was in his office before most commuters had poured their first cup of coffee.

'Kurt, I was about to call you. Admiral Sandecker told me about your successful mission. Congratulations to you and Paul.'

'Thanks, Rudi. Unfortunately, our job isn't over. Razov is the key to all this. I was wondering if you'd heard anything about his whereabouts.'

'That's what I wanted to tell you. The Mad Russian has come up for air. He and his super yacht are expected momentarily in Boston.'

'How'd you pick that up, through intelligence or satellites?'

'Neither one, actually. I saw it in the business section of the *Washington Post*. I'll read it to you:

Russian mining tycoon Mikhail Razov will arrive in Boston today to announce the opening of an international trade center. Razov, who is also a prominent political figure in his country, will host a reception for government officials and other guests tonight aboard his yacht, said to be one of the largest privately owned vessels in the world. The stop-off is part of a tour of major East Coast ports.'

'Thoughtful of him to save us time and energy,' Austin said.

'It doesn't fit with what I have heard about the gentleman. Wonder what he's really up to?'

'Why don't I go aboard and ask him?'

'You're serious?'

'Of *course*. It might do some good for him to know that we're onto him. Maybe we can shake the trees and see what falls out.'

'Just as long as you're not standing under them.'

Austin thought of Yaeger's suggestion about finding the master control center. A man like Razov would never let anything get far from his control. And his yacht was both his home and the headquarters of his worldwide corporation.

'We can't let an opportunity like this go by. I want to get aboard that yacht.'

'We could fix you up with some NUMA credentials.'

'That would be like waving a red flag in front of a bull. I have another idea. I'll get back to you.'

Austin hung up and dug in his wallet for a business card. Then he dialed the New York number on it.

'*Unbelievable Mysteries*,' the receptionist said.

He asked if Kaela Dorn had returned from assignments.

'I believe so. May I say who's calling?'

Austin gave his name and braced for a breath of icy air. He was surprised at the warmth in Kaela's voice. 'Good morning, Mr Austin. You certainly get up early in the day.'

'The early bird catches the worm, I've been told.'

'Never did like worms,' Kaela said. 'What can I do for you?'

'First of all, tell me why you're being so friendly.'

'Why *shouldn't* I be? You saved my life. Even better, you got me transportation back to Istanbul on Captain Kemal's boat.'

'Which wasn't exactly the *QE2*, as I recall.'

'Doesn't matter. On the way back, the captain told me about a wreck he knew of and took me there. It was big and old, and my guess is that it was originally measured in cubits.'

'Noah's ark?'

'Who knows? Who cares? We got the story, plus bonuses. So thanks again, and I mean it with all sincerity when I say, what can I do for you, even though you still owe me a dinner.'

'How about Boston baked beans?'

'I was thinking more of rack of lamb at the Four Seasons.'

'Anything you say. But I need your help first. There's a trade reception tonight aboard a yacht in Boston Harbor, and I need some press credentials.'

'Is there a story here?'

'Eventually. But not now.'

'Okay, but under one condition. I'm going with you. Before you say no, think about it.'

Austin thought about Kaela's sultry beauty for a millisecond. 'It's a deal. I'll catch a shuttle to Logan Airport.' He suggested a meeting time and place.

After they hung up, Austin sat back in his chair and stared into space, a distant expression in the coral-blue eyes. Finding Razov's central control system might be the breakthrough he and NUMA needed, but there was another reason he wanted to get aboard the yacht. *Boris.*

3 I

Boston, Massachusetts

Kaela Dorn waited at Commonwealth Pier over-looking Boston Harbor and watched the parade of limousines drop off a steady stream of VIPs who quickly lined up to be transported to Razov's yacht. She stood near a line of television vans whose satellite dishes and antennae sprouted from their roofs like alien vegetative growths. She was scanning the crowd when the tall stranger approached from behind and greeted her. Hardly glancing in his direction, Kaela replied with a polite hello. She regretted it a second later when he said in a wheedling nasal voice: 'Excuse me, but haven't we met before?'

She turned her full attention toward the man, thinking that he looked like a husky version of – what was that singer's name?

'No,' she said with a mixture of amusement and scorn. '*Never.*'

'I thought you'd forgiven me for missing our dinner date in Istanbul.' The voice had dropped several octaves.

Kaela gave him a hard look, especially the broad shoulders. 'Good Lord! I didn't recognize you.'

'They don't call me the Man of a Thousand Faces for nothing,' Austin said, with a devilish smile. He spread his arms wide. 'Is this what the well-dressed tabloid TV journalist wears?'

Austin wore black slacks, matching T-shirt and sports jacket and seventies-era RayBan sunglasses, even though it was night, and scuffed New Balance running shoes. He wore a gold neck chain, and his silvery-gray hair was hidden under a dark brown wig.

'You look like a Hollywood undertaker,' Kaela said. 'I especially like the wild hairpiece.' She squinted. 'What did you do to your face?'

'Putty. A necessary evil in the age of face recognition technology.'

Kaela raised an eyebrow, suddenly remembering the name. 'The only one they're likely to match you with is Roy Orbison.'

'I'll remember that in case someone wants my autograph. Now that I've passed inspection, how are you?'

'I'm fine, Kurt. It's good to see you again.'

'I'm hoping after business hours we can pick up where we left off.'

'I'd like that,' she said, with a flirtatious tilt of her head. 'I'd like that very much.'

Kaela wore a taupe pantsuit whose silky folds emphasized the curves of her body. Austin found himself being drawn in again by her exotic looks. With great effort, he put a lid on his amorous thoughts. For now, anyway.

'Then it's a date. Cocktails at the Ritz Bar.' He looked around at the milling crowds of men and women dressed for the black-tie affair. 'Ready to crash the party?'

Kaela hung a plastic laminated ID card around his neck. 'From now on, you're Hank Simpson, our sound man. It should be easy to fake. Dundee's job was mostly hauling equipment around and holding a mike boom. I'll help you set up. Mickey is going to meet us at the press boat. Just grab those cases and play dumb.'

'Dumb I can do,' Austin said. Snatching up the heavy metal suitcases as if they were feathers, he followed Kaela to a section of the pier where a PRESS sign had been nailed onto a piling. An open launch was coming in to pick up the next load of journalists.

The short, stocky figure of Mickey Lombardo came trotting over with a steadi-cam on his shoulder. 'I got some great shots of the Kennedys.' He recognized Austin despite his disguise. 'Hey, it's our guardian angel,' he said, with a grin. 'Good to see you again, pal.'

Austin held his finger up to his lips and glanced around.

'Oh, yeah, I forgot,' Lombardo said, lowering his voice to a stage whisper. 'By the way, I like your taste in clothes.' Like Austin, Mickey himself was dressed almost all in black.

'If anybody asks, tell them we're the Blues Brothers,' Austin suggested.

'Hate to interrupt your reunion, boys, but our ride is here,' Kaela said.

Austin picked up the sound-equipment cases and loaded them into the launch. The seats in the boat were set up in rows like a bus. Kaela sat between her two crewmen. Within minutes, the boat was filled with a diverse group made up of print journalists uncomfortable in their rented tuxes and blow-dried TV anchorpersons, each with an entourage of fawning assistants. The launch swung away from the pier and sped across the harbor, its place taken by another shuttle.

The arrival of Razov's yacht had attracted press coverage from all over the East Coast. The general public had learned for the first time of Razov's wealth and political ambitions, and his intention to open a billion-dollar trade center in Boston. But it was the physical manifestation of that incredible wealth, his huge and luxurious yacht, that invited the most interest.

The *Kazachestvo* was the biggest thing to hit Boston since the Tall Ships. Circling TV helicopters followed her entrance into the harbor and beamed aerial pictures around the world. An escort of fire-fighting boats sent fountains of water arcing into the sky. Hundreds of pleasure craft nudged closer, only to be shooed away by the Coast Guard patrols. When the yacht dropped anchor, it was greeted by boatloads of politicians, bureaucrats and businesspeople. But only the most important and influential guests were invited to the gala reception in the evening.

The Ataman ship was allowed to anchor between Logan Airport and the Boston waterfront, so guests arriving by plane could be shuttled to the party. The yacht blazed from one end to the other with colored lights that lit up the harbor. To celebrate the gala event, the local congressional delegation had persuaded the Navy Department to move the frigate USS *Constitution*, '*Old Ironsides*,' from her home at the Charlestown Navy Yard for a rare nighttime harbor excursion.

The old fighting ship normally left her pier only once a year, when she was turned around so that her sides weathered evenly. The annual turnaround cruise was done with the help of tugboats. But in recent years, after an extensive overhaul that had restored some of the original 1794 construction design, the ship had been taken for short cruises under sail for special occasions. Austin overheard one of the TV people say the frigate was scheduled to do a sail-by under its own power. A detachment of Marines and a gun crew were on board to fire off a cannon salute.

As the launch drew closer, Austin turned his attention to the yacht. It was as Gamay's photos showed, with a sharp V-shaped bow, concave stern and streamlined superstructure. He recognized the FastShip design that would allow Razov to move his headquarters and home anywhere there was water within days. The launch took its place in line behind several others, coming alongside the ship to a door on the side of the hull. Crewmen leaned from the opening and helped passengers out of the shuttle boats. The guests were passed onto official greeters, who barely glanced at their press credentials and sent them toward a stairway. Austin noted with perverse amusement that the TV anchors looked as if they had stood in front of a fan after the trip in the open boat.

With Kaela leading, Austin and Lombardo lugged their equipment to the main deck, which resembled a high-class block party. The press representatives passed through a gauntlet of young men and women, all dressed in maroon blazers, who looked as if they had been hired through central casting. They were handed press kits, novelty key chains in the shape of Russian wolfhounds and magnets with the Ataman logo on them. Thus loaded down, they were guided to a roped-off section in the fantail.

A handsome young man whose blazer had a crest on it, indicating rank, welcomed them to the reception. He said interviews were being set up in the media center with the governor and the mayor. Mr Razov would be giving no interviews, but would make a statement shortly. Knowing that free food and drink are the most persuasive bribes for favorable publicity, he directed them to the salon.

While the other press people stampeded toward the open bar, Austin and his crew set up their equipment near a rank of microphones and floodlights. When their work was finished, he took Kaela by her slim arm. 'Shall we join the other muckety-mucks?'

'In a minute,' she said. She guided him to the rail, where there was a view of the Boston skyline, the Customs House and the Prudential and Hancock towers. Her soft features were set in a grave expression. 'Before we go in, I want to ask you something. You were determined to get on board this boat. Does Razov have anything to do with the Black Sea sub base or those thugs who attacked us?'

'Why would you conclude that?'

'Please don't be coy with me. He's Russian. They were Russian. His operations are centered in the Black Sea.'

'Sorry, I can't tell you everything. It's for your own protection. But there is a connection.'

'Is Razov responsible for the death of Captain Kemal's cousin, Mehmet?'

Austin paused. There was no refusing the determined gaze of those amber eyes. 'Indirectly, yes.'

'I *knew* it. It's time that dirtbag is called to accounts.'

'I have every intention of making Razov pay for his deeds,' Austin said.

'Then I want a piece of the action.'

'You'll get your story. I promise.'

'I'm not *talking* about a story. Look, Kurt,' she said with frustration, 'I'm not some California Valley Girl whose biggest thrill was getting kicked out of the mall for smoking. I grew up in a tough hood and if I hadn't had an even tougher mother, I might be doing ten to twenty at Soledad now. I want to do something to help.'

'You've already helped by getting me on board.'

'That's not enough. It's evident. It's evident to me that you want to nail this creep to the wall. Okay, I want my hand on the hammer.'

Austin vowed never to get caught in the crosshairs of Kaela's gunsight.

'It's a deal, but tonight we're on Razov's turf. You keep a low profile. I don't want to expose you and Mickey to any danger. I'll work the ship on my own. Agreed?'

Kaela nodded. 'You'll have time while we're doing the interviews.' She grabbed his arm and guided him toward the salon door. 'But first I'm calling in the IOU on that drink you've promised me since the day we met.'

They joined the throng moving into the immense salon. For a moment, Austin forgot that he was on a boat. They seemed to have been transported a hundred years back in time. The salon looked like a throne room designed by a Las Vegas casino architect. It was a curious meld of Western civilization and Eastern barbarism. Their feet sank into a plush carpet of imperial purple that was big enough to cover several houses. Crystal chandeliers hung from vaulted ceilings that were covered with figures of cupids and nymphs. On each side of the room was a row of square-built columns whose sides were carved and covered with gold leaf.

The crowd was a cross section of Boston's powerful and influential. Fat, red-nosed pols whose bellies strained at the buttons of their rented tuxedos jostled each other for room at the huge center table, which groaned under the weight of Russian delicacies of every description. At the other extreme, painfully thin women sat at rococo tables and picked at their food as if it were poisoned. Waspish businessmen gathered in knots to discuss how best to help the wealthy Razov spend his money. Legions of attorneys, financiers, Beacon Hill lobbyists and staff people flitted from table to table like bees in search of nectar. At the far end was a dais, but instead of a gold throne it held a band that played a lively Russian folk tune. The musicians were dressed like Cossacks, Austin noted with discomfort.

While Austin and Kaela looked for a place to light, there was a roll of drums from the band. The public-relations man in the crested blazer took the stage, effusively thanked everyone for coming and said that their host would like to say a few words. Moments later, a middle-aged man wearing a plain blue suit climbed the stage and took the microphone. At his heel were two Russian wolfhounds – lean, regal-looking dogs with snow-white fur.

Austin edged closer for a good look at Razov. The Russian didn't look like an arch villain. Except for his hatchet-faced profile and deathly pale skin, he was quite ordinary. Austin reminded himself that history is full of men of unremarkable appearance who have rained unbounded misery on their fellow human beings. Hitler could have passed as the starving artist he once was. Roosevelt had called Stalin 'Uncle Joe,' as if he were a kindly old relative instead of a mass murderer. Razov began to talk.

Speaking English with only a trace of an accent, he said, 'I wish to thank you all for coming to this party honoring your wonderful city.' Gesturing toward the wolfhounds, he said, 'Sasha and Gorky are very happy to have you here too.' The dogs were the ice breakers he wanted them to be. After the crowd had responded with laughter and applause, the hounds were taken away by a handler. Razov waved good-bye to the dogs and grinned at the audience. He spoke in a deep baritone and with an authoritative manner. He had the gift of appearing to look people directly in the eye. Within minutes, he had everyone in the room hanging on his every word. Even the pols had stopped their gluttony to listen.

'It gives me great pleasure to be here in America's cradle of independence. Only a few miles from here is Bunker Hill, and a little farther, Lexington, where the shot was fired that was "heard 'round the world." Your great institutions of learning and medical centers are legendary. You have done much to inspire my country, and in return I wish to announce the opening of a Russian trade center that will foster the smooth flow of commerce between our two great countries.'

While Razov was going over the details of his investment, Austin whispered into Kaela's ear. 'Time for me to poke around. I'll meet you back at the launch.'

Kaela squeezed his hand. 'I'll be waiting,' she said.

Austin edged his way toward a side door and stepped out into the coolness of the night. With most people in the salon listening to Razov speak, the decks were virtually deserted. He bumped into only one person, a waiter who pressed a plate loaded down with sausages and boneless prime rib into his hand. Austin was going to throw the plate over the side as soon as the waiter was out of sight, but decided he'd look less conspicuous if he wandered around the boat with the plate in his hands.

He sauntered toward the front of the yacht until he came to a roped-off section. A sign in English hung from the rope: PRIVATE. The deck beyond the sign was in darkness. Razov had kept his strong-arm boys out of sight so as not to scare the guests. But as Austin was checking the off-limits area, a stocky man with the unmistakable bulge of weapon under his suit walked by. He saw Austin and said, 'Is preevat,' in a thick Russian accent.

Austin gave him a drunken smile and offered his plate. 'Sausage?'

The guard replied with a sour look and kept on his rounds. Austin waited until he was out of sight and prepared to duck under the rope. He turned at the sound of a light patter on the deck and saw two white ghosts sprinting in his direction. Razov's wolfhounds. Trailing their leashes, they jumped up on his chest and almost knocked him down, then stuck their long curved snouts into the plate he was carrying. He put the food down on the deck. The dogs noisily gobbled down the sausages and prime rib, licked the plate clean, then looked up at Austin as if he were holding out on them.

Someone was running toward them. It was the dogs' trainer. He said something in Russian that might have been apology, grabbed the leashes and led the dogs away. Austin waited until he was once more alone, then ducked under the ropes into the restricted area. He made his way forward, as silent as a ghost. With his black outfit he easily melted into the shadows.

After a few minutes, he stopped at a vent that was taller than he was by a foot. He reached into his pocket, brought out an object about the size and shape of a Palm Pilot and hit the On button. The small dial glowed pale green, and a set of numbers appeared. Yaeger's 'sniffer' was ready to go to work.

An excited Yaeger had called while Austin was getting ready to go to Boston. 'I think I know how to plug into the yacht's system,' Yaeger said. '*Wi-Fi*.'

Austin no longer blinked at the strange language Yaeger used. He assumed that computer geniuses like Yaeger were on another planet and sometimes they reverted to their native tongue. He'd asked for an explanation. Yaeger said that Wi-Fi was shorthand for the wireless computer networks that were coming into use at major complexes.

'Say you're running a big hospital,' Yaeger explained. 'You want your people to have access to vital information so that if they're away from their computers on the other side of the building, they don't have to go running back. You set up a wireless computer network that only covers the building or complex. The key staff carry laptop computers. They simply switch them on, tune in to the right frequency and they have instant access to the main system.'

'That's very interesting, Hiram, but what's it got to do with our problem?'

'*Every*thing. The Ataman yacht has Wi-Fi.'

Austin still wasn't sure where Yaeger was going, but Hiram's enthusiasm was contagious. 'How do you know this?'

'It's Max's idea, really. After we fell flat on our faces trying to decipher Ataman's code, she started to pull out everything she could find on the yacht. There wasn't a lot, because Ataman built the ship at its yard on the Black Sea. But the electronics were beyond anything the Russians had, so they bought American equipment and had it installed by a French team. Max got into the French company's file. They set up Wi-Fi for the yacht.'

'I can see a hospital using something like that, but why a yacht?'

'Think of it, Kurt. A boat that size is a community unto itself. Say you're the purser, and a question on the payroll comes up while you're away from your office at the other end of the boat. You flick on your laptop, and there you have it. Same thing goes for the chef. Maybe he's in his cabin and has to check inventory. Or you're the first mate and you're on break in the mess hall when you need information on who's manning a shift.'

'How's this help with our main problem, the missing password?'

'The password must be in that ship. If Max and I could plug directly into the network, we could take stuff out at our leisure and look closely at it.'

'What's stopping you?'

'A couple of things. First of all, the information is bound to be encrypted against unauthorized use. Second, the wireless signal is a weak one that only covers the yacht itself. I need somebody to place a "sniffer" on board.'

'You're talking computer weird again.'

'Sorry. A sniffer is simply a device that can tap into the network, pump up the signal and send it to the waiting arms of Max.'

'Impressive. You say the files would be encrypted. What's to say the code won't stop you again?'

'Nothing. But it's not a dedicated encryption like the one on the mystery ship. We can come in side-ways from different angles. And besides, Max is determined.'

'Nothing like a determined woman, even a cybernetic one. Where can I pick up these electronic noses?'

'There's a NUMA courier on the way over with a package. Instructions included.'

The instructions had been simple. Click the sniffer on, check to make sure it's picking up a signal, then use the magnet attached to the back of the transmitter to attach it. Yaeger had given him a second sniffer for backup.

Now Austin reached into the vent and placed the sniffer out of sight. Then he worked his way over to a lifeboat and felt his way down to where the davit joined the deck. He got down on his hands and knees and found a small hollow space in the steel support. He slipped the second sniffer inside and started to rise, when he heard a soft click on the deck behind him. Something hard pressed against the small of his back.

32

'You're getting careless in your old age, Kurt Austin. The next time it could be fatal.'

The hard pressure was removed from his back. Austin turned and saw the livid white scar on Petrov's face in the silvery moonlight.

'I aged at least ten years when you stuck that gun in my ribs, Ivan. A simple hello would have been sufficient to grab my attention.'

'It keeps me in practice,' Petrov said. 'I don't want to lose my edge.'

'Believe me, your edge is as sharp as ever. Who let you in my country?'

'Unlike your unsanctioned adventure in Russia, my visit here comes with the blessing of your State Department. I'm in the US on an agricultural trade mission for Siberian Pest Control and asked the local Russian consulate to include me on the guest list for this reception.'

'How did you find me?'

'I saw you leave the grand salon and followed you into the restricted area of the ship. Your face threw me off, I must admit, but it was impossible to hide those wide shoulders and that confident walk. I've been wondering, where did you get that incredible wig?'

'I bought it at a KGB yard sale.'

'I wouldn't be surprised at that the way things are going. May I ask why you were crawling about in the dark on your hands and knees?'

'I lost a contact lens?'

'Really? I don't remember your dossier saying anything about contacts.'

Austin chuckled and told the Russian about the electronic sniffers. Ivan was duly impressed and asked only that he be kept informed as information developed. 'I suggest that we rejoin the festivities,' he said. 'Most of the guards are watching the guests, but a few are making the rounds.'

Austin knew they were already pressing their luck. They moved toward the lights and music, taking advantage of every shadow or pocket of darkness. They saw only one guard and ducked behind a bollard until he passed. Moments later, they were strolling along the deck.

Petrov, who looked debonair in his tuxedo, lit up an American cigarette. 'What are your plans now?'

'You didn't see Razov's pet monk, did you?'

'I suspect that Razov prefers to have Boris stay out of sight on public occasions. He may or may not be on the ship. We're not likely to see him.'

'In that case, maybe I'll spend a few minutes talking to our host.'

'*Razov?* Do you think it's wise to play your hand here on his territory?'

'Maybe I can get him rattled enough to make a mistake.'

'I've heard it's not safe to play with rattlesnakes, but do what you wish. I think I'll wander around and enjoy the food and drink as long as I'm here.'

'You came alone?'

Petrov plucked a shot of vodka from the tray of a passing waiter. He slugged it down and smiled. 'I won't be far away if you need me.'

The party was going full-blast. Guests wandered about the deck with food and drinks. The Cossack band had switched from Russian folk tunes and was belting out a rock number. Petrov mingled with the crowd and disappeared like a leaf being swept away in a stream. Austin saw a knot of people, with Razov holding court at its center. He moved closer, wondering how he was going to get past the bodyguards flanking Razov. The pair of long-legged canines took the matter out of his hands. Razov's dogs jerked away from him and galloped toward Austin in a dead heat. As before, they jumped up, put their paws on his chest and licked his face. He managed to dislodge them with strategically placed hip blocks.

He grabbed the leashes and held them short to keep the rambunctious hounds under control. A moment later, the dogs' trainer came running up, this time with panic in his eyes. Austin was about to pass the leashes over when he saw Razov and his two bodyguards coming up behind the trainer.

'I see you've met Sasha and Gorky,' Razov said,

with a genial smile. He took the leashes from Austin and said something in Russian. The dogs obeyed instantly and sat by his side. Their haunches quivered as they fought their instincts.

'I shared some prime rib and sausage with them a while ago,' Austin said. 'Hope you don't mind.'

'I'm surprised they ate it,' Razov said. 'They dine on fare much better than most people's. My name is Razov.' He extended his hand and glanced at the name on the press pass hanging around Austin's neck. 'I'm the host of this little celebration.'

'Yes, I know. I heard you speak. Very impressive.' He squeezed the hand until the bones crunched and he saw Razov wince with pain. 'My name is Kurt Austin.'

Razov's face showed no emotion. 'The famous Mr Austin. You look nothing like I expected.'

'Neither do you. You're much smaller than I thought you'd be.'

Razov failed to rise to the bait. 'I was unaware you had changed to television work. The last I knew, you were employed by NUMA.'

'This is only a temporary diversion. I'm still with NUMA. We've been doing some treasure-hunting in the Black Sea.'

'I hope it was worth your while.'

'Someone beat me to a treasure aboard a ship called the *Odessa Star*.'

'That's too bad, but treasure-hunting is very competitive.'

'What I can't figure out is why someone who already possesses huge wealth would go through so much trouble to recover a few shiny baubles.'

'We Russians have always been fascinated by baubles, as you call them. We believe that beyond their intrinsic value, they impart a power to the possessor.'

'Treasure didn't do the tsar and his family much good.'

'The royal family was betrayed by traitors in its midst.'

'I assume you intend to return the treasure to the Russian people.'

'You know nothing about my people,' Razov said. 'They don't care for jewels. What they need is the firm hand of a leader who can restore their national pride and fend off those countries who are circling like vultures.'

'That's assuming your secret Operation Troika is a success.'

'There's nothing secret about Troika,' he said, with undisguised scorn. 'It's shorthand for my plan to open trade centers in Boston, Charleston and Miami. Look around, Mr Austin. There is nothing sinister about my business.'

'What about the massacre aboard the NUMA ship? Would you consider that sinister?'

'I read about it in the press. A tragedy, certainly, but I had nothing to do with that unfortunate incident.'

'I don't blame you for not taking credit for it. It

was a botched attack. You screwed up, Razov. Your mad dog got the wrong ship. I wasn't on the *Sea Hunter*, and your men murdered the *Sea Hunter*'s crew for nothing. Of course, you know all that by now.'

Austin saw a flash of anger in Razov's eyes. 'Really, Mr Austin, you disappoint me. You sneak aboard my ship in that ridiculous disguise, drink my vodka and eat my food, then repay my hospitality by calling me a killer.'

'I had another reason to come aboard. I wanted to look into the face of the murdering scum I plan to destroy.'

The mask of the affable politician melted away, to be replaced by the street thug. 'You destroy *me*? You're a mere flea.'

'Maybe, but there are many more fleas where I come from. And we all bite.'

'It will take more than NUMA and your government to stop me,' Razov said. 'When I'm through bringing Russia back to its former glory, the US will be like a puking, mewling child, a world beggar, its resources depleted, its leadership weak and confused –' Razov saw that he had gone too far and stopped suddenly. 'You're no longer welcome aboard my yacht, Mr Austin. My security men will escort you to the launch.'

'I can find my way. 'Til we meet the next time, Mr Razov.' He started to walk away.

Razov's lips parted in a feral grin. 'There isn't going to be a next time.'

Razov made a subtle gesture, and his guards started to follow. Austin let out a low whistle. The wolf-hounds perked up their ears and, with tails wagging, broke away from Razov, trailing their useless leashes. Austin grinned and looked Razov straight in the eye. The Russian stared at Austin with a look of pure hate. Austin turned and walked quickly toward the stern of the boat, merging with the crowd with the dogs at his heel. He realized that he had to lose the hounds. They were too conspicuous and would call attention to him.

He stopped and patted the dogs on their heads, then handed their leashes to a startled young woman wearing a maroon blazer. He whipped his wig and sunglasses off and tucked them in the woman's pocket.

'Would you return these to Mr Razov, please? With my compliments.'

Walking quickly, he made his way past the salon entrance and slipped through the crowd, almost bowling Kaela over.

'What's the big hurry?' she said.

'Get off the yacht as soon as you can,' he said.

'Where are you going?'

'Don't know. See you at the Ritz Bar in about an hour.'

Austin pecked Kaela's cheek and headed toward the stairs that would take him to the launch deck. He hoped to catch a ride on a launch, but abandoned that course. Two guards flanked the stairway, their eyes

462

scanning the crowd. Austin had assumed, wrongly, that Razov wouldn't risk an incident with all the people around. But Razov had spilled more than he'd intended and was willing to take the risk. Pushing his way back through the crowd, Austin was trying to gain a few minutes while he figured out an alternative escape route, when someone grabbed his arm.

Austin whirled and tensed his body into a combat stance. Petrov released his grip. The Russian was smiling, but his eyes were deadly serious.

'I think you'd better not go that way,' he said.

Austin followed Petrov's gaze. A guard was working his way through the crowd. He looked straight at Austin and spoke to a microphone in the lapel of his suit. Austin let Petrov guide him into one door of the salon, around the dance floor, then through the other door and out onto the deck. They headed toward a stairway, but this too had a tall guard stationed at it. The man had a hand cupped next to his ear, listening to his radio.

Wearing a broad smile, Petrov went up to him and said something in Russian. The guard responded with a suspicious glare and reached for the gun inside his jacket. Petrov drove his fist into the man's midsection. The guard doubled over, gasping for breath, and when he came up for air, Austin was waiting with a right cross. The big man tumbled like a big tree felled by a lumberjack.

Stepping over the fallen guard, they raced down the stairs to the deck below. Austin saw a door like the one used on the other side of the ship for the guest shuttles. Petrov worked the latch and pushed the door open. Austin wondered if they were going to have to swim for it, when a shaft of light fell on a powerboat. The motor was idling, and the man at the wheel grinned and waved when he saw Petrov.

'I took the liberty of arranging alternative transportation,' Petrov said.

'I thought you came alone.'

'Never trust a former KGB man.'

Austin scolded himself. Unlike Petrov, he had underestimated the determination of his foe. He had been so eager to confront Razov that he had neglected his own escape plans. He vowed to praise Ivan later for his meticulous attention to detail. He stepped from the ship onto the deck of the powerboat, Petrov followed and Petrov's man ratcheted up the throttle several notches. The boat surged forward, almost pitching Austin and Petrov into the water, as the snarling outboard motor pushed it up on plane.

Austin looked back at the brightly lit ship and chuckled as he imagined the reaction of Razov and his thugs to their escape. His triumph lasted only a second, however. Silent gunfire raked the boat, coming not from the ship but from the harbor itself. Though there was no sound, the muzzle flashes were clearly visible in the darkness, and the hail of bullets stitched their way across the body of the helmsman. He let out a soggy yell before he crumpled over the wheel, and the boat careened off at a wild angle.

Petrov pulled the man away from the wheel and Austin grabbed the helm. Spotlight beams converged on the powerboat. Razov was no fool. He'd stationed a picket line of his gunmen in boats around the yacht.

Another volley raked the boat. There was only one way past the guard boats, and that was *through* them, Austin concluded. He steered toward a gap between spotlights, and the boat shot between the picket line. Razov's guards held their fire for fear of hitting each other in the cross fire, but once Austin was in the open harbor, they let fly with everything they had.

The water around the fleeing boat exploded with miniature geysers. A few shots found the windshield and shattered the glass. Petrov clutched his head and fell to the deck. Austin ducked low and wrung every ounce of speed he could out of the motor. The boat was fast, but the pursuers were slightly faster. Spotlights were gaining on both sides. Austin glanced toward shore. They'd never make it . . . and then another possible refuge offered itself. Dead ahead, her masts and sails illuminated by deck lights, was *Old Ironsides.*

A volley of slugs from a flanking pursuer slammed into the side of the boat at the waterline and blasted a row of holes in the fiberglass. Austin tried to keep the boat on plane, but the holes were too big and the boat quickly swamped. The outboard motor pushed on until it died with a smoky gasp. The boat went under like a diving submarine. Austin found himself floating in Boston Harbor. Petrov went under. Austin dove after him, grabbed the Russian by the neck and pulled him to the surface, where he was greeted by a bright light shining in his eyes, and he could hear the sound of voices shouting.

Strong hands reached down, grabbed Austin by the arms and the scruff of his jacket and pulled him, dripping, from the chill water. He wiped his eyes and saw that he was in a double-ended boat about thirty feet long. A dozen men wearing white navy uniforms and black neckerchiefs pulled at long oars with practiced strokes. Petrov was stretched out at Austin's feet, blood streaming from a wound on his head. He gave Austin a weak wave.

'All you all right, sir?' said a young man who sat next to Austin in the stern, his hand on the tiller. Over his white sailor's uniform he wore a long black coat with brass buttons down the front, a black neckerchief and a shiny black-brimmed hat.

'A little waterlogged. Thanks for hauling us out of the harbor.'

The steersman extended his free hand. 'Josh Slade. I'm the officer of the deck on board the USS *Constitution*. We saw you from up there,' he said, pointing to *Old Ironsides*, which sat in the water a few hundred feet away, her three tall masts brightly illuminated by floodlights.

'My name is Kurt Austin. I'm with the National Underwater and Marine Agency.'

'What's NUMA doing in these parts?'

Slade gave him a funny look as he asked the question. Austin brought his hand up to his face and felt his fake nose. It was hanging half off from the effects of the dunk in the harbor. Austin ripped the nose off and tossed it over the side.

'Long story,' Austin said, with a shake of his head. 'How's my friend?'

'Looks like the bleeding has stopped. We'll give him first aid when we get back on board.'

Music from Razov's yacht drifted across the water. Austin hoped Kaela and Lombardo were all right. He saw no sign of the chase boats and their gun-happy crews, but instinct and experience told him they hadn't gone far.

'Did anyone see the powerboats that were following us?'

'Just a glimpse. They were right on your tail, but when you got into trouble, they disappeared. We couldn't figure out why they didn't stop to help. Don't know where they went. We were busy launching the captain's gig and didn't pay much attention.'

'Lucky you were here. It would have been a long swim back to land.'

'I'll say. Normally we wouldn't be out here this late. The *Constitution* does one turnaround cruise a year, on the Fourth of July. We were taking the ship out on a midnight cruise. Got the master gun team, so we can fire a twenty-one-gun salute. The governor and the mayor got the okay from the Navy Department for us to do a night-time sail-by. What

467

happened? We saw you zipping it along, but then your boat seemed to vanish from under you.'

Austin saw no point in beating around the bush. 'We were leaving the party yacht. Those boats you saw shot us out of the water and killed our helmsman.'

He stared at Austin as if he suspected his sanity. 'We didn't hear any gunfire.'

'They had silencers on their guns.'

'Come to think of it, we saw flashes of light that could have come from guns. We thought they were camera strobe lights. Who *were* those guys? Whoops,' he said, not waiting for an answer. 'Going to have to excuse me for a minute.'

Slade steered them around behind the *Constitution* under the white eagle and ship's name emblazoned on the stern. He maneuvered the boat under the davits that projected overhead like extended wooden arms. The rowers lifted the oars out of their locks and stood them in a vertical position, then attached the lines hanging down from the davits and winched themselves up to deck level.

With help from the deck crew, Petrov was extricated from the boat. The Russian had revived and was able to walk with the help of a sailor on either side. Someone made a mattress of life jackets so he wouldn't have to lie on the hard wooden deck. Another crewman gave Austin a coat to replace his dripping jacket.

Slade took his hat off and tucked it under his arm.

He was a dark-haired young man in his twenties, a couple of inches taller than Austin's six feet one. With his chiseled features and ramrod posture, he could have posed for a navy recruiting poster.

'Welcome to *Old Ironsides*, the oldest commissioned warship in the world, still manned by an active-duty US Navy crew.' The pride in his voice was obvious.

'Ay, tear her tattered ensign down! Long has it waved on high,' Austin said, quoting the first line of the Oliver Wendell Holmes poem, 'Old Ironsides,' that had inspired the nation to save the ship from destruction.

Slade grinned and quoted the second line, '"And many an eye has danced to see that banner in the sky . . ." Sounds as if you know your naval history, sir.'

'I know the ship fought the Barbary pirates and gave the British a major headache during the War of 1812. That she was undefeated in battle. And during the fight with the British frigate HMS *Guerriere*, cannonballs bounced off her sides as if they were made of iron.' His eyes fondly swept the two-hundred-four-foot length of the frigate, taking in the long bowsprit, the expansive spar deck with the neat rows of cannon and the two-hundred-twenty-foot-tall mainmast. 'Hope I look half as good when I'm her age.'

'Thank you. We take great pride in keeping her shipshape. She was built not far from here, launched in 1797. Actually, her sides were made of live oak from the southeastern US. Her hull is twenty-five inches thick at the waterline. Paul Revere did the copperwork and made the ship's bell. Don't mean to give you the guide routine,' he apologized, 'but we're awfully proud of the lady.' His face grew serious. 'Instead of giving you a history lesson, I should call the Coast Guard and let them know we've got an injured man on board.' Slade patted the pockets of his coat and frowned. 'Damn. My cell phone must have fallen out when I got in the gig. I've got a walkie-talkie we use to keep in touch with the tugboat when we're being pushed or towed. I'll ask the crew to relay a message to the Coast Guard.'

While Slade retrieved his handheld radio, Austin went over to where Petrov was stretched out on the deck. Someone had covered him with a section of sail. A crewman was keeping watch.

Austin knelt by Petrov's side. 'How are you feeling, *tovarich*?'

Petrov groaned. 'I have a splitting headache, as you would expect after having a bullet bounce off a corner of my skull. Why is it that every time I get too close to you, I get blown up or shot up?'

'Just lucky, I guess. Razov must have taken something I said the wrong way. Sorry that you lost your man.'

'I am, too. He wasn't a bad sort for a Ukrainian. He was aware he was in a dangerous business, though. His family will be well-compensated.'

Austin told Petrov to take it easy, then he rose and

walked to the thick wooden bulwark, the chin-high raised side that enclosed the uppermost deck. While he was scanning the harbor, Slade returned.

'Mission accomplished,' he said. 'The tug crew will notify the Coast Guard and the police harbor patrol. They'll ask them to send some EMTs over to take care of your friend. How's he doing?'

'He'll live. A half an inch lower and he would have lost some brain power.'

'Is he with NUMA, too?'

'He's a Russian trade representative from Siberian Pest Control.'

Slade gave him that funny look again. 'What's he doing in Boston Harbor?'

'Looking for Siberian pests,' Austin said.

Slade noticed Austin peering back toward where the tugboat was nudged up against the stern of the ship.

'The tug pushed us away from the wharf,' Slade explained. 'We were getting ready to raise sail after they got us into the outer harbor. We're supposed to do a run for the television cameras, then rendezvous with the tug and get a ride back to the navy yard.'

Austin was only half listening. He squinted into the darkness at the snarl of boat motors. The sound grew louder. Then he saw firefly points of light made by muzzle flashes.

Traveling in a line, three fast powerboats materialized and raced toward the stern of the sailing vessel. Then came the snap and whine of rounds ricocheting off the tugboat. Sparks exploded where the bullets struck the steel hull. The tugboat crew got over its surprise at being fired upon. With a roar of its engines, the tugboat went into reverse and headed off at full throttle. The boats circled the slower craft, riddling the wooden pilothouse with bullets. The tug slowed, traveled a few hundred feet before it stopped completely.

Austin clenched his fists in anger, helpless to prevent the cowardly attack on the innocent tugboat. He asked Slade to call the tug on his walkie-talkie. After several attempts, the sailor gave up.

'It's no use,' he said. 'Damn, why'd they attack those guys?'

'They know the tug was our only propulsion.'

Although the boats were out of sight at the edge of darkness, Austin could hear their idling motors. Then he saw the gun flashes, followed by what sounded like a hundred woodpeckers attacking the ship. Slade tried to lean over the bulwark to check out the noise. Austin pulled him down on the deck.

'Jeez, those idiots are *shooting* at us!' Slade yelled. 'Don't they know this is a national treasure?'

'We'll be fine,' Austin said. '*Old Ironsides* stopped cannonballs. A little automatic gunfire isn't going to sink her.'

'I'm not worried about that. I don't want my crew hurt.'

Austin had been listening with one ear to the gunfire. 'They've stopped shooting. Tell your men to keep their heads down and wait for orders.' Austin realized Slade was in command. 'I'm sorry. Those are suggestions. This is your command.'

'Thanks,' Slade said. 'Your suggestions are well taken. Don't worry, I won't fall apart. I was a Marine before they gave me this duty. I'm only here because I hurt my knee in an accident.'

Austin studied the young man's face and saw no fear, only determination.

'Okay, here's my take on that strafing run. They wanted to drive off the tug so we'd be dead in the water. They know they can't sink us. My guess is that they'll try to board us.'

Slade tucked his chin in. 'That's unacceptable. *No* enemy has ever come aboard the *Constitution* except for prisoners of war. You can be certain it's not going to happen on *my* watch.' He glanced around the spar deck. 'There's only one problem. The ship originally carried more than four hundred men. We're a little shorthanded.'

'We'll have to make do. Can we get the old girl moving?'

'We were about to hoist sail when we stopped to pick you and your friend up. The best we can get out of it is a couple of knots. *Ironsides* is no speedboat.'

'The main thing is that we establish even a little control of the situation. It will keep them guessing. Speed's not important. What about weapons? Any on board?'

Slade laughed and pointed to the cannon lined up

473

on both sides of the deck. 'You're talking about a *fighting* ship. Take your pick, thirty-two-pounder Carronades on this deck and twenty-four-pounder long guns below. Plus a couple of Bow Chasers. More than fifty cannon total. Unfortunately, we're not allowed to carry gunpowder.'

'I was thinking about something more practical.'

'We've got boarding pikes and axes and cutlasses. There are belaying pins everywhere. They make fine blackjacks.'

Austin told the young officer to do what he could. Slade gathered his men around, introduced Austin and told the crew that the people who shot up the ship might try boarding it. He ordered every light on the ship doused and told some of the crew to get aloft. They scrambled up the rigging and onto the yards, where they loosed the topsails. The inner jib was set and the ship began to move, on her own, at a speed of about one knot.

The sail crew dropped down to the deck and hauled up the main topsail yard. The 3,500-square-foot mainsail filled with the breeze, and the mast began to squeak. The ship crept along at the speed of a fast snail. Then the outer jib was set, followed by the fore topsail. The ship tripled its speed. The movement would pose no problem for anyone trying to board, but it gave the crew a modicum of control. In the meantime, weapons were being stacked on the deck.

Slade picked up a cutlass and felt the sharp edge

of the blade. 'Warfare was a personal thing back then, wasn't it?'

'Unless you know how to use that thing, this might be more practical,' Austin said, hefting a boarding pike, basically a long wooden shaft with a sharp metal spearhead on one end.

The crew split up into two parties, one for each side, and nervously kept watch. A party was dispatched to the fighting platform halfway up the main mast where Marines and sharpshooters used to rain death down on attackers. Austin paced restlessly back and forth, a belaying pin in his hand.

They didn't have to wait long.

The first sign of the renewed attack was the loud rapping against the ship's side. The attackers were trying to soften them up with automatic gunfire. The bullets chipped the black and white paint, but hardly put a dent in the two-foot-thick oak hull. The doughty old ship plowed through the water, brushing off the bullets as if they were a swarm of pesky mosquitoes. Like the Barbary pirates and the British navy, the attackers learned *Old Ironsides* was no pushover.

The attackers saw that their bullets were having no effect and stopped firing, instead switching on their spotlights, revving their motors and closing on their slow-moving target. Austin heard the boats thump against the hull. He had figured that the attackers would try to climb up the standing rigging that ran from the masts down the side of the ship like rope ladders, and when he saw a hand grab onto the bottom ledge of a gun port, Austin brought the belaying pin down on the attacker's knuckles.

There was a shriek of pain. The hand let go, and the attacker fell into the harbor with a loud splash. A face appeared on the other side of the gun port. Austin set aside the belaying pin and picked up a boarding pike. He tucked the spearhead under the man's chin. Austin was practically invisible on the darkened deck. The attacker felt the sharp point tickling his Adam's apple and froze, afraid to move.

Austin pushed the pike forward slightly, and the face disappeared. This time there was a loud thud, as the attacker fell into a boat. Seeing his gun port clear for the time being, Austin strode down the line of cannon. The ship's crewmen were using their boarding pikes with similar effect. Working in pairs, some of them tossed cannonballs over the side. Judging by the yells and crunching sounds, they were finding their mark.

Slade came running up, still wearing his cocked hat. 'Not one of those jerks has set foot on deck.' His sweaty face beamed with pride.

'Guess they're getting the point,' Austin said. A face appeared over the bulwark behind Slade. Before Austin could warn Slade, the attacker had hooked a leg over the side and was bringing his assault rifle to bear.

Austin threw the boarding pike like a Masai warrior taking on a lion. The pike struck the attacker in the chest, and he let out a cry of surprise and toppled back, his weapon firing uselessly in the air.

Austin grabbed a cutlass and leaped onto the nearest cannon, intending to cut the rigging to prevent it from being used as a ladder. As he brought the sword back, he heard someone yell:

'*Starboard!*'

The shout came from the fighting platform. The assault had moved around to the other side of the ship.

Two of Razov's men had climbed onto the bulwark and were unslinging their weapons, preparing to spray the defenders concentrated on the deck.

Acting on pure instinct, Austin slashed the line nearest to him, grabbed onto the loose end like Tarzan swinging through the trees and launched himself across the deck, his legs extended in front of him. The attackers looked up and saw a dark Batmanlike apparition flying their way. They tried to get their guns around, but Austin's feet struck them with the full force of his weight, and they pitched over backward. Austin reached the end of his arc and swung back, then dropped onto the deck amid loud cheers from the astounded crew.

'Wow!' Slade said. 'Where did you learn *that* trick?'

'Watching old Errol Flynn movies in my misspent youth. Is everybody okay?'

'Couple of cuts and bruises, but *Old Ironsides*'s deck has not been violated.'

Austin grinned and clamped the sailor on the shoulder, then looked around.

'What's that?'

'Boat motors,' Slade said.

They ran to the side of the ship and peered over. They could see three wakes. A cheer went up from the crew, but it faded when the boats came to a stop a few hundred feet away and the pinpoints marking muzzle fire began. But instead of aiming for the nearly impregnable sides of the ship, they were concentrating on the rigging. The sails were being shredded. Bits of rope and splinters of wood began to rain down on the deck. The observers scrambled down from their platforms.

'Those cowards!' Slade yelled. 'They can't board her, so they're going to rip her to shreds.' Tatters of sail fell on his head. 'We've got to *do* something!'

Austin grabbed the sailor's arms. 'You mentioned a twenty-one-gun cannon salute.'

'What? Oh, yeah, the two cannon on the foredeck. We fire them every morning and sunset. They're old breechloaders. We've jerry-rigged them to fire three-hundred-and-eighty-millimeter shells. But they shoot blanks, except for the time when someone forgot to remove a cap and we hit a police boat.'

'Our friends out there don't know they're blanks.'

'That's right.'

Austin quickly outlined his plan. Slade ran back and ordered the helmsman to steer a new course. The helmsman swung the wheel over, and the *Constitution* slowly came about so that its bow was pointed at the attack boats.

Slade rounded up his gun crew and they climbed down to the gun deck and hurried forward. Within moments, the forward cannon were loaded. Austin peered through the gun port and saw the attack boats lined up. They had been readying for another assault when the ship turned and came at them. With *Old Ironsides* taking the offensive, they seemed to be confused. Austin wanted them as close together as possible. The gap was closing. The boats started to move apart.

'*Now!*' Austin ordered. He stepped away and covered his ears.

Slade pulled the lanyards. There was a double roar, the foredeck was enveloped in smoke and the cannons leaped back, their recoil held in check by thick cordage. The gun crew had purposely left the caps in.

The bluff worked. The attackers saw the big black ship bearing down on them behind a cloud of purple smoke, heard the twin projectiles whistle through the air and saw the geysers of water. The boats sprinted out of the way like startled jackrabbits, then headed at full throttle toward the mouth of the harbor where they disappeared in the darkness.

The cannons roared again, with blanks this time, as the ship gave chase.

Even as the echoes faded, a mighty roar went up from the crew.

'Party's over,' Austin said.

Slade was grinning from ear to ear. The comment that followed might not have been in the same class of immortal words as 'Don't give up the ship' or 'Damn the torpedoes!' . . . but as Austin watched the departing wakes of the attack boats, he couldn't argue with the young sailor when he said, '*Old Ironsides* still knows how to kick ass!'

33

Washington, DC

Sandecker glanced around the Oval Office and reflected on the life-and-death decisions that had been made in the famous room. It was hard to believe that the political currents that swirled around Washington had their center within these quiet walls. On his last visit to the White House, he'd been treated as a pariah and warned to butt out of national security matters, but after NUMA had rescued the *NR-1*'s captain and crew and saved the White House major embarrassment, Sandecker had become the proverbial eight-hundred-pound gorilla. He lost no time throwing his weight around.

The White House's formidable appointments secretary hadn't hesitated when he called and asked to meet with the president on an urgent matter. The secretary bumped an ambassador and a congressional delegation from the president's busy schedule, and she never blinked when Sandecker asked that only the president and vice president attend.

Sandecker had politely refused the offer of a White House limousine and made the trip in a Jeep Cherokee from the NUMA motor pool. The receptionist had ushered the admiral, Rudi Gunn and Austin into the Oval Office and saw to it that a steward served them coffee on White House china.

As they waited, Sandecker turned to Austin. 'I've been meaning to ask you, Kurt. How did it feel to commandeer a national monument?'

'Quite the rush, Admiral. Unfortunately, with only two cannon in the bow, I couldn't yell, "Give 'em a broadside!"'

'From what I've heard, you and the *Constitution*'s crew acquitted yourselves with undeniable valor. *Old Ironsides* lived up to her glorious name.'

Gunn said with a twinkle in his eye, 'The scuttlebutt among the top navy brass has it that *Old Ironsides* is being commissioned as part of the Seventh Fleet. After she's patched up, of course.'

'I understand that the navy plans to retire an aircraft carrier in her favor,' Austin said, with a poker face. 'The Pentagon sees great cost-cutting opportunities in the use of sail and belaying pins.'

'Cost cutting would be a new one for the Pentagon,' Sandecker mused. 'What happened to the men who attacked you?'

'The Coast Guard and police scoured the harbor. They found three boats scuttled in the marshes on a harbor island, the hulls shot full of holes.'

'I understand there were some injuries.'

'The tugboat crewmen were wounded, but they had the presence of mind to play dead.'

'What of the Russian, the man you call Ivan?'

'He was only grazed by the bullet and is doing fine.'

'What did Razov have to say about these pirates?'

'Nothing. He cut his party short, kicked his guests off the yacht and sailed out of the harbor before anyone could ask him questions.'

'This Razov is a shifty character,' Sandecker said with a knitted brow. 'We've got our work cut out for us. We've been keeping an eye on him since he left Boston?'

Gunn nodded. 'Satellite surveillance had him heading at a leisurely pace along the Maine coast.'

'Just a gentleman yachtsman out for a cruise,' Sandecker said, his voice dripping with sarcasm.

'I've asked the satellite department to run the latest results over here for this meeting,' Gunn said.

The door opened, and a Secret Service man stepped inside. 'The boss is on his way,' he said.

A bustle of activity could be heard in the hall and President Wallace came through the door, wearing his trademark smile, his outstretched hand cocked for action. The towering figure of Vice President Sid Sparkman was a step behind. After a round of handshakes, the president settled behind his desk, and as usual the vice president drew up a chair close at his right elbow, emphasizing his place in the executive hierarchy.

'Glad you asked for this meeting,' the president said. 'Gives me the chance to thank you personally for saving the folks from the *NR-1*.'

Sandecker acknowledged the thank-you and added, 'Kurt and the others in the NUMA Special Assignments Team deserve the real credit.'

The president's eyes narrowed. 'I heard about that business in Boston, Kurt. What sort of a lunatic would shoot up *Old Ironsides*?'

'The same type of lunatic who would order the massacre of a NUMA crew, Mr President. Mikhail Razov.'

The vice president leaned forward in his chair as if he were using his body mass to intimidate. 'Mikhail Razov is a prominent figure in his country,' he said, his smile belied by the fierce expression in his eyes. 'You're talking about the man who might be the next leader of Russia. What evidence do you have that he's involved in *any* of this business?'

Austin leaned forward as well, emphasizing his broad shoulders. 'The *best* kind of evidence. An eye-witness.'

'I read the report on the *Sea Hunter* attack. The ravings of a hysterical woman,' Sparkman said, with a snort.

Austin felt the bile rising in his throat. 'Hysterical, yes; ravings, no. Razov's man Boris made sure we knew the attack was retribution for trespassing on the old Soviet sub pens.'

'I'm glad you used the word trespass, because that's what it was, an illegal violation of another country's national sovereignty.'

Austin's mouth widened in a grin, but his gaze had

the look of a lion regarding a wounded wildebeest. Sandecker saw Kurt ready himself to unsheathe his claws and deflected the attack. 'What's done is done, I'm afraid. We've got more to worry about now, gentlemen. The prospect of a plot against the United States. With all due respect, Mr Vice President, we believe that the man behind this threat is Mikhail Razov.'

'That's ridiculous –' the vice president said. The president silenced him with his hand.

'Razov expects to rise on the crest of a neo-Cossack revolution,' explained Austin. 'Claiming to be descended from the Romanovs gives him legitimacy in the eyes of his fanatical supporters, who will follow him to the death.'

'Any truth to his claims?'

'We don't know, Mr President. We do have evidence that the Grand Duchess Maria, one of the tsar's daughters, survived the Russian Revolution and went on to marry and have children.'

'Maria? The only one I've ever heard of was Anastasia,' the president said. 'Saw that Walt Disney picture.' He toyed with a pen on his desk. 'Fascinating. Does Razov have any proof to back up his bloodline?'

'I wouldn't be surprised if he had a birth certificate. The Russians have decades of experience forging documents under communist rule. We believe he will buttress his claim with the crown of Ivan the Terrible. The crown is said to bestow mystical power upon its wearer. Razov will say that only the rightful ruler of Russia would have the crown. Once he's in power, I doubt if anyone would bother him for a DNA sample.'

'He has this crown?'

'Maybe. We found a jewelry box containing a list of the tsarist treasures being carried on the *Odessa Star*. The crown was not included.'

'What about DNA?'

'Once Razov is in power, he could fabricate any DNA evidence he needed. It would be a simple thing.'

'The Russian people are pretty sophisticated, for all their problems,' the president said. 'Do you really think they'll buy a cock-and-bull story like that?'

Sandecker's lips tightened in a smile. 'As an elected official, you've had more experience than I have with the ability of politicians to bamboozle the public.'

The president cleared his throat. 'Yes, I see what you mean. He wouldn't be the first tinhorn dictator to sell his people a bill of goods. We know Razov is furious at the United States for trying to paint him out of the political picture. Sounds like he intends to call our bluff, use this so-called threat as a little black-mail to get us to pull back. Well, I've got news for Mr Razov. The United States won't be blackmailed. If we let Razov get away with this, there will be no end to the threats.'

'It may be more complicated than simple black-mail,' Austin said, recalling the story Petrov had told him about Razov's girlfriend. 'Razov had a fiancée, a young woman who was going to be his tsarina. She was visiting Yugoslavia during the NATO air raids on Belgrade and was accidentally killed by a bomb from an American plane. It's given him a deep hatred of the United States.'

Sandecker rejoined the discussion. 'What Kurt is saying is that Razov's animosity toward the United States goes beyond our efforts to frustrate his political career. My guess is that neutralizing the US fits in with his nationalist ambitions, but that he intends to satisfy his thirst for vengeance as well.'

The president leaned back in his chair and laced his fingers across his chest. 'It's the last part that interests me, Admiral. How's he propose to knock us out of the game?'

'We think Razov has found a way to release the energy stored in pockets of methane hydrates under the continental shelf off the East Coast,' Sandecker said. 'By destabilizing the shelf, he can cause massive underwater landslides that create *tsunamis*, giant waves that can be directed at specific targets.'

A look of pure astonishment crossed the president's face. He sat bolt upright. 'Are you saying Razov plans to launch giant waves against the US?'

'He already has. He sent that wave into Rocky Point.'

Turning to Sparkman, the president said, 'Sid, I signed off on the federal disaster aid to Rocky Point. Did anyone say it was connected to terrorism?'

'No, Mr President. Nobody I've talked to thinks

the wave was anything other than a natural occurrence. In this case, caused by an undersea earthquake.'

'Well, Admiral?' the president said to Sandecker.

'Perhaps if we heard from an authority on the subject, it might allay any doubts.'

'That seems like a good idea,' the president said. 'When can you line up your expert?'

'As long as it takes to summon him from the reception room. Actually, I've brought along *two* experts, Dr Leroy Jenkins, an oceanographer formerly with the University of Maine, and Dr Hank Reed, a geochemist with NUMA.'

'You never go anywhere without backup, do you, James?' the president said, with a smile.

'It's my old academy training. Why fire one torpedo when you can launch a whole spread? I've also taken the liberty of inviting NUMA's chief computer programmer, Hiram Yaeger.'

The president murmured an order over the intercom. A few minutes later, the Secret Service agent ushered Yaeger, Reed and Jenkins into the office. Yaeger was no stranger to the corridors of power and was little impressed by anyone who did not speak in terms of megabytes. In deference to the president's title, he had donned a well-worn Madras-plaid cotton sports jacket over his jeans and T-shirt and wore a new pair of desert boots. Jenkins had on his tan poplin suit from his college days and a new blue oxford shirt bought for the occasion. Hank Reed had made a valiant effort to subdue his Lyle Lovett hair, but even his suit and tie couldn't prevent him from looking like a troll doll.

If the president wondered at what may have been the oddest-looking assortment of human beings ever to visit the Oval Office, he was diplomatic enough not to show it. After a round of handshakes and introductions, he said:

'The admiral here was telling us about that *tsunami* business up in Maine. He seems to think the wave was man-made.'

Jenkins had been nervously playing with the knot of his tie. Under gentle prodding from the president, he spun out the story of the Rocky Point *tsunami* and his investigation as to its cause.

The president turned to Reed. 'Do you agree with Dr Jenkins?'

'*Totally.* I see no reason to doubt his conclusions. My research shows that force applied at specific points on the continental shelf could produce the results he's predicted.'

Austin jumped in. 'I've described the projectile I saw on the Ataman ship to some ordnance people. They suggested that it might be a concussion bomb with a shaped charge capable of great penetration. The thrusters drive it deep into the seabed. It might have multiple warheads similar to a nuclear ballistics missile.'

'You're not suggesting *nuclear* warheads?' the president said, with a look of alarm.

'From what I understand, it could be done with

conventional explosives. Some of the new ones are almost as powerful as a nuke. There's another thing. When I talked to the captain and pilot of the *NR-1*, they said Ataman had been using the sub to look for weak spots, faults and thin cover in the crust along the slopes and canyons of the continental shelf.'

'Where is this Ataman ship now?'

'Off the New England coast. I've asked our satellite people to look around. A courier will have the results here shortly.'

'I'll instruct my receptionist to send your person right in,' the president said. He turned to Sparkman. 'You're the mining man, Sid. You know anything about this methane hydrate?'

Sparkman, who had been quiet throughout the presentation, looked as if he were having acid indigestion. 'Yes, Mr President. It's basically frozen natural gas. Some people call it fire ice.'

'Let's get back to specifics, Dr Jenkins. What could we expect off the US coast?'

Jenkins looked preoccupied, as if another thought had occurred to him. 'Damage depends on the shallowness of water near shore, the shape of the bay, whether there is a river where the wave concentrates its energy.' He took a deep breath. 'It's possible that a wave might reach a height of one hundred feet after it hits the shore.'

The president looked shocked. 'That could cause unimaginable damage.'

'Unfortunately, there are worse things than *tsunamis*,' Jenkins said quietly.

'What could be worse than a giant wave hitting a metropolitan area?' the president said.

Jenkins took another deep breath. 'Mr President ... a massive release of methane could trigger large-scale global warming.'

'What? How could that happen? I thought it was just man-made causes we had to worry about.'

'That, too, but – look, let me give you an example. Back in the eleventh century, there was a huge "burp" of methane that released a giant amount of methane into the atmosphere and started a worldwide warming trend. The tropics advanced as far north as England and the sea may have extended as far as Arizona.'

The room was silent.

'Razov must know about the possibility,' Sparkman said, at last. 'Why would he do such a thing?'

Reed offered an explanation. 'The Russians have always wanted to warm the northern wastes of their country. It's an incredibly rich, but very harsh land. There was serious talk at one time of warming the waters off the Arctic with atomic energy to accomplish the goal. A temperate climate would allow vast development and settlement. At the same time, some people speculate that global warming would turn America's interior into a dust bowl.'

'My advisors have filled me in on global warming,' the president said. 'It's a very complex process, as I understand it. There's no guarantee it would turn out the way Razov wants it to.'

'Apparently, Razov is willing to take that chance,' Reed said.

'Good God!' the president said. 'That would be a disaster of unimaginable proportions.'

'It would be worse than that,' Sandecker observed. 'With his huge methane hydrate mining ships and a weakened US, Razov would be in a position to control the world's future energy supply. He could be the closest thing to a global dictator we've ever seen.'

'This man must be stopped,' the president said.

'A squadron of fighter planes would make short work of Mr Razov,' the vice president said.

'Do we have enough evidence to blast this ship out of the water, especially with the situation in Russia?' the president asked.

Sandecker said, 'That's an excellent point, Mr President. As we all know, Russia is in turmoil with Razov's right-wing forces battling the moderates. Razov would use any attacks against Russian ships to show that the US is the enemy. The moderates would be done for. Russia's nuclear arsenal would come under the control of the Cossack lunatic fringe.'

'But we can't let that ship carry out its mission,' the president said.

The receptionist knocked softly at the door, then opened it. A young woman rushed in with a folder in her hand. 'Sorry for the delay,' she said breathlessly. 'We ran into complications.'

'That's quite all right,' Sandecker said, 'but how complicated could it be to find one ship?'

'That was easy,' she said, handing over the folders. 'We picked up the target so quickly we decided to look at the rest of the East Coast down to Florida.'

'You found another ship, then?'

'Actually, sir, we found *three* of them in position off the East Coast. Another three appear to be on their way, and there seems to be some activity off the Pacific coast as well.'

'Thank you,' Sandecker said, dismissing the courier.

When she was gone, the president exploded. '*Three* ships? And more on the way? Damn! How will we know which city is the target?' The shadow of a cloud passed over the president's face. 'What if there is *more* than one target?'

Sandecker turned to Yaeger. 'Hiram?'

'Kurt and Paul did all the hard work,' Yaeger said. 'They gave me access to the encrypted files aboard the Ataman ship, but Razov was using a steganographic system. The communications were hidden within digital photographs – it's become a standard tool of terrorists because the images can be tough to decipher. In this case, it was a photograph of a Russian restaurant menu. It was part of what Razov called Operation Troika.'

'Razov told me that Troika was nothing more than a nickname for his plan to open trade centers in three US cities,' Austin said. 'There was nothing secret about it.'

'The menu hid his plans for the real operation,' Yaeger continued. 'The key to deciphering the code was on Razov's yacht. Thanks to Kurt again, Max and I were able to get into the yacht's central control system. We tracked down the binary code in a dark corner of the system. The actual operation is not Troika, but *Wolfhound.*'

Austin raised an eyebrow. 'Gorky and Sasha,' he said. Seeing the quizzical expressions around him, Austin explained: 'Those are the names of Razov's pet wolfhounds. He's pretty infatuated with the two mutts.'

The president said, 'I like dogs, too, but I'm more interested in the nuts and bolts of this operation.'

Yaeger said, 'The Wolfhound file indicated that the three ships would be off the cities of Boston, Charleston and Miami.'

'But . . . those are the cities where Ataman plans to open trade centers,' the vice president said. He seemed stunned.

'What better cover for an operation?' Sandecker asked.

Yaeger said, 'The admiral's right on the mark. I came across orders to evacuate Ataman personnel and interests in all three cities. Unfortunately, there was no information in the yacht's computer system about whether one city or all the cities are targets.'

'My guess is Boston,' Austin said. 'There's a major international financial conference going on right now at the Boston Harbor Hotel. It's being attended by representatives from all the countries that have been trying to undermine Razov.'

'Then the other ships are decoys?'

'I won't rule out the possibility that Razov means harm to all three cities, but Boston may be his prime target.' Austin opened a manila folder he'd been holding on his lap. He pulled out two transparent sheets and put them on the presidential desk. 'This is a map of Rocky Point. The other sheet is a mylar transparency of Boston Harbor and surroundings.'

The president laid the transparency over the map and swore under his breath. 'They're almost identical.'

Austin nodded. 'I think that when Razov chose Rocky Point to try out his wave-making machine, he picked a place as close to his intended target as possible.'

The president banged his hand down on the desk and reached for his phone. 'That does it,' he said. 'I'm calling an emergency meeting of the cabinet and Joint Chiefs of Staff to discuss air-and-sea strikes, no matter what the risks. We may have to evacuate those cities. How long do we have?

Hiram said: 'The operation is to be launched in less than twenty-four hours.'

Sandecker said, 'The panic of a mass evacuation may cause as many casualties as an attack. May I suggest a middle course, Mr President?'

The president's hand froze in midair. 'I'm listening, but I can't forget my duties as commander in chief.'

'We're not asking you to. From what we've heard,

the immediate threat is to Boston and possibly two other cities. According to Hiram's information, the command center is on the yacht. I propose that we disable the central control. As insurance, we send boarding teams aboard all three ships and deactivate the explosives. In the meantime, we can delay the arrival of the other ships, maybe under some pretense.'

The president scratched his chin in thought. 'I like it. Of course I can't give official approval of an operation in international waters. I need deniability in case things get dicey.'

'This wouldn't be the first time that NUMA has operated out of sight and sound of official channels,' Sandecker said.

'No, it wouldn't,' the president said dryly. 'What do you think, Sid?'

'Razov's treachery can't be tolerated. My first instinct is to blow him out of the water. I'd keep the attack subs and fighter planes ready to destroy him, his yacht and ships if the plan doesn't work out.'

'Fair enough,' the president said. 'Well, Admiral, looks like you have my "blessing." But no one outside this room can ever hear about it. Sid, I want you to get this thing moving immediately with special ops and the armed services.' He checked his watch and got up from his desk. 'Now if you'll excuse me, I've got a Boy Scout troop coming in from my home state for a Rose Garden ceremony.'

*

As the Oval Office emptied, Sandecker touched Sparkman's sleeve. 'I wonder if I might have a word with you in private.'

Sparkman gave him a troubled look. 'Sure, why don't we go outside and get some air? We can talk about how to keep the White House liaison with NUMA close to our vest.'

They walked out of the executive mansion to the south portico. Sandecker gazed around the manicured grounds. 'Beautiful setting, isn't it?'

'The prettiest sight in all of Washington.'

'A pity you will never get to live here.'

Sparkman laughed, but there was an edge to it. 'I have no intention of moving from the naval observatory. Couldn't afford the heating bills for this place.'

'Don't be modest, Sid. Everyone in Washington knows that you are the heir apparent after this president's term has expired.'

'There's no guarantee I'd be elected or even nominated.' There was something in his tone.

'You're being disingenuous. It's not a sin to have political ambitions.'

'We're all politically motivated in this town, even you.'

'No argument there.' Sandecker swung around to face him. 'But my ambitions aren't funded by a Russian madman, Sid. Tell me, what did Razov promise you? And don't tell me I don't know what I'm talking about. You've been caught with your hand in the cookie jar.'

Sandecker's bluff was convincing. Sparkman looked for a moment like he was going to bluster – and then he caved in completely, his face a mask of misery.

'I was going to get a big cut of the methane hydrates production off the United States. It would have been worth billions,' he said, his voice shaky.

'Now that you've heard the real reason behind those explorations, have you changed your mind?'

'Of course I have! You heard me in the Oval Office. I'm the one who took the hard line. I wanted to go after Razov tooth and nail.'

'I'm sure it had nothing to do with the fact that if Razov were blown out of the water, your secret would be safe.'

A wan smile crossed Sparkman's lips. 'You're not a man known to dillydally, are you, Admiral? All right. What do you want?'

'First of all, I want you to know that if one word of what transpired in the Oval Office this morning gets back to Razov, I'll see that you are pursued by the hounds of hell.'

'I may be greedy, but I'm not a traitor, Admiral. There is no way I would aid and abet Razov after what I've learned of his plans.'

'Good. Second, as soon as this is over, I want you to submit your resignation.'

'I can't –'

'You can and you will. Or else your role in this scheme will be played out on CNN twenty-four hours a day. Agreed?'

Sparkman's face had a haunted look. 'Agreed,' he whispered.

'There's one other thing. Tell Razov that the US is still trying to figure out why the *NR-1* was hijacked. A little disinformation couldn't hurt.'

Sparkman nodded.

'Thank you, Mr Vice President. I won't waste any more of your time. I know you've got a lot to do carrying out the president's orders.'

Sparkman squared his shoulders. 'I'll have someone from my office stay in close contact so we can coordinate our planning.'

The two men parted without shaking hands, with Sparkman heading back to the White House. Sandecker strode to the parking lot, where the others awaited him. He was angry at having to destroy a man's career, angry that Sparkman had been such a fool. His blue eyes blazed with a cold fire as he slid behind the wheel of the Jeep and said, 'Gentlemen, I think it's time we put Mr Razov's wolfhounds in the dog pound.'

34

Off the coast of Boston

'In the event I ever write my memoirs,' Zavala said, 'what exactly is going on?'

'This is a scientific mission being undertaken by Siberian Pest Control on a US Navy submarine, supervised by NUMA,' Austin said. 'Officially, it doesn't exist.'

'Maybe I *won't* write my memoirs,' Zavala said, with a shake of his head.

'Cheer up,' Austin said, glancing around the spacious wardroom. 'No one would believe you anyhow.'

Austin had to raise his voice to be heard above the raucous voices of a dozen tough-faced men dressed in black commando uniforms. They were at the far end of the room smearing black and green camouflage paint on their faces. The exercise produced laughter and jokes that rose in decibel level, stoked by slugs from the vodka bottle being passed around. Petrov, who was dressed for combat like the others, dabbed paint on his cheek, hiding his scar, and made a remark in Russian that provoked great hilarity among his men. One man started to howl and pounded him on the back with sufficient force to break the rib cage of an average person. Petrov grabbed the bottle and came over to Austin and Zavala.

Austin said, 'Sounds like amateur night at the Kremlin Comedy Club. What was the big joke?'

Petrov laughed and offered the vodka. Austin declined and Zavala said, 'Thanks, I'm a tequila man.'

Petrov seemed more in his element than Austin had ever seen him. 'I reminded my men of an old Russian proverb: "Live with wolves, howl like a wolf."' Noting Austin's blank look, he said, 'It's like your saying about birds of a feather.' Seeing that his explanation still fell short, Petrov said, 'I'll explain later.' He daubed Austin's forehead and cheeks with paint, Indian fashion. 'Now you're properly prepared for action.'

'Thanks, Ivan,' Austin said, completing the job. 'Sure you're up to a field operation?'

'Are you implying that I'm too old? As I recall, I'm a month younger than –'

'I know,' Austin said. 'My *dossier*. Don't be so touchy. I was thinking about your injuries from our fun night in Boston Harbor.'

'A wonderful battle. I will never forget the way you swung over the deck like Tarzan of the apes. I have a few scratches. Nothing that would slow me down.'

Austin jerked his head toward Petrov's men. 'Hope the same goes for your men. Maybe we should give them Breathalyzer tests.'

Petrov dismissed the comment with a wave of his hand. 'I would trust any of those men with my life, drunk or sober. You worry too much. A few shots of vodka before battle is a tradition in the Russian military. It was the secret weapon we used to defeat Napoleon and Hitler. When the time comes, my bandits will carry out the mission with precision and courage.'

Austin glanced toward a young sailor who had stepped through the door. 'Looks like that time is now, Ivan.'

The seeds of the joint operation had been hatched after Austin had returned to his office following the White House meeting. Petrov had been waiting for him. When Austin described the plan, Petrov immediately volunteered his men to board the yacht. Austin checked with Sandecker, who liked the idea and got an okay from the vice president. Russians boarding a Russian yacht would add another layer of insulation between the mission and the president.

The sailor surveyed the painted faces, trying to pick out someone in command. Austin waved him over.

'Captain says we're ready anytime you are.'

Petrov barked a command to his men. The transformation was startling. The horseplay came to a halt and the bottle of vodka vanished. The grins were replaced by firm jaws and stony expressions of determination. Hands reached for automatic weapons, and a chorus of metallic clicks echoed throughout the room as loads were checked. Within seconds, the ragtag gang had changed into a fierce-eyed fighting force.

Ivan gave Austin an I-told-you-so smirk. 'After you,' he said.

Austin grabbed the pack holding his Bowen, and with Zavala and the others behind him, followed the sailor to the control room. Captain Madison lifted his eyes from the periscope and said, 'We surface in exactly three minutes. The target is one hundred yards away. Seas look fairly calm. You're in luck, the clouds are covering the moon.'

'Thank you for allowing my men the use of your vessel, Captain,' Petrov said.

Madison scratched his head. 'This is a first for me, but if your country and mine can cooperate in space, why not under the sea?' He turned to Austin. 'Someone at NUMA's got a lot of pull. It's not anyone who can yank a US Navy missile sub off its usual patrol for what seems to be, if you'll pardon the expression, a renegade special-ops mission.'

The four-hundred-twenty-five foot *Benjamin Franklin* was one of four subs in its class that had been recruited because it was equipped for special operations. Even Sandecker's considerable influence wouldn't have superseded naval orders without approval, however masked, from the highest level.

Austin said, 'This mission wouldn't have gotten off the ground if it weren't crucial.'

'Good luck, then,' the captain said. 'We'll stand by

as long as we have to. Call us when you need a lift home.'

'You'll be the first to know.' Austin went over to a bank of computer screens.

'We're heading out, Hiram,' he said.

Yaeger sat in front of a keyboard where one of the sub's electronics people was explaining the vessel's computer setup. Sandecker had been reluctant to let Yaeger go on the mission, but Austin had pressed his case, saying that Hiram's computer expertise could be vital. The admiral relented after Austin had said he would bring Yaeger aboard only if the yacht's control center had been secured.

Yaeger shook hands with Austin and wished him good luck. 'I'm still working to decipher the last piece of code,' he said. 'I'll let you know if I break through the wall.'

At a signal from Austin, Petrov gave his men a series of commands. The boarding party made its way through the sub and crowded into the space under the loading hatch. A crewman climbed a ladder and opened the hatch cover, letting in a cold spray. Austin and Zavala went first, climbing through the hatch to emerge on the deck behind the sail. Petrov's men joined them and passed up two large plastic canisters. The canisters were opened, and compressed air hissed into the inflatable boats inside. The sub's crewman whispered, 'Good luck,' and the hatch cover closed with a soft clunk.

Moonlight, filtered by the clouds, gave the sea a

dark pewter cast. The tall sail, with its horizontal hydroplanes, looked like a giant robot from a science-fiction movie. Austin squinted through the gloom at the silhouetted yacht. Unlike its appearance in Boston Harbor, where it had been lit up like a Mississippi riverboat, the yacht was dark, except for a few lights on its radio masts and the yellow glow of cabin windows.

The satellites had watched the yacht change its course along the coast of Maine and head south, until it finally stopped off the coast of Massachusetts about fifty miles from the *Ataman Explorer I*, which was due-east of Boston. The other two Ataman ships had halted eastward of Charleston and Miami.

The men grabbed their paddles, pushed the boats off the slippery deck into the water and clambered aboard. Donning their night-vision goggles, they silently dipped their paddles, using precise strokes that propelled the bobbing craft through the mounding seas.

The cool air stabbed like an ice pick through Austin's layers of clothing and he almost regretted not taking a slug of vodka himself to warm his innards. He turned and looked back at the sub, which had slipped under the sea with hardly a gurgle. The sub would remain on station with only a few feet of its conning tower above the surface.

Within minutes, the boats were nudging the towering steel walls that formed the ship's sides. Austin felt like a minnow next to a whale. Ordinarily, he would say that the odds against the mission were considerable, but Max had leveled the playing field. As Yaeger had poked around in the yacht's electronic nervous system, he'd come across two very important connections. The first was the vessel's troubleshooting program. It was similar to the visual displays used in cars, only far more sophisticated. The system could tell the people running the yacht the status of the watertight doors, and the performance of the gas turbines, power flow and the other electronic veins and sinews that kept the ship running. Most important, Yaeger had located the central control room. Everyone in the raiding party carried a waterproof map of the ship, based on Max's snooping.

The second breakthrough was more prosaic but equally important. The yacht's payroll records had the names and titles of practically everyone on board. Since the yacht served as Razov's home and corporate center, he had a full complement of housekeeping staff, cooks, bookkeepers, accountants and secretaries. The ship's crew was unexpectedly small, indicating that the vessel was loaded with automated systems. Austin's interest had centered on a category that Petrov had translated to mean: 'nonregular crew.' In other words, Razov's private shipboard army of thugs, like those who had come after Austin in Boston Harbor. There were fifty of them, and their ruthlessness and loyalty were not to be ignored. Petrov insisted that the odds were nothing his men couldn't handle.

Stealth would be their primary weapon. They would silently slip aboard the yacht and race to the control center, which they would destroy with well-placed explosives. Opposition would be quietly neutralized. If they had to fight their way out, they had enough firepower and the element of surprise to put them on an even footing. At the same time, Austin and Petrov were realists. They knew that the odds of discovery were high, and casualties were likely on both sides. But given the stakes involved, it would be worth the losses.

The night-vision goggles the boarding party wore gave the ship and the sea a greenish tinge. Austin could see the water-level door he and Kaela had entered to attend Razov's party. It would be too risky trying to gain access through that door because the open portal would show up on the ship's visual display. Instead, they would employ the time-tested method used by pirates, castle stormers and commandos alike. Grappling hooks.

In their folded position, the hooks were tucked into metal tubes. When the grapple was launched like a mortar round, the hooks opened. The prongs were covered with foam rubber so that even someone standing a few yards away wouldn't hear them grab onto the rail of a ship.

Two grapples shot out of their mortars with quiet coughs of compressed air. The lines were tested. The ropes were taut, indicating that the grapples had engaged. Petrov's men pointed guns equipped with silencers toward the rail where anyone looking over would get a rude surprise. All was quiet, and they moved on to the next phase of the operation.

Austin and Petrov made the first ascent, not an easy task with their packs. They lunged awkwardly over the rail, surveyed the deck and saw it was deserted, then signaled the others to come aboard. Within minutes they were squatting on the deck like a flock of black and heavily armed ducks. Two men stayed with the boats.

The raiding party split in half. The group led by Austin took the starboard side. Those under Petrov's command crossed to the port side. Both units would advance and meet at a ladder at the base of the bridge. From there, the plan was to climb three decks to the control center located in a small room behind the wheelhouse. At this hour, only a skeleton crew should be manning the bridge. Austin gave Petrov the okay sign. Crouching low, their guns at the ready, both groups began to move forward.

Austin was encouraged at their swift progress, but they had just passed the grand salon where Razov had held his Boston bash, when a door opened without warning. Light spilled onto the deck, flaring in their night-vision goggles, Austin pushed the goggles back on his head and saw one of Razov's guards standing like a deer frozen in the headlights. The man clutched a bottle of vodka and his arm was around the shoulders of a young woman in a maid's uniform, his hand under the unbuttoned front of her dress. Her dyed red hair hung down over her face, and her bright lipstick was smeared. Austin realized he had provided for every eventuality except the human libido.

The man's drunken grin faded at the sight of the intruders with their painted faces and automatic weapons. As a professional gunman he knew exactly what was expected of him: *silence*. His female companion had no such restraint. Her mouth opened wide, and she let out an ear-piercing scream. Her lung power was opera-star level. Her second shriek was even louder, the howl easily drowning Austin's curses. She finally ran out of breath, her eyes rolled up and she crumpled to the deck in a faint.

As the echoes faded, the ship lit up like a pinball machine. Doors flew open at every level, and yells seemed to come from all directions. There was the sound of running feet and rough voices shouting orders, with a few more high-pitched screams thrown in for variety. Those were only the preliminaries. A second later, all hell broke loose.

35

The Sikorsky HH 60-H Seahawk helicopters raced side by side over the ocean like twin Valkyries, skimming so low their landing gear was splashed with spume from the cresting wave tops. The aircraft were painted in low-visibility gray, their insignia and markings toned down and almost invisible.

As he stared out the window of the right-hand helicopter, the platoon commander, Navy Lieutenant Zack Mason, reflected on the urgent phone call from Washington and the orders to scramble a special warfare task unit for a secret mission.

With his classic profile and soft-spoken manner, Mason could have passed for an investment banker. Under the patrician looks was a tough and competent warrior who had not simply survived the rugged SEAL training, but *thrived* on it. Still only in his thirties, Mason had been involved in missions that ranged from an aborted plan to shoot down Saddam Hussein's helicopter to security at the Olympics in Atlanta.

Officially, he was the leader of a SEAL group on the East Coast. Unofficially, he was liaison to the Joint Special Operations Command, an amalgam of SEALs, Delta Force and the 160th Special Operations Aviation Regiment known as SOAR. The shadow force maintained its own helicopter support. The assault teams specialized in attacking at-sea targets such as shipping or oil rigs. The joint command was authorized to conduct preemptive strikes against terrorists and terrorism.

The orders for the mission had bypassed the normal links in the chain of command. This job had been directly authorized by the secretary of the navy, who had handed the problem off to the admiral in command of the Naval Special Warfare Command in Coronado, California. The admiral had been told to avoid the usual red tape, and have the operations decisions made at the lowest possible level. Mason would report directly to Coronado from the field.

After Sandecker talked to him, Sid Sparkman had gone to the president and told him the truth about his connection to Ataman. He'd admitted to being seduced by the chance to make billions of dollars, but he'd said he had no inkling of Razov's plans against the United States. He'd handed in his written resignation, to be announced at the pleasure of the president. And he had offered himself up as a sacrificial lamb. If the operation blew up in their faces, Sparkman would take responsibility for the rogue action to contain the damage. Ever the pragmatist, the president pocketed the resignation, accepted Sparkman's offer and told him to call the naval secretary.

Based in Little Creek, Virginia, Mason's SEAL

team was chosen because it had been trained in boarding a ship at sea. The mission goal was simple: swarm aboard the ship without warning and deactivate a bomb. Mason knew that reaching that goal would be the hard part.

'Coming up on target,' the pilot said, with a lazy drawl, interrupting Mason's meditations. 'T minus ten minutes.'

Despite his calm demeanor, Mason couldn't avoid the adrenaline rush and excitement of a SEAL mission. He was what was known as an 'operator,' one who had joined the navy for action. He glanced at his Chase-Durer Swiss watch, turned and gave the men behind him a ten-fingered signal like a basketball player making a two-handed free throw.

Dressed in black uniforms, their exposed faces streaked with war paint, the SEALs were barely visible in the cabin's dim light. As an elite force, SEALs were given leeway in dress and weapon. Some wore 'drive-on rags,' Rambo-style around their heads, others the more traditional floppy hats with the brim turned up at front.

There was a rustle as the SEALs patted the pouches of their assault vests and laid reassuring hands on their automatic weapons. Most in the team carried Colt automatic rifles, the shortened version of the M-16 that fired rounds with no cartridges, allowing them to carry more ammunition. One man, who was built like a bull, carried the M-60 E3, a light machine gun that normally requires two men to operate. Another was armed with a 12-gauge shotgun whose slugs could penetrate metal. In addition to his own rifle, the explosives expert carried a rucksack that contained C-4 plastic charges and fuses.

Mason commanded the sixteen-man platoon that would board the starboard side. His executive officer, '2IC,' for second in command, headed the group that would secure the port deck. No matter how heavily armed they were, thirty-two men composed a small attack force for a target as huge as the *Ataman Explorer.* The last thing the SEALs wanted to do was get into a firefight with a vastly superior force. Their main weapon would be surprise; their allies would be confusion and shock.

'Comm check,' Mason said. Like the men in his platoon, he carried a Motorola MX300 radio with throat mike and earpiece. The men answered in order of their seating. Mason counted the answers. Sixteen. Everyone was connected. His 2IC called in from the other helicopter. He and his men were ready.

Mason slipped a cell phone out of his assault vest and punched out a number. The phone used a special encryption algorithm that connected Mason directly to the other assault teams.

As Mason's unit headed due east of Boston at the chopper's maximum speed of one hundred forty-five miles per hour, the other squadrons were on similar missions to the south. The Delta Force was in the group off of Charleston, South Carolina, and an air force special operations regiment was in the southernmost track east of Miami. On this mission, the navy would be in charge. Which meant Mason was calling the shots. If he got taken out of action, the Delta leader would take charge, then the SOAR officer.

'This is Omega One,' he said. 'Come in, Omega Two.'

'Omega Two, and how are you?'

Mason smiled at the bad rhyme. On joint training exercises, he had come to know and respect the Delta Force leader, a wisecracking African-American named Joe Louis, after the great champion boxer.

'We're right on schedule, Joe. T minus ten.'

'Roger. Hey, Zack, couldn't the navy brass come up with something more imaginative than *Omega*. Maybe something like the Three Bears?'

'Doubt if the admiral would like being called Goldilocks. Besides, it was the air force's turn to name this mission.'

'Figures. Fly boys. T minus eight.'

'Call when you make visual contact.'

'When we do, I will call you. Over and out.'

Mason punched another button and got Will Carmichael, leader of Omega Three. In contrast to Louis, Carmichael went by the book. Even his spontaneous comments seemed to be programmed. He reported that his team was right on schedule, then added, 'Pieceacake.'

Mason knew from hard experience that dropping out of the sky onto a huge and possibly heavily armed moving ship in open ocean and disarming an unknown explosive was not exactly a piece of cake. They had rehearsed boarding vessels at sea dozens of times, but this was the real McCoy. The mission depended on delaying detection until the last possible moment. The HH 60-H helicopter was ideal for the job. It was relatively quiet, had an infrared jammer and suppressor system, a radar threat-warning receiver and other electronic eyes and ears. In addition, the helicopter had sharp teeth: two M-60 machine guns and a Hellfire missile system.

'T minus four,' the pilot's voice droned.

Mason turned and held up four fingers. It was an unnecessary gesture because all his men were plugged into the helicopter's communications system, but he did it for emphasis. The tension was so thick he could have cut it with the knife at his belt. It seemed only seconds passed before the pilot said, 'Visual contact.'

Mason donned his night-vision goggles and ordered his platoon to do the same. He made out the silhouette of an enormous ship plowing wake through the sea. He called the other teams to report visual contact. Both had sighted their targets. He said he would call as soon as he was aboard the LZ, military shorthand for landing zone, and quickly slipped his phone back into its pouch.

They were seconds away from their target. At the last moment, when it seemed as if they were going to slam into the side of the ship, the Seahawks cut their speed, swooped up and over the vessel and hovered over each side of the wide stern deck. Thermal-imaging viewers scanned the ship for heat areas that would indicate human presence. Satisfied the deck was clear, the pilot maneuvered the aircraft past the masts and antennae and hovered at fifty feet.

Every man knew that this was when the teams were at their most vulnerable. As they had practiced dozens of times, the SEALs dropped a two-inch-thick rope that was secured to the hoist bracket down to the deck, then they donned heavy welder gloves. Mason stood in the door, got a good grip on the line and jumped. Using the upper body strength that was a product of rigorous SEAL training, he checked his controlled fall before his feet touched the deck, quickly moving aside to avoid the next man down.

Both helicopters were emptied within ninety seconds. As soon as they hit the deck, the boarders threw their gloves away. The first four men down adopted a circular formation that was reinforced as the others joined them. The helicopters darted off like startled dragonflies and hovered a few hundred yards from the ship on either side. They would await the word that the ship had been secured, or that the mission had failed. Their orders were to evacuate the assault team and sink the ship with well-placed missiles.

Mason swept his eyes around. He was glad to see that the ordnance expert, Joe Baron, had made it safely. Mason could handle explosives in a pinch, but Baron was a pro. The lieutenant pulled a light stick from his vest and snapped it back and forth so that the chemicals inside mixed and glowed a cold blue. He waved the light stick to let the port team know all was well. His signal was returned a second later. Radio talk would be kept to a minimum as they swept the ship from one end to the other.

Mason got on his cell phone.

'Omega Three. Stern LZ secured. No assets encountered. Report in, Omega Two.'

'Omega Two. Stern secured. No one home, so we will roam.'

'This is Omega One. Proceed according to plan and cut out the lousy poetry.'

'Roger,' Louis answered, although it must have killed him not to say 'Dodger.'

'Omega Three. All A-OK.'

Mason ordered the teams forward. They broke into two squads on both sides. One squad formed the base element, taking up firing positions to protect the other group as it raced forward. Then the assault team became the fire team and the other squad leap-frogged ahead in a maneuver that quickly covered ground.

Within minutes, they had rendezvoused in the bow of the ship with the port team. Mason ordered his 2IC to probe the bridge and superstructure while he took his squad to the decks below. Using the same leapfrog technique, Mason and his men made rapid progress through the storage areas and holds. They stopped in front of one door that was welded shut.

Since they couldn't get in, no one could get out, so they moved on. They burst into the boiler room with guns ready. The engines were going, but there was no sign of boiler men or engineers.

A voice crackled in Mason's earpiece. 'Up Squad. Gone through the crew and officers' quarters. Beds all made. No one here. Spooky as hell.'

'Boiler room. Engines are purring away. No one here either.'

The squads continued into the ship, and still they encountered no one. After a thorough search, they climbed back to the main deck.

The voice of the 2IC came onto Mason's radio. 'Lieutenant, I think you should get up to the bridge as quickly as possible.'

Moving quickly, Mason led his team to the wheelhouse. On the way, they passed men who were stationed on the decks and wings of the bridge keeping watch.

'Anything?' Mason said to the man who carried the shotgun.

'No, sir.'

Mason made his way into the wheelhouse. The 2IC and several of his team were waiting for him. Nothing seemed out of place. 'What did you want to show me?'

'This is it, sir. *Nothing*. There's nobody here.'

As he looked around at the computer monitors glowing with blue light and the blinking faces of the digital readouts, the truth dawned on Mason. He and

his men were the only human beings on the great
ship.

Calls were coming in from the other Omega teams.
Louis and Carmichael reported that the *Ataman II*
and *III* were deserted. As he listened to the reports,
Mason detected a change in the ship's movement.
He was sure of it. The ship had stopped its forward
motion. He went over to the big window that over-
looked the deck and stared out into the darkness.
Something was definitely happening. He couldn't be
sure, but the ship seemed to be moving laterally.

'Lieutenant,' one of his men called. 'Look at this.'

The man was standing in front of a large computer
monitor. Pictured on the screen was what looked like
an archery target. The image of a ship was slightly off
to one side of the bull's-eye. The ship was turning
on its axis as it moved closer to the center of the
concentric circles. Red lights flashed intermittently
on both sides of the ship image. The situation became
clear to Mason in an instant. The ship was a *drone*.
The vessel and its sister ships were being controlled
from another location.

Mason ordered his 2IC to secure the bridge and
called the choppers and told them to land. Then he
instructed Joe Baron to assemble with the squad
members trained in explosives on the foredeck. He
called the other Omega teams and instructed them
to proceed to the main objective, the bombs. Mason
raced down to the first level and led the way inside

the ship, with Baron and the other SEALs pounding down the stairs behind him until they came to the sealed door they had seen on their first exploration.

The lieutenant checked their location against the ship's diagram. They were outside the bomb chamber. Baron got to work right away and taped strips of plastic explosive C-4 onto the door. He inserted the blasting cap into the puttylike material and ran an attached wire around a corner. Mason and the other men cleared out of the area and squatted a safe distance away, with their hands covering their ears. Baron squeezed the M-57 firing device attached to the other end of the wire. A loud, hollow thump echoed through the passageway.

They rushed back to the smoking door, now marked by a ragged-edged square hole. Baron, who was as skinny as an eel, easily wriggled through. The others handed their packs to Baron, then squeezed through the opening after him. Flashlight beams stabbed the darkness. Then someone found a wall switch, and the chamber was flooded with light.

The SEAL team was standing on a platform with a large rectangular opening in the center. The missile hung down through the opening from the ceiling, held in place by gantries that extended from the walls like helping hands. There was silence as the men gazed with awe at the huge cylinder. The light gleamed off the metal skin and the rotor housings.

'Look sharp. No time for sightseeing!' Mason barked.

Baron ran his fingers over the surface of the missile. Then he inspected the intricate network of hoses and electrical connections that snaked down to the missile from a hole in the ceiling. He sucked his breath in. 'Man, I've never seen anything like this.'

'The question is, can you deactivate it?'

Baron grinned and rubbed his palms together. 'Does the pope live in Rome?'

'No, actually he lives in the Vatican.'

'Close enough.' Baron dug into his pack, pulled out a stethoscope and plugged it into his ears. He listened at several points on the outside of the missile, smiling and frowning like a heart specialist examining a patient.

'She's all dressed up and ready to go. I can hear humming.'

'What about those connections?' Mason asked.

'Fuel and electrical. I could cut them, but that might tell this baby it's operating on its own.'

'In other words, it might start the launch.'

Baron nodded. 'I've got to cut the heart out of this thing.' He ran his fingers along the slightly raised edge of a panel on the side of the missile. Then he dug out a set of tools from his rucksack, and after a couple of tries found a lug that fit the nuts holding the panel cover on. Using a battery-operated wrench, he started to unbolt the panel cover.

Like a sportscaster broadcasting play-by-play, Mason kept up a running account of Baron's work for the other teams, instructing them to stay one step behind. His men, in the meantime, had scoured the area and come up with one-inch cable they'd found in a storeroom. They ran the cable under the thrusters, hoping to rig up restraints on the projectile.

Baron was making slow progress. He stripped some bolts that had rusted in the dampness of the big room and had to use a special attachment to get a grip on them. He was leaning against the missile, his head close to the exterior. All at once, he stopped his work and listened.

'*Crap*!' he said.

'What's wrong?' asked Mason, who'd been peering intently over Baron's shoulder. Baron started to answer, but Mason stilled him with a hand signal. The 2IC was calling from the wheelhouse.

'I don't know if this means anything, Lieutenant, but all the screens and panels are going crazy up here.'

'Stand by.' Turning to Baron, he said, 'That was the wheelhouse. The instruments are showing unusual activity.' Mason cocked an ear. A loud humming that grew in intensity filled the chamber.

Baron looked around as if he could see the sound. 'The damned thing is about to launch.'

'Can you do anything?' Mason said evenly.

'There's a chance. If I can get this panel off, maybe I can sabotage its activation circuit. Stand by with those wire cutters.'

Baron unscrewed another bolt and was working on the next one when they heard a new noise, like the grinding of great gears. The sound was coming from below. They looked down, which probably saved them from eye damage when the electrical conduits and hoses blew off the sides of the missile a few feet above their heads. They dove onto their stomachs. Below them, the moon pool gates started to move apart.

Then the rotors inside the thruster housings began to whir.

As the moon pool fully opened, there was another explosion and the gantries holding the missile blew off. The jerry-rigged cables snapped like thread and the loose ends sliced the air and would have decapitated anyone in the way.

Then the bomb dropped.

Voices were yelling in Mason's ear. The other teams were seeing similar developments. Joe Louis was yelling. 'Omega Two. Bomb has dropped.'

Then Carmichael's voice came on. 'Omega Three. So has ours.'

Mason and his men crawled to the edge of the opening once occupied by the bomb and stared down. Waves and froth created where the missile splashed into the sea and its thrusters dug in. As they peered into the dark roiling sea, it was as if they were looking into the bowels of hell.

36

Petrov's lead man, a giant whom Austin had nick-named Tiny, stepped forward and drove the wooden butt of his AKM into the side of the guard's head. The guard's legs turned to rubber and he crashed to the deck. Figures were running toward them. Some-one flicked on a flashlight that caught Austin in its beam. An AKM burped once. At a firing rate of six hundred rounds per minute, even a short burst was deadly, especially at close range.

The flashlight skittered across the deck, but in its quick flicker, Razov's men had sized up the strength and position of the assault group. White-hot muzzle bursts blossomed in the darkness. They dove for cover. In the stroboscopic effect created by the fusil-lade, Petrov's men looked as if they were moving in slow motion.

Austin and Zavala hit the deck belly first and rolled over until they were behind the protection of a bollard. Bullets shredded the air over their heads and rico-cheted off the big steel mushroom. Austin hauled out his Bowen and blasted at a moving shadow, unsure if he'd hit anyone. Zavala pecked away with his H and K. The muzzle bursts became more scattered, indicating that Razov's men were spreading out.

'They're trying to outflank us,' Zavala shouted.

Tiny, who was on his belly a few feet away, was waving to get their attention.

'Go!' he bellowed. 'We hold position.'

Austin had his doubts. Tiny and his men could defend the narrow deck for a while, but like the Spartans holding the pass at Thermopylae, they too would eventually be outmaneuvered. Tiny jerked his thumb over his shoulder. The gesture needed no translation. *Get moving.* They let off a few more rounds, then inched backward on their elbows and knees until they were under a lifeboat davit.

With Razov's men still shooting at their last position, they got to their feet and dashed heads-down toward a salon door. It was unlocked. They stepped inside, weapons cocked. The crystal chandeliers were dark, and the only illumination came from a series of wall sconces. In their yellow glow, Austin could see the outlines of tables, chairs and settees. They crossed the dance floor to the opposite side. Austin paused. Petrov's men might be in the vicinity, and it could be a lethal mistake to surprise them. He called Petrov on the radio and gave him their position.

'Sounds as if you stepped into a hornets' nest,' Petrov said.

'Couldn't be helped. Don't know how long Tiny can hold them off.'

'You might be surprised,' Petrov said, without concern. 'Come through the door onto the deck. We'll be watching for you.'

Austin clicked off, opened the door and stepped out. There was no sign of Petrov or his men. Then dark shapes detached themselves from the shadows where the commandos crouched. Petrov came toward them. 'You were wise not to stick your heads outside. My men are a little edgy. I've sent a few around to the other side. We should hear from them in a –'

He was interrupted by the thud of exploding grenades. The gunfire became more sporadic. 'Evidently, my men have thinned out the ranks of the opposition,' he said. 'I suggest you proceed to your objective. Do you need any help?'

'I'll call you if we do,' Austin said, moving toward a ladder that went up the side of the bulkhead on the bridge superstructure.

'Good luck!' Petrov called out.

Austin and Zavala were halfway up the bridge when the chilling reports started coming in from the Omega teams. He stopped to tell Zavala the bad news coming in through his earpiece.

'The bombs have dropped,' he told Zavala. '*All* of them.'

Zavala had taken the lead and was hanging on to a ladder to the next deck. He turned at Austin's words and let out a long string of curses in Spanish. 'What now?'

In answer, Austin jerked his arm up to shoulder level and pointed his gun at Zavala, who froze in place. The Bowen barked. The slug passed within inches of Zavala's head and the breeze created by its passing ruffled his hair. A heavy object plunged from above and crashed to the deck with a thud. Zavala blinked the light spots out of his eyes and stared at the Cossack spread-eagled on the deck. A saber lay a few feet from the man's outstretched hand.

'Sorry, Joe,' Austin said. 'That guy was about to cut you down to size.'

Zavala ran his fingers through his hair on the side the bullet had passed. 'That's okay. I always wanted to part my hair on this side.'

'There's nothing we can do about the bombs,' Austin said somberly. 'But we can deal with the murdering scum who launched them.'

Austin took the lead, and they climbed higher until they were under the wings that extended out from either side of the wheelhouse. They split up, with each man taking a wing. Austin sprinted up the stairs. With his back to the bulkhead, he edged up to the open door and peered around the corner. The spacious wheelhouse was lit by red night-lights that washed the interior in their crimson glow.

The wheelhouse seemed deserted, except for the solitary figure of a man who stood in front of a large computer monitor, his back to Austin, apparently staring at the screen. Austin whispered into his radio, instructing Zavala to keep watch while he investigated. Then he stepped inside.

Razov's wolfhounds must have smelled him. They rushed out of nowhere in a flurry of clicking claws and wagging tails and pounced on Austin. He pushed them down with his free hand, but the dogs had spoiled all hopes of a silent entry. Razov turned and frowned at the dogs' attention to Austin. He gave a sharp command that brought the dogs whimpering back to his side with their heads low and tails between their legs. His thin lips widened in an evil smile.

'I've been expecting you, Mr Austin. My men told me that you and your friends were aboard. It's good to see you again. Pity that you had to depart so abruptly on your last visit.'

'You might change your mind when we blow your operation out of the water.'

'It's a little late for that,' Razov said. He pointed toward the monitor. The screen was subdivided into three vertical segments. On each section, a blip was rapidly descending toward a wavy line at the bottom.

'I know you've launched the bombs.'

'Then you know there's nothing you can do. When the missiles hit bottom, the thrusters will drive them into the sea floor, where they will explode, releasing the methane hydrate, collapsing the shelf and triggering *tsunamis* that will destroy three of your major coastal cities.'

'To say nothing of launching your mad scheme to trigger global warming.'

Razov looked startled, then he smiled and shook his head. 'I should have known you would figure out my ultimate goal. No matter. Yes, Siberia will become the breadbasket of the world, and your country will be so busy licking its wounds and trying to feed itself that you will no longer be able to mind Russia's business. Maybe we might sell you Siberian wheat, if you behave.'

'Would Irini have agreed with your insane plot?'

The smile disappeared. 'You're not fit to speak her name.'

'Maybe not.' Austin pointed the Bowen at Razov's heart. 'But I can send you to join her.'

Razov spat out a command. The curtain that divided the main section of the wheelhouse from the chart room parted, and two men came out, a bearded Cossack and Pulaski, who had hijacked the *NR-1*. Machine pistols at the ready, they moved around behind Austin. Then the curtain parted again. A tall man dressed in a long black robe emerged. He gazed at Austin with deep-set eyes and licked his lips, as if he were about to feast. He said something in Russian; his voice was deep and sonorous, as if it were issuing from a tomb.

A chill danced along Austin's spine, but he kept his gun leveled at Razov.

Razov seemed amused at Austin's reaction. 'I'd like you to meet Boris, my associate and closest advisor.'

The monk grinned at the mention of his name and spoke in Russian. Razov translated. 'Boris says he's sorry he didn't meet you when he boarded the NUMA ship.'

'You don't know *how* sorry I am,' Austin said. 'He wouldn't be standing here now.'

'Bravo! A fine attempt at bluff. Put the gun down,

Mr Austin. As we speak, your companions are being eradicated by my men.'

Austin had no intention of relinquishing his gun. If he had to, he'd go down in a hail of machine gun fire and take Razov and Boris with him. He wondered where Zavala was. While he pondered his next move, he heard Yaeger's voice in his earpiece.

'Kurt, can you hear me? There's still a chance. I've been working on the code, the section I couldn't figure out. It's about the bombs. They won't explode until they're activated. Can you hear me?'

Still keeping the Bowen trained on Razov, Austin glanced at the monitor. The blips had come to rest on the ocean bottom. Razov saw where he was looking. 'The deed is done, Mr Austin.'

'Not quite,' Austin said. 'The bombs are harmless unless they're activated.'

Razov's face betrayed his surprise, but he recovered quickly. His features contorted in a mask of rage. 'True – and you will have the privilege of witnessing the activation. Too bad you're about to die knowing that your feeble attempts to stop my grand scheme have failed.'

Razov gave an almost imperceptible nod of his head. In response, Boris stepped over to a keyboard next to the monitor, and his long fingers reached out for the keys. They never made it.

Austin swung his revolver away from Razov, aimed at the monk's hand and squeezed the trigger. The effect at close range was devastating. The hand exploded in a shower of bone and blood. Boris stared down in disbelief at the bloody stump. An ordinary mortal would have crumpled to the deck. Instead, Boris let out a feral cry of rage and glared at Austin with hate burning in his eyes. He reached under his tunic with his left hand and pulled out a dagger. Paying no heed to the blood flowing from his mangled hand, he went for Austin.

The other men cocked their machine pistols. Boris shouted a warning. He wanted Austin to himself.

Austin couldn't believe the man was still standing. He raised the Bowen, intending to finish Boris off with a bullet between the mad, staring eyes, but without warning his arms were pinioned by his sides. Pulaski had grabbed him from behind.

Boris was so close Austin could smell the animal odor of the unwashed body and the foul breath. Boris smiled, showing a mouthful of rotting teeth, and raised his knife to strike.

Forcefully, Austin ground his heel into Pulaski's instep. Pulaski grunted with pain and his grip loosened, and Austin bent his knees and drove his elbow into the man's side. Pulaski let go completely, then Austin brought the long barrel of his revolver up so it was mere inches from the Russian's chest, and squeezed the trigger. The impact of the heavy bullet hurled Boris back and he slammed into the bulkhead and fell to the deck.

Then Pulaski brought the butt down on the side of Austin's head. Austin saw every star in the galaxy and he crashed to the deck and blacked out for a second, but the intense pain kept him at the edge of consciousness. Through blurred eyes, he saw Razov tapping out a command on the blood-splattered keyboard. He felt the recoil of the gun in his hand and blacked out.

Pulaski bent over and lowered his machine pistol to Austin's head to administer the coup de grâce, but Zavala's Heckler and Koch stuttered from the side door. Pulaski went down, with the Cossack right behind him.

When Austin regained consciousness, Zavala was kneeling by his side. The wolfhounds had cowered in a corner when the shooting started. Now they came over and licked Austin's hand.

'Sorry I didn't get here sooner. I had to take care of a couple of Razov's goons.'

Austin brushed the dogs gently aside. 'Where's Razov?' he said, looking around.

'He slipped out the other side while I was trading gunfire with the Cossack guard.'

With Zavala's help, Austin got to his feet. He glanced at the bodies of the dead Cossack, Pulaski and Boris, then went over to the computer. The screen was a pile of splintered glass. 'The bombs had to be activated from here. Razov was typing out the command to trigger the explosions. I got the control computer with a lucky shot.'

Zavala smiled. 'I hope he's got a thirty-day warranty.'

Austin got on the radio to Petrov. 'Ivan, are you there?'

'Yes, we're here. Any problems?'

'A few, but we took care of them. How are you doing?'

'They made the mistake of trying to outflank us. We were waiting for them. It was what you Americans call a turkey shoot. I lost a few men, but it's now only a question of mopping up.'

'Good work. Boris is dead. We stopped the bombs from being activated. Razov is on the run. Keep an eye out for him.'

'Yes – *wait*. There's a helicopter taking off.'

Austin could hear the clatter of rotors above the sporadic gunfire. He stepped out onto the bridge wing in time to see a black helicopter soar over the ship. He raised his pistol, but the masts interfered with his aim. Within seconds, the helicopter had merged with the darkness.

Something nuzzled the back of Austin's knees. The wolfhounds wanted attention and food, not necessarily in that order. He holstered his gun and scratched their heads. With the two white hounds trailing behind them, he and Zavala made their way down to the main deck to rendezvous with Petrov and his men. Maybe he could find a plate of sausages for his new pals.

37

England

Thirty-six hours later, Lord Dodson sat up suddenly in his leather chair, blinked the sleep out of his eyes and looked around at the familiar dark paneling of his study. He had dozed off reading a new biography of Lord Nelson. He muttered to himself. Sign of old age. Nelson's life was anything but boring.

A noise had jarred him from his slumber; he was sure of it. All was quiet now. Jenna, his housekeeper, had left a short while before. The house had no ghosts that he knew of, although it sometimes creaked and mumbled. He reached over and plucked his cold pipe from the ashtray and considered lighting it. Curiosity got the best of him. He replaced the pipe and put his book aside, rose from his chair, unlatched the front door and stepped out into the soft darkness.

Great luminous clouds were moving across the moon and stars peeked out here and there. There was no wind. With his hand, he stirred the wind chimes outside the door. No, he thought, the tinkling sound they made wasn't what had awakened him. He went back into the house. As he shut the door, he froze at the ragged cracking noise from the kitchen.

Had Jenna returned without his knowledge? Impossible. She was going to tend to a sick sister, and her
family took precedence over work.

Dodson quietly went back into the study and
removed the hunting rifle from above the fireplace.
With trembling hands, he rummaged through a desk
drawer until he found a box of shells. He loaded the
rifle and made his way to the kitchen.

The light had been left on. He stepped inside, and
his eyes went immediately to the broken window
pane in the back door. The floor was littered with
shards of glass. The sharp sound could have been
someone walking on a broken piece of window. *Bur-
glars.* Damned cheeky breaking into a house with
somebody home. Dodson walked over to the door
for a closer look. As he was bending over to examine
the damage, he caught the reflection of movement in
an unbroken pane.

He whirled around. A man had stepped out of the
pantry, pistol in hand.

'Good evening, Lord Dodson,' the man said.
'Please give me your rifle.'

Dodson was cursing himself for not checking the
pantry first. He lowered the rifle and handed it over.
'Who in the blazes are you and what are you doing
here?'

'My name is Razov. I am the rightful owner of a
valuable object that you have in your possession.'

'Then you've made a big mistake. Everything in
this house is mine.'

The man's lips widened in a sardonic smile. '*Everything?*'

Dodson hesitated. 'Yes.'

The man took a step closer. 'Come, Lord Dodson. It's not dignified for a proper English gentleman to be caught in a lie.'

'You'd better leave. I've called the police.'

'Tut-tut. Another lie. I cut your telephone line after I had a little chat with your housekeeper.'

'Jenna? Where is she?'

'In a safe place. For now. But if you don't start telling the truth, I will have to kill her.'

Dodson had no doubt the man meant what he said. 'All right. What is it that you want?'

'I think you know. The crown of Ivan the Terrible.'

'What makes you think I have this – what is it? Some sort of Russian crown, you say?'

'Don't try my patience with your futile bluff. When I failed to find the crown with the other tsarist treasure on the *Odessa Star*, I did what any experienced hunter does. I backtracked. The crown was with the tsar's family until they arrived in Odessa. But the tsarina had a premonition that she and her family would never complete their journey. She wanted to make sure that even if the family died, the crown would find its way to a surviving Romanov who would use it to reclaim the Russian throne. She entrusted the crown to an English agent.'

'That would have been long before my time.'

'Of course, but we both know that the agent was in the employ of your grandfather.'

Dodson started to protest, but he could see it was indeed futile. This man knew everything. 'The crown is nothing to me. If I give it to you, I must have your word that you will let my housekeeper go. She has no knowledge of any of this.'

'I have no use for the old woman. Take me to the crown.'

'Very well,' Dodson said. 'Follow me.'

Dodson led the way to a hallway and opened the doors of a walk-in closet. He cleared out the winter jackets and other clothing hanging in the closet, then he pushed boots and shoes aside and stepped in. He lifted a section of floor and pressed a button set under the wood. The back wall of the closet slid noiselessly aside. Dodson turned on a light, and with Razov close behind, he descended a winding staircase made of stone blocks. They were in a stone-walled chamber about fifteen feet square. Rusty iron brackets stuck out of the walls.

'This is the original Roman cellar. They used it to store wine and vegetables.'

'Spare me the history lesson, Lord Dodson. The *crown*.'

Dodson nodded and went over to a pair of brackets set in the wall. He twisted them both clockwise. 'This is the unlocking mechanism.' He ran his hands down the stones until his fingers found a depression.

Then he pulled and a section of wall, actually an iron door faced with inch-thick stones, creaked open. Dodson stepped back. 'There's your crown. Exactly where my grandfather put it nearly a hundred years ago.'

The crown sat on a pedestal that was covered with purple velvet.

'Turn around and put your hands behind your back,' Razov ordered.

He bound Dodson's hands and ankles with duct tape and pushed the Englishman down on the floor so that he sat with his back to a wall. Then Razov tucked his pistol in his belt and reached inside for the crown. It was heavier than he thought and he grunted with exertion as he hugged it to his chest.

The sparkle of the diamonds, rubies and emeralds covering the domed crown was matched by the glitter in Razov's greedy eyes.

'Beautiful,' he whispered.

'I always thought it was a bit gaudy myself,' Dodson said.

'*Englishmen*,' Razov said with contempt. 'You're like your grandfather, a fool. Neither one of you could appreciate the power you held in your hands.'

'On the contrary. My grandfather knew that with the tsar's family dead, the appearance of the crown would inflame passions and bring out any number of claimants, legitimate and *otherwise*.' He looked pointedly at Razov. 'Other countries would be drawn in. There would be another world war.'

'Instead, we got more than half a century of communism.'

'It would have come in time, anyway. The tsarist regime would have withered from corruption.'

Razov laughed and placed the crown on his head. 'Like Napoleon, I crown myself. Behold, the next ruler of Russia.'

'I only see a little man making a vulgar display of wealth.'

Razov's serpent's eyes went flat. He cut another piece of duct tape and slapped it over Dodson's mouth, then he picked up the crown and climbed up the stairs. At the top, he paused. 'You must have read Poe's "The Cask of Amontillado." Where the victim is sealed up forever? Perhaps someday your bones will be found. I leave you here in place of the crown. I'm afraid I must dispose of your housekeeper.'

He stepped through the closet door and into the hallway. His hands were both full with the crown, so he didn't close the secret panel in the back of the closet. He would deposit the crown in the back of the car, come back and seal Dodson off for eternity, then kill the housekeeper and dispose of her body in the river.

As Razov carried his burden toward the back of the house, he heard a rap at the front door. He froze.

Zavala's voice called out. 'Lord Dodson. Are you home?' Then the knock again, louder this time. Razov turned and headed for the kitchen.

Dodson had left the door unlocked when he went out to see if the wind was blowing. Zavala and Austin stepped inside, guns in their hands. Zavala called out again. They made their way down the hall and stopped at the open closet where light streamed from the secret chamber. They exchanged glances, then Austin stepped inside, Bowen at ready, and descended the stairs while Zavala covered his back.

Austin saw Lord Dodson sitting on the floor and peeled the tape from the Englishman's mouth. 'Are you all right?'

'Yes, I'm fine. Go after Razov – he has the crown.'

Austin used his Buck knife to cut the tape binding Dodson's hands and feet, and they climbed from the cellar. Dodson smiled when he saw Joe. 'A pleasure to see you again, Mr Zavala.'

'Nice to be back, Lord Dodson. This is my partner, Kurt Austin.'

'I'm very pleased to meet you, Mr Austin.'

'The back door is open,' Zavala said. 'He must have gone that way.'

Dodson looked worried. 'My housekeeper. Have you seen her?'

'If you're talking about the large and very angry lady we found tied up in the backseat of a rental car, she's fine,' Austin said. 'We sent her for the police.'

'Thank you,' Dodson said. 'Razov may try for the river when he finds his car is gone. There's a boat there he may use in an attempt to escape.'

Zavala started for the back door.

'Wait,' Dodson said. 'I know a better way. Come with me.'

To the puzzlement of the NUMA men, Dodson led them back through the closet into the underground chamber. He twisted two more wall brackets and opened another section of wall. 'This is an old escape tunnel. It comes out at the bottom of a dry well near the river. Use the hand and footholds to climb out. You may be able to get to the boat ahead of that dreadful man. The crown will slow him down.'

'Thank you, Lord Dodson,' Austin said, ducking his head as he slipped through the door.

'Don't go into the river after him,' Dodson called out. 'The shallows are dangerous to walk on. The mud is like quicksand. It can swallow a horse.'

Austin and Zavala barely heard the warning as they bent into a running crouch and made their way through the tunnel. They had no flashlight and had to feel their way down the narrow, sloping passageway. The smell of stagnant water and rotting vegetation grew stronger. The tunnel ended abruptly, and if not for the shaft of moonlight they would have slammed into the curved wall.

Austin groped around the stones and found the foot and handholds, then they climbed over the low walls around the well and saw the small boathouse silhouetted against the river's sheen. They made their way to the river and took up their stations on either side of the pier.

Before long, they heard the pounding of feet and heavy breathing. Razov was running their way. It seemed as if he would walk directly into their trap, but as he neared the pier, a patch of sky opened in the clouds and the riverside and Austin's pale hair were bathed in a silvery light. It was only an instant, but Razov veered off to avoid the ambush and ran along the banks of the river.

'Stop, Razov!' Austin shouted. 'It's no use.'

The crackle of broken branches came from ahead as Razov crashed through the bushes bordering the river. They heard a splash. Austin and Zavala followed the sound until they stood on the grassy bank that rose a few feet above the river. Razov was trying to ford the river, but had only made it a few yards from shore before his feet became encased in the soft bottom mud. He had tried to scramble back to land without success. Now he stood in the water waist deep, facing the bank, the crown still clutched in his arms.

'I can't move,' he said.

Austin remembered Dodson's warning of quicksand. He found a limb broken off a tree and extended it toward Razov. 'Grab this.'

Razov was sinking almost to his armpits, yet he made no effort to reach for the branch.

'Drop the damned crown!' Austin yelled.

'No, I've waited too long. I won't let it go.'

'It's not worth your life,' Austin said.

The water had reached Razov's chin, and his reply was unintelligible. He lifted the crown high and placed it on his head. The weight only served to push him under the surface more quickly. His face disappeared until only the crown was visible, seemingly floating on the water, its surface glittering with a silver fire. Then it, too, disappeared.

'*Dios mio*,' Zavala said, reverting to his native Spanish. 'What a way to go.'

They heard a huffing and puffing. Dodson had retrieved his rifle and ran toward them with a flashlight.

'Where is that scoundrel?' Dodson asked.

'There.' Austin threw the useless branch into the river where Razov had disappeared. 'The crown, too.'

'Dear God,' Dodson said. He pointed his light at the brown, muddy water. Only a few bubbles marked Razov's position and soon they, too, were swept away by the slow-moving current.

'Long live the tsar,' Austin said.

Then he turned and walked back to the house.

38

Washington, DC

Austin rowed in the misty golden light, so intent on his strokes that he barely noticed the powerboat that crossed the river until it took up a position behind him. Austin stopped and the boat did the same. He wiped the sweat off his forehead, took a pull from his plastic water bottle and rested on his oar handles, squinting against the glare. As he gazed back at the unmoving boat, Austin began to wonder if life still pulsed in a stray tentacle of Razov's vast organization.

As a test, he started to row. He had only taken a few strokes before the boat stirred and followed him again, keeping an even distance. He let the scull coast to a halt. The powerboat stopped again.

A quick glance up and down the river told Austin he was on his own. The river was empty of boats, which was why he rowed so early. Austin set the scull into a wide easy turn and pointed the needle-sharp bow back the way he had come. He picked up the pace, keeping in mind that rowing was more technical precision than power. As he drew nearer, he saw that the boat had a white hull, although he couldn't tell how many people were aboard. He pulled harder, and the scull shot toward the boat with the unerring accuracy of a cruise missile.

He was nearing a section of shoreline that bulged into the Potomac like a beer gut. Austin knew that the current flowing near the knob of land described a peculiar curlicue that could suck an unwary boater in close to land before spitting him out. Although his rowing created a straight-line illusion, he was actually being drawn closer to the bulge.

On his next stroke, Austin kept one oar out of the water and used the other as an impromptu rudder. The scull veered suddenly and he finessed the abrupt change in direction without overturning, pointing the scull toward land.

He heard the angry buzz of the outboard motor.

He had hoped to catch the watcher off-guard and hadn't expected such a swift reaction. The powerboat quickly rose up on plane. Austin saw he'd never make shore and that he'd be at his most vulnerable, broadside to the approaching boat. He jettisoned his original plan, did another quick turn and sent the scull directly *toward* the fast-approaching powerboat.

The boat was slightly shorter than the scull, but seen from water level it seemed to loom like the *QE2*. Any collision with the arrow-slim scull would be as devastating as an encounter with an ocean liner. Austin hoped that the boat would veer off at the last moment, or at the worst, that the hulls would come together with a glancing blow. Just when they seemed about to collide, he hoisted one oar on his shoulder as if preparing to throw a javelin, and braced himself.

The motorboat throttled back, came off plane and settled down in the water, where hull resistance brought it almost to a stop a few feet away. Austin heard a familiar barking laugh and looked up to see Petrov's cold-chiseled face looking down at him. The Russian was wearing a baseball cap and a Hawaiian shirt with palm trees and bikini-clad women on it.

Austin replaced the oar in its outrigger. His heart was still thumping in his chest. 'Hello, Ivan. I was wondering when you'd show up again. How'd you know I'd be out here?'

Petrov shrugged.

Austin smiled and said, 'You might be interested to know that I checked into *your* dossier. Seems you've only become Ivan Petrov in the last couple of years.'

'As the poet said, what's in a name?'

'When do you leave for home?'

'Tomorrow. Your president has turned the tsar's treasure over to my country. I'll be returning to Russia as a hero. There's even talk of political office. With the disappearance of Razov, his Cossack forces are in disarray and the moderates have a chance of staying in power.'

'Congratulations. You deserve it.'

'Thank you, but to be honest, can you really see me sitting in the parliament?'

'Guess not, Ivan,' Austin said. 'You'll always be a man of the shadows.'

'Do you blame me? It's where I belong and where I'm the most comfortable.'

'Maybe you could answer a couple of questions before you take on your next identity. Was Razov really descended from the tsar?'

'That's what he was told from his father's death-bed. When he met Boris, the mad monk saw it as a marriage made in heaven. We have definite proof that Boris was directly descended from Rasputin.'

'The *original* mad monk?'

Petrov nodded.

Austin shook his head in amazement. 'And Razov?'

'His father was ill-advised. The village priest who kept the family records was a bit of a drunkard. He had heard the story of the tsar's daughter surviving, and used it to pry vodka money from Razov's father.'

'So there were no descendants from Maria.'

'I didn't say that.' Petrov's lips widened in an enigmatic smile.

Austin raised an eyebrow.

'The Grand Duchess Maria had two descendants who are still living. A man and a woman. I've talked to both of them. They are happy in their lives and aware of the repercussions that would result if they revealed themselves. I will respect their wish for privacy. Now I have a question. How did you know Razov was headed to see Lord Dodson?'

'We searched his yacht and found some papers indicating that the crown had been sent to Dodson's grandfather. We hopped a NUMA jet to England.

Razov was traveling alone, luckily. I don't think he wanted anyone to know he had to steal the crown. Sorry we couldn't save it.'

'Don't be. It's probably better off where it is. If ever an inanimate object harbored a malignancy, that was it. Every one of those jewels was paid for with the blood and sweat of the serfs.' Petrov watched a hawk making a lazy circle over the river and said, 'Well, Mr Austin –'

'Kurt. We're beyond formalities.'

Petrov saluted. 'Until we meet again, *Kurt.*' He kicked up the throttle and raced down the river until the boat disappeared around a curve. Austin resumed his rowing and was back at the boathouse in a few minutes. He stowed the scull and climbed the stairs that took him to the main level. Stripping down to his shorts, he made a fresh pot of Jamaican coffee and gathered the ingredients for a gourmet breakfast.

'You're certainly an early riser.'

Austin turned to see Kaela Dorn coming down the stairs from the turret bedroom. She was wearing a silk pajama top and a smile.

'Hope I didn't wake you,' Austin said.

She came over and inhaled the fragrance from the coffeepot. 'I can't think of a nicer way to wake up.' Her brow wrinkled as she traced some of the scars on Austin's tanned back with her fingers. 'I didn't see these in the dark last night.'

'You had your eyes closed.'

'So did you. I must say we made up for all those dates we didn't have.'

'Hope it was worth the wait.'

She kissed him lightly. 'Was it *ever*.'

The coffee was ready. He poured two steaming mugs, and they went out on the deck overlooking the shimmering river. The air was fresh and clear. Austin raised his mug in toast. 'Here's to your new career with CNN.'

'Thanks to you. It never would have happened without my exclusive on the Ataman plot. I'm going to miss Mickey and Dundee, though. I don't know how I can repay you.'

He gave her a Groucho Marx leer. 'You already *have*.'

'You mean to say that you gave me that exclusive just so you could get into my pants?'

'Can you think of a better reason?'

She put her finger on her cheek and cocked her head. 'No. Not really.'

Austin had called Kaela before he left London to tell her he was coming home. They'd arranged to meet in Washington after he reported to NUMA. As promised, he gave her an exclusive on Razov's plot. He had to leave out some details, but she had enough leads to chase down on her own. The story ran for three nights on all the networks, and all at once Kaela was the hottest journalistic property in town – so much in demand that Austin was surprised when she called and suggested they get together for dinner at a quiet inn in the Virginia countryside. The reunion had then shifted to Austin's boathouse, and nature had taken its course.

Austin excused himself and went to the front door, which looked out on a rolling green lawn. He gave a whistle, and two white blurs shot out of a copse of trees and raced across the lawn. The excited wolf-hounds followed him back onto the deck.

'What are you going to do with these characters?' Kaela said, scratching Sasha's bony head.

'They'll be my houseguests for the time being. I'll find a new home for them when I go on my next assignment. In the meantime, I'd like to take you on a boat ride.'

She laughed lightly. 'What kind of boat do you have?'

Austin said, 'NUMA and I recently came into possession of a very large yacht.'

She put her arms around him and gave him a long and lingering kiss. In a husky voice whose tone was unmistakable, she said, 'Just make sure they have room service.'